Love and Mutiny: Tales from British India

Love and Mutiny: Tales from British India

Anne George

Love and Mutiny: Tales from British India is a work of fiction, based on the Sepoy Mutiny, also known as the First War of Indian Independence, which occurred in 1857. While this work is situated in the context of the historical events, persons and places in the revolt of 1857, all events and characters in the plot are fictitious and any resemblance to any events or persons, dead or living, is a matter of pure coincidence.

For information on how to purchase copies, please visit annegeorgebooks.com.

Cover designed by Jennifer Quinlan, Historical Fiction Book Covers.

Cover Images:
Mitoire, Benoît Charles, *Samoylova Yuliya*, 1825. Accessed from: http://commons.wikimedia.org. Ⓢ

Norie, Orlando, *The 78th Highlanders at the taking of Sucunderabagh, Siege of Lucknow*, 1857. Accessed from: Anne S.K. Brown Military Collection, Brown University Library. Ⓢ

First edition

ISBN: 1-7322698-1-5
ISBN-13: 978-1732269811

Printed in the United States of America

DEDICATION

To my precious Zachary

CONTENTS

CHAPTER ONE

VISITING CALCUTTA

E dwina Hardingham stared, transfixed, as the rain pattered relentlessly on the enormously tall windows of her sister's home in the city of Calcutta in India. It was the beginning of March, and although the summer had just begun, it was already sweleringly hot. The rain made the day somewhat bearable. Her eldest sister's confinement had brought the family away from their home in the cool comfort of Simla—at the foothills of the Himalayas—to the bustling city where the eldest Hardingham daughter, Katherine, had made her home. Edwina missed her pleasant walks in the gardens around her home in Simla. She especially missed the company of Christopher, her cousin and closest confidant.

Christopher had remained in Simla along with Edwina's father, Arthur Hardingham, who was preoccupied with his business affairs. Simla in March was mild and pleasant, carrying with it the fragrance and promise of spring, she reflected. Edwina's thoughts trailed off as she gazed at the downpour outside. The rain was a merciful respite from the scorching heat of an early summer's day in Calcutta. She breathed deeply as the scent of wet earth wafted through the air. The peacocks in the garden called frantically and the males strutted their flamboyant plumes before the retreating hens. The *koels*[1] calling outside her window all morning had promised this welcome reprieve, given as they are, to

---

[1] A glossary giving a brief explanation of non-English words may be found at the end of the book.

calling out plaintively before it rains. For the present, the heat of the summer was momentarily subdued.

Her reverie was interrupted as her *ayah*, Shanta, clucked and demanded why she had not finished her tea. It had become cold now and they would have to make her some more. Edwina had not wanted any breakfast that morning, having been kept awake all night by the oppressive heat and the arrival of her newborn niece in the early hours. She realized that she would welcome some tea, now that the earth had relinquished its mantle of heat. She smiled at Shanta and asked in soft accents for more tea. Her smile, charming and dimpled, never failed to disarm her old nurse. Shantama, as Edwina liked to call her when they were alone, had served her family faithfully since Edwina was born. She had been retained as a '*daye*,' or a wet nurse for Edwina. Her own child, a boy, had succumbed to cholera early in his infancy. Her husband had been taken away by the illness too. Disease and starvation, so rampant amongst the poor in India, had wiped out most of the old woman's family. In the Hardingham household, she had found a haven. To Edwina's parents, she was somewhat of a saviour to their child.

Englishwomen who came to India quickly found that their adopted home, while exotic and alluring, often exacted a heavy toll from their children. The heat and illnesses prevalent in the warm clime quickly conspired to claim the lives of scores of their children and the celebration for the birth of a baby could quickly turn into a funeral. Faced with the prospect of losing their new infant to starvation, Arthur and Elizabeth Hardingham quickly sought the services of a *daye*. Unlike other European families, however, the Hardinghams had not sought to eradicate all traces of the *daye's* presence in their child's life once the need for her had passed. They were not terrified that their child would become a *Hindustani*, unacquainted with English ways. They saw India as their home, and easily accepted the inevitable intersection between Indian and European life. They wore Indian garments at home, ate the delectable preparations of the land with relish, and had an easy association with the people of India, regarding many noble Indian families as their friends and acquaintances.

When her services as a *daye* were no longer needed, Shanta was retained as an *ayah* for the Hardingham children. The bond between her and Edwina was strong, with Edwina regarding her with a particular fondness that traced back to her earliest memories. As the youngest child, Edwina was the recipient of great favouritism at the hands of her *ayah*. As *ayahs* were wont to do, Shanta had cossetted and petted Edwina throughout her childhood, nursing her devotedly through several pernicious childhood illnesses that had threatened to take her to her grave. As Edwina and her two sisters grew into womanhood, she stayed on in the family and presently waited on Edwina as her abigail. The family servants were deeply loyal to and loved the Hardinghams. And, although Arthur and Elizabeth Hardingham treated their servants with uncommon courtesy, caring for sick stable boys and pensioning retired servants generously, their youngest daughter, Edwina, seemed to have a deep and singular attachment to their Indian staff, and especially to Shanta. She was indispensable to the women of the Hardingham household, and traveled with them to Calcutta to assist in the inevitable commotion that accompanied Katherine's confinements.

The eldest Hardingham daughter at six and twenty had become a hardy matron, having brought three other children, all boys, into the world before the newest addition to the family. She appeared to thoroughly enjoy motherhood and was a devoted parent, running the risk of being decidedly *unfashionable* in her social set. Her husband, George Markham, was a member of the Bengal Civil Service, in the Railway Branch of the Public Works Department of the Government of India. Under Governor General Lord Dalhousie's eventful administration, a system of Railways, having been inaugurated in 1853, was now expanding rapidly across India. Currently, Mr. Markham was preoccupied with plans for inaugurating the Railway service between Howrah and Hooghly. Lord Dalhousie doubted that the Railways would ever become profitable for the East India Company, and like him, Markham had his misgivings.

Rarely away from his work, at his chamber in Dalhousie Square in the heart of Calcutta, he was anxious to return to the papers and drawings that awaited him there. Presently, he fled from the commotion in the sitting room, precipitated by the arrival of his infant daughter early in the morning, taking refuge in the library. It was here that he found Edwina, staring out at the rain drenching the world outside. The clamour of the three boys begging to be allowed to see their new sister could be heard as Shanta opened the door, bringing Edwina a fresh tray of tea and toast. Seeing Markham in the room, she hesitated and nervously muttered that she had brought only one cup. He waved her aside, wanting nothing but to be left alone. Edwina smiled at her brother-in-law and the two of them sat in grateful silence, enjoying the fleeting calm. Edwina knew she would be wanted by Katherine's bedside soon, and savoured the quiet moment and her tea.

Soon enough, she was summoned to help Katherine and hurried away leaving Markham to himself. Upstairs, she found Katherine ensconced in a becoming nightgown, surrounded by a great quantity of pillows, and being fussed over by several *ayahs* and her mother and other sister, Anne. Edwina chuckled at the sight. She had worn an unquestionably matronly cap, but the quantity of blonde ringlets that tumbled from underneath it gave her a decidedly roguish look. She appeared to be enjoying the fuss immensely.

'Why, Kate! I do not think you are ever as happy as when you have just brought an infant into the world! To be sure, you must make sure to have lots of children in your lifetime,' teased Edwina.

'How can you say such a thing when I suffer so in this heat?' demanded Kate. 'But of course I am delighted, I now have four children.' This last part was said with great relish and a glow of contentment.

Her sister, Anne, rose impatiently from her chair as Edwina approached.

'Where have you been? It has been so tiresome to sit here all morning!' Noticing her mother's frown, she hastily added, 'I am sure poor Kate would have liked some tea and to have you to talk to, as well.'

The middle child, Anne seemed to be the most self-absorbed of the Hardingham sisters. She was closest to Katherine, and confined her conversation with Edwina to demands and summons. Like Katherine, she had a mass of blonde curls. But she was decidedly the prettier of the two, with impossibly long eyelashes and a perfectly curved mouth. She had come out earlier in the year, and had soon built a coterie of loyal followers. These faithful gentlemen, in keeping with the best traditions, called at hours that while fashionable in London, were unquestionably the hottest times of the day in India! They came alone, and sometimes in pairs, and scarcely a day passed when Anne Hardingham did not find her book filled with engagements. She flirted artfully, keeping everyone

one of her admirers hopeful, and yet, never favouring one over the other. Although she was markedly *open*, she was never vulgarly coquettish, and unlike other dizzy young women who had come out, she was weighing her options with a remarkably cool head. If she was partial to any one of her suitors, it was not readily apparent either to them or to any of the Hardinghams. Anne Hardingham had decided on making a good match and to this end, she had spent several months at her sister's home in Calcutta, where some of the best matrimonial prizes in the East India Company were to be won.

Edwina had neither the beauty of Anne nor the fetching disposition of Kate. She was quiet where one was noisy, and forthright where the other was demure. She had fixed opinions and was not content to let others decide her thoughts. Her dark hair quite glistened in the sun and gave her a striking appearance, but it sadly did not curl in the fetching manner of Kate's and Anne's hair. Her mouth was curved, but tightened around the corners, giving her an air of decision. And whilst her brown eyes hinted a lively sense of humor, few ever saw their gleam. Consequently, she was declared to be pleasing, but not a *Beauty*. Sensing Anne's impatience to be free of her service to Kate, Edwina quietly said she was sorry for dawdling over her tea and would now take her place.

At this, Mrs. Hardingham softly remarked, 'I don't think you were quite *dawdling*, dearest. And besides, you were awake most of the night.' And, before Anne could bridle at her mother's suggestion that Edwina had done the most, she added, 'It is good you have come; you are needed here, for it will soon be time for Anne's gentlemen to be calling, although I daresay few will venture out in this downpour!'

Torn between arguing that she had gone above and beyond the call of duty in Kate's service, and prettying herself for her daily retinue of admirers, Anne lingered by her chair. But her mother's suggestion that the gentlemen might be hindered from their daily devotions by the deluge annoyed her. Declaring herself to be unbearably hot, Anne hurried out of the room.

Mrs. Hardingham sighed, 'Poor Anne! The rain does good to all but her.'

Kate placidly replied that the rains would be sure to cool Anne down too, but Edwina saw the twinkle in her mother's eyes as the two of them exchanged a quick glance. Like her youngest daughter,

Elizabeth Hardingham housed a keen wit in a calm and mild-mannered demeanor. Unlike Edwina, however, her passions were not quickly aroused. She had not the flashing outrage in her eyes when seeing an injustice done and she did not seethe inwardly, as Edwina sometimes did. She did, however, examine the world around her with a keen eye, often finding amusement in the everyday goings on of domestic life. Anne's petulance when Edwina was preferred over herself, or Kate's self-assured conviction that she was naturally more talented and capable than her younger sisters amused her. Edwina's quiet pliability around her sisters failed to deceive her. She knew her youngest daughter to be resolute and occasionally, surprisingly passionate, but always sensible, and unfailingly kind. While she mused on these lines, the newest member of the family was aroused from her sleep by the sound of the bell at the front of the house. As she urgently demanded sustenance, Kate attended to her needs.

Although a great many English families sent their children away to school in England, the Hardinghams had decided to delay the inevitable for as long as they possibly could. Instead of sending their children to England, as most British parents living in India did, Mrs. Hardingham had undertaken the education of the children herself. She had been aided in her endeavours by a European tutor whose services were retained at an outrageous sum of eighty-five hundred rupees (Twelve hundred pounds) a year! Indeed, Calcutta was a frightfully expensive place, with European lawyers and tutors demanding inordinate fees for their services. Although their decision to keep their children in India had netted them the ire of relations from both sides of the family, they were firm about not wanting to be separated from their children. Perhaps it was the loss of their three oldest children in infancy, or their feelings of loneliness as exiles in a new homeland, or perhaps it was the detachment that they witnessed between the parents and children of many English families in India, but whatever the cause, the Hardinghams, contradictory to the prevailing wisdom of their times, sought fiercely to keep their children close by.

Moreover, while friends and kin had warned them that their children would grow into 'little savages,' Arthur Hardingham and his wife persisted in the conviction that their course of action was advantageous. Thus, apart from a short six months spent in England in her fourteenth year, during which she had come to cuffs with a 10-year-old cousin who insisted that India was filled with 'heathen savages,' Edwina had spent the entire of her nineteen years in India. Her violent outburst at her ill-informed cousin had solidified the conviction among her relations in England that her parents had made a grave mistake in her education and upbringing in what must surely be an extremely savage land to have produced so fierce and incontinent a girl. For her part, Edwina herself simply saw herself as an Indian of a different caste, in a land where a great many castes existed, and took umbrage at the unchristian and harsh language with which the unfortunate young man had described what she saw as her homeland and her people. No European family was ever as glad to set foot on Indian soil as the Hardinghams when their brief stint in England had come to a close and they returned to India. The Hardingham girls were none the worse for their mother's tutelage. A capable woman herself, she had instructed in them in English, mathematics and geography. They had learnt French and some Portuguese as well, and each was skilled at playing the pianoforte. Indeed, they had been prepared well for marriage and as such would have been quite at ease in the finest household in England.

The bell at the front door of the house was tugged at a second time—with some impatience. Hearing it, Anne was mercifully roused from her sulks by the chimes and Markham currently found himself greeting Captain John Lovelace of the 5th Bengal Cavalry. The rain had made exercises impossible and he had ostensibly decided to call on his friend Markham, to congratulate him on the birth of his infant. Kate's physician served in the army, and news traveled fast among officers. Lovelace's eyes, however, darted towards the doorway frequently, as if expecting someone to enter. A quiet man of stern manner, Captain Lovelace seemed to be the most unlikely of Anne's suitors. While the others fawned and wrote poetry to her, Captain Lovelace was grave and proper whenever they met. Her manner to him, while always welcoming, was never too warm. For his part, he was unsure whether this was due to a genteel reserve, which elevated her charms in his esteem, or a coolness towards him, which served as somewhat of a damper. Since her manner had not given him reason to think too ill of his prospects, he pressed on, with disdain for many of his dandified competitors. Today, he was the only one who had come to pay obeisance to Beauty, and she rewarded him with her warmest smile.

'Captain Lovelace! Why, how kind of you to call! I had not expected us to have any callers in this dreadful weather. How surprising it is to find you here!'

Captain Lovelace's gratified response was drowned in a hoot of undignified laughter from Markham who declared, 'Lord, Annie, stop your fustian! Surely you are not dressed in your finery for your own gratification!'

While Anne managed a rigid smile at her brother-in-law, she was saved from answering him by Captain Lovelace who remarked that attire that must appear to be finery on other women was rather commonplace for a person as exquisite as Miss Hardingham. Markham thought to himself that he had not taken Lovelace for a mooncalf, while Anne found herself musing that she had never found him so gallant and charming before. And because no one else had visited to pay her homage that day, she rewarded him with a great many tinkling laughs delivered from behind her little fan, and with the fluttering of lowered lashes whenever he paid her one of several compliments. The result of that afternoon's visit was that in the weeks to come, Captain Lovelace felt much emboldened to frequent the Markham residence as often as possible. This led Markham to remark to his wife and mother-in-law that he would not be surprised if Anne should find herself wed before long. He expounded on the advantages of the match, as Lovelace was well connected in England and a member of the Crown Forces with a very promising career. Mrs. Hardingham, pleased to see Anne's prospects look so favorable, now turned her attention on how to situate Edwina. She must be brought out as soon as Anne became engaged. Perhaps they ought to prolong their stay in Calcutta, to that end, she mused.

As the capital of the East India Company in India, Calcutta was certainly the hub of great activity. The bazaars were vibrant and colorful, the buildings old and large, and the society generally cheerful and thriving. Officers of the East India Company and Crown Forces were everywhere and as such, a woman looking for a husband could certainly land a prize catch in this city. The Hardinghams had spent many years in Calcutta prior to their removal to Simla and were consequently quite intimately acquainted with many respectable families in the city. Invitations to balls were plenteous and Mrs. Hardingham was certain Edwina would have no difficulty in the matrimonial *market,* once introduced to society. For now, she scarcely had a day when she did not receive an invitation to visit an old childhood friend. Once Katherine's child was delivered, she promptly accepted several welcome invitations to the company of old friends.

Her brother-in-law frowned on them, as many of these friends were Indians. He could not fathom how a genteel and well-born family could know so many low and vulgar persons. While the Hardinghams respected their Hindu and Mohammedan friends, recognizing that many of them had nobler origins than what the Hardinghams themselves could lay claim to, in Markham's eyes, they were simply 'natives,' and as such, entitled to no more than condescension from what he believed was a superior race of persons. His wife had not noticed that all those of their acquaintance were Europeans. She simply lived in the assumption that unlike herself and her sisters, her dear Markham knew very few Indians because the principal part of his life had been spent in England. Early on in their marriage, Markham perceived what he interpreted as a peculiar attachment to the natives on the part of his in-laws, when a careless remark about the coarseness of these persons had quickly been countered by a fierce rebuke on the part of his mother-in-law and youngest sister-in-law. He had learned quickly that the sentiments of the Hardinghams on this issue, although disturbingly liberal, would best be respected and henceforth, was cautious in expressing his disapproval over the predilection of his sisters-in-law to consort with native women.

This morning, Edwina was delighted to pay a visit to her childhood companion, Ruksana Begum, the daughter of Zayed Reza Khan, a prominent merchant in the city who was related to the erstwhile *Nawab* of Bengal, and a close friend of Arthur Hardingham. Accompanied by Shanta, she giggled nervously as their chaise made its way through narrow streets and then through the hectic bazaars. They made a quick stop at Burrabazaar, a favorite haunt of Europeans. This morning, she would pick up some silk for new dresses. The best fabric in India could be had at these bazaars. The *durzis* were adept at creating marvelous copies of patterns sent from England, although Edwina noted wryly, that European women were apt to comment that they always seemed to make some subtle changes to the style so the garments never looked quite the same as they did in England. Perhaps, she reflected, it was their way of expressing their resentment against the rule of a foreign power that had overrun their centuries-old nation and ways of life. The Hardingham women were not much affected by the vagaries of their *durzis*, for at home, they often wore Indian clothing, finding them infinitely more comfortable and pleasing than European attire.

This morning, as she called on Ruksana Begum however, she was attired in a demure muslin dress of the latest fashion in England, albeit subtly altered by the local *durzi*! The chaise arrived at the gates of the stately *haveli* and Edwina and Shanta were directly driven to the main entrance of the house. Unlike many wealthy Indians, Khan had not demolished his ancestral home to rebuild a modern Victorian-style mansion. Edwina noted with gratification that the rambling estate where she had spent many happy afternoons playing with her friend remained unmolested by the dictates of modern fashion. Nor had the ravages of time left their mark, for a brilliant army of gardeners and servants kept the house and gardens in impeccable condition within and without. As the chaise drew up to the front of the mansion, she was greeted by a veiled figure, hurtling down the stairs at her.

'Edwina! You've come at last! Why did you not come the first week you arrived in Calcutta?' shrieked Ruksana Begum as Edwina and Shanta were ushered into the *zenana* of the house.

Her nurse shuddered in horror at the unladylike squeals the two girls emitted as they leapt into each other's arms. In vain she attempted to replace her charge's fallen veil on her head.

'My dearest Ruksana! You have grown into a great lady! I can hardly recognise you. It's true then? You are to be married soon?' asked Edwina breathlessly.

'Yes, and am I not a great beauty?' returned the artless and rather vain Miss. Khan.

At seventeen, the honorable Ruksana Begum had grown into a dazzling beauty and preparations for her nuptials were underway. She was to be wed to a noble from the family of the *Nawab* of Hyderabad. Already her grandmother and aunts complained she was in danger of turning into an old maid, but her father countered that an illiterate young woman would do no credit to the family she married into and would indeed shame the family of her birth. He had spent great sums of money on procuring the finest European tutors for his daughter, despite the censure of relatives who were aghast at a woman being educated and worse, by a foreign male being allowed to enter the women's quarters. The tutors were forbidden to look on their ward and instruction must occur through a tall curtain that hung from the ceiling to the floor, and with five or six maids in attendance. The unspeakable Miss Khan took sore advantage of this system, often planting a maid in her seat before the tutor arrived and making off with Edwina into the sanctuary of the mango trees in the garden.

'Do you remember how we tried to dislodge mangoes from their branches high up in the trees with my catapult?' asked Edwina.

'I most certainly do,' replied Ruksana. 'But best of all, I remember you striking my brother with your stone one afternoon. That was a shame, for we got found out and my father installed the old curmudgeon to watch me after that, and I never got away from my miserable lessons ever since!'

Edwina glanced at the old nurse who sat nearby, but she merely nodded, guessing that her young mistress had made reference to her. Fortunately, she had not attained any comprehension of the English language by osmosis through her presence in all of Ruksana's education.

'Yes, it's a shame, you were forced to improve your mind after all,' countered Edwina with a laugh.

'Let's play a game of *parchisi* before we partake of luncheon,' suggested Ruksana enthusiastically.

Edwina acquiesced readily and the two spent a very pleasant morning together. Lunch was a grand affair. They were joined by several of her aunts who stared at Edwina, with delight. Edwina was used to this, remembering how, when she was young, she liked to stare at the beautiful ladies in the *zenana*, where males from outside the family were forbidden to enter. The lovely women often stared out at their strange European visitors through latticed windows and their giggling could be heard by the men and women who sat in the stately drawing-rooms. Unlike other Europeans who found this disconcerting, Edwina's mother simply took her daughters past the veils and sat with the women. After the initial curious gazes were exchanged, the women discovered that they had an inevitable common thread of concerns that revolved around men, children and domestic life, and many close friendships were forged between Mrs. Hardingham and her hostesses.

In the manner of Mohammedan families, they ate communally, dipping their bread into the same dish. Like many English, Edwina's palate had grown to dearly love Indian food. She found English fare prodigiously dull and indeed, mostly Indian dishes were prepared in the Hardingham household. At Katherine's home, Markham fastidiously clung to English dining and as such, Edwina never ate heartily when visiting her sister's home. After lunch, the women walked arm in arm through the large gardens in the estate. The menservants were instructed to refrain from entering the part of the gardens where the women walked and the maids walked in tow. A sentry was posted at the east end to allow them to walk in privacy. They chatted at length, with Ruksana asking Edwina many questions about her life in Simla and Edwina enquiring about her husband to be and her new life in Hyderabad. Ruksana had never met the young man, in accordance with Indian customs.

'But,' she confided, '*Abba Huzoor* showed me a likeness of his made by an artist and he is very handsome.'

The two women giggled as they conjectured what the future held for them. Their meeting was pleasant and Edwina was loath to part from her friend, but she knew she must relieve her mother and assist Kate in her place. They hugged in parting and the two women smiled tearfully at each other as they realized that they should probably not see each other again for a very long time.

'Perhaps Papa will bring us to Hyderabad for a visit some day and we can meet then,' suggested Edwina and the two faces brightened visibly.

She sank back in the waiting chaise and sighed over all the friends she had made and parted from since her family's departure to Simla. But, she reflected, women often parted from their friends when they were wed. Indian customs dictated that a woman adopt her husband's family as her own, and relegate her relationship to her own family as secondary. In consequence, most of her relationships prior to wedlock were likely to remain formal and marginal. Perhaps, then, such partings were inevitable. And, while the European wife in India may find herself isolated from her family of origin by geographic distance, she found herself sheltered in a cocoon of strong bonds with other European women. Loneliness was never something that ailed them in Calcutta, or indeed, in Simla. The society was vibrant and most families found their time crowded with many social engagements.

The chaise made its way through the heat of the afternoon back to the Markhams' residence in Chowringhee, a fashionable area close to Fort Williams that was inhabited by wealthy Europeans. Edwina decided that this evening she would not take the evening air in the Eden Gardens as she was accustomed to, for she felt excessively tired and wished to take a nap. The streets were impossible to pass, with scores of shoppers thronging the bazaars, seeking provisions for an upcoming festival. The coachman, Sunder Singh asked if she would prefer a quieter route through side streets, although that would take longer. She agreed, relieved that they would be able to move through from the heat quickly. The afternoon heat and the heavy meal soon weighed her eyelids shut and her head rested on her nurse's shoulder as the horses trotted sedately down the quiet by-lanes of the busy city.

Soon, they were in a shady, tree-lined street where a few houses loomed in the distance, surrounded by high walls and large trees. The occasional call of birds in the trees above did not arouse her and neither did the soft breeze playfully teasing the ribbons of her bonnet. In the space of a half-hour, they would find themselves at home. Suddenly, she was jolted awake by the chaise swerving violently. The horses appeared to have been panicked and Sunder Singh shouted in Hindustani for them to keep still.

Shanta screamed as she observed a rider appear alongside and grab the reins out of the coachman's hands. The elderly woman instinctively wrapped her arms around Edwina, shielding her from the onslaught of hands reaching forth into the chaise. Rapidly the women found themselves surrounded by seven or eight armed men, their faces covered by masks. One of the men reached into the now stationary chaise, but was thwarted by Sunder Singh, who lunged at him with his whip. The man lashed at him with a sword and for a moment, the men froze. To Edwina's horror, the elderly coachman slid off his perch as a line of blood appeared along his neck and arm. Her screams died in her throat and she sat in frozen terror. The men now turned their attention to the two women in the carriage. Shanta hoarsely asked them who they were and what they wanted. The one who had struck the coachman appeared to be their leader, and in menacing accents he ordered the old woman out of the chaise.

'We have no quarrel with you. Leave now while you may, for we respect your grey hairs,' said one of the men.

'Do you then have a quarrel with me?' asked Edwina in flawless Hindustani.

The men were taken aback at her fluency in their native language and glanced at each other. Sensing her advantage, Edwina swallowed hard to keep her voice from trembling.

'Why is that? What have I done to you?' she pursued.

'It is not you, you loathsome creature,' he replied. 'It is what you foreign devils have done to us. You have robbed us of our women, our lands and our livelihoods. What remains for us, but to beg and steal?'

'I have robbed no one, and neither has anyone in my family done so! And as for being a foreigner, I was born here and this is as much my land as yours. Do not hide your cowardice under the guise of vengeance for you are a despicable wretch to attack an unarmed old man and two defenseless women. You are nothing but a thug and furthermore, you should go home and wear your wife's bangles, if you have one, for you are but a coward!'

This last insult, which in India insinuated that a man should dress as a woman for he was as weak and cowardly as one (though in truth, Edwina often thought she found a great many women far more courageous than the men around them; but in the heat of the battle, this did not signify, as insult him as best she could, she must), found its mark. The men's momentary hesitation vanished. One of them reached in and grabbed her reticule, while another seized her arm. Her nurse shrieked and hurled herself on the man's arm, scratching and striking at him with all her might. In the momentary confusion, he drew back and Edwina, using her parasol, struck him in his eye. Incensed, he bellowed and made as if to hurl himself onto her, but suddenly froze as a shot rang out in the air. He wheeled around on his horse. The men with him roared and charged behind the chaise, but were soon repelled by someone who also appeared to be on horseback. Another shot rang in the air and the two women cowered in their carriage. Soon, the commotion intensified, with the sound of shots, the clink of swords, the neighing of horses and the thundering of hooves filling in the air. Someone was rescuing them. It appeared to be a great number of people, as she saw the men suddenly flee, riding their horses hard into the narrow streets that lay beyond, deserted this hot afternoon. The coachman lay dead on the ground by the side of their carriage and all appeared to become quiet in an instant. In the quiet that followed, a horse and rider appeared to Edwina's left. She shrank back as he leaned into the chaise, but relaxed when she saw a kindly face. It was a European gentleman. The man stood still, taking in the terror on her white face, and the droplets of blood on her hand from the struggle.

'Are you alright, Madam?' he asked. "You appear to be hurt, and your servant has a gash upon her forehead that must be attended to. If you tell me where you are headed, I will conduct you there in safety. Here is your reticule.'

His coolness helped her collect herself and she looked down at Sunder Singh. The sight of her apparently dead coachman affected her deeply and she reached out to receive her reticule with trembling hands.

Swallowing, she answered, 'I am quite well, sir. I thank you for your assistance. Perhaps, you will be good enough to have your men attend to my coachman. I am afraid he has been killed and he was a good man.'

'There is no one here with me, but I shall presently see to your coachman myself,' replied the stranger, dismounting his horse and going to the right of the chaise where the coachman's crumpled body lay.

Edwina marveled that he had battled the whole band of attackers solitarily, but presently, was too distracted by the sight of the elderly coachman's body to speak. The stranger lifted the old man and with tenderness, laid him in the chaise. To her great relief, he informed her that the man was still alive and with the help of a surgeon, would soon be set to right. He was informed they were residing at the home of George Markham, and having deposited the two women into the chaise and secured his own horse to the back of the vehicle, he possessed himself of the reins and proceeded to drive the chaise to the Markham residence.

The two women sat in silence, drained of all energy. Edwina mopped the blood from her nurse's brow, holding her handkerchief as a compress to stanch the flow of blood. Her nurse weakly scolded that her beautiful silk handkerchief was now ruined and she should not have done so. Edwina ignored her, continuing to hold the cloth in place until the wound stopped bleeding. She glanced at the coachman who was still unconscious. Her heart filled with foreboding at the sight of his lifeless form. Sunder Singh had been her father's coachman when the family lived in Calcutta. When they left for their new home in Simla, he had stayed on to serve Kate's household. She recalled how he had spent many hours when they were children, amusing them and walking their ponies as they learned to ride. She felt her throat tightening as a sob threatened to break out. Shanta held her gently, soothing her sore hands, which had been grazed in the violence earlier.

The carriage came to a stop before the women realized they had arrived home. The watchman at the gate stared mystified at the sight of his master's chaise being driven by a European gentleman. For a moment, he stood gaping, not comprehending the man's command that he open the gate to the Markham's mansion. The sight of Shanta leaning out of the window of the chaise, ordering him to comply with the *sahib's* request at once and to make himself useful, however, soon sent him scurrying and the gates were quickly opened.

As they approached the house, two servants ran to the chaise to help Edwina out of it. Taking in the scene, both of them abandoned the injured persons in the chaise and ran within, in a great panic, shouting out the news to the residents. Soon, the entire household, with the exception of Kate and the children, was at the door, agitatedly enquiring what had befallen them. The tall stranger quietly explained the day's events to Markham. Markham was overpowered by the news and exclaimed that this was horrifying. Anne began to cry hysterically and was soon joined in the endeavour by four maidservants. Only Mrs. Hardingham remained still and quiet. She turned to her son-in-law and told him to fetch a surgeon to attend the coachman at once. Markham hesitated. A British surgeon could scarcely be expected to attend to a wounded native coachman. Reading his thoughts, she softly directed him to seek the assistance of a friend who was a surgeon in the army. She was certain he would not refuse an old friend. She then turned to the stranger and asked him to carry the man into his quarters around the back of the house. Sunder Singh's wife, a sensible woman, went directly to prepare their rooms for her wounded husband. The surgeon arrived soon and tended to his wounds. They were deep, but not fatal. The sword had thankfully missed his arteries and with careful tending, the man's wounds would heal in time. He had sustained a blow to his head as he fell and that was what had kept him unconscious. Shanta was seen by the surgeon and her brow bandaged.

It was discovered that the stranger's name was William Grayson. The chaos of the afternoon having subsided, he was begged to stay and dine with them that night, but declined, agreeing instead to partake of tea, and promising to dine with them the next day. Markham, having regained his composure, proceeded to send for the Sergeant of Police. A report was made and Grayson described the men in as much detail as he could. They all wore black clothes.

'They were armed with swords and one was injured in his arm by my dagger before they rode off into the streets by the side,' Grayson informed them. Since these streets were not too wide, it was expected that they could not hide there for very long. 'They might still be in the city at this time,' ventured Grayson. 'Perhaps an armed search party might be sent to recover them.'

The Sergeant shook his head. 'They appear to be a gang of dacoits. We have been hearing of these dacoits for some time. They have likely disbanded and melted away into the city by now and it will be nearly impossible to find them. We can, however, see if our informants in the city report the appearance of men in black clothing on horseback within the city. If one is wounded, he might be more easily spotted,' he said.

Edwina had listened to this exchange quietly, but her brow bore a puzzled frown. 'They did not appear to want to rob from me,' she said. 'Rather, they appeared to be insurrectionists of some sort, who were rebelling against the British, for they declared their intention to kill me because they thought I was a foreign intruder in their land.'

This announcement made the Sergeant start with alarm. 'That puts the matter in a more urgent light. These men must be caught to prevent civil unrest,' he answered quickly.

Grayson, however, took a more cynical view of the men's intentions. 'They are more likely thugs who have infiltrated the city and are trying to rob innocent citizens. Such men often mask their base intentions in noble rhetoric,' he argued.

The group stared at him incredulously. The notorious *thuggees*, a violent cult of bandits, had been suppressed some twenty years ago, by

Lord William Bentick, the then Governor-General of India. Their legend was still alive in the memories of the people, however.

'I do not suggest these are the very *thuggees*,' he added quickly, noting their alarmed expressions. 'Rather, they seemed like a similar assembly, dressed as they were in a uniform of some sort. Perhaps it is a group of dacoits that wishes to revive the cult of the *thuggee*. Besides, they did seem to want to make off with your reticule, did they not, Miss. Hardingham?' he asked.

Edwina recalled that one of the men had indeed grabbed her reticule and that Mr. Grayson had restored it to her after they were put to flight. She breathed a sigh of relief, saying, 'Yes, one of them did, as I recall.'

This seemed to relieve the spirits of the entire group. The men were a group of dacoits and they had happened upon an enticing prize that afternoon, as the unarmed chaise had entered the quiet lane. 'There has been a spate of robberies in the city in quieter streets. The Commissioner has already ordered greater patrolling of these streets. To be sure, these men will make a blunder soon, and then we will catch them,' declared the Sergeant.

Edwina was grateful for the calm perspective put forth by Grayson. Indeed, the entire company seemed reassured. The Sergeant left the Markham residence relieved that he was merely chasing robbers and not traitors to the Crown!

The sobriety of the company gradually dissipated and gave way to a more convivial mood. In the stately drawing-room, surrounded by her mother and sister and the three gentlemen, Edwina felt the terror of the day loosen its hold on her. The regaining of consciousness by Sunder Singh and the absence of any ill effects sustained by her nurse served to lighten her mood. She had washed and had changed her dress and her slight wounds were attended to. She wore a silk dress of pale pink and when she entered the drawing-room, she felt Mr. Grayson's eyes follow her across the room. She glanced at him shyly and his eyes met hers. He smiled kindly at her and said that he hoped she was none too worse for the wear after the day's adventures.

'Because of your kind aid, I find myself safe at home. I admire your courage and I thank you for your kindness,' she replied in a quiet voice.

He bowed and gravely declared himself to be very much in the debt of the brigands who had allowed him to make such a pleasant acquaintance. His smile was reassuring and soon, she felt much at ease in his presence. His profile might be regarded as exceedingly handsome, and his person pleasing. The openness of his countenance, along with the laughter in his blue eyes and the ready dimpled smile at the corner of his fine-set mouth gave the impression of a very handsome and good-natured man. That he was extremely brave had already been established, and overall, all the present company perceived him as a handsome man with excellent address. Markham declared him welcome at his home at any hour, and Mrs. Hardingham repeated her gratitude to him for his assistance. On his departure, Markham immediately made plans to include him in the dinner party that was to be held that week in honour of the Hardingham ladies who were planning to effect their departure to Simla shortly.

He thought it would be capital if Edwina's Mr. Grayson made the acquaintance of Anne's Captain Lovelace. Anne immediately blushed and declared that he was not 'her' Captain Lovelace, and that Edwina had barely become acquainted with Mr. Grayson this day and he could not very well be 'her' Mr. Grayson, and that it was too provoking of him to tease them so after such a trying day! Edwina nodded in agreement with Anne, but smiled at her brother-in-law. She felt strange pleasure in hearing her new friend described as 'her' Mr. Grayson. When they had parted, she had wondered when she would see him again. Perhaps it was the banter of the dinner table, or perhaps it was the horror of the day's events, but that night, Edwina slept fitfully, tossing and turning profusely. She dreamed that Mr. Grayson had kidnapped her and was carrying her away into the hill country of Simla. But she was not distressed in the least and appeared to enjoy his company, making no protests along the way. Such nights of troubled sleep are often followed by days of listlessness and Edwina, after being reassured that all was well with the coachman and her nurse, remained in her bed for the good part of the next day.

That evening, they were joined at dinner by Mr. Grayson. He wore a fine-cut suit of black. His cravat, with a vast quantity of folds appeared to be in the latest fashion of London. His short ankle boots with their pointed toes were *de rigeur* and appeared to have been cut from the finest calfskin. He wore a large sapphire ring on his right hand and altogether presented a picture of the highest elegance. Edwina wondered that his cravat did not wilt in the heat. Markham's cravat hung crumpled around his neck, soaked in his perspiration. Mr. Grayson did not appear to perspire. Indeed, he appeared impervious to the climate and his person did much credit to his tailor's accomplishments. His family was found to belong to the peerage. He had come to India three years ago to make his fortune and find adventure.

'I have found both and perhaps so much more in India,' he declared.

This was said with a glance in Edwina's direction. His eyes appeared to follow her every move and quite often that evening, she found herself conscious of his gaze. Whenever she looked at him, he met her eyes with a smile in his and she found herself blushing more than once. And more than once, she found herself standing next to him, out of earshot of the rest of the company. Each time, he paid her some compliment and she found herself feeling warmer, as the evening progressed. When Markham announced the approaching dinner in honour of his soon-departing in-laws, Grayson appeared to be distressed to hear that the ladies were soon to depart Calcutta. On hearing that their destination was Simla, however, he broke into a smile. To their surprise, they discovered that he planned to visit Simla soon and was in fact, a frequent visitor there.

'How strange that we should not have met before, then!' said Anne.

'I only visit during the summer. I'm afraid I cannot face India in her summer glory and must retreat to the hills when the plains heat up,' he replied. 'But perhaps,' he added, 'there is more to entice one to Simla than merely the cool air.'

The significance of this remark was not lost on the rest of the company and Edwina found herself blushing again. Anne noticed the exchange of looks between the two. Though she was surprised that her plain younger sister had secured such a dazzling conquest, she good-naturedly felt pleased by it. Besides, she found Captain Lovelace to be rather dashing himself. He was in attendance tonight, and spent every moment at her side. His solicitousness was gratifying and Anne was close to admitting to herself what the others perceived as patently evident—that she was very much in danger of falling in love with Captain Lovelace. This evening, however, all eyes were on Mr. Grayson.

His manners served to delight all those present and Mrs.

Hardingham was pleased at the prospect of meeting him again. He would be visiting Simla the following month and it was decided that he would call on the Hardinghams as soon as he arrived there. In the days that followed, Markham gleaned from his friends that he was on the lookout for a wife as he had a mind to settle down. Apparently none of the fashionable women he had met in London or in India had caught his fancy. But, he appeared to be very much taken up with Edwina—his calls had been frequent and Mrs. Hardingham found herself facing the possibility of settling two of her daughters in matrimony, rather than just the one. And although she was a sensible woman who felt that young people's feelings should be allowed to take their due course, she could not but feel pleased at the prospect of Edwina's marriage. Everything about Grayson was pleasing and she wished her husband to make his acquaintance without the smallest delay.

It was therefore with much gratification that three weeks later, Elizabeth Hardingham departed for Simla with Edwina and their servants. It had been decided that Anne would remain at Kate's side, a suggestion she welcomed heartily. The journey to Simla was taxing but otherwise unremarkable. The difficulty of traveling in a horse carriage on roads that were bogged with mud was something all European women became accustomed to as they lived in India. They journeyed by chaise, accompanied by soldiers who were traveling north. They broke the journey in Delhi and then in Chandigarh, with the last leg of the journey up the mountain roads. In Simla, one mainly travelled by horseback. The Hindostan-Tibet road was nearing completion and would allow easy access through the hills of Simla. Although the Hardinghams possessed a phaeton, it was seldom used, for many of the roads were impassable except on horseback or on foot. Until the previous decade, wheeled carriages were forbidden for all except the Viceroy, who spent the summers in the cool climes of Simla along with the entire administration. The Hardinghams, like other year-round residents of the 'hill station,' as it was referred to, looked forward to easy access through the various towns at the Himalayan foothills, upon completion of the Hindostan-Tibet road. Edwina reflected on the term 'hill station.' Her race had chosen to reduce the mighty Himalayas to 'hills,' and to refer to the towns on their foothills as 'hill stations.'

Perhaps, she thought, *it reassures us that we have indeed conquered a land that we suspect is unconquerable.*

CHAPTER TWO

RETURN TO SIMLA

Simla was crowded during this time of the year. Its temperate summer clime led to its being regarded as a sanatorium. Its coolness and breathtaking beauty made it the refuge of the British who found the summer heat of the plains unbearable. They came in droves to the towns at the foothills of the Himalayas, reminiscent as they were of scenes in England and Scotland. The wildflowers and apple orchards, coupled with dizzying views of snowcapped mountains, made life in India tolerable for those who had no love for the country and no wish to remain here. Many a homesick Englishman who refused to see himself as a part of this strange and alien land saw touches of Surrey in the hill station, cherishing it as a symbol of the world he had left behind. Simla stood out among the hill stations because it was by far occupied by the wealthy and prominent. It also had a reputation for great scandal. Women whose husbands remained in the plains on business in the summer months were everywhere, along with a bevy of young ladies who had traveled from England to find suitable husbands. These members of the 'fishing fleet' as they were known, were most often the targets of gossip about scandals whether real or imagined. Bachelor officers and civil servants obligingly toured the Simla circuit, making for a very active rumour mill that often found its way to Calcutta.

For the Hardinghams, however, this place was their home. They chose to reside here year-round and long after the summer residents retreated to the plains. When the winter snows came, the land transformed itself into an enchanted realm, unrivaled in splendor. But, the snows were several months away and until then, there were plenty of thrilling occupations to indulge in. Picnics, balls, riding, and day excursions consumed one's time. The community was tightknit, especially among the year-round denizens of the land.

Edwina and her mother resumed their routines quickly and were glad to be home again. Mrs. Hardingham was especially devoted to her husband and could not bear to be parted from him. A daughter of a clergyman, Elizabeth Hardingham was devout, gentle and known for great kindness. As a younger son among many sons of a Colonel who had retired after service in the Bengal Army, Arthur Hardingham, not surprisingly, chose to journey to India with his new bride, in search of fame and fortune. Both had certainly smiled on him, as he now controlled a trade that extended between the Malabar Coast and Calcutta. He had avoided a career in the Army and had instead made a fortune in spices and calico. He was joined by his younger brother, who tragically perished from dysentery along with his wife, leaving their son Christopher in his care.

Presently, Mr. Hardingham was pursuing the promise of cultivating tea on a large scale in Darjeeling, another town on the foothills of the Himalayas and a day's journey from Simla. It seemed a risky venture, but his uncanny talent for scenting a good business prospect urged him to persevere. Time would tell if he was right or not. Already, there were efforts underfoot to cultivate tea in Darjeeling, and a good deal of interest had been evinced by the government in tea cultivation. But, not until a year's harvest would they know if the idea was a sound one. For his part, Mr. Hardingham was unruffled on the imprecise nature of the business. Succeed or fail, he had already accumulated a sizeable fortune and would not be severely jeopardized if tea failed him. Perhaps he would be a trifle inconvenienced, though, he reflected wryly. He was glad to have his wife and youngest daughter returned to him. Edwina appeared to be glowing in the mountain air and he was greatly pleased by the prospect of a favorable alliance for her, as his wife had recounted to him.

Edwina rejoiced at being returned to Christopher's company. They resumed their morning walks and she regaled him with an account of her time in Calcutta.

'How I wished I could have joined you there,' he said, as he heard of her adventures.

A weak constitution from childhood had left him confined to the sickroom for most of his life and his physician had warned him away from the heat of Calcutta. The death of his parents early in his infancy had left him in the care of his father's brother. Edwina's parents looked upon him as the son they never had. His relationship with Edwina had always been close. His gentle nature lent itself easily to nurturing his youngest cousin, who was put upon inexorably by her two elder sisters. As children, he was her protector when they tormented her. Now, when the teasing of childhood was past, he had become her friend and ally in every scheme.

'Oh, but it was nothing compared to the beauty of our beloved Simla. We were there principally to aid Kate, and my enjoyment of our journey was incomplete in your absence, dear Brother!' she replied, noticing his pensive expression.

Presently, she expressed her delight that the hunting season was yet in progress. Game was plentiful in the foothills of the Himalayas—pheasants, deer, and all sorts of wild birds. Christopher's presence allowed her to follow the hunt for pheasants, but he was soon tired, despite his enthusiasm for the outdoors.

'Do you think, perhaps, that we shall be able to hunt sometime? Uncle John has plans for a *shikar* for a tiger. He says I may go with them. Will you come? Say you will, for Papa will certainly be more apt to countenance such a scheme in your presence!'

The *shikar* was a favorite pastime of the members of the East India Company, and Edwina relished the thrill of the hunt as much as many men who found themselves in a country lush with game and characterized by natural splendour. To her delight, Christopher acquiesced. There was almost nothing he would not do for his cousin!

They did not have to wait very long to fulfill Edwina's wish, for that Sunday, the Hardinghams were paid a visit by Mr. John Knowles, a second cousin to Arthur Hardingham. Mr. Knowles was an employee of the Simla Municipal Committee and like the Hardinghams, a year-round denizen of the hill country. He was an avid sportsman and had built a reputation for being an excellent shot. He frequently participated in the more dangerous exercise of eliminating man-eaters in the surrounding hill country and had bagged quite a few dangerous trophies. He lived alone, having lost his wife many years ago, in childbirth. The child had not survived and Knowles had endured his twin losses by spending many weeks encamped in the forests surrounding his home. Today, he was besieged by his niece and nephew. No sooner had the men joined the ladies after dinner, than Edwina gestured at Christopher to begin the attack.

'Do you plan to go on a *shikar* sometime, Uncle John?' began Christopher with a self-effacing cough.

'Perhaps,' replied his oblivious uncle between sips of Sherry, before proceeding to expound on the recent events in the British expedition against Persia, to his cousin. 'Lieutenant-General James Outram's decisive command has no doubt secured the Crown a resounding victory. I'd say we'll have no more trouble on that front,' said Mr. Knowles.

Impatient with her cousin's ineffective incursion into their conversation, and anxious to steer the discussion away from war, a subject that never seemed to fail to enrapture the men, Edwina hastily interjected, 'When precisely do you plan to embark on your *shikar*, Uncle John? Christopher and I are of a great mind to join you.'

This declaration had its intended effect as her uncle and father turned quickly in her direction. Mrs. Hardingham's arched brows were belied by a twitching mouth. Her uncle suppressed a smile at the sight of Mr. Hardingham's grave countenance.

'What's this, child? You propose to follow a hunt without my permission?' her father asked.

'Oh no, Papa! I should never dream of going without your permission. I merely hoped that, since Christopher is keen on joining a *shikar*, you would trust me to the care of Uncle John. I am certain I would be of great use to them, were I to accompany them.'

This last part was said with a pleading glance in the direction of her uncle who was now shaking with mirth at the sight of Christopher's crimson face and Edwina's abject gaze. Her father glanced in his nephew's direction. There were not many exertions that Christopher undertook. Denying the boy the pleasure of a *shikar* he was desirous of going on, seemed unreasonable. He himself would not be able to go on one for the time being. He was much too occupied with business matters and he was starting to develop the gout. Accompanying John might be the only way for Christopher to enjoy a hunt, he thought.

'Besides, there cannot be much harm in my merely accompanying a hunt, for I am certain that neither of them would allow me to do anything that was truly dangerous,' added Edwina, pressing her advantage inexorably on.

Faced with an appeal that was based on the merits of the men present, Mr. Hardingham turned helplessly to his wife. Perhaps she would say with womanly distress that she could never be at ease at her daughter's foray into the kingdom of so ferocious a beast.

He was sorely disappointed in this, for Mrs. Hardingham was a woman with a lively spirit. She was inclined to insist on her own attendance at the *shikar* as a prerequisite for Edwina's presence there. But, she knew that would be rather too great a concession to anticipate from her amiable, but wary, husband.

So, she simply said in beguilingly soft accents, 'If she is in your care, John, I do not see the slightest harm in the excursion. And Christopher, I know, will be glad for her company.'

Thus overruled, Mr. Hardingham sighed and leaned back into his chair, taking solace in a glass of Port. The young persons quickly assailed their uncle with queries on how and when the expedition would be undertaken. Plans were quickly made and it was agreed that they would embark on the *shikar* in four weeks. They would travel to the surrounding forests in the lower slopes of the hill country and encamp there. Game was abundant in these parts, especially the *chital* and *sambar* that were the preferred prey of the tiger. They would be joined by their uncle's friend, a Mr. James Henry Davenport. He was also an avid sportsman and John Knowles felt that he would rather prefer to be accompanied by another accomplished marksman when entrusted with the young persons, in the jungle.

The journey promised to be taxing, as they could travel only part of the way by horseback. The rest had to be accomplished on foot and on elephants, with the group striking camp at sundown. Undaunted, Edwina beamed with pleasure at the prospect of the weeks ahead. Many preparations would have to be made. They would need ammunition, provisions and other supplies. But, Edwina was no stranger to life in the wilds. She had spent several summers hunting for wildfowl with her father and uncle. They had often encamped in the jungle and Edwina discovered that tent living suited her very much indeed! Sleep eluded her till late that night and she penned a letter to Anne in her thoughts. Anne would wish to be a member of their party, she knew. But, by the time word reached her in Calcutta, they would have returned from their adventures. She would be much too busy at any rate, to sit down to write a letter, she reflected, as she drifted off to sleep.

The following morning, Edwina waited impatiently for Christopher to join them at breakfast. She wished to go riding, and couldn't imagine why he was uncharacteristically late this morning. She swallowed a little tea and toast hastily, keeping a keen eye on the door, awaiting his appearance. When he did not arrive, but instead rang for his tea some twenty minutes later, Edwina hastily finished her tea and went upstairs to see him. He was still in bed and seemed lethargic and pale and wanted nothing but some tea. Her eagerness to leave with him was replaced by concern for him.

'Christopher! Are you ill? You seem paler than your nightshirt,' she said, looking alarmed.

'I am well, my dear. 'Tis nothing but a headache,' he said with as much cheer as he could muster. 'I did not sleep very well last night. Nothing but what a little rest will cure, which I propose to engage in, after I have had my tea. But, you were hoping to ride this morning!' he remarked, as he observed her in her riding habit, a look of dismay clouding his face.

'Yes I was, but that is nothing. I wish to see you recovered from this tiredness. Shall I read to you?' she asked, as she plumped his pillows.

'No, thank you, Eddie. I should like very much to be quiet, for all sounds hurt my head.'

Shanta arrived with his tea and she poured him a cup. She quietly prepared a cold poultice for his forehead, knowing how to minister to him, as she had done countless times before.

He held her wizened hand on his brow and sighed, saying in Hindustani, 'Just so, Shanta. You always know how to heal me!'

Shanta smiled and gently said, 'Of course I do, young Master. I have reared you from when you were a tiny little thing, no bigger than my arm!'

He closed his eyes and seemed to find relief. Shanta nodded to Edwina to leave him to rest and she noiselessly obeyed her nurse. When it came to tending sick Hardingham children, Shanta was very much in charge, and no one, not even Mr. Hardingham, questioned her authority.

Edwina found her mother on the landing of the stairs, making her way up, to Christopher's room. 'He is suffering from one of his headaches, Mama, and Shantama is presently taking care of him. He wishes to be left to rest,' she said.

'Does he require anything?' asked Mrs. Hardingham anxiously.

'No, I do not think so. He has had his tea and Shantama has prepared him a poultice. I'm afraid there remains nothing to be done, but for him to rest,' she answered.

'Do you think I may visit Mrs. Ashton this morning, then?' her mother asked.

Mrs. Ashton was a close friend and she and Mrs. Hardingham had been friends since they were in the schoolroom. Her husband was a Captain in the army and she was currently ill from the ague. She had contracted it when in the plains during the winter and her condition had not improved much since her removal to Simla.

'By all means, go, Mama. There is nothing to be done, and Christopher always recovers from his headaches by taking a nap. I myself plan to go riding, if I may,' said Edwina.

'Who is to accompany you?' asked Mrs. Hardingham as she made her way downstairs.

'I shall ask Madho to follow me on the new mare,' she replied.

Madho was the senior groom; he often accompanied Edwina when she rode, if Christopher's health did not permit him to ride. Mrs. Hardingham was satisfied and she left to visit her friend. Edwina proceeded to the stables, and called for Madho. He did not seem to be there. She walked around to the back and found the new groom, cleaning out a saddle.

'Where is Madho?' she asked.

'He has gone with *Sahib, Memsahib,*' he replied.

She recalled that her father had some business that morning that would take him to the neighbouring town of Kalka. The journey to and fro would take the best part of the day and Madho would not be back in time to accompany her. She decided to ride alone. Although her parents required that their daughters be chaperoned when outside their home, they did not put too fine a point on etiquette.

'Saddle my horse,' she said to the lad and proceeded back to the house to procure her riding crop.

Upon returning, she found her mare saddled and ready for her. She mounted lightly, with minimal assistance from the boy, and pulled the veil of her bonnet over her face, for it was a sunny day.

She followed her usual path, skirting the town, and choosing the trail that edged the woods. She breathed in the smell of the pines around her with a contented smile. She was delighted to be back in her beloved Simla, after the chaotic bustle that she had become accustomed to in Calcutta. She passed a few hill women, who were cutting grass for their cattle. They walked in single file, baskets daintily perched atop their heads, holding their sickles in one hand and their veils in place with the other. She marveled at how they managed to keep their baskets perched as they were, without the use of their hands. They turned at the sound of hooves and stepped aside to give her room. She called out a greeting to them as she rode on. They gestured and called back to her as she passed them.

It was a glorious day and a profusion of birds and butterflies surrounded her on the hills. She spied a *chital* feeding at the side of the path, fleeing, as she neared the place where it stood. As she drew near a bend in the road, she spied a large tree trunk in her path. It had become dislodged and had come crashing down on the road the night before. She was tempted to jump, and was confident in her mount. But, she hesitated. The trunk was wide and there were several sharp stones and small rocks immediately in their path, beyond the fallen trunk. If they did not clear them, she might injure her horse. She reined in her horse and veered to the right, deciding to ride in the woods for a short space until she could safely get back on to the path. There was no road to follow, and the ground was uneven, requiring her to ride deeper into the woods to get a safe footing. She made her way over grassy tufts and soon saw a herd of *chital* scatter as she disturbed their grazing.

She traversed to the left, as she instinctively knew that she had left the road from that direction. The meandering through the woods made this hard to do. Suddenly, she wasn't sure that the road was to her left anymore. She thought it might be directly behind her, but could not be sure. She felt slightly uneasy at not being able to see the road and wondered if she would be able to retrace her steps. *Perhaps I should have headed back when my path became blocked and headed out in a different direction,* she thought. She pursed her lips as she slowed her horse down. She leaned out and grasped the branch of a tree and snapped a twig on it, in two, to mark the spot. She continued to do this every eight or nine feet, so she would be able to mark her path, should she decide to retrace her steps.

She kept moving towards her left when, to her horror, she saw a tree with a snapped twig hanging from a low branch. She had been moving in circles! Suddenly, the woods did not seem beautiful anymore. The chirping of the birds, musical and marvelous thirty minutes ago, sounded menacing and melancholy now. She knew there were leopards in the vicinity, and although they were likely to engage in the pursuit of food only at night and to rest during the day, she felt uneasy at being in their terrain unarmed and alone.

'This cannot be happening!' she exclaimed to herself. 'I must simply keep a cool head and move in the direction of the sun, for it is still morning,' she said, leaning forward to stoke her horse as she whinnied at the sound of Edwina's voice.

But, the direction of the sun was hard to determine under the dense cover of trees. She thought of the women she had passed on her way. Surely they would also try to circumvent the log and pass through the woods. She listened closely to discover any human sounds from the vegetation around her, but heard nothing.

She continued on, trying to find her way back to the path she had come from, marking her way by snapping twigs on the lower branches of the trees she passed. Suddenly, she reined her horse in and froze, for she thought she had heard the neighing of a horse. She could not tell which direction it had come from, as sounds seemed to reverberate in the woods, until they came at one from all directions. She opened her mouth to call out, but suddenly decided against it. She remembered her recent mishap in Calcutta. She must not call out, until she was sure that there was no peril here. She gently stroked her horse, speaking in a low voice to steady her, and stood still, waiting to see what was beyond, in the distance.

There was no mistaking it. It was the sound of a horse, cantering now, and then gently trotting, no doubt as the terrain grew rougher. It was getting nearer and Edwina held her reins tightly, preparing to either greet the rider or to turn and flee, should the need arise. She gripped her riding crop tightly, thinking it would have to serve as a weapon if the person now approaching intended harm. She would have the element of surprise in her favour, as the rider was not expecting her presence. She glanced wildly around her, wondering which direction she should flee in, when abruptly, the sound ceased. Had she been spotted? Was she now being stalked by a mysterious rogue, she wondered. Her heart pounded as she looked around her, but there was no sign of anyone in the midst of the trees.

Suddenly, a duet of roars and barks emitted from a pair of Hornbills on the branch above her head and simultaneously, the sound of a shot rang out, ricocheting in the trees. The twin sounds had the effect of panicking her horse, and it reared instantly and fled in a terrified gallop. She clutched her reins and did her best to stay seated on her horse. She tucked her skirts away from the saddle horn, knowing that she would be dragged if they were to become entangled. She locked her legs together, gripping the pommels as best she could, imploring her horse to stop. She didn't dare jump off because of the closeness of the trees around her. She was terrified that they would crash into a tree, as it was. Without warning, she came upon a narrow clearing and her horse charged straight into a horse standing in the midst of it. Edwina felt the impact of its teeth against her arm, as the startled horse swerved to avoid them. It reared, but was soon reined in by its rider, who drank in the scene rapidly and thinking very quickly indeed, raced after her and grabbed her reins, using his horse to interrupt her mare's frantic dash. The exhausted mare soon found itself blocked in between a tree and the other horse. Its master's compelling voice and control of its reins brought it to a stop at last, and Edwina slid off, trembling violently.

She glanced gratefully up at her rescuer. He evidently was a gentleman and not a bandit or other such malignant person, as she had feared, and she smiled weakly, thinking that her earlier terror had been needless.

He strode to her side and held her arm, asking, 'Are you well, ma'am?'

He was an Englishman, dressed smartly, although not necessarily in the latest fashion of the season. His black hair was tangled over his dark brows. His swarthy complexion betrayed that he had been a native of her country for some time. Now that the terror of the moment had passed, she found herself staring at him. Being able to breathe again now, she thought him a very striking man. His shoulders were broad and despite his tall stature, he moved with ease and grace.

'Thank you, sir! I am quite well. I am slightly unnerved, but shall be myself presently,' she replied, with a wan smile.

Evidently, her artless investigation of his person had not gone unnoticed, and she swiftly became aware of him glancing over her lazily in return, taking in her hair that had now partly come undone beneath her bonnet and her scarlet riding habit. He seemed to be studying her figure and she blushed angrily, finding his gaze insulting.

She felt disconcerted now and moved away from him towards her horse, and prepared to mount, when he stood before her and grasped her hand, saying, 'Here, you seem injured.'

He was referring to a tear on her sleeve, where her arm had struck the mouth of his horse.

'It is nothing, I assure you. The tiniest scratch,' she said, freeing her arm from his grip. She made as if to mount her horse, but he continued to block her path, looking down at her mockingly.

'If you would be so kind as to step aside, sir, I should like to mount my horse,' she said tersely.

He stepped aside without a word, and as she struggled slightly to mount, she felt his arms steady her waist. She hurriedly settled herself into her saddle, leaning down to stroke her horse, speaking to her in a gentle voice. Looking up, she saw him looking at her through narrowed eyes.

'What on earth were you doing, tearing into me like that? You scared away my *chital*,' he exclaimed, with great annoyance. Before she could answer, he continued, with a sneer, 'And what are you doing here, alone and unattended? Perhaps you are here on an assignation? No doubt with a gentleman, of some means, hopefully? Or, perhaps you wished to make *my* acquaintance! Do you make a custom of charging into gentlemen to make their acquaintance, madam?'

'I assure you, sir, I am not here on any assignation, as you so *delicately* put it, and I had not the slightest intention of making your acquaintance! It was quite haplessly forced upon me by the agitation of my horse, which I might add, I may thank you for, as it was your shot that panicked it,' came her outraged reply.

'Come, come! Why don't we dispense of the affectations of propriety, as unchaperoned ladies of the *fishing fleet* are quite often rather unreserved in my experience,' he said sneeringly.

Edwina's colour heightened and she grasped her crop tightly, till her knuckles were white. How she longed to strike his mouth with it. He was a most odious and hateful man!

She answered in a strained voice, 'Your *experience*, sir, is no doubt of a most coarse and dishonorable nature. I would scarcely deign to acquaint myself with the depth of it. While I owe you no explanation, I will tell you this: I am a lady, the daughter of a gentleman, who would doubtless have you flogged for your insolence. I have spent the good part of my life in this region. In this place, I have never felt the need for a chaperone, not until today, that is. I tell you this because I wish to dissuade you from making any further vulgar observations, should you be so tempted! And, although I abhor having to ask you for any assistance, I must ask you to point me in the direction of the road, for I am lost. Of course, if you insist on acting like a boor, I would vastly prefer to wander lost in these woods, until my father seeks me out, for I doubt that these woods have any dangers worse than your acquaintance!'

She stopped, partly because she was out of breath and partly because she could think of no more heated words to say. His eyes seemed to be laughing although his face did not change expression. Taking in her white knuckles clutching her riding crop, and reading her thoughts, his mouth twitched slightly.

'Rest assured madam, your charms are not so great as to cause me to forget I am a gentleman. You are quite safe in my company. I shall conduct you to the road as soon as I have recovered the deer I have shot. I should doubtless prefer to save the good men of Simla the ordeal of conducting a search for a silly female who chose to go careening through the forest unattended,' he said contemptuously, as he strode towards the deer he had lately shot, unlike its lucky companion that had escaped.

Edwina was now dangerously quiet. Those who knew her well knew that once the heat of rage was past, she became silent with a white fury. When she was thus angry, she could be oblivious of hurt to herself or to others. At present, she was helpless. While she was desperate to ride on, away from this lunatic, his words had stung. She had made a foolish choice, not in deciding to ride alone, but in departing from the path and into the woods when alone. She knew her father would not be home until sunset and a search party in the dark would be unsuccessful. Besides, she was not keen to spend the night alone in this ominous place, which seemed to intimidate one so, even in broad daylight. She bit her lip and refrained from responding to his insult.

Instead, she said in a low voice, 'Thank you for your generous offer to conduct me back to the road. I gratefully accept.'

The sarcasm in her words made him chuckle, but he said nothing, quickly loading the dead deer onto the horse, instead. She silently waited as he mounted and followed as he made his way back to the path. How she wished she had brought along her pistol. She must remember to carry it with her whenever she rode. She would dearly love to shoot him in the back. She wasn't bound to a gentleman's code of honour, after all. Why couldn't she shoot him in the back? The thought that that would constitute an unladylike course of action flitted through her mind, but was hastily dismissed. Envisioning him shot by her made the journey pleasant, so imagine it the more she did. Each time they passed a low branch, he swung it aside, not waiting to hold it for her as she passed. Several times, she had to duck, in order to avoid being struck by a swinging branch. Each time, she mentally increased the tortures she would accord him. Not only would she shoot him, but also ride over his body as it lay on the ground! Thankfully, they found themselves back on the path, close to where the fallen tree lay, before long.

He turned to her, asking, 'Well, which way to your house, now?'

She icily replied. 'Thank you for your assistance with my horse and with finding my way back, sir. It delights me greatly to inform you that I shall not need it anymore!'

With that, she set her horse on a furious gallop. She heard his horse start to canter, but she went frantically on, not looking behind her. She reached a path that cut through the Hardingham estate and veered onto it, before he could make his way around the bend and catch sight of her. She had the impression that he was not really following her. His bay stallion could have easily caught up to her smaller mare, but she did wish to find out whether or not she was his quarry.

She found herself in front of the house in a few minutes and rode towards the stables. She had been gone for three hours, but no one would have been worried by her absence, for Mrs. Hardingham was still away. As she neared the house, she became aware of two of the menservants standing outside the house talking animatedly with a stranger. The man was a *dâk* runner. He had brought with him a letter for her father from Calcutta. The letter was sizeable in bulk and bore the new 4 *anna* stamp with the image of Her Majesty, Queen Victoria. The penmanship on the envelope was unmistakably Markham's. She was immediately curious, frustrated that she would have to wait at least until after supper to hear its contents from her father. Perhaps there was a letter from Anne addressed to herself within it. And surely there was news of the children, particularly the new infant. But, she would not open it until her father gave her leave to do so. She hastily gave the *dâk* runner a generous reward of five *annas* for his effort. The man gratefully *salaamed*, while the head steward, Haridas shook his head at her naiveté; but she hurried on in, directing the two servants to feed the man.

The men gladly retreated to the wing of the house that contained the kitchen. After their meal, they sat down to rest in the shade of a large chinar tree outside the kitchen. Reclining on their *charpoys* and softly sucking on their hookahs, they listened as the man entertained them with tales of his adventures as a *dâk* runner. The *dâk* runner carried the post, often at peril of his life. There was usually a relay of conveyors, with each group of men carrying their cargo in a palanquin suspended on a pole, balanced expertly on their shoulders. The journey for each group of bearers carried fresh dangers and excitements.

'Frequent has been the night where we hid from bandits intent on attacking us, as we ran with the *dâk*,' he informed them. 'One time, we hid in a cave on seeing a band of dacoits,' he continued, as their eyes widened.

The men listened enraptured as he told them of his brush with death as he crossed a river filled with *muggurmuch*.

'Sometimes we lose the mail to these evil men, but the *sahibs* are fiercely angry when that happens,' he lamented. 'Why did you not journey with a caravan of travellers? Why were you so careless? That is all one hears from them. Never do they recognise the hardships of a *dâk* runner's life,' he said, shaking his head. 'The *sahibs* are ever quick to kick a hungry man in the stomach,' he continued.

Haridas and Manohar Lal, the other servant, nodded gravely. They ruminated on the *dâk* runner's words.

Then Haridas spoke, 'You are right. A great many *sahibs* are cruel and unfeeling. Even here in Simla, such cruel ones are to be found. However, not all the *sahibs* are unkind. Hardheenghamm *sahib* is not so, for he treats us with kindness.'

After waiting for a reasonable amount of time, for he was the younger of the two, Manohar Lal added, 'That is most true, Brother. We are well-cared-for here. And the *memsahib* treats us as her children. Why, only the other day, I had a gash on my arm and she was most solicitous in pouring ointment on it and forbade me from working until it healed. That was most trying for the household, for we are the only menservants here, with the exception of those who work in the stables, that is—'

He paused for a breath and was met with a stern look from Haridas, who was the senior of the two. The younger man was given to great loquaciousness and Haridas shrewdly assessed that he had just started his speech and, if left unchecked, would wax eloquent on this and a great many subjects. As head steward of the house, he carried precedence in the household, by virtue of having served the Hardinghams for a great many years. And although the norms of Indian hospitality demanded that he treat the visiting *dâkwallah* with great courtesy, he was not inclined to disclosing too many details about the household to a stranger. Manohar Lal discreetly lowered his eyes in deference to the older man.

'Your words are true. I have seen the generosity of the young *memsahib* with my own eyes,' replied the *dâkwallah*, retrieving the coins Edwina had given him, from a pouch fastened to his crimson cummerbund, where he had deposited them earlier. 'And besides, it is not just the *gora sahibs* who are heartless. The *zameendars* are cruel too. They extort outrageous taxes from the poor farmers, even when there is a drought. My wife's brother is a farmer and his fields were dry from the drought last year. The ground was parched and the heavens did not lend him a single drop of rain. He had no grain to feed himself and his family. But the *zameendar's* men whipped him when he could not pay his *lagaan*. The poor man hanged himself. His widow and unlucky children live on the mercies of the others in the village. My father was a farmer too, crushed underneath the weight of the *lagaan*. I swore on his funeral pyre that I would never be a farmer. The life of a *dâkwallah* is dangerous, but infinitely better than that of a farmer,' he said.

The men listened with moistened eyes. The man's story was truly sad. What was to become of his wretched wife and children, they wondered. They talked at length of the prices of grain and agreed that the rulers did nothing for the poor of the land. Their conversation lulled and the *dâkwallah* settled on the *charpoy* for a nap, as the men returned to their chores. He would wait for Mr. Hardingham's reply and leave the next day, staying the night in Haridas' cottage, for Manohar Lal's wife had gone to her mother's home to bear their first child, and there would be no hospitality suitable for a guest there. Haridas' wife would feed them and prepare them a *paan* to chew on after their meal and gently rock the *pankha* to keep the men cool as they talked.

Inside the house, Edwina laid the letter on her father's desk. The excitement of receiving the letter from Calcutta served to somewhat ease the disquiet from earlier in the day. She rang for a cool glass of lemonade, and enquired after Christopher. He was still asleep and she sat down and awaited the return of Mrs. Hardingham. She did not have to wait long, for her mother returned with Christopher's physician in the space of a half-hour.

'Mama! You are returned. It has been such a morning!' she exclaimed as her mother entered the sitting room where she was, reclined on a chaise lounge.

'Why, Edwina! Is something amiss? Is Christopher well?' asked her mother with alarm.

On seeing the doctor, Edwina quickly caught herself. Sitting up, she answered 'Oh yes, yes! Certainly, ma'am! He does very well. I have been told he is still napping which always bodes well for him when he has his headaches.'

She glanced in the direction of the doctor. Sensing that the conversation would have to keep until they were alone, Mrs. Hardingham steered the doctor towards Christopher's bedchamber, leaving Edwina to reflect on the events of the day.

When they returned downstairs, her mother pleasantly informed her, 'Christopher is well. He is quite recovered. Doctor Willoughby says he will be well enough to partake of dinner with us.'

'Quite so, ma'am, but he must refrain from any form of strenuous activity. I will not recommend bloodletting, for it is an unprofitable exercise. I have, however, an excellent remedy here containing valerian and mustard. A few drops of this with some brandy will give him respite and cause him to slumber for a while. When he awakes, I'll wager he'll be himself again,' he said, thrusting a bottle into Mrs. Hardingham's hands.

'Will you not partake of luncheon with us, Doctor Willoughby,' asked Mrs. Hardingham.

'It would be my pleasure ma'am, for the food at your fine table is always the best in Simla,' came his pleased answer.

'You are most kind,' she answered, 'and you have revealed yourself to be an admirer of simplicity, for we do not indulge in grand repasts here,' she said with a smile.

Their meal comprised of a fiery mulligatawny soup, a roast fowl, mutton curry and rice, fried fish, that most delectable of Indian deserts—the rice pudding, *Kheer*—a very good cheese, fresh bread and butter and an exceptional claret. And while delightful to the palate, it was austere in comparison with the fanfare with which other Anglo-Indian families dined. Englishwomen who came to India were astonished by the cheapness of foodstuffs in India. Half a goat could be procured for as little as one rupee! Consequently, the most unrefined persons coming to India from England could afford the greatest delicacies, and mealtimes were occasions for demonstrating great fanfare, with sixteen or seventeen courses served at a single meal. The commonest Anglo-Indian families living in India could afford to live like the best families in England. The Hardinghams, on the contrary, were possessed of an aversion to affectation and excess and dined well, rather than wantonly. To their guest, the meal was a refreshing departure from the rich fare he was accustomed to when he partook of his *tiffin*.

Following his departure, Mrs. Hardingham turned to Edwina and asked directly, 'Now, dearest, pray tell me what the source of your disquiet was when I returned this afternoon.'

Edwina paused to sit down, searching in her mind for an answer.

'It was merely the anxiety of Christopher's malaise, Mama. It was rather a hot morning and I was perturbed by the continuation of his distress when I returned. It pains me to see him suffer so,' she said.

She had decided not to disclose her unsettling encounter with the offensive person she had met earlier. Her mother would be agitated by the intelligence, and would no doubt censure her for riding unchaperoned.

'Did you have a pleasant time?' enquired her mother.

'To be sure, I did, for a great profusion of birds were to be seen everywhere. Pray, how does Mrs. Ashton do?' she asked, praying silently that her mother would not discover Madho's departure for the day with her father.

Mrs. Hardingham however, was too tired to notice her slight deception.

'She is well now and was glad to see me today,' she answered. She was accustomed to a siesta after her luncheon and retired summarily to her bedchamber, summoning her maid to tug the cords of the *pankha* hanging above her bed, to cool her as she slept, for it was a hot day. Edwina herself felt her eyelids droop from the exertions of the morning and followed her example.

The custom of taking afternoon tea that was pervading England had found its way to India and, to their delight, Christopher was able to join them, refreshed from his nap. He sat beside Edwina on a settee as she sat bent on her needlework.

'What adventures have I forfeited today, Eddie?' he asked with a smile.

She gave him a look filled with meaning, nodding at her mother.

He walked towards the large window on the furthest corner of the room exclaiming, 'How good it is to be able to look outside without feeling oppressed by the light. Come, sit by me, Eddie.'

She complied and in a low voice, apprised him of the happenings of the morning. He listened gravely, becoming alarmed when she described the stranger's coarse treatment of her. 'Why Eddie, you have been a silly chit, wandering around in the woods without a proper escort! Consider the grave danger you were in!' he chided.

'Pray do not scold me, Chris, for I should not be able to bear it after such a trying day. You must not tell Papa about it, for it will put him into a rage,' she pleaded.

'Don't be such a goose. I should never betray you! Don't fret, love, I shan't scold you anymore, even though you *have* been excessively foolish,' he said, pinching her chin with a kindly smile. 'I should like to get my hands on that rogue's neck, though,' he said, his eyes hardening.

'Well he cannot be thought of as too base, for he *was* a gentleman and he *did* rescue me,' she said grudgingly.

'That is true. You should probably be still lost in the jungle had you not happened on him. Still, his conduct does belie breeding!' he remarked.

Edwina found her secret very nearly discovered when, at supper, her father following a disclosure of his activities that day and receiving a full report in return from Mrs. Hardingham about Christopher's recovery, turned to her and said, 'Edwina, you must have had a monstrously dull day, with your cousin confined to his bed all morning.'

She was sure her mother would remark that she had been riding, and he would instantly enquire who her escort was. And although he had disapproved of her riding unescorted in the past, he would not be unduly perturbed by it. What she loathed was to give her mother the impression that she had been deliberately deceptive. That would surely arouse a great deal of unwelcome curiosity in their breasts.

She was saved from answering by Christopher who, pretending not to hear his uncle's question to Edwina, interjected, 'Uncle Arthur, how is your *munshi*, Mohan Das? Will he not return to Simla? Our affairs are shockingly tangled by his absence.'

His uncle was immediately drawn to a discussion of business affairs for he too was concerned by the necessity of his clerk's having to be away from Simla. The man had temporarily been placed in charge of the tea cultivation that they were experimenting with in Darjeeling.

'Ay, it's time we had him back here. Perhaps we should employ another person to manage the affairs in Darjeeling,' he replied.

Edwina breathed out softly, thanking her cousin silently for his protection. Following their supper, the family was at last able to inspect the contents of Markham's letter. Mr. Hardingham read it silently, his face betraying no expression. When he finished, he handed it to Mrs. Hardingham who read it aloud. There was a message from Kate, describing the children's health and her own forays back into Society. She had heartily resented her seclusion, necessitated by her recent childbearing, and appeared to be thrilled to be returned into the arms of Calcutta Society. Anne's letter, consequently, contained a detailed description of the excitements that she had lately partaken of, including several balls she had attended.

She made mention of missing Edwina, saying, 'I often think about Eddie, especially when I have to attend a ball. For none can fashion my hair as prettily as she does.'

'Anne's affection for you is sincere in that she sincerely misses you whenever she requires something. Consider how lonely she might have been had you not been born, Eddie,' her father remarked with a twinkle in his eye.

'Arthur! Consider how unkind a picture that paints of her, and is Edwina of so little consequence that she is only thought of when one requires assistance?' his wife remonstrated in shocked accents.

'Come now, Lizzie. You know that I jest,' he replied soothingly. 'Meanwhile, the real news we have today is that Anne's young man has sought my permission to offer for her. Markham seems to approve of him, although I might add, that would distinguish the chap as prodigiously dull!' he said.

'You are determined to tease me tonight, my dear,' said Mrs. Hardingham disapprovingly. 'George is an excellent man and is quite devoted to Kate. He may not possess a keen wit, but I hardly think he is dull. Besides, Anne has most certainly developed a *tendre* for this young man, if my eyes are to be believed.'

'You are certain of Anne's feelings in this matter?' he asked.

'I am not in my dotage just yet, Arthur. I imagine I can still whiff love when it passes me by,' she countered smartly.

Her words were greeted by a shout of laughter by her husband and nephew. Edwina giggled.

'Indeed Mama, you are quite the romantic. I wonder if you are not fancying their attachment, because you wish very much to be in love yourself,' she said mischievously.

'Nonsense, child! There was never a woman more blasé than I. I have never had much use for Romance,' she retorted.

'So saying, you wound me with an incurable wound,' said her husband with mock seriousness. 'Would you have me give them my blessing?' he asked.

'Yes, most certainly, for he is a respectable man and it is what, I believe, Anne wishes greatly,' she replied, adding, 'Now, it is time for

Edwina to be presented, for it will not do for her not to have the good fortune of developing a *tendre* of her own!'

'I do not have the slightest wish to form a *tendre*, Mama,' she answered calmly, not for a moment missing her mother's intended meaning. 'I am convinced, like you, that nothing is more tiresome than a Romance. I dislike balls, and I believe I am quite content to dwell here with the three of you.'

'Stop talking gibberish,' ordered her father with a chuckle. 'There is not a young woman I have known who is not forever yearning for a ball. Perhaps what you are angling after is a ball of the first stare. We must take you to London so you can attend the season at Almack's. I hear that the formidable arbiters of that temple have slipped into a decline and their grip of the place has loosened. We should quite easily obtain a voucher for you there, Eddie,' he teased.

'Ah, but that would be of no avail, I'm afraid Papa. For I have it on good authority that Almack's is no longer *de rigueur*. I'm afraid its allure has deteriorated with the departure of its patronesses. I might very well end up an old maid, were I to be presented there,' she replied laughingly.

'That would not do in the least, for I am certain you should be the most disagreeable old maid! I'm afraid there is nothing to be done, but to present you to society at the earliest possible instant! We shall have to settle for a ball for you in Simla,' said her mother. 'It's settled then. You shall be presented here, and perhaps you can visit Kate in the winter, for the pace of Society picks up in Calcutta when the weather is cool,' said her mother.

Mr. Hardingham nodded saying, 'Anne must return home, then. And Captain Lovelace may pay his respects whenever he finds leave from his duties.'

'As to that, I am not at all certain that she would care to be parted from him, or from Society for that matter,' warned Mrs. Hardingham. 'I daresay we would do well to apply ourselves to Edwina's ball. The enjoyment will be welcome for Christopher,' she added.

Edwina was pleased by this. She hated to see her cousin excluded from the amusements of life. A ball would be perfect entertainment for him. The thought of its consequence for him weighed far more with her than her own gratification.

'In that case, we simply must have a ball! I am sure to find something to wear among all the dresses we purchased in Calcutta. When will it be, Mama?' she asked, pleased with the prospect of it now.

Her mother smiled, answering that they would need at least three weeks to prepare for it.

The following day, she embarked on a stroll with Christopher through the Cart Road, recently constructed by Lord Dalhousie. She was pleased to encounter several acquaintances on their walk. She passed the wives of several colonels and captains. The latter nodded at her, while the former looked icily away.

'It would appear, dear Christopher, that you and Papa are not important enough, for no lady of consequence in Simla will condescend to our acquaintance,' said Edwina with a giggle after one such pretentious matron passed them by without so much as a nod.

'On the contrary, Eddie, I believe it is you they find vastly unbecoming, for these ladies are wont to be quite convivial towards me when you are absent,' he countered with a twinkle in his eye.

'Oh! In that case,' she retorted, 'I must warn Mama and Papa, for your fortune may be endangered by the wiles of a mercenary female!'

This prompted a chuckle from her cousin. He was quite wealthy with an income of eight thousand pounds a year, left in the trusteeship of his uncle until his twenty-eighth birthday. In Simla, however, where social consequence was rigidly determined by the military rank of the officers, wealth and fortune did not inevitably open the doors to Society. Fortunately, the Hardinghams did not care for such snobbery and had cultivated a small cluster of intimates with whom they shared a genuine attachment.

'I suppose I *could* hope for a matrimonial prize after all, couldn't I?' he asked lightheartedly.

'Well, I suppose you might catch a very *desperate* woman from the officer-set, but you must not expect her to be very accomplished,' came the reply.

This last part was said with such a serious expression that her cousin convulsed with laughter that rendered him breathless for the space of a few minutes.

Neither of them perceived the approach of a gentleman from the rear. Not until they heard her name called did they look at the man who was now walking abreast, to their right. To her surprise and delight,

Edwina found herself looking up into Mr. Grayson's striking countenance. He was attired in a dark frock coat over lighter trousers and low-heeled shoes, along with a soft-crowned grey hat. He presented a picture of great elegance and Edwina was instantly conscious of the plainness of her white muslin gown. His smile was dazzling and she felt her stomach tangling into a thousand knots. Oddly, she wished she presented a more stylish appearance this morning.

'M—Mr. Grayson,' she heard herself stammer, 'how do you do?'

His reply was given in a calm and collected tone, and at last, her tongue came unglued and the words rushed out all at once, 'How delighted I am to see you again. I had not thought to see you again for several weeks. This is most welcome!'

Her momentary confusion surprised her cousin and signaled at once to him that the stranger was special. He quickly gathered that this was Edwina's rescuer. He had been made aware of the chilling events that had occurred in Calcutta, but nothing in Edwina's words had indicated the formation of a friendship with her champion.

'Mama has been telling Papa about you and you simply must call on him as soon as you are able,' she continued, slowly becoming aware of Christopher's surprised expression.

But, she could not contain the pleasure that brimmed over. She had thought often of William Grayson and now, when he was before her in the flesh, could not treat him with maidenly reserve.

'Allow me to introduce you to my cousin, Christopher Hardingham,' she said, warmly.

The two men bowed formally, but Grayson soon put the younger man at ease with his genial manner.

'I had formed the intention of calling on your father this morning, when I suddenly saw you. Perhaps I may accompany you on your way your home?' he suggested smilingly.

On their way to the Hardingham home, Christopher enquired whether the bandits who had attacked his cousin had been apprehended.

'Sadly there was no trace of them to be found. That is often the case in Calcutta. The criminal finds a safe haven in the bustling streets and bazaars and employs the art of camouflage, making him virtually impossible to apprehend,' answered Grayson.

The conversation turned to more pleasant topics as Grayson

interviewed his hosts about possible diversions in Simla. On realizing that Christopher's ill health often hindered him from his favorite pastimes, he soothingly replied that India's climate was apt to diminish one's pursuit of more active pleasures. Mrs. Hardingham was greatly pleased to see Grayson again. She had wondered about what had kept him away from Simla all these weeks. She was sure she had not been mistaken in thinking there was a romance budding between Edwina and him. She greeted him warmly and introduced him to her husband as the gallant gentleman who had rescued Edwina from peril in Calcutta. Studying the man, Mr. Hardingham found him quite amiable. His manners were pleasant, and while there was something lofty about his carriage, he seemed careful to avoid the impression of hauteur. On the contrary, he seemed eager to please. Mr. Hardingham enquired of Grayson's parents.

'I regret to say, sir, they are both deceased. They were drowned at sea on a voyage to England from India. I returned to settle their business affairs, but found myself seduced into staying in this enchanting land of promise,' he said.

'This must have come as a great shock to you and to your brothers and sisters,' said Mrs. Hardingham gently.

'I have no brothers or sisters, ma'am. I was the only child of my parents. Perhaps that made my journey into this land so much more inevitable.' This disclosure served to arouse the sympathy of all present.

'It pains me to hear that you have faced such harsh circumstances. Nevertheless, perhaps God will use your sad experiences to bring some great good to your life. It has often been my observation that it is in our darkest moments, when Heaven seems the farthest away, that the kindness of God shadows us the most,' said Mrs. Hardingham kindly.

'You are extraordinarily kind, ma'am and entirely correct, for I believe the hand of Providence has given me fortitude through much hardship. The kindness of my friends makes me look upon life with great optimism,' he replied with a smile.

His cheeriness in the face of such harsh experience elevated him in the esteem of his new acquaintances. He became a regular fixture in the Hardingham residence, walking and riding with Christopher and Edwina, dining with the family and forming an agreeable fourth at whist when Christopher was too tired to play. He had extracted from her a promise of two dances at the ball. But, that did not seem to satisfy him for very long.

'I should like to dance every dance with you, Miss. Hardingham,' he said softly to her as they played a game of Écarté one evening.

'I don't think you can, for Papa is most strict about such things,' she said with a smile.

'In that case, I shall dance with no one but you that night,' he replied.

'You shall present a rather odd appearance, in that case, Mr. Grayson, for no one dances just one dance at a ball!' she declared with a smile.

CHAPTER THREE

THE BALL

The ball was a modest affair, by Calcutta's standards. Still, it was well attended for it was the height of the season, when Simla was brimming over with Europeans who had fled what they described as the 'fiery climate of the plains.' In addition, the Hardinghams were as highly regarded for their consequence as for their wealth. The reputation of Edwina's grandfather, Colonel Hardingham, had certainly stood them in good stead, for they were eagerly sought after by much of the fashionable set in Simla. Moreover, while some officers and their wives might scorn their inclusion into Society, a great many families recognised their refinement and considered themselves honoured to receive an invitation.

Edwina was attired in a silk taffeta dress of the softest shade of cream with a full gathered skirt, a rounded open neckline and short puffed sleeves. A profusion of peach rosebuds were embroidered onto the fashionably longer bodice and the skirt, and scattered across the trimming of her neckline. She wore a pair of coral earrings fashioned in gold. A coral and diamond girandole fastened to her bodice completed her toilette. The fiery hue of her jewellery stood out against her dark hair, which was worn in an unaffected chignon, with a lock of hair on the side framing her face. She blushed at the proud glint in her father's eyes as he caught sight of her.

'Why, my dear, you are certainly very pretty today. It is too bad your sisters are not here to bear you company,' he exclaimed.

Christopher smiled down at her, saying, 'Step lightly as you dance tonight, Eddie. For, I am certain you will tread on many gentlemen's hearts before dawn!'

She laughed, retorting, 'I believe it's the gentlemen's toes that will suffer and not their hearts, for I am a sadly unsatisfactory dancer.'

The room was bedecked with dozens of paraffin lights, ensconced in glittering globes of glass that hung from the ceiling. The reflections of the multitude of flames on the dazzlingly attired women made the room seem ten times more brilliant. While the European women shone, it was the Indian ladies, several of whom were present at the ball, who truly bedazzled all, decked in *sarees* woven of metres of silk and gold. The Hardinghams had several distinguished Indian friends and they had graced the occasion with their presence. Some were the relatives of noblemen and others simply old friends. Several of the women huddled in a secluded section of the room, unable to reconcile themselves with the strange customs of the English that allowed respectable women to dance in public and worse, with unrelated men. One of them, a relative of a princess from the kingdom of Patiala smiled shyly at Edwina, when the latter was presented to her.

'I have brought you a small gift,' she said, handing Edwina a beautiful jewelled box.

'I am most fortunate to be the recipient of such a magnificent present as this!' exclaimed Edwina, smiling with pleasure.

The box was studded with gems and contained two containers of the most choice *attar*. Edwina gasped at the magnanimity of the gift. Her guest, bedecked in sparkling earrings, necklaces and nose rings that glittered with her every movement smiled at her obvious pleasure. Edwina looked at the women wistfully, wishing she could herself be dressed as they were, in the finest silks, the softness of which was unbelievable. She found most European attire drab in comparison. Tonight, however, she was somewhat satisfied with her apparel.

Although she was not vain in the least, she found herself delighted by the approving glances cast in her direction. She was seldom noticed when in the company of her dazzling sisters. And while she heartily wished that they could be here tonight, she felt a heady rush of triumph rise within her. *So this is how it feels to be admired*, she thought to herself.

Grayson, in a finely cut dress suit, appeared a remarkably striking figure and his attention to her was even more flattering. She stood up with him for a quadrille and was conscious of many envious glances from the young ladies present. When the dance concluded he declared himself devastated, for she would stand up for no more than one other dance with him after this.

He said, 'Then I shall dance the waltz with you. Until then, I must go and find consolation by talking to your charming father,' casting a telling look at her.

'Oh, but you must dance with the other ladies present here tonight,' she protested, ignoring the implication of his words, though a flush was slowly creeping across her face. She continued, 'I think it would be imprudent if you were to ignore the rest of the ladies present.'

He seemed much struck by this and said, 'Quite so! It wouldn't serve to give the females present too much fodder for gossip. Perhaps I should dance with that insipid wallflower sitting there,' nodding in the direction of a quiet and plain young woman who was sitting unobtrusively, watching the dancers whirl past her.

The lady was Grace Appleby, the daughter of Major John Appleby who was serving in a regiment fondly referred to as the Bombay Sappers. They were acquaintances, although not intimate, for their residence was in Ahmednagar and they only visited Simla in the summer every year. Edwina looked reproachfully at him, uneasy at the unkindness of his words.

He gave a chuckle and reassured her saying, 'You are too kind a being. I overheard that person speak ill of you. I cannot countenance ill-natured creatures. I must always be loyal to my friends. But I shall speak no more ill of her for you have too generous a nature to abide that.'

Edwina was puzzled by his words. She could not imagine that a person as quiet and gentle as Miss. Appleby would speak ill of anyone.

Perhaps she has perceived herself slighted in some way. Or, perhaps Mr. Grayson has misunderstood her words. I should go and speak with her so she will not be displeased with me any longer, thought she.

She was prevented from this by her next partner and when the dance was concluded, she was approached by Grayson who said amicably, 'I misspoke. Miss. Appleby is a most amiable creature. I believe it was not you that she was speaking ill of, but some other lady who has indulged in some great scandal, occasioning the death of her father from a stroke!'

Edwina was relieved to be made aware of the absence of ill will towards her, but was prevented from conversing with Miss. Appleby by her standing up for a dance with another gentleman. Mr. Grayson's incursion into her corner of the ballroom had not gone unnoticed and had resulted in a great many women regarding her with jealousy. It had also invited the notice of several gentlemen who felt a keen necessity to outdo their dashing rival, with the result that Miss. Appleby found herself playing the part of a wallflower no more.

Edwina's card was full and she danced with a great many gentlemen, until she felt quite exhausted. Grayson was gallantly fulfilling his promise to eschew scandal and was dancing with a dazzled lady. The room was hot and Edwina suddenly felt she needed to rest. Glancing down at her dance card, she was relieved to see that Christopher was to dance the next two dances with her. Looking around, she spied Christopher talking to an old friend, Frances Hawkins. Miss. Hawkins had recently become engaged to a Captain and she was excitedly informing Christopher about the new home that he had purchased for her in Calcutta.

'Edwina, you are dazzling!' she exclaimed, catching sight of Edwina.

'Ah, but I can scarcely match the glow on your countenance, Fanny,' Edwina replied graciously. Happily, her friend was spoken for at the next dance and Edwina put her hand on her cousin's arm, begging him to take her outside for a spell.

'What, and forego the opportunity to dance with you?' he asked with mock sorrow.

'Oh do not tease me, Chris, for I am intolerably warm and might swoon. Think how tiresome you should find it to tend to me then!' she replied.

'Not to mention how many belles I shall miss dancing with if I had to waste my time waving smelling salts under your nose!' he retorted, leading her out to the quiet verandah.

To their surprise, they found her parents and her uncle standing there with a guest.

'Frightfully hot in there, isn't it?' remarked her father taking in her flushed face. 'Your mother threatened to faint if I did not bring her out into the cool air for a moment,' he added.

Edwina and Christopher burst out laughing, and Christopher

exclaimed, 'Why, Uncle Arthur, I believe it is some sort of conspiracy, for Edwina herself said that to me not five minutes ago.'

'On the contrary, I believe it accentuates the veracity of my claim that the room was uncomfortably hot, for Mama needed some respite too. I am surprised that all the ladies present here tonight have not insisted on being escorted out into the verandah,' returned Edwina.

'Heaven forbid! That would make the place deucedly crowded!' responded her uncle, adding, 'Here, Eddie, allow me to present to you my old friend, James Henry Davenport. If you recall, he will be accompanying us on the *shikar*,' he said, turning to allow his friend access around the pillar and to where Edwina stood.

She turned to curtsey and froze as she looked up at the face of the man bowing to her. Standing in front of her was not the avuncular gentleman she had assumed her uncle's sportsman friend to be, but a young man with a familiar face. To her horror, the man looking amusedly down at her was the insolent stranger she had encountered in the jungle not many days ago.

'You—!' she uttered incredulously, before she could prevent the words from escaping her mouth.

A horrified expression had taken possession of her face. She opened her mouth to say something and then closed it, becoming aware that the rest of the party was looking at her with great surprise.

'Is something the matter, Edwina?' asked her mother gently. 'Are you acquainted with Mr. Davenport?'

Edwina swallowed hard, casting about desperately in her mind for a reply. That the man was her uncle's friend put the matter in a completely different light. No doubt her father and uncle would, should they hear of that day's events, take a dim view of her departure from the road into the jungle, unescorted. His uncivil words would only embarrass her, if repeated. The fact that she had concealed the incident from her parents would dismay them. No matter what was said, she would emerge from the episode looking very shabby indeed.

She took a sharp breath, but before she could say anything, Mr. Davenport smoothly interjected, 'You are quite right madam. Miss. Hardingham has had the misfortune of seeing me pass by here recently, attired in a somewhat raggedy fashion. No doubt, she believed me to be in dire straits and wished to bestow some charity on me and is now vastly astonished to find I am not a deranged fakir. That she even recognised me is somewhat remarkable.'

Edwina stared at him, greatly mystified. She felt a sort of awe at the glibness with which he seemed to have taken hold of the situation and explained himself. She would think it a rather strange explanation later, but for the moment, she marvelled greatly at his coolness.

'I was thrown off my horse and trespassing through your land, when she saw me pass by. Not wishing to be presented to a lady when I seemed so shabby, I hastily walked away before she could offer me assistance,' he continued casually. 'I hope you will forgive me for trespassing through your land, Mr. Hardingham, and you Miss. Hardingham for my dishevelled appearance and indecorous manner,' he finished, with aplomb.

'Nonsense, Mr. Davenport, If there's anything to forgive, it's that you did not march in here and demand our assistance!' exclaimed Mr. Hardingham.

'Were you badly hurt, Mr. Davenport,' asked Mrs. Hardingham anxiously.

But, before Mr. Davenport could respond, her uncle interjected, 'How in heaven's name did *you* get thrown off a horse, Davenport? I'll be dashed if you weren't in your cups. Were you? Come to think of it, I believe you'd stay mounted even if you *were* to take a seasoning! What happened?'

Edwina and her mother looked at each other, slightly amused and slightly embarrassed.

'Ah, John, that is a base accusation, indeed,' responded Mr. Davenport smoothly. 'I do not make it a habit of being intoxicated, much less of riding when so. I trust you will be kind enough to disbelieve Mr. Knowles' caricature of my character, Mrs. Hardingham,' he said gravely, with a bow, even as Mr. Hardingham and Christopher chuckled.

Mrs. Hardingham smiled, saying, 'Of course I shall, Mr. Davenport. Any friend of John's must certainly be of an unimpeachable character, and you certainly do not seem the exception.'

'And any faults that might appear in you are undoubtedly the deleterious effects of my cousin's acquaintance,' added Mr. Hardingham with a laugh. They continued to converse, with Edwina discovering that like her father, the man had made a substantial fortune through trade that extended across the country.

Mrs. Hardingham presently became aware of her duties as a hostess. Turning to her husband, she said, 'Arthur, we must return inside at once. I believe it is excessively unbecoming of the four of us to be standing out here when our guests are inside. Mr. Davenport, John, if you will excuse us, we will return within. John, you must not whisk Mr. Davenport away tonight before I have had the opportunity of becoming better acquainted with him.'

Edwina and Christopher, started to follow her as she walked in on her husband's arm, but Mr. Hardingham turned to them saying, 'Stay and converse with him, Christopher, for you might wish to be better acquainted with him before you depart on your *shikar.*'

Christopher nodded, turning towards Mr. Davenport. But he had walked up to Edwina, and was now bowing to her, saying, 'May I have the honour of the next dance, Miss. Hardingham?'

Edwina looked at him in some confusion. She wished above all else to avoid exchanging words with this strange and unpredictable man.

She suppressed an impulse of gratitude which demanded that she thank him for rescuing her from great mortification and the certain censure of her father and mother, turning instead to Christopher and saying, 'I beg your pardon, sir, but I cannot, for I have promised the next dance to my cousin.'

Christopher had taken a liking to the tall stranger his uncle had called his old friend. His thoughtful interjection in the face of his cousin's bewilderment on being introduced to him earlier had not gone unnoticed. His polite manner and quiet confidence had instantly won Christopher's trust.

'That is of no consequence, Eddie. I would be glad to forfeit my opportunity to dance with you, to Mr. Davenport,' he said, turning sharply in the direction of the ballroom, as if catching sight of someone familiar.

'Oh, but I have promised every other dance tonight and shall not be able to dance again with you then,' she said, silently berating herself that she had not had the presence of mind to declare Grayson as her next dance partner.

'Nonsense, Eddie. You and I can dance every evening after dinner if you so wish. Tonight, you must enjoy the opportunity of making a great many more acquaintances than mine,' he said absent-mindedly, very much in the tone of a dismissive sibling, walking indoors as he spoke.

Before she could reply, he was gone. Had she declared Mr. Grayson to be her next partner, she could have escaped, she thought ruefully. *Considering how obtuse Christopher is being, however, he would be sure to announce that I was mistaken and that it was he and not Mr. Grayson who had the next dance, and he would then tell me that he was glad to forfeit his dance to Mr. Davenport,* she thought resentfully, feeling very trapped indeed. The dictates of civility however demanded that she curtsey gracefully and accept Mr. Davenport's arm.

To her dismay, the next dance was a Waltz. Although several elderly persons considered it most risqué, the popularity of the Polka had ensured that it had acquired respectability even here, in Simla. It was now commonplace at every ball, but Edwina found herself wishing it were still outlawed from ballrooms, as she felt Mr. Davenport slip his arm around her waist and pull her to him. She rested her hand reluctantly on his arm, alternating between the hope that she did not step on his toes, and the fervent wish that she did indeed do so. Bruising his feet at the risk of being thought a deficient dancer seemed an inviting prospect, but she would not disgrace her mother's careful tutelage and waste the vast sums of money lavished on the dancing master. Her thoughts were soon interrupted.

'It is customary for a lady to converse with her partner as she dances, Miss. Hardingham. And I have it on good authority that you *are* a lady and the daughter of gentleman,' he said, his eyes dancing with merriment.

'That is an accusation I can bear to sustain, while you, sir, must find it unexceptional to be accused of *not* being a gentleman!' she retorted with asperity. She was as surprised as him by the harshness of her words.

He cocked an eyebrow at her and said sardonically, 'That is a serious charge, Miss. Hardingham, but quite baseless, you will agree, for ladies do not travel unchaperoned, and gentlemen always rescue ladies in distress. I daresay you will not disagree that *my* conduct has surely not contradicted that of a gentleman.'

She felt her colour rising, but his next words surprised her. 'Come, now, Miss. Hardingham, why do we not put the disagreeableness of our earlier encounter past us. You and I shall be seeing a lot of one another in the days to come, for I am told you and your cousin are to accompany Mr. Knowles and me on a *shikar*. Allow me to beg your pardon for my incivility to you that day in the jungle,' he said, with so much grace, that she felt quite ashamed at her outburst.

'I beg your pardon, sir,' she said in a subdued tone. 'And, thank you for your intervention earlier, although you are a shockingly untruthful person who has sadly misled my parents,' she added, with a mischievous smile.

He laughed and she saw that it made his face seem younger and very kind. He looked to be about thirty, but perhaps he was younger, she thought.

She spied Christopher close by with a stunning partner, a lady she had never seen before. Edwina saw she was dazzlingly beautiful, and it did not take long to observe Christopher's worshipful gaze fixed on her. She wondered if the lady was the reason why he had so unceremoniously abandoned her to dance with Mr. Davenport. His manner at the doorway had been one of a man who saw someone compelling whom he was previously acquainted with. But, she wondered, where could he have made the acquaintance of so fair a creature? He was looking at her with a strange expression that she had never seen before, and Edwina felt determined that she must make the lady's acquaintance.

Her attention was drawn back to her present circumstances by Mr. Davenport saying wryly, 'Perhaps you find me a poor substitute for your cousin, Miss. Hardingham?' Her frequent glances in her cousin's direction had not gone unnoticed by him.

'Oh no,' she replied hastily. 'You are a much better dancer than he. Although, I'm afraid your toes will be quite injured before the dance is concluded, for you will find me an indifferent dancer,' she said apologetically, as he gently manoeuvred her around a turn.

'On the contrary, you are a most proficient dancer—of the Waltz, at least—for you are extremely pliable. When dancing the Waltz, only one person can lead,' he replied sincerely.

She knew he was not a man to pay one a compliment lightly, and she blushed with pleasure. He looked down at her with a warm look in his eyes, and she found his gaze both gratifying and disconcerting at the same time. She was greatly relieved when the dance came to a conclusion.

She looked around the room and found Christopher leaning solicitously over a fair head, offering the lady a cup of punch. She hesitated, wondering whether she should approach them, but decided against it. Christopher had not presented her to the fine creature. She would not force her acquaintance on the lady.

As Mr. Davenport escorted her to her mother's side, she found Grayson at her elbow, saying, 'Miss. Hardingham, I believe the next dance is mine.'

He bowed on being presented to Mr. Davenport and then, turning to Edwina, he said with a speaking glance, 'I had particularly hoped to stand up for the waltz with you this night. I fervently hope they may play it again.'

Edwina coloured at both his words and the tone in which they were said, wondering how he could be so indiscreet. Mrs. Hardingham looked surprised for a fleeting moment, but schooled her features instantly. Edwina glanced up at Mr. Davenport and saw him looking at her with hooded eyes.

'I believe the waltz is as good a dance as another, Mr. Grayson. Will you not agree?' she asked coolly.

He bowed in acquiescence colouring slightly. As he escorted her to the dance floor, Edwina's eyes followed Mr. Davenport across the room as he withdrew to the room that housed the refreshments. They danced the polka and she soon found herself enjoying immensely as Grayson was an excellent dancer.

When she sat down to rest, Grayson immediately offered to procure her some refreshment and she gratefully nodded, requesting for something to quench her parched throat. The refreshments were lavish, and cleverly arranged at Mrs. Hardingham's direction, in such a manner as to prevent any of their Indian guests from being offended.

'Keep the nourishment on one table entirely devoid of the meat of any animals. Our guests who eschew the ingestion of foods that are abominable to their religion must find foods that are palatable to them. If they are presented separately, that will assure them they are not polluted,' she had instructed the servants.

Accordingly, mounds of *pakoras* were placed innocuously besides large quantities of cucumber sandwiches, so that none of the guests, Indian or Anglo-Indian, were aware that foodstuffs prepared with meat had been placed in separate locations to avoid wounding the sentiments of the Hindoo guests. Mrs. Hardingham had wisely eschewed all food made from pork this evening and as a result, the Mohammedan guests were also at ease.

'Edwina, you look marvelous,' said a voice beside her. Looking up, she saw that it was Colonel Parks, an old friend of her father's. His father had served alongside her grandfather many years ago in India, and the relationship between the two families was close.

'Colonel Parks, how do you do?' she asked. 'And you, dear, *Begum Sahiba?*' asked Edwina, rising to address his wife.

The normally taciturn wife of Colonel Parks became instantly animated, at her respectful greeting, saying, 'I am very well, child. My heart is especially warm to see you look so radiant.'

Edwina grasped her hand, begging her to sit beside her for a spell. Edwina felt her face warm with shame as she noticed a number of European ladies scatter away from their vicinity, as if fleeing contagion. Mrs. Parks was a Mohammedan lady who had converted to Christianity to marry Colonel Parks. And unlike many Englishmen who had taken Indian consorts on the understanding that they were to be 'temporary wives,' he had behaved nobly and treated his wife, as a gentleman should his lady. They were shunned by many of the Simla set who lamented on the predilection of some officers to lowering themselves by forming vulgar connections with the natives. Colonel Parks was impervious to their snobbery and usually avoided their companionship. In the Hardingham household, however, he knew his wife to be welcome and treated with the respect due a gentleman's wife. He had wandered to Mr. Hardingham's side, having deposited his ignored wife in Edwina's company.

'I am so honoured to be in your company, *Begum Sahiba,*' she said, resolutely holding the older woman's hand, as if to defy the superciliousness of the European women who were casting disapproving glances in their direction.

Mrs. Parks smiled gratefully at Edwina, who always addressed her with the Urdu equivalent of 'Madam' whenever they met.

'You are growing lovelier each day, child. It will not be long now before some handsome prince snatches you away from us,' she said fondly.

As the musicians played another quadrille, Edwina became aware of her next partner, Captain Jeffery Gardner standing at her elbow.

'May I have the honour of this dance, Miss. Hardingham,' he was saying.

Edwina looked perplexedly at him. To refuse him would be grave incivility, but to abandon Mrs. Parks when no one else in the vicinity was inclined to socialize with her was tantamount to betrayal, she thought. She looked for her mother, but saw that she was presently dancing with her uncle.

While she desperately looked at the man, hoping to convey to him her predicament, she heard Mr. Davenport say, 'How do you do, *Begum* Parks?'

To her surprise, Mrs. Parks and Mr. Davenport appeared to be old friends.

'How do you do, James? It is a pity my sons could not be here tonight, for they will be sorely disappointed they missed your company,' she said smiling on him with the fondness bestowed to a favoured son.

Edwina conferred a thankful smile on him, as she excused herself from Mrs. Parks' company. He simply sat down beside Mrs. Parks and proceeded to converse with her.

The gentleman dancing with Edwina seemed to be greatly struck by her person. He had not noticed her before, having been secretly smitten with her sister, Anne. Tonight however, there was something decidedly different about the youngest Miss. Hardingham. She was radiant and self-assured. He did not wish to appear to stare too pointedly at her.

'I'm amazed at Colonel Parks for bringing *her* here,' he said, casting about in his mind for some morsels of casual conversation.

Edwina stiffened imperceptibly saying coldly, 'I am afraid I fail to catch your meaning, Captain Gardner. Can you possibly be referring to *Mrs.* Parks?'

Impervious to her displeasure, the man blundered on saying, 'I should have imagined that by now, he would have realized that there is no welcome for that poor lady in circles such as these. For, she is rejected by those of her own race as well as by European ladies of superior standing. And while the dictates of civility demand that he be invited, courtesy on his part would require a sensitivity to the feelings of others.'

It had not occurred to him Captain Gardner that the members of this exceptional family would harbour sympathies for the unfortunate Mrs. Parks. Consequently, he was rather taken aback by Edwina's reply.

'I believe that it is not incomprehensible that a gentleman might choose to attend a ball in the company of his wife. Mrs. Parks *is* his wife, is she not? I assure you, sir she is quite welcome in this house,' she said icily.

Comprehending her displeasure at last, he immediately ceased to pursue this line of conversation.

Changing the topic and having caught sight of the mysterious object of Christopher's evident adoration, she asked pleasantly, 'Do you know who that lady is, who is standing by your sister, Captain Gardner?'

'She is Miss. Diana Johnson, a relation of Colonel Pendleton; she is Mrs. Pendleton's cousin,' he answered stiffly.

When the dance was concluded, he sighed audibly and relinquished his partner willingly. She turned to make her way back to Mrs. Parks' side, but found that she was not at the spot where they had conversed earlier. She felt a hand on her elbow and turning, saw Christopher smiling down at her, his face flushed with excitement.

'Oh Eddie, there is something I should like you to know. No, actually, there is *someone* I should like you to know,' he said, his voice trembling with excitement.

'Why Christopher, you seem vastly pleased. Can you be referring to Miss. Johnson?' she asked airily.

He stared at her mystified. 'How on earth did you know? Are you acquainted with her? Why did you not introduce us?' he demanded.

'I could ask the same of you, could I not?' she asked archly.

He seemed mortified by this and smiled sheepishly at her. 'You are right. And now, be so kind as to tell me how you made Miss. Johnson's' acquaintance,' he begged.

He spoke her name with such reverence, that Edwina was hard pressed not to laugh.

The intensity in his eyes made her answer in an even voice, 'Oh, I have never been presented to her. I merely know her name. I had to enquire who she was. ...'

She left her words incomplete, not explaining why she had felt that need. He was too excited to ask her to explain herself. 'A *colonel's* relation, no less, Christopher?' continued Edwina, gurgling with unbridled mirth and unable to restrain herself any longer. 'Pray tell, how did you even come to be in the company of so exalted a being?'

Her cousin laughed nervously. 'I believe I would not be presumptuous in calling her a friend, whom I may add, I think you will like very much,' he said diffidently.

'You have made a new friend when I was in Calcutta? How did this happen? And why did you not give me the slightest inkling that your heart was becoming entangled with someone in my absence, all these days?' she asked in a more serious tone. He felt himself colouring rapidly.

'Oh, she is simply someone who needed assistance with finding her party at church. I believe she is a distant cousin of the colonel's wife. Our meeting was quite accidental. She became separated from the colonel and his family after the service, and in the downpour, seemed quite lost. I merely assisted her to her carriage. Since then, we have often encountered each other on The Mall or on the Cart Road ... but it has always been quite fortuitous, I assure you. ...'

He faltered, remembering his banter with his cousin a few days earlier on the subject of the aloof members of Simla society.

'We were formally presented to each other at a dinner at Captain Gardner's house, for she is intimately acquainted with Miss. Gardner,' he added hastily, lest he give the impression of impropriety in their conduct. And then, noting a slight hint of hurt in her eyes, he added, 'As to letting you know that my heart was becoming *entangled,* why, I did not dare hope that she was aware of my existence. Not until tonight. ...' he finished, in a half guilty and half elated tone.

Dinner was now served and they proceeded to dine, exchanging feverish whispers though the lavish feast comprising of mostly Indian dishes.

After dinner, he took Edwina aside and said, 'How shall we contrive to form your acquaintance with her? She is currently occupied between two gentlemen.'

'Well, then you must present her to Papa and Mama and she must be invited to take tea with us soon,' she said.

'That is a splendid idea!' he said warmly. 'In fact, that is precisely what I intend to do right now.'

He walked towards Miss. Johnson and having exchanged a few words with her chaperone, escorted her back to where the Hardinghams stood, saying, 'Aunt Elizabeth, Uncle Arthur, Uncle John, Edwina, may I present to you, Miss. Diana Johnson.'

The ladies curtseyed gracefully. Miss. Johnson was indeed comely. Her eyes were a cornflower blue, and her skin pale and translucent, with a hint of pink. Her dress was fashioned in the latest design in London. Her hair seemed to be styled by an accomplished lady's maid. They were joined by Mr. Davenport and Mr. Grayson. When presented to these gentlemen, she smiled and lowered her lashes fetchingly. Indeed she was breathtaking, Edwina thought. It was evident why Christopher was so entranced by her. She was chatting easily with Grayson, describing her journey from England. Edwina found herself wondering if Mr. Grayson and Mr. Davenport also found her appealing.

They must, for neither of them appear to be blind or in their dotage, she thought with a small sigh.

Christopher seemed satisfied that he had conquered the awkwardness of first disclosure. That he was especially attentive to this lady was evident, but now that the acquaintance had been formed, he would let it cultivate naturally, taking its own course.

He turned to Davenport saying, 'I've been meaning to ask you, Mr. Davenport, how comes my uncle to address you as his *old* friend, considering that you do not appear to be more than five years my senior?'

Davenport and Knowles chuckled.

'I have known him for a very long time, ever since he was young enough to sit on my knee,' said Knowles. 'That endows me with the right to call him an *old* friend. And besides, his father was a very close friend. After his passing, James and I have carried on that bond of friendship faithfully,' he added.

Mr. Davenport's face had softened and Edwina was struck by how youthful it made his face appear.

'John has been a great support to us since our loss ten years ago, and I find myself very grateful for our friendship,' said Davenport quietly.

Edwina found his words touching, for she sensed he did not lightly display his sentiments. She felt pleased by his regard for her uncle, for she herself held him in high esteem.

'That is well, sir, for then you will be willing to endure our company on the *shikar* without indulging in the temptation to shoot us, for Uncle John is immensely fond of Edwina and me,' said Christopher.

'On the contrary, I might actually shoot you to rid my friend of a tiresome brat. I am certain he will thank me later,' he replied with ready laughter dancing in his eyes.

Christopher beamed, feeling gratified to be addressed with such familiarity by someone who seemed very much a man of the world. Christopher asked him several questions about the nature of the *shikar*, weapons and ammunitions that must be carried and the necessity of bringing along an adequate number of bearers. He evidently admired Mr. Davenport, and spoke to him with a deference accorded by an adoring younger sibling to a highly accomplished older brother. This surprised Edwina greatly, for she knew Christopher to be naturally reticent. He had only just begun to warm towards Mr. Grayson, and even then, did not confer on him esteem but rather, treated him like an equal.

Miss. Johnson was enthralled on hearing of the proposed *shikar*. 'Oh how I have longed to go on a *shikar*,' she said in longing accents.

'Perhaps you might join us, Miss. Johnson, for we are to embark on one soon,' said Christopher breathlessly.

Aside from an initial flicker of surprise, Mr. and Mrs. Hardingham betrayed no emotion. Grayson's face remained expressionless while a tiny frown appeared on Davenport's brow. The ripple that had imperceptibly passed through the company tickled Edwina and she hastily suppressed a giggle. Sensing Christopher's mounting embarrassment and Edwina's growing merriment, Mrs. Hardingham came to his rescue.

'This is a very good plan, Christopher. I do not see any objection to this scheme, providing, of course, that the Colonel feels amenable to the suggestion, given that there is not a female to chaperone the young ladies on this expedition. I believe Edwina would benefit greatly from the presence of another young lady on this expedition. A companion can make the hardships of the wilderness quite palatable. That is, if John feels equal to the task of minding two girls, instead of one,' she said.

Mr. Knowles declared he had not the slightest objection to taking another person on the *shikar* and with that, the discussion was diverted from Miss. Johnson and back onto the subject of hunting rifles, allowing Christopher a few moments of respite from the scrutiny of the others, which he detested heartily. Following Miss. Johnson's inclusion in the party, Grayson inevitably found himself a member it as well. That he described himself as a good shot made him a more welcome addition to the group in Mr. Knowles' eyes.

As the guests began to depart after the evening had ended, Miss. Johnson took her leave of the Hardinghams. She had been escorted hither by Captain Gardner, his sister and their aunt. As she sunk her exhausted head into her pillow, Edwina found herself calling to remembrance Christopher's lovelorn gaze that followed Miss. Johnson as she set off with the Gardners. Edwina desired greatly to further her acquaintance with Miss. Johnson, for her impression on Christopher was becoming clear. Besides, it was of the greatest importance to acquaint oneself with the members of one's hunting party!

Edwina did not have to wait long, for on the following day, they received an invitation to dine at the Colonel's residence that Saturday. This was an unusual occurrence, for wives of officers preferred to consort with each other and even then, laid great store by the rank of their husbands. Such condescension could mean only one thing: that Christopher had fixed their interest as a good catch. The Hardinghams found the Colonel and his wife haughty, but Miss. Johnson made every effort to delight.

She was lovely, with flaxen hair and a heart-shaped mouth. Her dimpled laugh tinkled musically through the room and she seemed eager to please her new acquaintances. She was especially solicitous towards Edwina and waited attentively on her. Edwina thought her pleasant, but could not help noticing that her conversation was never profound. There was a certain shallowness of manner and occasionally, Edwina discovered, she was prone to looking sideways at Christopher over her fan. Towards the rest, her manners were pretty and she was easily pleased. But, when conversing with Christopher, she fluttered her eyelashes at him and laughed coquettishly at the most commonplace remark.

'I thought you might wish to accompany Edwina on the *shikar*, Miss.

Johnson. I recall you mentioning that it was your greatest wish to experience one while in India,' said Christopher in a low voice. They were seated close to the fire, within Edwina's earshot.

'Why, Mr. Hardingham, how gallant of you to remember my words and care for my wishes so!' she answered coyly.

Edwina was struck by how unlike her cousin she was. Where he was grave, Miss. Johnson seemed frivolous, and where he was intense, she seemed rather shallow. Still, she was aware of the warm glow that spread across Christopher's face when he looked at her and when she addressed him. Edwina was determined to like her. With that end in mind, she fortified Christopher's invitation to her with one of her own.

Miss. Johnson begged her cousin to permit her to accompany Miss. Hardingham on the *shikar*. The Colonel reluctantly agreed, partly because he seemed quite uninterested in the goings on in the life of his wife's cousin. She belonged to the 'fishing fleet' and if she stood the chance of making a good match, it would not do for him to stand in the way, for she did not have a large income to her name. Christopher's fortune, the Hardinghams' respectability, and John Knowles' reputation as a sportsman would have to be sufficient justification for him to acquiesce.

Mrs. Pendleton, though greatly in awe of her own consequence, was not entirely insensible to the advantages of an alliance with young Hardingham and was keen to fix her cousin's interest with him. She encouraged her cousin to accompany the group and now, their *shikar* party was set with six persons. Edwina reflected that her companions would be convivial and although she had her reservations about Mr. Davenport's geniality under tense circumstances, she was certain that his friendship with her uncle guaranteed some redeeming qualities in him.

The days following the ball were spent in anticipation of the upcoming *shikar*. They were met with unanticipated bad news, however, for Christopher's physician had prohibited his proposed excursion. He had recently suffered from several unbearable headaches and was still frail. The doctor warned that his constitution would not withstand the grueling treks and the excitement that would be inevitable at a tiger hunt. He seemed deeply disappointed, but when Edwina suggested that they abandon their plans, hastily demurred.

'Miss. Johnson will be *most* devastated should we cancel our plans.

We must go on as planned,' he said in a low voice when the rest of the family was out of earshot.

'I am most concerned to be deprived of your company, especially when we find ourselves in Mr. Davenport's. He is liable to be cross as crabs when it suits him,' she confided.

He looked at her greatly mystified. 'Why, Edwina, you are mistaken. He is surely nothing but amiable!' he replied incredulously.

She eyed him with disfavour, endeavouring speedily to relieve him of his misapprehensions.

'On the contrary! He is the crossest and most uncivil person I have met,' she declared, informing him of the true identity of his new friend.

He was the boorish stranger she had encountered in the jungle not long ago! However, Christopher's unceasing confidence in Mr. Davenport's geniality persisted, to Edwina's annoyance. She was perplexed by her cousin's inexplicable intransigence. For Christopher to disbelieve her and roundly insist that a perfect stranger—or a brand-new acquaintance at best—was to be believed over her, seemed insupportable.

'I am convinced that you are mistaken about his character, somehow,' he said, firmly. 'I believe you will be safe in his company, wherever that may be,' he declared with pig-headed loyalty.

Edwina smiled. It was unlike Christopher to form a deep attachment to someone lightly. And, she could not very well argue with his assertion that she would be indisputably safe in Mr. Davenport's company.

'Besides,' he said urgently, 'at all costs, the *shikar* must go on as planned, for I could not bear for Miss. Johnson to be disappointed.'

She nodded and echoed his statements when Mrs. Hardingham suggested the *shikar* be postponed for Christopher could not accompany his cousin, saying, 'I believe that would be cruel to Miss. Johnson, Mama, for she has come to greatly anticipate our proposed excursion. And besides, we are in the protection of my uncle who has been akin to Papa to me throughout my life.'

Mr. and Mrs. Hardingham were much impressed by this line of reasoning and Christopher shot her a grateful look. With disaster averted, the plans for the *shikar* continued.

Edwina vowed to deepen her acquaintance with Miss. Johnson, no matter how unexceptional she found her. To that end, she invited Miss.

Johnson to take tea with her quite often over the next few weeks, and the two young women embarked on what promised to be a friendship. Determined to like her, Edwina began to recognize several excellent qualities in her new friend. She was vastly amiable, determined to be pleased by those around her and quite gentle in her disposition. And, while she did not possess a great degree of knowledge on a variety of subjects and was, Edwina thought privately, entirely too pliable and indecisive, she evidently was possessed of the kind of disposition that could make any young man happy. Christopher possessed strength of mind and character and was eternally affable. He would provide a wonderful counterweight for Miss. Johnson's lack of decision. She would rely on him and he would be her guide. The conviction that they would be enviably happy together began to settle in Edwina's mind and she looked forward with enthusiasm to their upcoming adventure.

Eager to recognise the birds that they should encounter, Edwina decided to spend one afternoon in the library. She was particularly keen on perusing the *Himalayan Journals*, recently published by noted surgeon and naturalist, Joseph Dalton Hooker. Edwina was a keen reader, and spent much time in the library. Mr. Hardingham despised the idleness that was so widely predominant among the British in India. While he relished sport and entertainment as much as the next person, he had enforced in his home the principle of industry, insisting that while he occupied himself with trade, the members of his household apply themselves to useful occupations.

He was ably assisted by Mrs. Hardingham who was devoted to charitable endeavours. This morning, she was on an errand of mercy, visiting the sick child of the head groom, carrying confections that would be sure to cheer the patient in his sickbed. Edwina was instructed to oversee the preparation of the noonday meal and had spent a busy morning assisting the cook and instructing him on new creations. She was glad for the respite in the library and rang for some tea. Oddly, her book was not on the shelf. Unless Christopher had taken it out of its shelf, she was sure no one else would want it. She paced past the shelves, her eyes probing for the missing volume.

'What do you seek, *Missy Sahib?*' asked Shanta, as she poured her some tea.

'I am missing a book that I was reading but yesterday, Shantama,' she replied with a perplexed frown on her brow. 'Do you know where Chris *Sahib* is?' she asked.

'He is not reading any book, for he has been toiling all morning with *Bada Sahib* in the office,' Shanta replied, handing her the cup. 'Perhaps he took it last night and left it in his bedchamber? Or, perhaps it was *munshiji*,' suggested Shanta, for he was reading here last night.

Edwina was pleased to hear of the return of her father's *munshi* to Simla. Mr. Hardingham and Christopher had lately been greatly preoccupied by business affairs, and were finding themselves hard-pressed to manage their rising commercial endeavours across India from the far reaches of the Himalayan foothills. Edwina had never pictured the elderly clerk as given to reading English works, but perhaps he had recently become interested in them.

'Forgive me, madam. Are you looking for this book?' asked a voice from the doorway.

She turned and beheld a tall Indian man with a very familiar face standing before her. He held the book she was seeking in his hand.

'Yes, indeed I am,' she responded, mystified and casting about in her mind to discover who he was, for he was quite familiar.

'I told you, it was likely *Munshiji*,' said Shanta in a satisfied tone. 'Why have you taken the book from the library? Did you not know that *Missy Sahib* reads here every morning—for she is most learned? She is not a little child anymore, so you should be mindful of her comfort,' she scolded, looking at the young man not unkindly as she left the room.

'I am truly sorry. Please forgive me,' the man said with embarrassment.

'Is that who you are—the *munshi*? But what has become of Mr. Mukherjee?' asked Edwina greatly puzzled, for this man was not Mohan Das Mukherjee, her father's faithful clerk.

'My father has retired and I have taken his place in your father's service,' he replied.

'You cannot be Sharat Mukherjee!' she exclaimed.

'But that is exactly who I am,' responded the young man with a smile.

'Oh you are so different now—you have become a *babu*. Do you remember, we used to play together as children, you and I?' she asked, delighted to renew her acquaintance with a former playmate.

'Yes, I remember, Miss. Hardingham, and allow me to remark you have grown into a fine lady,' he replied.

'Don't be deceived Mukherjee! She's no such thing,' said Christopher with a chuckle as he joined them.

'Do sit down and have some tea with us,' invited Edwina. 'It will be wonderful to talk of old times.'

Mr. Mukherjee hesitated, saying, 'I could not dream of doing something as impertinent as that. Thank you for your kindness.' His manner was simultaneously diffident and proud.

'What on earth do you mean? How could your having tea with old friends be construed as impertinence?' asked Edwina, baffled by his manner.

'I would hardly dare to describe you as my friends for I am but your servant,' he said somewhat bitterly.

'What has gotten into to you, man? The three of us were famously inseparable as children and you and Edwina were used to write to each other for the longest time. You are employed in my uncle's service now, but why should that prevent us from renewing our friendship?' demanded Christopher with asperity.

'Friendships must, of necessity, exist betwixt those who are equals. I am well aware that members of your race perceive the natives of this land as inferior to yourselves. How then can you expect a true friendship between us? Now, if you will excuse me, young Master, I will return to my books,' he answered.

The bitterness in his voice and the blazing of his eyes were perplexing.

'Mr. Mukherjee, I cannot answer for others of my race, only for myself and perhaps, my family,' said Edwina. 'For my part I will say this: you have gravely misjudged us. We are of two different races, but no less equal in God's eyes. And while there are bound to exist some differences in our lives owing to the variances of cultural experience, can there not be an alliance of thoughts and of the highest moral principles between us? You are in my father's employ, and you are also a friend of my childhood. There is not the slightest impediment to our friendship, and you are free to pursue our acquaintance once you have discharged your daily duties. That is my view on this matter,' she finished.

The gravity of her manner and the sincerity with which the words were uttered had the effect of causing the young man to relent. He made his way from the doorway to a small table where they were seated.

'You must forgive the severity of my words. My experiences have been bitter,' he said sadly.

'Then you must tell us, your old friends, all about it,' she said sympathetically as she handed him a cup of tea.

'It is a harsh tale, but not uncommon for men of my generation. As you know, my father had educated me after the manner of the English. But, no job that I am qualified for is open to me, for the highest and best positions of service are reserved for the English. It is the story of many men – we find ourselves educated beyond the professions that are left open to us. Were it not for the kindness of your father in employing me, I should find myself languishing in some small office in Calcutta, slaving away for a *Sahib* for a pittance, while he fritters away the days in sport and entertainment,' he said. Christopher shook his head in disappointment, waiting for him to continue. 'The situation is the same for my uncle. He is a *Sepoy* in the army, but cannot advance to a higher rank, for the officers must be Englishmen and the number of them swells daily, leaving very little room for the promotion of Indian soldiers to the rank of Commissioned Officer. My uncle has long waited for the promotion to *Soobedar*, but now that it is imminent, he is too old and must retire,' he continued.

'That is expressly unjust, but I am afraid that with increasing political power, the East India Company is apt to overlook the principles of fairness that are necessary in good governance,' said Christopher gloomily.

'I am distressed to hear of this undeserved hardship you face. In this house, and among us, I hope you will find your merits appreciated and your worth valued,' Edwina added.

He smiled and his manner became more cheerful.

'Did you find the book to your taste?' she asked, gesturing towards the book he had come to return.

'I am afraid my answer will disappoint you. I am filled with remonstrance today,' he said apologetically.

'No, go on. I am most eager to hear what you think of it,' she urged.

'Well, to begin with, it is a profound and marvellous treatise on the natural glories of this land. But, occasionally, the writer intersperses his views on the land with a disparagement of the peoples he encounters and our customs,' he said.

'No doubt you will find expositions written by visiting Englishmen to be riddled with their prejudices that compel them to compare everything they observe in this land to England,' Christopher remarked. 'Perhaps there are authors among those of us who live in India whose works might prove more impartial. Edwina, you are the expert on such matters. What books can you recommend to Mukherjee that are commendable for their absence of blind prejudice?' he asked.

'As to that, I am not at all certain. Whilst every English person who has ever lived in this country aspires to being a writer, not every person loves this land—until they return to England, that is. I believe that writing a journal is the foremost occupation of the English, and affords one a favourable pastime upon returning to England, if the numbers of expositions on India by Englishmen are any indication. I have, however, enjoyed excessively the works of Miss. Emma Roberts, a poet who has lived in India. Perhaps you will enjoy this book,' she said, rising to procure *The East India Voyager* from the bookshelves against the far wall. 'I believe you will find her thoughts comforting for they divulge the profound reverence of many Europeans for this land, along with their fervent hope that this land's glorious history might be revived and that perhaps the helping hand of the European might assist this,' she said.

He took the book reluctantly, for he was loath to believe that the European was capable of demonstrating the slightest degree of respect for his land and his people. When he left them, Edwina and Christopher bemoaned the direction that East India Company's actions were taking.

'It is becoming apparent that with increasing power, we are losing our admiration for this land and her people. A strange sort of arrogance appears to possess us, leading us to believe erroneously that we are in some way superior to those around us,' Christopher lamented.

She answered quietly, 'That is quite so. Perhaps the time will come when the people of Hindostan will oust us from here. Although I must say, this arrogance is not new. I remember reading somewhere that Lord Auckland was horrified some thirty years ago at the excessive cruelties meted out to the poor villagers by the indigo planters during his tenure as Governor-General. I remember reading of a planter who set his hounds on the villagers for sport, and laughed as the men desperately and vainly attempted to outrun them. I shudder to think what the future holds for those of us who see this land as our home. For, indeed, I cannot conceive of England as my home. I found it cold and dank and could not wait until I returned home to India.'

'You could write your memoirs—as all the fashionable ladies do—reminiscing about the warm sun and the loving and devoted retainers of India, whilst you shiver by a fire in the winter in Yorkshire,' said her cousin mischievously, for he could not bear for her to be gloomy.

Her dimples flashed and she retorted, 'Yes, and when your gout distresses you—as indeed it does all old men—I shall read you my memoirs on the *shikar*.'

CHAPTER FOUR

THE SHIKAR

On the morning of the *shikar*, Edwina awoke to the flute-like sounds of *monal* calling outside her window. She remembered that Christopher would not be accompanying them and this dampened her enthusiasm to some degree. Still, she was sure she could expect some adventure in the company of Mr. Grayson and she definitely was keen on furthering her acquaintance with Miss. Johnson. Only Mr. Davenport gave her cause for concern. He had apparently had reservations about Miss. Johnson's inclusion into their party, when it was proposed, and was about to remark on it—adversely, she was sure—but had decided against it when her uncle had supported the plan. She was not certain how long her uncertain truce with him would last and could only hope that his proffered apology to her at the ball had been sincere.

On the day of the hunt, the entire party met at the Hardingham home. To Edwina's dismay, Mr. Davenport seemed irritated this morning and in a hurry to leave. His manner indicated that he perceived that the presence of the various members of the party would diminish his pleasure from the *shikar*. He exchanged no more than a few words with Grayson and merely bowed politely in Miss. Johnson's direction. He seemed to have an easy rapport with Mr. Knowles' men, Kartar Singh and Makkhan Singh. They treated Davenport with the same deference they accorded her uncle and this puzzled her. The men had been in her uncle's employ since his stretch as a Civil Servant in the Punjaub province, and had served him loyally for many years.

They were Sikhs, natives of the Punjaub region, and they did not easily yield their respect to those they met. Although far from their native terrain, their unflinching bravery and unquestioning loyalty to her uncle made them indispensable to him, and he would not foray into so dangerous an exercise as a *shikar* for a tiger, in their absence. They were also excessively reserved, keeping their conversation with the gentle hill-folk who accompanied them as porters, at a bare minimum. They carried the guns and ammunition, along with the heaviest tent equipment, and appeared to notice no one apart from her uncle and Mr. Davenport.

They began their expedition on horseback along the few passable roads that dotted the hills. Mr. Davenport rode in front, leading the party, while Mr. Knowles followed in the rear. Grayson rode with the two ladies, alternating conversation with them whenever they slowed to a trot. He was most gallant, often enquiring about whether they needed a rest. Miss. Johnson seemed to be a poor horsewoman and as such, Mr. Grayson was especially considerate of her comfort, frequently requesting Mr. Davenport to slow the pace at which they travelled. At one particularly narrow turn, Miss. Johnson who seemed dangerously close to becoming unseated from her horse, looked perilously close to tears.

'I say, Davenport,' Grayson exclaimed, 'do you suppose we might slow down a bit, considering the ladies are quite worn out? I dare say there's no need to maintain such a devilish pace. I'm sure the tiger will keep, don't you think?'

This was said with a smirk that was met by a cold stare from Davenport, who glanced at the women and wordlessly tugged on his reins to slow his horse down. Edwina could not help but notice the scorn in his eyes and she felt herself getting warm with indignation. Still, she acknowledged that the manner in which the request was made was apt to chafe him. She was puzzled that so gracious a man as Mr. Grayson should behave so truculently. The two men had not seemed to like each other from the beginning. Mr. Davenport had made it clear that his presence at this *shikar* was a favor to his friend and he would prefer to enjoy the sport in the company of accomplished sportsmen and not that of ham-fisted sightseers. He drove the party on at a merciless pace and seemed impervious to Miss. Johnsons apparent privations or Mr. Grayson's protests. Mr. Grayson did not appear to be much of a sportsman. He rode stiffly and appeared to be ill at ease and much discomfited, although Edwina thought he presented a fine figure in the saddle.

Mr. Davenport has been discourteous to us and deserves to be treated with no more civility than he has accorded us, she thought, resolving at the same time to command his respect by not requiring any special consideration on the grounds of her being a member of the fairer sex.

Soon, the horses were abandoned and the journey proceeded on the relative safety of the backs of elephants. They would only go as far as they could on the backs of the elephants. Rocking to and fro in the howdah, listening to the mahouts' gentle commands to the elephants, Edwina breathed deeply, inhaling the scent of the grasses and flowers that had sprung up everywhere. It was near the end of April, and already the warmth of summer had descended on the earth. They continued along gurgling springs that progressed into raging torrents as they danced through rocks and ravines.

Miss. Johnson did not appear to be enjoying the sights afforded by nature. She complained unceasingly about the movement of the elephants and the climate. Camp was set up each night along the springs and *nullas*, where Knowles and Davenport sat patiently at their fishing lines, rewarded each time with a catch that fed them and the servants. Seated around the fire and sipping their tea, Edwina and Diana were conscious of the jungle sounds around them. They had travelled for three days and now, the jungle was filled with the unmistakable traces of a tiger. The hysterical cackling bark of the *langurs* high up in the trees and the agitation of the Himalayan wildfowl signaled the presence of their quarry nearby. The explosive flight of the scattering *kala titer* and the *monal* corroborated that something was moving in the undergrowth in the distance. Their presence had surely been detected and the tiger would give their camp a wide berth, as tigers usually do in the wilderness.

'Only a man-eater would seek out humans,' Knowles informed the group.

This seemed to alarm Miss. Johnson, who nervously glanced over her shoulder asking, 'Could there not be one stalking us as we speak?'

'In my experience, a tiger will not hunt men, unless it is sick or old. There have been no reports of a man-eater in these parts, Miss. Johnson. I should hardly have brought you here, were there any danger of us encountering one. I hope you will not tax yourself on that score,' came the soothing reply.

But, Miss. Johnson was not comforted. She planted herself between Edwina and Mr. Grayson and ate very little of the delicious roasted fish that they partook of. Mr. Grayson betrayed a brief glimpse of apprehension when he reached nervously for his rifle, but caught himself when Knowles chuckled and said that that was quite unnecessary as the tiger was more desirous of avoiding an introduction to him than vice versa. Grayson relaxed immediately, and proffered comfort to Miss. Johnson in the form of an offer to read to her from Lord Tennyson. He read from *Fatima*. She stared at him transfixed, as he read, her mouth softening into a wistful smile that made Edwina strangely uncomfortable. But, she was also elated with the promise of adventure the following day. She listened closely as her uncle and Davenport discussed their plan of action.

Machans had to be constructed in the trees first. The ladies would hunt from the safety of these perches. Knowles and Davenport would first stalk the tiger on foot, with the rest of the party following on elephants, at a distance. When a tiger was discovered, the ladies would be hoisted onto the *machans*. The elephants would be used to conduct a beat in the cover, forcing the tiger to move in the direction of the *machans*, thus providing the ladies with the best shots. If anything went wrong, Knowles and Davenport would follow hard on an elephant and shoot the animal themselves. They decided to construct two *machans*. Grayson offered to stay on one *machan*, in case the lady on the other *machan* missed her shot.

At this, Miss Johnson's eyes widened. 'Do you mean that either Edwina or I will be left alone on a *machan*?' she asked querulously.

'Do not worry, Miss. Johnson, for you shall not be left defenceless. I shall sit with you on your *machan*, and when the tiger passes us, I shall be sure that it does not get far. That is, of course, if Miss. Hardingham should have no objection to being left alone on her *machan*,' came Grayson's soothing reply.

'I do not mind in the least, sir. Diana *does* seem to be in great need of your company,' she replied, in a strangely cold voice.

After she had spoken, she became conscious of Davenport's contemptuous glance in her direction. Edwina blushed. His eyes seemed to say, *You have been found out! I see that you are out of sorts—you are in love with Mr. Grayson and he does not seem to notice you when in Miss. Johnson's company.* Odious man! She hated him now. She flashed a dazzling smile at Grayson and Miss. Johnson, to remove the sting of her words.

Thankfully, Diana had hardly noticed the affront, misinterpreting Edwina's comment as commiseration. She was preoccupied with the ills that she imagined had befallen her. 'I do not think it would suit me at all to see a tiger by my *machan*. Why, I hope we never see any of the dreadful beasts at all,' she said in a lamenting tone.

'I'm surprised to hear you say that, Diana. After all, we have come a great way into the jungle and you have complained of being so very ill-used when seated upon our elephant, that I should imagine you would want to actually shoot a tiger for your trouble!' said Edwina with a touch of asperity, growing more and more impatient with her cousin's new friend every minute.

As she glanced in the direction of Mr. Davenport, she noticed that his eyes held a look of amusement. But, at that moment, she did not care what he thought, or what had made him smile at her. She had a dislike of women who demurred at vigorous tasks and made themselves seem weak before men. Throughout their journey, she was determined that she would command the respect of Mr. Davenport—a feat that would be rendered impossible if he and her uncle were forced to play nursemaid to the ladies! She had uncomplainingly travelled, without a murmur about any discomforts she may have experienced. Diana seemed unaccustomed to the pace of the expedition and frequently demanded that they be let down from their howdah to stretch their legs. Always, Grayson concurred with her. Anxious not to appear fragile, Edwina stood with the men, glancing nonchalantly at her companion. Each time, she had spoken little, lest they discover that she too was drained by the journey. However, unlike Mr. Grayson and Miss. Johnson, she was vastly enjoying herself and delighted to be a part of the expedition. Miss. Johnson's wish to avoid encountering the object of their journey incensed her greatly.

This time, her outburst was not lost on Diana, who stared at her wide-eyed. That she perceived herself ill-used was evident in the flush that slowly spread across her flustered face and the tears that began to well up in her eyes. Edwina felt instantly ashamed. She remembered that whilst she had grown up in India and had frequently hunted small game in the jungles with her father, Miss. Johnson had only recently arrived from England and was as such, inclined to perceive her land as a strange and bewildering place with strange customs, enigmatic people and debilitating weather.

'Forgive me, Diana! My words were harsher than I had intended them to be. I am fatigued and spoke rashly. I beg you to forgive me!' she implored warmly.

For a moment, Miss. Johnson looked at her petulantly. However, she glanced at Grayson who was looking at her with an inscrutable expression and quickly schooled her expression into a forced smile saying, 'There is nothing to forgive, Edwina, dear! It is I who needs forgiveness. Unaccustomed as I am to arduous journeys, I am exhausted and spoke selfishly. Forgive me, dear friend!'

Peace having been restored, Miss. Johnson begged to be excused, for her tent was ready and she was quite worn out. Edwina stared miserably at the fire, as her uncle and Mr. Knowles resumed a dispassionate discourse on their ammunition. Her father and uncle had educated her in marksmanship. Their weapon of choice for this *shikar* was a Pattern 1853 Enfield with .577 calibre Minie bullets. At nearly four-and-one-half kilos, it was an unusual weapon for a young woman to use, but Edwina's father had insisted that each of his daughters master the use of a sturdy hunting rifle as a condition for being allowed to accompany *shikars*. Consequently, she was an expert at handling her rifle.

The conversation did not distract her from the feeling of hollowness that seemed to have engulfed her inmost being. Two weeks ago, she had been overjoyed at encountering Mr. Grayson again. There had been such joy and now … now, she had behaved in a manner that most certainly conveyed to him that she was impetuous and exceedingly intemperate. She no longer seemed to have a thrill course through her being when she saw him. Perhaps she was not very partial to him, as she had imagined earlier. That he did not harbour a preference for her was made apparent by the attentions he had lavished on Miss. Johnson. She was aware that Grayson was approaching her and had taken a seat beside her. She looked at him, fully expecting censure and his next words surprised her greatly.

'You have suffered the meanest of manners with the greatest

equanimity, Miss. Hardingham, and I applaud you,' he said in a low voice.

'Oh, but I should say, *my* manners left much to be desired,' said Edwina in a stricken voice.

He seemed surprised. 'How noble you are to say such a thing, for all day, we have heard nothing from a certain person, but complaints about the terrain, the elephants, the thickness of the branches we brushed against, and indeed everything! To be sure, I have tried very hard to take this burden off your hands by offering mine in exchange. I am certain you will have noticed that. I suppose those who fish in Simla cannot hunt in the jungles here.'

This last remark seemed somewhat harsh, but his eyes looking down on her were tender and full of solicitude. She felt her stomach entwine into knots again. He had not succumbed to the charms of Miss. Johnson. On the contrary, he had found her trying and was trying to relieve *her, Edwina*, from Miss. Johnson's cross complaining! She felt her heart soar again. She glanced in Davenport's direction and saw that he was looking at her with an inscrutable expression. *I do not care!* thought she. *I shall not let him mar my pleasure, for I am very happy indeed, to hear that Mr. Grayson has been so mindful of my comfort!* However, alongside her pleasure at these thoughts, she could not quite shake off a feeling of uneasiness that had descended upon her. Mr. Grayson seemed to make a great many spiteful remarks about other ladies in her presence and Edwina had far too much of a distaste for gossip to turn a blind eye to this!

She turned and smiled at Grayson, saying, 'You have paid so much thought to my comfort; how can I thank you?'

'Will you be safe alone in your *machan*,' he asked with a worried expression. 'I am surprised that they plan to leave one of you alone. Forgive me for my plainness of speech, but I'm afraid Miss. Johnson will be a sore trial to us, were she the one left upon the *machan* alone, and so, I am afraid it will have to be you.'

'I am not in the least bit afraid,' she replied, noticing again, his disparagement of Miss. Johnson, despite his attentiveness towards her all day. 'Uncle John would scarcely put me in harm's way! Rest easy, sir, I shall be quite safe, for I am, I assure you, a very good shot!'

'Of that I have not the least doubt. But, I shall venture to say it is not your uncle who is responsible for the less than satisfactory arrangements planned for tomorrow. I fear the *shikar* has been overrun by others,' he said quickly, with a nod in Mr. Davenport's direction. She did not think Mr. Davenport's plans unsatisfactory, but was not inclined to quarrel with William Grayson.

On her cot that night, she thought of the transformations that had occurred in the opinions the members of the party had had about each other. She had thought of Grayson as her fearless champion, but could not be blind to his predilection for petty gossip. She thought of his words about Miss. Appleby at the ball, and this night, of the coolness with which he had disparaged Miss. Johnson. To be sure, she deserved it, and he had avowed that he strove to minimize the impact of Miss. Johnson's complaining upon herself, but Edwina could not feel relief for his apparent solicitousness towards her.

His manner suggested duplicity, for she could not shake off from her mind images of his attentiveness to Miss. Johnson. True, they might be simply manifestations of gallantry from a gentleman, but his words about Miss. Johnson spoken in private to Edwina seemed to belie all gallantry. That he should lend his succour to Miss. Johnson and then later denounce her privately to Edwina seemed somehow ungallant. *A fortnight ago, I felt myself dazzled by his virtues, but now I question his moral fibre. How fickle I am. Surely, there is no man who is devoid of imperfection?* she chided herself.

Meanwhile, she reflected, Mr. Davenport seemed more the leader of the party than ever. He had quickly proved to be an expert on the land and entirely capable of leading them safely through this exciting pursuit. His kindness to the men and their admiration of him was not lost on Edwina. *Surely, a man so loved by his servants must have some qualities of mind that endear him to them. I would surmise that he is kind and generous to those he approves of and trusts, and faithful to those loyal to him. But, I find him as uncivil as I ever did, and my opinion of him remains unchanged. Perhaps I am not quite so fickle, after all!* she mused, as she drifted to sleep.

The night seemed fleeting and she was awakened by the screeching of jungle fowl. She scurried to ready herself, not wanting to lose a moment and not wanting to delay the rest of the party. They were already up, consuming vast portions of *kichidi,* or kedgeree as the English liked to call it, prepared by Haldi Ram, a most excellent cook.

Edwina hungrily ate the tasty meal, relishing the subtle flavor of the rice and *moong* lentils. When the party was finally ready to begin the day's adventure, John Knowles headed towards the brush with his two men.

That there was a tiger in the vicinity had been established by the calls he had heard in the early hours of the morning. He would try to stalk this animal mostly by following the signals made by the jungle inhabitants. He led the trail on foot, followed by the rest of the party who were in the relative safety of the elephants' howdahs. Miss. Johnson was seated upon a different beast from the one Edwina had chosen.

Mr. Davenport had stridden into Edwina's howdah and suggested that Miss. Johnson and Mr. Grayson follow on another one, 'for it will be safer for you to ride behind our animal,' he said.

Edwina felt a twinge of disappointment, for she had hoped to share the thrill of the hunt with Grayson.

'I trust you are not afraid, Miss. Hardingham?' Davenport asked, when the elephant was in motion.

'Not in the least, sir!' she replied pertly.

'That is just as well, for we are in a dangerous place now. Should we chance upon the tiger before you are seated upon the *machan*, ours will the elephant it will charge at first. I do not believe the other two members of our party would be able to deal with that prospect with composure, but I trust I may count on you to keep a cool head?' he asked levelly.

Torn between a desire to defend Mr. Grayson as a person who possessed a great deal of composure and a sense of pride that he had thought her level-headed, she answered simply, 'Yes, I believe you may. But,' she continued, 'I was unaware that tigers charged elephants.'

'A cornered tiger, Miss. Hardingham is a very dangerous animal. It will most certainly charge anything it perceives as a threat,' he replied. 'I know of an instance where a tiger leapt up to the elephant's head, leaving a large gash on the mahout's foot.'

'Certainly it did not try to drag him off the elephant?' she asked in horrified accents.

'Oh, but indeed, it did. The elephant, however, was an exceedingly brave specimen. He shook off the tiger and trampled her to death. I have heard on more than one occasion of a tiger springing as high as the howdah,' he said.

Hearing her gasp, he asked, 'Perhaps I have miscalculated your mettle, and should allow you to join the others behind us, Miss. Hardingham?' His mocking expression infuriated her.

'Pray, do not concern yourself about my mettle, sir. I am quite capable of protecting myself and—should the need arise—I would certainly offer you my protection,' she said acidly.

The smile in his eyes reached his mouth and incensed her further. But, he changed the subject, drawing her attention back to their prey.

'The tiger has evidently made a kill during the night,' he said pleasantly.

'How could you know that?' she asked, fickly forgetting her resolve to ignore him for the rest of the day.

'It now roams unconcealed. That is a sure sign that it has eaten and does not wish to stalk prey. Were it on the prowl for prey, it would take great pains to hide from its victim,' he replied.

'How can you know that it roams unconcealed, for we have seen no sign of it,' she asked.

'Oh, but there are signs of the tiger everywhere, Miss. Hardingham. Listen to the sounds of the jungle around you and tell me what you hear.'

'I hear animals and birds,' she replied, puzzled.

'Do you not hear the barking of the *langur* and the warning call of the jungle fowl? Each one of them is warning the others in the jungle that the king of the land passes by,' said he.

She listened with her eyes closed, and in the distance, heard the sporadic call of animals as the tiger passed in their vicinity. She opened her eyes and looked at him with wonder.

'If we follow in the direction of those calls, we should encounter the tiger,' she said.

'We do not wish to overtake it, precisely, for that would be dangerous. First, we will find its kill and then set up the *machans* close to the kill. The men will set up a beat on the other elephants and we will drive the tiger towards you,' he answered.

He continued describing the movements of the tiger as they listened to the call of the animals. He pointed to the trees around, naming them in Hindustani and English and telling her their uses. This one was poisonous, while the other was medicinal. The local *vaid*, or doctor, would harvest many of these, but they needed the escort of a great number of villagers, armed with pickaxes and sticks, for no one would dare venture into the tiger's lair alone. As she listened to him, she was struck by his intimate knowledge of the jungle around him. He seemed to be perfectly at home in his surroundings, carrying himself with an air of assurance. *What if a tiger were to leap at our howdah*, she wondered silently. She felt sure that he would remain unruffled and would send the animal to its death instantly. She shuddered involuntarily, praying that they would be spared that excitement.

She found herself glancing back at Miss. Johnson and Mr. Grayson. They seemed to be uncomfortable. Mr. Grayson was mopping the sweat off his brow and wore an expression of displeasure. He clutched his rifle and cocked it at the slightest sound around him. He looked ill at ease in his surroundings and she was puzzled by this, given how comfortable he had seemed when they first met in Calcutta, and when he had been introduced to her father. She caught herself thinking that unlike Davenport, he would be unable to withstand the onslaught of a charging tiger that leapt as high as his howdah.

She was displeased, wondering why she was comparing the two men. Surely Mr. Grayson was a fine shot, as he had said, and would be able to handle himself creditably should a crisis arise. Her thoughts returned to Davenport. Again, she found herself yielding him her grudging admiration. He seemed to be in charge of himself and of her and she wondered how he would approach the tiger if it appeared suddenly. She did not have to wait long to find out.

At that moment, her uncle signaled the procession to a halt. They had discovered the tiger's pug marks in the soft earth ahead. It was accompanied by traces of a kill that had been dragged by it over some distance. Davenport instinctively stood up to alight from the howdah and join his friend. He was checked by a signal from Knowles to remain where he was, with a nod in Edwina's direction. They had to be silent now, communicating mostly through gestures, to avoid alerting the tiger to their presence, for then, it was sure to flee.

Davenport understood the unspoken request. His friend wished him to remain with his niece and refrain from having the elephant kneel to permit him to alight, as that would place her in a most vulnerable position. He resumed his pose of alert watchfulness as he took his seat across from her. The men cocked their rifles and looked around them. They approached the brush ahead with the greatest care, never taking their eyes off the undergrowth. Knowles chose a circuitous route into the bushes to avoid being surprised by a charging tiger. The jungle around them was calm and in the distance, they heard alarm calls of animals. This made them reasonably sure that they were safe for now. Kartar Singh signaled with a waving arm that he had found the kill.

It was a *sambhar* and its half-eaten carcass lay concealed expertly in the bushes. Now, the general radius of the tiger's presence could be estimated. It would be sure to return to its kill. But, they would not leave an encounter with it to chance. The men moved quickly, constructing the *machan* on which the women would be hoisted. It was necessary to construct more than one *machan* and to place a gun on each, to ensure that there would be more than one opportunity to fire a shot. Mr. Grayson assisted Miss. Johnson up one *machan,* while Davenport aided Edwina up the other. Her uncle and Mr. Davenport would mount a beat atop their elephants, accompanied by the four other elephants which the porters sat on. The alarm calls had momentarily ceased.

'The tiger has probably stopped to rest. No doubt it is resting, for we do not hear any more alarm calls. The tiger will sleep for an extraordinarily long time during the day, for it hunts at night,' Davenport informed Edwina as he left her upon the *machan.*

The men on the elephants formed a wide ring around where the alarm calls had last sounded. Then they started to make a great deal of noise, calling loudly, clapping and playing drums. Often, the men who conducted the beat went on foot, but today, John Knowles did not want to court the slightest risk. The women's presence necessitated that caution preside over the entire exercise. Accordingly, the men moved closer, tightening their ring, leaving only one possible direction for the tiger to escape—towards the waiting *machans.* Suddenly, a porter shouted that he had seen the tiger in the rustling undergrowth. The men drew their elephants closer, in an ever-tightening semi-circle. Abruptly, the tiger bolted out from behind a tree and straight in the direction of the *machans.*

Edwina heard a call, a signal that they had agreed upon, that would signal the tiger's arrival in her direction. Her throat went dry as she peered through the sights of her rifle. Her *machan* was sturdy and stood a good ten metres above the ground. But she was suddenly conscious of being alone on her perch, facing a very fierce beast, which was enraged by fear and would tear apart anything that threatened it. As the minutes dragged by, seeming like eternal hours, her heart pounded louder and louder, until she was quite deaf to all other sounds. Suddenly, she heard a shot ring out from her right. Immediately, there was a deafening roar and the tiger bolted in the opposite direction. A sudden movement to her left caught her eye. But, by then, he had moved too far to the left and could not be reached by her shot in his direction.

Evidently, either Grayson or Miss. Johnson had fired a shot and hit the tiger. In the dead silence that followed, Edwina waited for one of them to speak. Then she called out, 'Mr. Grayson, Miss. Johnson, are you alright? Did you hit the tiger?'

'I certainly believe I did,' came Grayson's reply, in a voice brimming with pride.

'Is it dead?' asked Edwina. 'I don't know. It bolted into the jungle. It will probably bleed to death,' he replied glibly.

'But, what if it does not die, at least not immediately?' asked Edwina, with alarm.

'It don't signify,' came the shocking reply. 'The point is, I shot the beast singlehandedly, and on my first hunt too! Even if I don't have its hide, it will yet make for a most droll story at my club,' he chuckled.

Miss. Johnson, deadly silent until this point and clutching her smelling salts, giggled weakly. Edwina froze for a moment, allowing the weight of his words to sink in. A wounded tiger was on the loose. Although her sportsmanship hitherto had been restricted to hunting wild fowl and the odd *chital,* she knew the indelible code of sportsmanship: one did not leave a wounded animal in the wild, particularly not one that was a predator. The jungles were dotted with pockets of village settlements and even in the remotest parts, there lived small, isolated groups of people, who were now in great peril and would remain so until this animal was tracked and destroyed. She recalled with a shudder, her uncle's account that man-eaters were typically wounded animals.

She did not respond to Grayson's words, feeling quite at a loss for words. That the pleasant and charming Mr. Grayson was not a sportsman by any stretch of imagination had rapidly become apparent to her. He was a gentleman who was a skilled marksman. Sadly, the knowledge of how to shoot skillfully did not qualify one as a sportsman. She remained silent, hopelessly watching for any traces of the tiger's return, knowing fully well that it would not venture back to the spot where it had just been attacked so violently. Now, the task of the party would be the dangerous one of tracking a wounded and enraged tiger and finishing Mr. Grayson's unfinished business.

She heaved a sigh of relief as she heard a call from her uncle as he approached. 'We are safe, Uncle John. But take care for we do not know where the tiger lies for Mr. Grayson has shot him,' she shouted to him.

Soon, a procession of elephants approached. 'Where's the tiger?' asked Davenport.

'I shot him!' rang out Grayson's exultant reply.

'Where is he?' asked Davenport, looking nonplussed.

'Oh, he made off into the jungle. Licking his wounds in a corner somewhere, I expect,' he answered.

A frown appeared on Davenport's brow. 'You injured him, but did not kill him?' he asked, looking around the undergrowth with a look of foreboding.

'I suppose you have killed every single animal you've ever shot?' Grayson asked sneeringly, as he descended from his *machan*.

'No, I have not,' came Davenport's quiet reply.

Knowles added, 'That is not uncommon in a *shikar*. But, we must now track it and ensure it is dead.'

'*Track it?*' asked Grayson in incredulous accents. 'Surely you're not suggesting we follow a wounded tiger that's furious with us for gifting him a bullet? Come, sir! Surely you will agree, that's a fool's errand. I assure you it will bleed to death on its own.'

At this point, both men stared at him, stunned. 'We *cannot* leave an injured tiger in the jungle, close as we are to the villages around us. Surely you see that?' asked Davenport in a strained voice.

His words stung Grayson. For days this man had driven them through the jungle, turning what Grayson thought should have been a pleasant excursion into an arduous journey. He resented Davenport's self-assurance in the wilderness, and while unaccustomed to taking second place to other men, he was not oblivious of the fact that Mr. Davenport cast a large shadow wherever he went.

He presently felt the eyes of both ladies fixed on him and said, quite rashly, 'I see nothing at all, my good fellow, except someone who is perhaps bitterly envious at not having had a crack at it himself! And besides, you can count on it, the natives who choose to reside in these wild parts are apt to be quite capable of defending themselves.'

Davenport's countenance darkened, and the corners of his mouth tightened. He opened his mouth to speak, but was cut off by Grayson who unwisely blundered on, deluded by the exhilaration of the hunt into thinking that he was second to no man in masterfulness, and urged on by a pent up resentment of Davenport that he had carried these past few days, for being the one to whom all the party, particularly the women, deferred to.

'I must say, you fancy yourself quite in charge here, do you not?' he asked sardonically.

Edwina cringed at the unmerited allegation and at his foolhardy assertion that the villagers in the jungles would be able to defend themselves against an enraged wounded tiger. His utter callousness towards the gentle hill-folk who lived in little hamlets in the forests horrified her. Davenport and her uncle exchanged a quick, shocked glance. That he had missed the tiger was not remarkable. The best sportsmen missed or superficially wounded their targets. The angle one was in, the lighting, the time of the day and the speed of the passing animal all created variations in one's ability to kill his quarry. A sportsman who injured his prey without killing it, however, was honour-bound to follow it and finish the task. What galled them was Mr. Grayson's cavalier attitude towards this part of the exercise. He was unconcerned with the effect his actions would have, choosing only to gloat in the dubious distinction of simply having wounded the animal.

Davenport ignored the last remark and turned to Knowles saying quietly, 'Let us go on, John, with your two men. We will need to leave the rest behind for their safety and so we don't alert the animal to our presence.'

Knowles nodded, relieved that he was accompanied by his dependable friend.

'Do you propose to leave us here alone?' asked Miss. Johnson in a timorous voice.

The gravity of the situation had become apparent to her, and she was suddenly terrified of being in this place, open to attack at any moment. Indeed, she wished she had not listened to Grayson and descended from her *machan*, even though she didn't feel entirely safe, even up there.

'You should get onto an elephant, Miss. Johnson,' Davenport said kindly. 'Mohan! *Memsahib ko howdah pe charrao*' (Mohan! Help the lady onto the howdah), he commanded the mahout. 'It will perhaps be safest for all of you to head towards our camp,' he continued. 'And Miss. Hardingham would do well to alight from her *machan* and join Miss. Johnson,' he said, looking at Edwina.

She read derision in his eyes. *We find this fool foisted upon us, thanks to you*, they seemed to say. She felt flustered and ashamed. It was true. William Grayson had been introduced to her uncle as her friend and now, as her friend, he had behaved in an unmanly fashion and she felt partly to blame.

'Will we be safe in the camp?' asked Miss. Johnson plaintively as Mohan, the mahout, assisted her up into the howdah.

Mohan, assuming the ladies would ride separately, as they had done before and that Grayson would accompany the other *sahibs* to track the wounded tiger, had his elephant rise after Miss. Johnson had entered her howdah. Kartar Singh had produced a ladder and Edwina quickly alighted from her *machan*. He waited for Raja, the mahout of the elephant she had ridden on earlier to seat his elephant, to permit Edwina to enter the howdah. But, the elephant, named Chanda, would not kneel. Raja coaxed her, continually issuing commands, gently tugging on her ear with his hook, and prodding with his feet, but she was strangely disobedient. Raja tugged harder on her ear and she folded her front legs. Kartar Singh grabbed hold of the sides of the howdah and leapt within, intending to grab Edwina's hand and hoist her inside, when suddenly, Chanda stood up erect before he could take hold of Edwina's arm.

Glancing absently at the strangely defiant pachyderm, Davenport answered Miss Johnson's fearful question, saying 'Most certainly you will be safe, Miss. Johnson. Besides, you will be in the care of a most accomplished shot who seldom misses, though he may kill nothing.'

Grayson was quick to respond to the barb.

'Now see here,' he began.

But, Davenport had turned away from him, looking perplexedly at

Chanda. His own elephant seemed to be getting unnerved by Chanda's strange behavior. He decided to dismount and see what the problem was, but his elephant refused to kneel, as well.

Meanwhile, Grayson launched a harangue against Davenport, saying, 'You've got no right to speak to me that way. You're not—'

He was cut short by a shout from Knowles. 'The tiger! It's behind those bushes. Quick, Grayson, take Edwina up the *machan*. James, aim to your left. It's right around those rocks!'

The effect of her uncle's words was a tumult of events around Edwina. William Grayson bounded up the ladder and onto the *machan*. Edwina followed him, tucking up her skirts and preparing to mount the ladder, when Grayson, fearing that the tiger would be able to follow him up the *machan* by means of the ladder, kicked it down. Edwina veered to avoid it crashing on her. She did not stop to wonder why he had done that, moving towards the next *machan*, desperately hoping that Kartar Singh had left a ladder there. But alas, he had used the same ladder for both *machans* and it now lay on the ground. Edwina struggled to lift it up, when she heard a low blood-curdling growl behind her. She turned slowly and saw the tiger, not fifteen yards away. The elephants, now panicking, began to back away, and neither Knowles nor Davenport could take aim from atop them. Both were terrified of firing a shot without hitting the tiger, knowing that the sound of a gunshot would simply infuriate the animal further and he would charge Edwina in the blink of an eye. They must not fire until they were sure of hitting it. Only Grayson, seated on his unmoving perch had a clear shot.

Knowles called out to him, 'Shoot, man! For heaven's sake, shoot!!'

But, Mr. Grayson appeared to be frozen with the terror of having been within striking distance of the cat and sat with his rifle fused to his hands.

Edwina said in a low voice. 'Hand me your rifle, Mr. Grayson.'

But he seemed to have become both deaf and mute.

The tiger inched forward, as if to cut Edwina off from the cover of the startled elephants. Perhaps it was the sense of pandemonium that prevailed as *mahouts* and *sahibs* yelled their commands, but the well-trained elephants failed their masters today. Edwina felt the blood drain from her face. She knew she must not show her back to the tiger, but facing him was terrifying, even as her eyes widened involuntarily. She pursed her lips, determined to stay calm, thinking to herself, *Uncle John will come and get me. He will not leave me here to be slain by this beast. Uncle John always rescued me when I was a child and stuck up a tree. He will not abandon me now.*

But, she felt herself choking and a sob of terror threatened to break free. Still, she stood in absolute silence, waiting for what would come next; she was aware of a dull thud coming from the direction of the elephants. Someone or something had fallen, perhaps from off an elephant. She did not take her eyes off the tiger, however. The tiger twitched its tail, signaling that it was ready to attack, when the armed men atop the elephants suddenly fired several shots in unison. It was momentarily distracted and then, the enraged tiger prepared to spring. As he crouched, Edwina suddenly found Davenport planting himself between her and the tiger. He shoved her roughly to the right and himself swung to the left. As he did so, he fired a shot. The tiger leapt overhead and crumpled on the ground behind them. He quickly fired a second shot into the animal's head to ensure that it was indeed dead. It had already been weakened by a great loss of blood, which had worked in their favour.

Edwina felt her knees start to buckle, but as she leaned forward, she felt Mr. Davenport's arm around her waist.

'Are you alright, Miss. Hardingham?' he asked gently, with a look of great concern.

She could not reply for her throat was dry and speech had temporarily abandoned her. She trembled violently and opened and closed her mouth several times without being able to speak. He swung her gently up in his arms and carried her towards the elephant that had recently been so insubordinate. But now, Chanda was calm again. Indeed all the elephants had regained calm at the sight of the dead tiger. Kartar Singh reached down to hold Edwina, and together, he and Davenport seated her within the howdah. Davenport put his arm around her shoulders and gently offered her a drink of water from a container in the howdah. Kartar Singh alighted to make room for his master Knowles, who was shaking with shock. A seasoned hunter, he had often encountered peril nonchalantly before. But today, he was unnerved. To watch a loved one at death's door is particularly chilling and can excite terror in the bravest breast.

'Edwina, my child, are you alright?!' asked her uncle in an agonized voice.

Edwina saw tears stream down the crevices of his wrinkled cheeks.

With effort, she answered, 'I am quite well, thank you, Uncle John.'

He grasped her hands in his and asked in a choked voice, 'Are you injured, child?'

'No, sir. Pray, do not be uneasy on my account. I am just a little shaken. I shall presently be myself again,' she replied.

She felt grateful for the support of Davenport's arm around her waist and leaned weakly into his shoulder.

Turning to Davenport, her uncle said, 'James, I am deeply in your debt for your valour. You have saved us all today from unimaginable horror!'

'Nonsense!' said Davenport cheerily, 'It was Miss. Hardingham who saved the day. Never have I ever seen someone stand so coolly and stare a tiger down. Your calm certainly put off the animal's charge, Miss. Hardingham.'

His tone was warm and his eyes looked down on her admiringly. The colour that had deserted her face came rushing back and she blushed adorably. Suddenly, she was conscious of being extremely near to him and leaning into his shoulder. She demurely lowered her eyes and moved herself away. His arm instantly dropped from her waist, as he shifted himself onto the seat opposite hers. But, his eyes remained fixed on her face and when she met his eyes, she imagined a fleeting look of tenderness, before his eyes became guarded again.

'How can I ever thank you, Mr. Davenport? You risked your life to save mine,' she said in a soft voice.

He seemed unable to speak, as if disarmed by her gentleness.

'I am glad you are unharmed,' he replied quietly.

'I feel I am to blame for this day's events,' said Knowles in a stricken voice. 'How could I have asked you to alight the *machan* with a wounded tiger on the loose?'

'It's hardly your fault, John,' said Davenport. 'Not one of us could have expected the animal to return to the site of his injury.'

Edwina nodded in agreement, saying, 'To be sure, Uncle John, none of us had the slightest inkling that he would return, except perhaps, the elephants.'

'I should have read the signs of their agitation. They were warning us that the animal was close by,' he replied remorsefully.

Davenport was about to reply when they heard a shout from Makkhan Singh. He had heard a rustle in the shrubs where the tiger had lately emerged from. This time, the men were prepared and all aimed their rifles at the brush. Davenport and Knowles descended speedily from the elephant and moved in the direction of the sound. It was faint and could not have been made by a large animal. Still, the two of them proceeded with caution, making a detour to the far left of the bushes, where a large tree stood. Moving further left, they inched their way around, keeping their eyes fixed on the brush, where they could see the tall grass rustling. Suddenly Knowles gave a shout and dropped his rifle. He walked straight behind the tree and leaned down into the bottom of a large bush. When he emerged, he held a tiny tiger cub that could have been no more than three weeks old.

'Our tiger was a female, and here's why she returned to the scene of our hunt!' he exclaimed.

A hum of excited chatter filled that section of the forest as the party discovered the explanation for the tiger's uncharacteristic behavior. Edwina had witnessed the whole incident from the howdah and scrambled down her elephant to hurry to her uncle.

'It was a mother!' she exclaimed.

She turned to look at her late foe. The tigress was sprawled on the ground and the men were preparing to rope and hoist her up an elephant. Edwina felt an overwhelming sadness envelop her heart. This noble animal was a valiant mother. Though injured, she had returned to the scene of the injury and had faced her attackers with courage. She had planted herself between her cub and the people who threatened both, her and it. And now, this defenseless creature had been orphaned and left bereft of its mother.

'Edwina, are you alright? You should not have descended from your elephant, for you are most pale,' said Knowles as he hurriedly put the cub down and strode to her side.

'Oh, Uncle John! How cruel we have been!' she sobbed. 'We have killed this beautiful creature that was such a devoted parent. How can we find such an act pleasurable? Indeed, there is no sportsmanship in killing so magnificent a beast merely for pleasure.'

Her uncle put his arms around her shoulder and gently led her back towards the elephant. 'Come, come, my dear. You are quite overwrought. This day has been truly distressing for you,' he said soothingly.

'What is to become of this poor little creature? Is it to be left to fend for itself?' she asked weeping.

'Rest easy on that score, Miss. Hardingham. By no means shall this poor animal be left defenseless in the jungle. I am certain that the Maharajah of Ranthambore would be delighted with the gift of a tiger cub,' said Davenport gently as he offered her his handkerchief.

She felt somewhat comforted that the cub would not be abandoned. But, she vowed to herself, *Never again shall I participate in the killing of such a noble beast purely for pleasure!*

They became aware presently of Grayson approaching them. Davenport looked at him with cold contempt, while Knowles' face was covered with heated fury.

But, before either of them could speak, Edwina said kindly, 'Mr. Grayson, I hope you are none the worse for wear after this day's events.'

His pale face reddened with shame and he stammered, 'M—M—Miss. Hardingham, I—I have behaved truly shabbily. I have n—n—no right to ask for your forgiveness, or indeed of—of yours Mr. Knowles and Mr. Davenport.'

Davenport opened his mouth to reply, but he was again prevented by Edwina who said, 'Do not tease yourself about today's happenings, sir. This might have happened to anyone. Besides, I consider myself still in your debt for the courage you displayed in Calcutta. Surely today's events cannot overshadow those of that day. Indeed, I will not allow it to be so among friends, for that is surely what we are!'

Davenport cast a look of incredulity at her, but said nothing. He quietly turned to the men and proceeded to make arrangements to mount the dead tiger and the cub onto the elephants. Knowles wished to make his feelings known to Grayson, but restrained himself, as he felt a warning squeeze from his nieces' arm which was on his own.

'Thank you, Miss. Hardingham, for your generosity. I have not always been this way,' Grayson said in a low voice. 'On losing my parents, when I was on my way to India, our ship was assailed by a vicious storm. There were insufficient boats for passengers to escape in, and whilst I was in one of them, I was roughly cast out of it by a strong sailor. Ever since, I have experienced great terrors and in moments of peril, I find myself irrationally overcome by a paralyzing dread.'

'That is most distressing, Mr. Grayson. You have indeed suffered much. Doubtless it is this event in your past that accounts for your fear today. Do not tax yourself by thinking of it,' Edwina replied in sympathetic accents.

Grayson shot her a look of gratitude as her uncle steered her towards her elephant. He was prevented from accompanying her by a forbidding glance from her uncle, who presently seated himself beside her. Mr. Grayson reluctantly climbed into the howdah where Miss. Johnson sat. She had missed much of the excitement as she had fainted, revived and then fainted again. She felt quite displeased that she had been left unattended and had not been revived by one of the gentlemen. But, she did not dare alight her howdah and stayed in it, torn between petulance and terror. She was gratified by Grayson's solicitous inquiries on her well-being.

'I am holding up as best I can, under the circumstances, Mr. Grayson, despite being sorely neglected,' she complained. 'Miss. Hardingham was safely on the ground. Why, practically everyone had their guns on that beast and there was no *real* danger of it harming her, whilst I was being dashed about on this dreadfully uncomfortable perch. And yet, no one has bothered to enquire after my welfare. Mr. Davenport has no gallantry to speak of and Mr. Knowles seems to be too old to be gallant. I am certain, however that I may expect more chivalry from *you*, sir!'

Grayson was somewhat taken aback. He had not expected to be thought of as more preferable a companion than the two brave men who now refused to acknowledge him. The suggestion that perhaps Edwina had not been in any real danger was overpoweringly seductive, and he surrendered to its appeal, believing it to be a fact, and consequently, absolving himself of any misconduct. He felt considerably cheered and devoted himself to fussing over Miss. Johnson, who was extremely grateful and becoming more enamoured by him with each passing moment.

The journey back to camp was uneventful. However, the sounds of the jungle now took on a new meaning for Edwina. She wished

Davenport was in their howdah—to identify the different authors of the birdcalls that filled the air—she told herself. Her eyes darted back frequently to the elephant behind her, upon which he rode. But, her view of him was obscured by the frame of his howdah. He had not addressed her after their conversation with Grayson. She could not help feeling that he disapproved of her friendliness to Grayson. That he believed Grayson to be beneath his contempt was amply evident, but she desperately wished not to be cast in the same light as Grayson— because she felt so indebted to Mr. Davenport, she told herself.

Although surprised by Grayson's cravenness, she was not unduly perturbed by it. She was not at all surprised by Davenport's bravery, either. From the first moment they had met, he had struck her as a masterful and courageous man. The motive for the deference accorded him by Makkhan Singh and Kartar Singh now became apparent. She was sure he would have conducted himself with the same courage regardless of who was facing the tiger, but she found herself wanting to believe that his actions were especially fervent because she was the one. Why she wished this, she wasn't sure. She speculated that perhaps it was due to the great admiration he had excited within her today. She was grateful for the silence in which they travelled, as it afforded her moments of introspection. The journey to their camp seemed fleeting and before long, they were seated in front of a fire as the servants served them hot tea and biscuits. Edwina retired to her tent for a short nap.

When she emerged, the men were preparing dinner. Davenport had procured some wildfowl and the men were presently roasting them. Haldi Ram, the cook, had brought several herbs and spices with him and soon, a savoury fragrance assailed their camp. She looked around for Davenport or her uncle, but neither of them was in sight. She made herself comfortable around the fire, chatting with Haldi Ram about his delicious concoctions. She heard footsteps from a path that led into the dense jungle and saw, to her surprise that her uncle and Grayson had gone for a walk together. That they had not had a pleasant time was apparent from the glower on her uncle's face and the sullen expression on Grayson's.

Oh dear! she thought, *Uncle John has given him a dressing down. And he seems to be in the sulks. I shall have to cheer him up, or it will seem uncivil of me.* She did not relish the idea of spending the remainder of the evening cheering Grayson. She was forestalled, however, by Miss. Johnson who emerged from her tent, bestowing a radiant smile on Grayson.

'Mr. Grayson! Will you not take my arm? I do so wish to take a small walk to the stream, to stretch my legs. I'm afraid the rattling my bones have received on that beast has quite stiffened them and a walk will do me good.'

Edwina looked warily at the surrounding thickets. The sun would soon set and an orange glow had already begun to bathe the forest. Animals that hunted in the night would soon be on the prowl and a stroll in the jungle, away from the safety of the campfires, would be ill-advised.

Surely Uncle John or Grayson will forbid it, she thought. But to her surprise, neither man said anything. Miss. Johnson's appearance provided them both a welcome reprieve from the acrimony of the situation. Grayson gratefully took Miss. Johnson's arm and led her off into a small path bordering a dense thicket. To Edwina's relief, her uncle nodded to both his men, signaling that they were to follow the feckless pair into the jungle. They noiselessly skirted the path, following them in the cover of the brush, without giving their presence away.

Edwina felt relieved that she did not need to spend the evening in Grayson's company. Her eyes darted towards Davenport's tent, but there was no sign of him.

Finally, when she couldn't contain herself, she asked, 'Is Mr. Davenport well, Uncle John?'

He looked up from his book, 'Why, yes. He's washing by the stream.' He seemed surprised by her question.

'It's just that I thought he was in his tent, and I wished to thank him again,' she hastily supplied.

He seemed satisfied. 'Is that why you keep looking in the direction of his tent? He will be here presently, m'dear,' he said.

He was proved right by the appearance of Davenport. He had washed himself and his hair was dripping wet. He had taken off his coat and was in his shirt sleeves. His linen shirt was wet in places, signifying that he had bathed in the stream, but had not dried himself, simply wearing on his clothes and trusting the warm setting sun to do its job. On catching sight of Edwina, he seemed self-conscious and hastily put his coat on. He bowed slightly in her direction and strode on into his tent. Edwina's shoulders drooped and she leaned forward to pour herself another cup of tea. He emerged from his tent a half hour later. His hair was now dry and neatly brushed back.

He seemed in command of himself again and he walked up to the fire and seated himself beside Knowles, saying, 'Do we leave at dawn, John?'

'Eh?' uttered her uncle, 'Oh yes. But, what have you done with the tiger?' he asked.

'It's being skinned as we speak,' answered Davenport, observing Edwina's silent shudder from the corner of his eye.

'And where is the cub?' she asked, looking at her uncle.

'The cook has fashioned him a bottle out of a goatskin and he has been fed. He is to sleep in Haldi Ram's tent,' said her uncle.

She started to rise, wishing very much to play with the little cub, but her uncle prevented her, saying, 'James thinks it will not do to get him accustomed to humans as the Maharajah may wish to rear him for his gaming reserve.'

The thought that the delightsome little creature was to be reared solely to be hunted, unsettled Edwina. Still, what else could be done? Were he to be abandoned in the jungle, he would most certainly not survive the night. And while every Englishman in India, and a good many in England would consider a tiger a wonderful prize, it was improbable that any would rear one as a pet. Indeed, she wasn't certain that such a beast could be domesticated at all. She had heard of one family that had reared a tiger in their home, but the animal had become savage in its adulthood and had to be kept in a cage. That was perhaps the fate that awaited the little cub. No one could tenderly cherish it for very long, and yet, forsaking it now seemed cruel.

I suppose we should kill it ourselves to save it from a cage or from being hunted when it grows up, she thought with a shiver. She felt something touch her and when she looked up, saw that Davenport had put his coat around her shoulders. Yet, he said nothing to her, turning away to stoke the fire.

'Thank you, Mr. Davenport,' she said softly.

But, he remained with his back turned to her, as if he did not hear her words.

Her uncle was roused by her voice and said, 'James, Edwina was most anxious to speak to you when you were bathing. She looked so intently at your tent, I thought she would march right in,' he chuckled. 'Tell him what you wanted to, Eddie,' he said.

Davenport turned to her with a surprised look in his eyes. She felt herself colouring rapidly. Thankfully, the light was fading and her face would not be too visible.

'Oh, I just wished to thank you again, Mr. Davenport, for your kindness to me today. I am very much in your debt,' she said.

His expression did not betray any emotion, and he merely bowed saying, 'It was my pleasure, ma'am.'

She wished to say more to him, but could not think of anything to say. They were rejoined by Grayson and Miss. Johnson who seemed to have had a pleasant walk. Haldi Ram soon announced that dinner was ready and the group sat down to a quiet meal.

How quickly everything has changed, thought Edwina. *When first we entered this wilderness, I was determined to court Miss. Johnson's friendship and Mr. Grayson's admiration. And now, neither of them appeals to me as a friend!*

She was disheartened by Diana's growing familiarity with Grayson. Not because she wished to be the recipient of his admiration herself, as she had before, but because she knew that Christopher had developed a partiality for this shallow and vain creature. Still, it was best that she had revealed her heart before Christopher could fall *very much* in love with her. She prayed silently that the damage was not already done and that her dear cousin was not already in the desperate throes of love.

CHAPTER FIVE

FEARFUL TIDINGS

Edwina was relieved to be returned to her home. She decided to keep the events of the past few days to herself, choosing only to enlighten her parents on the pleasant details of the excursion. Her plan was short-lived, however. Her uncle dined with them the day after their return and rapidly informed them of the events that had transpired during the *shikar*.

'I wanted to give that scoundrel a dressing down he would not forget in a hurry, and dash it all, I would have very nearly come to blows with him, had it not been for Eddie's continued kindness to him,' he said, freshly annoyed at remembering his niece's inexplicable graciousness to the newly revealed coward.

Mrs. Hardingham grew pale and her husband paced the room. Both he and Christopher were made furious by Grayson's cravenness. Mr. Hardingham glared at Edwina from under bushy brows.

'Edwina, what I fail to understand is why you chose to conceal these matters from us. Was it your intention to continue your acquaintance with Grayson? Are you so much in love with him?' he asked angrily.

Edwina turned crimson red. 'Papa!' she exclaimed in a horrified tone. 'That is a most unjust reflection. I marvel that you suspect me of being capable of such base motives. Indeed, I have never been *in love* with Mr. Grayson and it is my fervent prayer that I never shall be. I wish never to be in his company again. In fact, I pity him and cannot but reflect that his state of mind must be a wretched one. On my initial encounter with him, I became indebted to him for saving me from the brigands in Calcutta. That debt blinded me to his callow nature. I was oblivious of the lack of gentlemanliness in him when he made unkind gossip, and I was blinded to his duplicity when he. ...'

She checked herself, for she was about to blurt out that Grayson had been duplicitous in his treatment of her and Diana, maligning her to Edwina's face, while performing the rôle of an intimate friend before Miss. Johnson. She could not bear to unmask Miss. Johnson heartlessly before Christopher.

'In all, I have behaved with him as a lady should, remembering always his kindness in Calcutta. I could not allow his act of kindness to be overshadowed by an act of cowardice for that should be ungracious behaviour in a lady. I do not like him, but nothing would induce me to behave uncivilly towards him,' she finished.

'Quite so, my dear. You have behaved exactly as you ought. Indeed Mr. Hardingham, I am dismayed by your accusation. Consider that Edwina has been exhausted by these events and must have wished above all else to put the horrors of the incident as far away from her mind as she possibly could, although I must say, my dear Edwina, that your failure to confide in us is sadly unsatisfactory, and is no doubt the reason for your father's outrage,' interjected her mother, torn between disapproval of her husband's unduly harsh words, and her daughter's reticence.

Christopher said remorsefully, 'I am truly mortified that it was my absence that allowed this rogue to impose on the kindness of Edwina and Miss. Johnson. I shudder to think how these two gracious ladies have been ill-used by Mr. Grayson's cowardice.'

Again, Edwina's desire to avert disappointment in those she loved was thwarted by her uncle.

'Balderdash!' he retorted, with a snort. 'She's a widgeon if I ever saw one, and ever eager to be imposed on by that coxcomb!'

'Whatever can you mean, Uncle John?' asked Christopher in a trembling voice.

'I found Miss. Johnson most sympathetic to Grayson. He never abandoned HER for a moment, be it on the *machan* or on the elephant, and for her part, she never ceased for a moment to make sheep's eyes him. What they found to mutter to each other, I'll never know,' elaborated his uncle obligingly.

Christopher digested this silently, betraying no emotion. His aunt, who had surmised his sentiments, shook her head sadly. Brother and sister had been ill-used at once!

When they were alone, Christopher took Edwina's hands in his, saying, 'Now I understand how your admiration turned so quickly into loathing. Your heart has been injured, dear Eddie, as has mine. My pain is greater, knowing that you suffer.'

'No! You mistake me, Christopher. Mr. Grayson's charm seemed alluring for a few brief moments, but he never captured my heart and indeed, has done my sentiments no harm. If you must grieve, do so for your own heart, dear cousin, as do I. For, it is you who have suffered the most,' she corrected him gently.

He seemed both pleased and crestfallen at the same time, relieved that she believed herself unhurt, and deeply hurt by the fickleness of Miss. Johnson who had given him every reason to expect that his suit would be favourably regarded. The days that followed seemed to drag on, until one day about two weeks later, they received an unexpected visit from Captain Lovelace.

The distress caused by the recent events was soon forgotten and the Hardinghams welcomed him with no small excitement. He arrived with his batman, carrying an introduction from Markham. Mrs. Hardingham was elated to see him again, declaring that he needed no introduction when visiting her home. He bowed to Edwina, complimenting her on how the mountain air seemed to have brought a bloom to her cheeks.

She smiled, and asked, 'I trust my sister and brother-in-law are well?'

'More importantly, is Anne well?' interjected Christopher playfully.

Captain Lovelace maintained his composure and stolidly replied, 'Mr. and Mrs. Markham and their children and Miss. Hardingham are all in the best of health. There is a letter addressed to your father from them.'

While his answer was exceedingly proper, Edwina and Christopher found his lack of emotion insipid.

'There is not a spark of passion in him that I can detect!' declared Edwina when she and her mother were alone.

'That may be true,' responded her mother calmly, 'but we can be quite certain that a spark of passion is not what Anne desires. She desires to make a good match with a respectable man from a family of consequence. In this, she is not ill-advised. You will agree with me, my dear, that we would be hard-pressed to find a suitor more eminently respectable than Captain Lovelace. I believe that they will be very well suited. You would do well to take a leaf out of Anne's book and seek a respectable man, instead of the rakes you have been inviting into our midst,' she said with a twinkle in her eye.

Edwina chortled, saying, 'Oh no, Mama! I shall never take credit for Mr. Grayson's being in our midst. For it was *you* who invited him to my ball!'

Seeing her so unencumbered by regret, her mother smiled, adding gently, 'Well, dearest, I believe that when you marry, it shall be for deep, enduring, unending love and because you have found a man with that spark of passion that you seek. I wish you may find it before very long.'

Edwina smiled, but said nothing.

They were to dine that night with her uncle and Mr. Davenport. Davenport had been most disinclined to join them, but Mr. Knowles had persisted and he reluctantly acquiesced. Captain Lovelace had come to Simla expressly to seek Mr. Hardingham's permission to pledge his troth to Anne. He was in a haste to leave after acquiring Mr. Hardingham's blessing, declaring that he was needed back in his regiment without delay, citing the fermenting of civil unrest in parts of Oudh and Meerut. Mr. Hardingham however, was insistent that he tarry and dine with them, wishing to introduce him to his cousin and to Mr. Davenport. Captain Lovelace, it turned out, was previously acquainted with Mr. Davenport. Their fathers had been acquainted and the two men had met briefly on a few occasions in their youth. Captain Lovelace seemed pleased to renew his acquaintance with Davenport, although he was surprised when Mr. Hardingham announced his betrothal to Anne in front of Davenport.

Seeing his surprise, Mr. Hardingham declared, 'I shall keep no secrets here for we are among friends.'

Mr. Hardingham had liked Davenport when first introduced to him, but his heroic rescue of Edwina permanently sealed his friendship with the Hardinghams, who were overcome not just by his reportedly brave actions, but also by his quiet modesty afterwards. They had thanked him profusely, and although he was evidently embarrassed, he received their expressions of gratitude graciously, saying quietly that he was glad that

Miss. Hardingham was unharmed. Furthermore, he was quick to add that Edwina's calm response had done much to alleviate the situation.

Edwina had greeted him shyly, and he had said little to her all evening. She contrived to seat herself beside him during dinner. But, he gave his entire attention to her mother who sat on his left, turning only occasionally to nod or make a quick observation to Edwina. After dinner, when the ladies withdrew, Edwina threw a quick, beseeching look at Christopher to encourage the men not to linger too long over their Port, and was surprised when he shook his head reproachfully at her. She sat with Mrs. Hardingham in the drawing-room, but it seemed like the men were a long time in coming. They were certainly relishing their Port, she thought, pacing the floor.

'Edwina, you seem disquieted,' remarked her mother. 'What is the cause of this anxiety?'

'Oh! Well … I actually hoped to inquire of Captain Lovelace more thoroughly after Kate and Anne and of course the children, for he seems in the greatest haste to make his way back to the plains,' she said, thinking to herself that her words did not sound convincing.

But her mother appeared satisfied. She sat down, bending over her embroidery to hide her anticipation. But, she was distracted, listening for any signs of movement near the door, starting whenever the servants brushed against it and pricking herself often.

At last, the men rejoined them. She shot a disapproving look at Christopher who shrugged and made his way next to her.

'I did my best,' said he. 'But, even Uncle John refused to drink another glass of Port after his third—and you know how *he* can drink longer than anyone. Uncle Arthur accused me of trying to get him bosky when I kept plying him with Port. That's when I had to stop prevaricating. Although why you have such an aversion for an amiable chap like Davenport *after* his valiant rescue of you, I will never fathom. You really must try to get over this prejudice, Eddie,' he said reprovingly.

She stared uncomprehendingly at first and then, gradually, his meaning became clear. She had signalled him to guide the men into the drawing-room quickly and he had supposed that she wished him to detain them from it as long as he possibly could. She was possessed of a strong desire to box his ears! He had assumed she wished to avoid Mr.

Davenport's company because she had declared her dislike of him before the *shikar*. Now, everything had changed, but of course, he had not realized it. She opened her mouth to explain but a thought occurred to her and she changed her mind. Mr. Davenport was standing at the far end of the room, conversing with her father and he made no move to so much as turn in her direction.

She turned absently to Lovelace who was presently asking her about the *shikar*, for some mention of it had come up at dinner. She answered his questions mechanically, looking at the far end of the room, whenever she could do so undetected. She saw Mr. Davenport rapt in conversation with her father. Sometimes she felt he was watching her, but whenever she looked in his direction, he seemed wholly occupied with the conversation he was engaged in.

At long last, Davenport made his way to where Edwina sat.

She looked up at him and smiled warmly, saying, 'Mr. Davenport, I have not had the chance to speak with you tonight. I trust you are well? You are quite the hero in this house, you know.'

He stared at her for a moment. His eyes seemed arrested. 'I am doing quite well, Miss. Hardingham, as I hope are you,' he answered.

She searched about in her mind for words to say to him, but none would come. She was desperate to detain him, but she lacked the skill to do so. Where Anne would have artfully communicated her interest with the flick of the wrist and a fan, Edwina was tongue-tied and suddenly shy. She lowered her eyes, appearing to regard her embroidery with a recently discovered zeal.

'I trust you are greatly pleased to receive good news of your sisters in Calcutta,' he remarked, conversationally.

'Oh yes! We had not expected to see Captain Lovelace—not today that is,' she finished somewhat awkwardly.

He nodded, encouraging her to continue.

'Captain Lovelace informs us that there is some civil discontent preparing in the plains,' she said, unable to think of anything else to say.

Overhearing her, Knowles turned to Lovelace asking him what was afoot.

'Oh, it's the beastly natives. Some rubbish or the other about tallow from cows and pig fat in their cartridges. The matter was attended to and Colonel Birch, the Military Secretary ordered that they were to use whatever grease they pleased, but that's only served to make them suspicious that we've ruined their caste and defiled their religion, in the first place. Their rogue leaders fan the flames of discontent. What they want is an iron hand to whip them out of their laziness.'

While the others listened in silence, Edwina's eyes flashed and she stiffened, as her embroidery slipped unheeded onto the floor.

Forgetting the tender thoughts that were flooding her person a few moments ago, she wrathfully declared, 'I would hardly think that the Indian *sepoys* are *lazy*, Captain Lovelace. If indeed that is what they are, why on earth does the mighty British army employ them? Could it be that we rely on their strength to conquer their land? Consider that a small minority of us rules this vast land with the aid of a small number of loyal and industrious men. If we are unwilling, after such exacting demands on their services, to accord them the dignity of treatment as equal partakers of this land's best, then I hardly think we can be surprised that they choose to chafe at the bit!'

'Promotions for sepoys are non-existent, reserved as they are for the English. And yet, we expect their unflinching loyalty without any rewards in return, and find it surprising when a brave lot choose to tell us we are not needed by them any longer? And as for these persons whom you unjustly label 'rogue leaders,' no Englishman who is governed by a sense of what is right and just can deny that the Doctrine of Lapse has been a most imbalanced and unjust means of expanding the interests of the Company. How can we brandish our race's superior claims to rule this land when we so effortlessly disregard every moral principle that we declare is what makes us superior to those around us? Depend upon it, Captain Lovelace the East India Company has vastly merited civil unrest on its hands!' she finished, with fury.

Mrs. Hardingham paled while Mr. Hardingham cleared his throat. Only Mr. Knowles sat calmly, nodding his head in agreement. Davenport did not betray his sentiments, but there was a strange light in his eyes as he regarded Edwina. Captain Lovelace stood up, crimson red and enraged. For someone who displayed no spark of passion, his face appeared to be demonstrating a vast amount of it now. He restrained himself with the greatest difficulty.

'Have a care, Miss. Hardingham! I hardly think someone in your position should venture to speak words that amount to treason against

England! You cannot be aware of what you say,' he exclaimed with as much composure as he could muster.

'And pray tell, what position exactly is that, sir?' she asked icily.

Before he could respond, Christopher interjected pleasantly, 'Such talk of moral principles and scruples is apt to give one indigestion—especially after that wonderfully rich curried mutton that my dear aunt presented us at dinner. It all sounds exceedingly more dangerous than your *shikar,* dear cousin. Were you aware, Captain Lovelace that several of the persons assembled here have recently been on a *shikar,* and have bagged a handsome trophy for their trouble? Two of them, to be precise, for there was a cub as well, was there not, Uncle John? Tell us what became of it,' he asked.

For a second, a look of contempt flickered in Captain Lovelace's eyes, but Mr. Knowles began to recount the tale of the tiger cub orphaned by them and was ably assisted by Davenport who had imperceptibly placed his chair in such a manner as to obstruct Lovelace's view of Edwina. The shift in the conversation had the effect of calming Captain Lovelace's temper. To his credit, he was very much in love with Anne and he was a gentleman. That he should find his future sister-in-law so intemperate had come as a great surprise to him.

Nothing in her manner or deportment had conveyed to him that she was given to so much unladylike passion. *Besides being woefully ignorant, she is unrestrained in her expression of these ignorant sentiments,* he thought. Mercifully, he reflected, her sister was nothing like her. In Anne, he would find an amiable wife who was conscious of the impropriety of a lady expressing extreme views on matters of politics. He did not wish to impair his address with her parents and gradually, allowed himself to become drawn into the conversation.

The heat of the moment having passed, Edwina gradually began to feel the ill-advisedness of her outburst. Although her parents continually gave her leave to speak freely in their presence, she was aware that restraint in a lady's speech was obligated by Society. She had mortified her parents and Anne. She hoped fervently that he would not cry off, thanking Heaven silently that Anne was so comely that there was small chance of that. She was sorry for her outburst, even though she believed what she said was just and true. Suddenly, it dawned on her that her comportment had more than likely left an unpleasant impression on Mr.

Davenport as well. This was a lowering reflection and suddenly she wished she could slide out of the room unnoticed. She raised her eyes to look at him, but he was occupied in a description of the hunt.

By now, Captain Lovelace was mollified and trying to make peace with Edwina asked, 'How is your friend, Mr. Grayson, Miss. Hardingham? I recall him mentioning to you that he would take the opportunity of calling on you in Simla. Did you include him in your *shikar*?' he asked.

Turning to Davenport, he said, 'Perhaps you have heard that Miss. Hardingham was viciously attacked, on peril of her life, by brigands in Calcutta. She was valiantly rescued by a Mr. Grayson, a most amiable man with excellent address—he's generally regarded as one of the handsomest fellows in Calcutta,' smiling knowingly at Edwina in a full-scale attempt to hand her an olive branch.

Glancing desperately at Mr. Davenport's back, Edwina silently prayed that he would not consider Mr. Grayson as a favorite acquaintance of the family, for she knew Mr. Davenport heartily despised him and she had no wish to be cast in the rôle of his friend.

She responded in an even tone, 'Yes, Captain Lovelace, he has called upon us.'

'I hope you included him in your party, for a braver fellow one would be hard-pressed to find,' said the inexorable Captain Lovelace.

'You are quite right,' she answered flatly, glancing at Davenport as she did so.

He had stood up and walked towards the mantlepiece, where he appeared to be conducting a close examination of a magnificent painting by Francesco Renaldi that hung over it. He did not betray any emotion and she felt confident that her unenthusiastic responses conveyed her absence of interest in Grayson. Captain Lovelace made his apologies, retiring to bed early, for he wished to commence his journey home before dawn.

As she bid goodbye to Mr. Davenport when they parted, she looked up at his face, smiling warmly. His face was reserved and his smile nominal. Edwina's heart sank to her stomach. He had found her outburst uncivil—she was sure of it. She had spoken self-indulgently, thinking only of herself and her need to say what was right. She had not considered that her words might occasion the displeasure of her guests and the embarrassment of her family. With a downcast heart, she tossed and turned in her bed that night, as sleep eluded her. She slept into the late hours of the morning and was awakened by Shanta who had become alarmed that she was not awake. She stayed in bed, swallowing the tea and toast Shanta insisting on bringing her.

'What ails you *Missy-sahib*?' she asked. 'Your heart is heavy. Tell me, who has hurt you?' she asked soothingly.

Edwina's eyes suddenly welled up, her heart aching in response to her nurse's tender solicitude. 'I have been most disrespectful to our guests, Shantama. I have disgraced the family,' she said forlornly. 'Has Captain Lovelace left, for I must apologize to him?'

'The soldier left this morning. He's a puffed-up one, *Missy-sahib*. I saw him berate Madho for trying to groom his horse, saying no one but his own servant may touch his horse. He even started to strike Madho, when *Bada Sahib* calmed him down,' she said, referring to Mr. Hardingham. 'And my dearest child, you could never bring disgrace on this family, for you are the light of everyone's eyes,' she said soothingly. 'Hush! Do not cry. It is a beautiful day. Eat something and go outside for a walk with your brother,' she urged.

Between her soothing words and the tea, Edwina regained her composure. She made her way directly to her father, as soon as she had dressed.

'Papa! Can you forgive me for my incivility last night?' she exclaimed upon entering the room.

He looked up at her puzzled and then as comprehension dawned on him, said, 'Before you launch into a lengthy declaration of contrition, Edwina, let me tell you that I was most pleased by your words. That Lovelace is a pompous popinjay. Do you know, he had the effrontery to attack Madho this morning for touching his horse? I was very near to telling him where he could go with his horse. Dash it all! I am beginning to wonder at Anne's common sense!'

'Oh, but Papa! I was most intemperate!' she declared.

'Nonsense! Is that why you look so Friday-faced?' he demanded.

'You said nothing to him that everyone in the room, including your mother, did not wish to say,' he said.

'I'm afraid I left a poor impression on Mr. Davenport,' she said in a low voice.

'I doubt that, for he's a man of good sense and loves this country as much as we do. If he *did* think ill of you, that would show poor sense on *his* part, and not yours!' he said emphatically.

She felt her spirits rise. She must look for her mother and give an account of herself to her. She found her in the kitchen, discussing with the maid how much butter to churn that afternoon.

Seeing Edwina's face, she smiled at her, saying, 'Why so woebegone, my dear? I would expect you to be in high spirits this morning, after your resounding triumph over our poor Captain Lovelace!'

Edwina smiled wanly.

'I'm afraid I am far too disappointed in myself to be in high spirits, Mama. I don't think I shall ever be able to face Captain Lovelace or converse with him again, without feeling a great sense of mortification!' she said.

'Humbug! All we have to do is to do is to ply him with Port and loosen his tongue! He will then babble on about the superiority of our race and you could then freely and unabashedly ring a fine peal over him again,' she said, making Edwina chortle with laughter.

'Oh dear! I must have seemed a harpy. I am most ashamed of myself,' she said with a rueful smile.

'Nonsense!' replied her mother. 'He deserved a set down for his unkind words. And now, perhaps you will cast off your sad countenance and accompany me to visit Mrs. Ashton, for she is ill again.'

Edwina readily agreed, relieved to be able to take her thoughts off the events of the evening before and the certain disapproval of her conduct by Mr. Davenport. They busied themselves with preparing for their visit, planning to take with them what they could to relieve Mrs. Ashton's family.

'Captain Lovelace has desired leave of your father to marry Anne at the earliest. Your father has consented, but is insistent that the wedding shall take place at Christ Church here in Simla. He has instructed Anne to return to Simla without delay,' Mrs. Hardingham informed Edwina as they made their way to the Ashton's home

'But, Anne will want time to purchase her trousseau in Calcutta and will desire to stay there until it is completed,' Edwina pointed out.

'That is what I told your Papa this morning. He conceded that she must come home as soon as her trousseau is complete. I do wish I could assist her now, for she must need a mother's guidance. I will simply have to trust Kate to do my part,' her mother said pensively.

'Oh, you can depend on it, Mama, Kate will make sure of it that Anne has the best trousseau in all of Calcutta, for you know how eager she is to dress us all in the finest fashion,' she reassured, alluding to Kate's frequent complaint that Edwina's attire was far too plain to do her features credit.

The two women smiled at the recollection of Kate's penchant for vanity.

The subject of Anne's return emerged after they had dined that night, and Christopher asked in a low voice, 'Are you trembling with trepidation, Eddie? I should quit the house before Anne gets here and head for the mountains. The village folk there might give you shelter and you will find their company vastly gentler than Anne's, once she has discovered your ill-usage of her beau.'

This was meant as a joke, but Edwina's eyes widened involuntarily.

'Do you think she will be very angry? I was counting on her being far too preoccupied with the excitement of preparing for matrimony,' she said.

'Of course, she will be too distracted to care for it. Don't be such a wet goose. I am only funning,' he said impatiently. And then, seeing the worry in her eyes, he added quickly, 'Come, do not be sad, my pet. You know I meant no harm.'

She smiled at him and he was relieved.

He continued to tease her, saying, 'You will be glad to know that I told Mukherjee this morning that we have him to blame for your shocking harangue. For it was he who filled your head with these notions that you dispense. He is accordingly remorseful for his actions.'

'Chris, you are most unkind and exceedingly untruthful,' she told him with a severity that belied the twinkle in her eyes.

They discovered that Mr. Mukherjee was still at work, in Mr. Hardingham's office for he had some private business to attend to the next morning and would be gone for the best part of the day. Mrs. Hardingham instructed Shanta to carry him his supper in the office, and Christopher and Edwina accompanied her to see if he wished for anything else. He was surprised and delighted to see them both. Despite his evident admiration of Edwina's spirited reprimand of Captain

Lovelace, he discreetly refrained from alluding to it, guessing shrewdly she was mortified by it.

Instead, he asked, 'Miss. Hardingham, can I impose on your kindness for a very great favour?'

'What is it?' she asked.

'I am bringing my wife here from the foot of the mountains where her father has brought her to. She is to live with me here, in my quarters. I wonder if I may presume to appeal to you to teach her English?' he asked.

'Your *wife*!' exclaimed the cousins in unison.

'Come now, this is doing it rather too brown, Mukherjee. You have contrived to wed on the sly and failed to invite us to the *dawat*?' asked Christopher skeptically.

Mr. Mukherjee blinked at him uncomprehendingly.

Edwina explained, 'Mr. Mukherjee, Christopher believes you are deceiving us. How could you have contrived to be married when you have been in Simla the whole time? Would we not have been invited to a great *dawat* if you truly were wedded?'

He smiled, saying 'Oh, I was wedded about twelve years ago, when I was a lad of ten. My bride, of course, remained with her parents until she came of age. And although they were ready to send her to me when she turned twelve, I insisted that she stay with them until I could obtain employment. I also expressed to them my desire that she be educated and taught to write and read. I know that they have honoured my wishes, but her knowledge must be greatly lacking, for not many *pundits* will devote pains to instructing a young girl in the village. Her father wrote to me declaring that he cannot keep her in his home any longer, for it is a great shame for them that she has not departed to her husband's house after having come of age. She is now eighteen and we must begin our life together.'

Although they were aware that this was not an uncommon practice, Christopher and Edwina were nevertheless astonished.

'In that case, you are to be felicitated, Mr. Mukherjee. I am sure that Mama and Papa would be most delighted to hear of this,' Edwina said, mustering her wits.

'Oh, they already know about it,' he replied. 'Your father was kind enough to send me a gift when I was wed as a child. Now, he has most generously promised to increase my wages, for I will now need to support a wife.'

Whilst they did not comprehend everything about their adopted homeland, the Hardinghams had vowed to endeavour to respect it as best they could, and Edwina and Christopher refrained from discussing the matter privately. Edwina assured Mr. Mukherjee that she would be delighted to teach his bride English. She spent the remainder of the day compiling a list of books that she would suggest that the young lady read.

The next morning, Edwina hurried to the garden at the rear of the house, before the heat of the afternoon made outdoor activity uncomfortable. She was impatient to tend her vegetables that were springing up. She worked eagerly, humming to herself and loving the feel of the soil in her fingers. She loved the endeavours of the summer. In a few months it would be too cold to cultivate her vegetables or her roses. In the midst of her labours, she looked up, as she heard the sound of a rider. Her father was no doubt returning from his morning ride. She made her way to the front of the house, wiping her fingers on an old rag. To her great surprise, the man who was striding towards her was not her father, but Mr. Davenport.

Edwina's surprise gave way to mortification as he swept off his hat and greeted her. She was wearing an old green muslin gown that had lived out its life, and that Kate had begged her to consign to flames two years ago. Her fingers were muddy, and she wore no gloves. Her hair had become disorderly as wisps of it had escaped from under her bonnet. She was acutely aware that she presented a shockingly ragged appearance.

'M—Mr. Davenport, how do you do?' she mumbled, attempting to effect a retreat towards the back of the house.

To her dismay, he followed her, saying, 'I hope your father is at home, Miss. Hardingham, for I must speak with him at once. It is a matter of the utmost importance.'

She looked up at his face and saw that he looked very grave indeed. She felt a great uneasiness descend upon her, without knowing why.

'He is out riding, but will be home presently, for he has been gone for over an hour. Will you allow me to conduct you into the house? I will ring for tea at once—I desire tea,' she said, as he started to refuse.

Her sudden air of decision prevented him from saying anything further and he sat down in the drawing-room where she left him momentarily, as she departed to make herself more presentable. Mrs. Hardingham and Christopher found him pacing there when they joined him a few moments later.

He was greatly perturbed, but did not seem to wish to divulge the reason for his visit to any of them, apparently wishing to speak with Mr. Hardingham alone. Edwina joined them quickly, grateful for the cup of tea her mother offered her. Tea always made life seem better, no matter how horrid it threatened to be, she thought.

After an interval of ten minutes he stood up forcefully, saying, 'Perhaps I should follow Mr. Hardingham's path. If you would be so kind as to tell me the general direction in which he rode, I might overtake him on the way and disclose my business to him.'

Mrs. Hardingham was prevented from answering by the sound of her husband's return. Davenport eagerly shook hands with a puzzled Mr. Hardingham, saying, 'Forgive my intrusion into your home at this early hour, Mr. Hardingham. I must speak with you at once, in private.'

Edwina's sense of dread heightened as the two men withdrew. She waited anxiously, when a few minutes later, her father returned, much agitated, into the drawing-room.

'There is a mutiny afoot in the plains,' he said. 'Mr. Davenport has heard that the Bengal Native Infantry has rebelled. By the time this news has reached us, Calcutta may the scene of great violence,' he said.

The import of his words sank in slowly, as the three persons in the room stared at him wordlessly.

Suddenly, Mrs. Hardingham cried, 'Anne and Kate and Markham and the young ones! Are they in danger?'

'I believe they might very well be, for Davenport says he has heard reports of great bloodshed and ferocity,' said her husband in a trembling voice.

'Are Europeans subject to such violence?' asked Mrs. Hardingham.

'Especially them,' replied her husband in a tortured voice.

Edwina became pale. Her knees seemed to buckle under her and she sat down suddenly. She was dimly aware of Mr. Davenport's hand on her elbow and mechanically swallowed a gulp from the glass of water he offered her.

She found her voice and said faintly, 'Something must be done, Papa. For, we cannot wait for the *dâk* runner to bring us news. Someone must go to Calcutta.'

'I shall go at once,' announced Christopher. 'I shall—'

He was cut short by Davenport who interposed, 'No need. I am setting forth for the plains within two days. I will take three of my sturdiest and best men with me. I have come to enquire about the address of your daughter in Calcutta. I will do my best to escort them safely back to Simla,' he said.

'I will go with you,' said Christopher at once.

'I will do so, as well, for I must ascertain the safety of my daughters,' Mr. Hardingham added.

'If you do, you will slow me down, for I plan to ride furiously until I reach there. I told John the same thing when he wished to accompany me. Recollect too, that your daughters are not deserted, for they have Captain Lovelace to protect them. He will no doubt secure their welfare instantly,' he said gently.

Christopher nodded, overcome by the knowledge that what his friend said was true.

'But, how come you plan to go to Calcutta?' Edwina asked suddenly.

He swallowed and answered in a strained voice, 'My sister is currently at Danapur, where she has been residing in the home of Mrs. Edens, a distant relation, whose husband is a captain in the Bengal army. He is situated in Danapur. While the revolt broke out initially at Barrackpore, there is news that there has been unrest in Delhi, as well. If the disquiet has spread as far west as Delhi, I have to consider the possibility that Danapur might be affected too, for it lies in between these two places.'

This is seemed like an entirely reasonable train of thought. 'But how came your sister to remain in the plains during the summer?' Christopher asked.

Davenport's face seemed anguished and he suddenly appeared much older. 'We had planned to set sail for England in July and I thought it would be unwise for her to travel up to the mountains and then back again so soon. I presumed that the heat and the ardours of the journey would tax her,' replied Davenport. 'But now, I heartily regret that course of action and wish I could somehow undo it! Not wishing to leave her alone in Calcutta, I escorted her to the home of Captain and Mrs. Edens in Danapur. They have been our guests at Simla in the past, and Mrs. Edens and my sister, Jane, have always enjoyed an easy companionship, for Mrs. Edens is but four years older than Jane,' he added.

Edwina recalled that after the death of their father, he had become his sister's guardian. Their mother was deceased for some time now and she was his sole relation. She struggled to find words of comfort, but none came to her lips. Without thinking, she placed her hand on his arm.

'I hope you find her unharmed and thank you for your kindness in inquiring after Markham's household,' she said at last.

Davenport looked down at her, his eyes momentarily arrested. There were tears welling up in her eyes and he was certain they were as much for his unfortunate circumstances, as they were for her own.

'Thank you! I hope to return to you soon with good news. We must be hopeful in the grace of God,' he said to all in the party, although his eyes seemed to linger on Edwina for the most fleeting moment.

'Godspeed, Mr. Davenport! May God be with you!' said Mrs. Hardingham, squeezing his hand.

Davenport nodded and departed, riding at a furious pace and disappearing from their view as he made his way past the *deodar* trees that lined the path that lead to the Hardingham home.

Edwina sank back onto the sofa, trembling as the implications of Davenport's communication began to grasp her mind. She was deeply agitated about the safety of the members of her family in Calcutta and of Davenport's sister. But, added to her distress was a gnawing ache in her heart that Mr. Davenport was riding into the midst of this danger.

She had not told him that she loved him and that she wished above all else that he may be spared the least hazard, that he may return to her safe and sound and that she did not believe she could ever be happy apart from him. Indeed, propriety had forbidden her to speak thus and she was sure that he held no tenderness in his heart for her. But, regardless, she wished she had told him at least this—that she wished him a safe journey and hoped he would return unharmed. She was unable to indulge in more than a moment's sorrow, however, as her mother sank to the floor, weeping silently. Christopher and Edwina rushed to her side.

'Depend upon it Mama, it is nothing. Davenport was right in taking the matter seriously, for he is his sister's guardian. But, I hardly think that the entire Bengal army is surrendered to the mutineers. No doubt, it is the work of some men who have been unjustly treated and hope to obtain justice,' said Edwina.

'While I hardly think that Davenport is a man to exaggerate, I am inclined to agree with Edwina, Aunt. Consider that Davenport is likely to respond with a greater degree of urgency to *any* report concerning the safety of his only sister, regardless of how obscure the circumstance might be,' added Christopher in a low voice.

She clung to their words, drawing comfort from them, stalling the terrors besieging her mind. The human soul is apt to cling to any hope, regardless of how bleak it may be. Mrs. Hardingham forced herself to repudiate the facts that Davenport had presented to them, choosing instead to hope against all hope that her loved ones were safe and that her loving prayers had protected them from doom. She busied herself with the matters of her household, spending much of the day in the kitchen quarters and in counting the linen returned by the *dhobi*. Mr. Hardingham retreated into his offices for a while, but before long, decided to summon Edwina and Christopher to his chamber.

'Is everything well, Papa,' Edwina asked with a look of foreboding.

'I have something to tell you, but this must be kept from your mother,' he said. 'Davenport did not disclose the full extent of the missive he received from the plains to you this morning. In private, he revealed to me certain dreadful facts that have chilled my heart. He received word from his stewards overseeing his affairs in Delhi, that several European women and children have been slaughtered there. General Anson received a communication on Tuesday, as he dined with several guests at his house, that Delhi is under siege One of those guests is a friend of Davenport's and his account accentuated the urgency of the situation,' he said gravely.

'While these facts are horrifying, indeed, Papa, we must not allow ourselves to be unduly alarmed. Delhi is a great distance away from Calcutta and it does not follow that a tumult in Delhi must of necessity be reciprocated with one in Calcutta,' said Edwina.

Her voice trembled as she spoke, although she remained calm.

Her father shook his head, saying, 'I wish that were so, child. But the terrifying part of it is that it was the sepoys in mutiny from Meerut who burned down the bungalows of European families in Delhi. As you heard, Davenport has informed us that the trouble started in Barrackpore, which is a short distance from Calcutta. I'm afraid that Calcutta cannot be unharmed if the violence has spread from there all the way to Meerut and Delhi.'

Edwina could not argue in the face of such reasoning. Desperate though she was to believe that all would be well, the magnitude of the problem was rapidly becoming apparent to them all.

'Perhaps it is just a few isolated men scattered across the country who are enraged and the course of events will soon dissolve away?' asked Christopher, despondently.

'Davenport says that General Anson sent men to the plains, although he himself tarried in Simla until he could get further word on how things stood. Davenport informed me that this morning, the general has departed for Umbala with 6,000 men who were in the hills to elude the heat of the plains. Such concerted effort on his part can only mean that the situation is much worse than even he imagined,' Mr. Hardingham responded, sinking his face into his hands. After a few moments he added, 'Davenport was insistent that I discuss the matter with him in private for he was anxious to avoid distressing the ladies. I can perceive the wisdom of concealing some of these matters from your mother, but you, my dear children, must be fully aware of what is occurring. I know that you are a person of resolute disposition, Edwina and that you will not crumble beneath the weight of these facts. Indeed, I beg you to remain strong, for Christopher and I will depend on you, and we do not have the slightest wish to conceal any of these matters from you.'

'You can depend on my discretion and on my mettle, Papa. For now, we must, as best as we can, shield Mama from these particulars,' she answered, putting his hand lovingly to her cheek.

There were so many questions she wished answers for, but there was no way to obtain them for the news would take far too long to reach them, especially if the journeys of *dâk* runners were now hindered. There was a new telegraph line, but it only ran from Delhi to Umbala, which was a good five hundred furlongs away from Simla. And, whilst a telegraph system was available that linked Calcutta with Bombay, Agra and Lahore, no communications were forthcoming through it, at least not at present.

'It is not inconceivable that that the telegraph station at Calcutta has been rendered unworkable by some means, if there is a rebellion underway,' Christopher pointed out unhappily.

The days that followed passed in a blur, as the Hardinghams waited desperately for news from Calcutta. That Sunday, they attended services and found the church filled with women who had come to lift up prayers for their men who were advancing against a presently indefinite menace in the distance. Small assemblies of women huddled together, seeking solace from one another and exchanging what titbits of information they could. Their anger against the Indians was unanimous, with the exception of a few individuals, such as the Hardinghams, who had no thought on their minds, but to secure the safety of their families.

'What is that woman doing here?' demanded Miss. Gardner, on beholding Mrs. Parks, who had come to attend the service.

Her brother, Captain Jeffery Gardner was currently part of General Anson's force marching towards Umbala and she seemed greatly angered at the presence of Colonel Parks' Indian wife in their midst.

'I believe that she has come to offer prayers, as we have,' said Mrs. Hardingham, greatly astonished by her tone.

'It's these horrid persons that have got us into this calamity,' she said with vehemence.

'Why, Miss. Gardner, surely you are aware that her husband is currently on his way to Umbala under General Anson's command. She is truly in the same predicament as we,' answered Mrs. Hardingham gravely.

She had come to know of General Anson's advance from her husband who had thought the intelligence would put her mind at ease. Miss. Gardner shrugged discourteously and distanced herself from their company. Edwina and Mrs. Hardingham were mortified by her incivility and they endeavoured to engage Mrs. Parks in conversation. She responded mechanically to their solicitous inquiries, but her eyes betrayed the hurt she felt.

Edwina was pained by the thought that the gulf between the English and the people of India could only widen from such a mindset as Miss Gardner's. The strain of unknown happenings in the plains seemed almost too much to bear. She tried not to think about Davenport or her family in Calcutta, but distracted herself with familiar undertakings around the house, instead. Sitting by the window in the library, an opened, but unread book on her lap, she mused about where Davenport could be.

'Miss Hardingham, forgive me, I hope I am not disturbing you. The master is not keen to transact any business today and I wished to procure a book from the library,' she heard the *munshiji* say.

'Not at all, Mr. Mukherjee, I should be glad for your company,' she replied despondently. 'How is your wife? When do you wish to commence her English lessons?' she asked mechanically.

'Once the present distress is past, we can find ample time for her instruction,' he answered quietly. 'I wish you to know I am truly sorry to hear of the circumstances the members of your family in Calcutta may face,' he added.

'Thank you, Mr. Mukherjee. I cannot believe our land faces an hour such as this,' she said sadly.

'But surely you are not surprised at this turn of events, Miss. Hardingham, cognizant as you are with the affairs in the plains?' he asked, somewhat surprised.

Seeing her perturbed expression, he added gently, 'You once gave me leave to speak as an equal and as a friend in your presence. Today, I will put that invitation to the test. The present circumstances are more injurious to the White man, than to the sons of this soil. Surely you can see that it is the Company that faces a dark hour, and not this land. The East India Company and India are not the same entity, Miss. Hardingham. You will see that in centuries to come, this hour will be prominent in the history of India, for this was the hour that the people of this land decided to say to the foreign power that rules us that the predicaments foisted on us by them cannot and must not continue.'

She turned pale at his words, 'Mr. Mukherjee, surely you do not identify my parents and this family with the harshness of sections of the government? Surely you are not saying that it is justice that my family faces this moment?' she asked tremulously.

'No, I am not, Miss. Hardingham. I am saying to you that unfortunately, those of your race have created untold hardships for the people of this land, that you must sadly pay the price for. It is the penalty for being English, just as we have for centuries in this country paid the price for being Indian. I am also saying that despite the harsh and unjust rule of the East India Company, I do not see you or your loved ones as guilty of any crime. I am saying that my fervent wish is for their safety and wellbeing. I had come to offer you comfort, but I am afraid, I have hurt you by my opinions. Forgive me!' he said remorsefully as a tear rolled down her cheek.

'There is no need to ask for forgiveness. I said you were free to speak your mind always and you did. I do not like what you say, however, for I see myself as much a child of this country as you are,' she said in a saddened voice.

'I believe you speak from your heart, Miss. Hardingham, but what you say is not true. As long as Company rule exists in our land, you will never be one of us. It pains me to say that because I hold you and the members of this home in the highest regard,' he said gently.

'Oh, I think it is what *you* say that is not true, Mr. Mukherjee! But that does not signify. We can agree that we disagree and remain good friends, can we not?' she responded firmly.

'That is quite true,' interjected Christopher in a low voice.

He had slipped into the library unnoticed and was shocked by the words uttered by his father's clerk. He looked at him sternly, not because he believed that he had crossed a line of decorum, but quite simply because he had made his dear Edwina sadder than she already was.

'I am afraid I have given you offense, sir,' said Mukherjee.

'Yes, you have. But not because of what you have said, but because you have grieved Edwina at this present hour of sadness,' he said reproachfully.

'That was certainly not my intention, Mr. Hardingham. I merely wished to present the facts to my friends,' he said.

'And what might those facts be?' asked Christopher hotly.

'Just that this hour speaks of a cry for freedom from the tyranny of the English crown,' he said softly.

Then, looking at their despondent faces, he added, 'And that I wish more than anything for this hour to be past so that the members of this family might be spared further distress. Forgive me for any hurt I may have caused.'

As he left the room, he turned and said to them, 'My words should have been inconceivable in any other circumstances and with any other English persons. You have truly treated me as your equal and for this I am grateful.'

Edwina and Christopher sighed, puzzled and disconcerted by his words and his unexpected truculence. It seemed to Edwina that some great change was coming upon the land and it did not bode well for them. Their trepidation was intensified the next day, upon the discovery of a letter that Mr. Mukherjee had left in the library, addressed to Mr. Hardingham. To their great consternation, Mr. Mukherjee had quit their household. His letter brought some alarm to Mrs. Hardingham and Edwina. It said:

Dear Sir,

It pains me to inform you that I have decided to quit your service and your household. I debated whether to leave instantly, without any communication to you about my reasons for doing so, but have decided against it. You have been extremely kind to my father and to me. Unfortunately, while my father, as is the manner of his generation, believed himself to be bound to you in loyalty and for our family to be bound to yours for all generations, I do not believe this.

I believe that as an educated Indian, I have the right to seek profitable employment, earn good wages and live with freedom and dignity. The British race, of whom you are an unfortunate member, has made this impossible. Modern Indians are educated beyond our employability. Jobs that we are qualified for are given to the sahibs. There is no greater injustice than one's motherland being held ransom and one being forced to beg for equality from an invading power.

While I do firmly aver that you and your family are in no way personally responsible for the injustices that the British mete out against Indians, you are nevertheless, by your very presence in my motherland, contributors to the injustice. Consider how you live in this fine house in Simla. The very best houses and land may only be bought by the British. Indians are forced to live in the most crowded settlements in town and in undesirable houses that are packed into the hillside. No Indian, no matter how rich, may purchase the better tracts of land. Given the disparity of our circumstances, no British person can live in this country with an untroubled conscience. The fact that you reside here and enjoy the wealth of the land makes you guilty of the crimes perpetrated by the most prejudiced persons of your race.

Forgive me for my plain speech. It hurts me to say this to one who is like a father to me in some ways. I am going to join the revolt against the British. I wish greatly that no harm ever comes to you or your family. I advise you to return to England, for this is not your home and it never shall be!

Sincerely,
Mr. Sharat Mukherjee

Edwina reeled at the contents of the letter. Its tone was unmistakably hostile. She took great umbrage at Mr. Mukherjee's suggestion that this was not her home and she was unwelcome in it. This was the only home she had ever known and she had a great love for it and its people. She too wished for the betterment of conditions for the people of India and for the East India Company to reform its practices. Mr. Hardingham had not amassed his fortune through dishonesty or oppression. He had conducted honest trade, and even in the absence of the East India Company's hegemony, they would have prospered in their undertakings, for he and his late brother were most industrious. The threat the letter carried, of harm that might be inevitable to the British in India as a result of the revolt was greatly unsettling to the ladies.

To add to the strain they felt, Mr. Davenport sent them a letter indicating that his journey had been hindered owing to the fact that his men who were to accompany him became sick from cholera. Not wishing for an epidemic to sweep through his domestic staff, he was forced to stay behind and oversee their care as well as ensure that proper hygiene was maintained to prevent the spread of the infection. He had read that cholera was spread through association, although the physicians declared that it was caused by bad air and smells. He recalled a physician in Patna who had treated a great many cases of cholera, asserting that it was contact with sick persons that spread the disease. That man had enforced a policy of isolating sick persons and many of his patients had recovered. Davenport ordered that the sick men be placed in a separate cottage in the care of two sturdy women who had experience nursing other patients. The men were hill-folk whose families were a half-day's journey away, but Davenport did not wish to send them home, for he was convinced that they would carry the disease to their remote hamlets. While his diligence paid off without further illness among his staff and a recovery among his men, he was delayed by three weeks from his journey.

The absence of news from the plains deprived him of sleep and he presented a somewhat haggard appearance by the end of that period. He was greatly relieved when his good friend Mr. Knowles offered to send his own men, Makkhan Singh and Kartar Singh, with him. Davenport gratefully accepted, as he would be hard-pressed to find two braver or abler men. He sent word to the Hardinghams the next morning that he was to depart on his journey, accompanied by Mr. Knowles' men. The news had the effect of elevating the mood at the Hardingham residence for all, except Edwina, who was greatly concerned for his safety and wellbeing. Notwithstanding, she was relieved that he had not contracted cholera!

The days dragged on interminably as they waited for some news from the plains. The odd report that wafted up to Simla contained ominous portents. There were tidings of mayhem and chaos and in some places, while the Company troops were said to be gaining the upper hand, in others, there were gruesome events where none were spared, and even the littlest infant and weakest woman put to the sword. Mr. Hardingham shared such news as he received rather sparingly with his wife and daughter, but he and Christopher carried the weight of most of the grim tidings. He found his nephew a no small source of comfort in this hour of grief, grateful to find in him a strong and loving son. Where the weakness of his constitution made him unable to ride boldly into the plains to rescue the family, his strength of mind and courageous disposition made him a source of great encouragement, and Mr. Hardingham noted with pride that he had reared the lad well.

CHAPTER SIX

DESCENT INTO TURMOIL

The dread that had descended upon the Hardinghams was not unfounded, as the events that unfolded would reveal, for it was indeed a turbulent time in India. Events had come to a head and there was no turning back for those who had begun the rebellion. Battles and war were not alien to this land, for scores of kings and emperors had strove to conquer this rich land before. From the fabled Aryans of old who were believed to have migrated to India from the regions near the Caspian sea, over three thousand years ago, India had witnessed the incursions of several invaders past. The famed exploits of Alexander of Macedonia were legendary. But, he had left India, for the most part, as he had found her, untouched—except for monuments he erected. Whilst India remained largely unspoiled from his intrusion, the journey exacted a heavy toll on his armies.

The Arabs had come next, bringing with them their religion of Mohammedanism into this land. They were followed by the Turks and then by the Afghan Mahmud of Ghazni, who launched a campaign of terror, plundering the land seventeen times, in raids that extended over a span of twenty-five years. The powerful kingdoms of the north disintegrated and it was only the valiant Rajpoot kings who offered the pillager any resistance whatsoever. Nevertheless, they too were far too factious to withstand his onslaught. Whilst the kings of the various kingdoms in India were dismissive of the impact of this latest invader, it was he who laid the foundation for the arrival of other Mohammedan kings. Muhammad of Ghor, another Afghan king came, but unlike

Mahmud of Ghazni, this invader did not seek to plunder the wealth of the land to carry it back to his home. Not for him were the pleasures of profits from the loot sold in the Persian markets. Why expend energy on raiding a rich land year after year, when you can make it your own? Ghori made his kingdom in India, and the kings of the north were made to realize that his kingdom was no passing threat.

The legendary leader of the Rajpoot kings, Prithviraj III met the new menace in battle and vanquished him. Sadly, the noble Rajpoot king made the fatal error of pardoning his foe and releasing him from captivity. Ghori fortified himself with an army of Turcik slaves and returned the following year, this time to win the battle, mortally wounding Prithviraj Chauhan. Ghori's slave became the next king and declared himself the Sultan of Delhi. Had the kingdoms of the north been more apt to set aside their rivalries, the new threat might have been stemmed. But the kings of the north, as most kings are wont to do, fought relentlessly among themselves, jealously guarding their little parcels of land and striving to uphold their hegemony over small and sometimes obscure kingdoms. The result was that yet other threads of language, religion, food, dress, art and music were woven into the fabric of the land. And when Babur, the king of Kabul, bringing with him artillery and cavalry—hitherto unknown to Indian warriors—defeated Ibrahim Lodhi the then Sultan of Delhi in 1526, the empire of the Moghuls was fashioned in India.

That dynasty had endured ever since and welcomed European traders into their courts. Courted for centuries by merchants and empires wishing to enrich themselves with her treasures through trade, Hindostan was no stranger to the European. The Portuguese were the first to try to trade with India. Admiral Vasco de Gama had arrived on his ship *San Gabriel* to the port of Calicut. Upon his return home, his cargo of spices fetched many times its value in the market, whereupon the Portuguese returned to the Malabar Coast, this time with an armada of thirteen ships under the command of the famed military commander Pedro Alvarez Cabral. The twenty cannons mounted on the bow of each of his ships obligated the weak Zamorin of Calicut to sign a treaty with Cabral, allowing the Portuguese a firm foothold in the spice market of India that lured the nations of Europe into the perilous high seas.

The British Empire was, by comparison, a late entrant into the ports of India, for it was not until the Battle of Swally, where Captain Thomas Best routed the Portuguese, that the English had, after ten voyages, finally secured trading rights in this prominent and opulent land. Having set out from Gravesend in England on the first day of February in 1612, he reached Surat, which was the principal port of the Moghul emperors, in the September of that same year. Captain Best arrived as an emissary of His Majesty, King James I, seeking permission from the Moghul emperor, Jehangir, for the British Empire to trade with India. However, ere his message could reach the emperor's court, four Portuguese galleons intercepted the English ships. In the battle that ensued, Captain Best was said to have run three of the four aground. Having come out the worse from the skirmish, the Portuguese lost face considerably in the Moghul court. Emperor Jehangir, perhaps impressed by the feat of Best and his men, and perhaps eager to seize on an opportunity to oust the enemy of the Mohammedans from the land—for the Portuguese were known to hate the Moors and all those who espoused their creed and vexed those who made pilgrimage to their shrine in Mecca—invited the English to establish trade in India.

English trade was forever changed after this, for now, spices, silk, indigo, saltpeter and jewellery came to be available, for the first time, in plenteous supply in England. The clamour for luxurious goods, hitherto reserved for the nobility, became louder as silk and cotton, once exorbitant in value, now came within the reach of a wider swathe of the populace in England. The Honourable East India Company, established to consolidate trade in the East Indies, soon set itself up as the sole purveyor of trade in these parts, responding to this insatiable yearning for riches from faraway lands.

The voyage from trade to political power was a relatively smooth one, as empires began to crumble in succession to make room for the new traders who started to control larger portions of land, imposing their rules of trade and commerce on the populace as they did so. As the Moghul Empire began to fragment, and administration of the provinces fell into the hands of its *Soobedars*, the East India Company began its ascendancy in India. And while the French and the Dutch also arrived, seeking their share in India's wealth, it was undoubtedly the British East India Company that held sway, armed is at was, with inordinate powers including the maintenance of private armies, the powers to forge and cease alliances with native kings and to mint its own coins in India. Over the course of a century, the land steadily fell under the power of the British Empire, and Madras, Bombay and Calcutta—all prominent cities in the land—fell one by one into the lap of the English.

Sometimes kings were vanquished honourably in battle. At other times their close associates were bribed to betray their sovereigns, as had occurred in the Battle of Plassey. Lord Robert Clive routed the *Nawab* of Bengal, Siraj-ud-daulah, by bribing his recently demoted commander Mir Jaffer to lift not a finger to aid his master during the battle between the *Nawab* and the English. The *Nawab*, betrayed in battle fled for his life, but was treacherously murdered. As reward for his perfidy, Mir Jaffer was crowned the *Nawab* of Bengal in his master's stead!

Through might and through guile, through treachery, bribery and sheer courage, inch by inch, kingdoms of the north and the south gradually came under the suzerainty and often the direct rule of the East India Company. They were not unaided in these endeavours by the natives of the land, who whether for the lust of thrones, or for vengeance, aided their new allies. The daring ambitions of the members of the East India Company were often matched by the ruthless political ambitions of local kings, who solicited the aid of rival European powers to wage wars against each other.

For their part, the English bred jealousies and rivalries, waging proxy wars that eventually led the Company's rule to extend across the far reaches of the land. Kingdoms that were left unconquered were placed under the rule of symbolic kings, anointed for their posts by the new Machiavellian force that had swept through the land. Vast fortunes were to be made by the English hero who returned to England after successfully expanding the influence of the English Empire in India— Robert Clive was granted a peerage and prodigious sums of money on his return to England. So much so that by the end of the eighteenth century, for the first time in its history, India became one land, ruled, for the most part, by one ruler, instead of the fragmented assortment of large and small kingdoms vying for power that it once was.

The British had built factories to manage their trade in all the large cities. In time, the areas surrounding these factories came to be the inhabited by European men and women who came to seek their fortunes in India. These military garrisons, the *cantonments,* became the hub of English life in India. The people of the land lived in the fringes of the cantonments, trading with the English and serving as domestics. While conquering the land was easy, governing it proved to be quite another matter. Invested as it was, with the charge of profitable trade on behalf of the Crown, the East India Company was ill equipped to deal with the governance of a vast body of subjects. The interests of profiteering are apt to be at odds with those of the care of indigent subjects.

What resulted was a system where the sole aim of governance was the collection of taxes, often forced. Land tax was raised—sometimes fivefold—to ensure that sufficient revenue was earned for Britain. Opium and indigo were deemed profitable for cultivation over grain. The result was the infamous Bengal Famine of 1770 where, in a period of prolonged drought, and in the absence of grain reserves, a third of the population of the land perished from starvation and no effort was made to succour them through the provision of foodstuffs. No small blame was laid at the door of Company officials, who had seen the land and its people as fit for little above pillage, magnifying their consequence and purses through the use of unfair trade monopolies and oppressive taxation. It was argued that Lord Clive's unscrupulous machinations as Governor of Bengal had set a precedent for corruption and larceny. Since that time, for nearly one hundred years, no successful challenge to Company rule had presented itself, although nearly forty small scale rebellions had erupted in assorted places across the land.

Davenport thought on these matters as he made his way to the plains. *Surely, in the history of India, this uprising against the government is a first,* thought Davenport, as he made his way with his men towards the plains. His presumption was inaccurate, but he might have been forgiven for surmising thus, for in his lifetime, the British Empire's rule in India had appeared to be a fact of common existence and it was not inconceivable for the Englishman who had been bred in the land, to presume that the way things now were was the way they had always been. His mind went back to Edwina's passionate decrial of the state of affairs when the matter of the discontented sepoys had arisen.

To be sure, Davenport loved this land and her people. For, it was the place where he had spent the principal part of his existence. This was his homeland. He was a just man, unfailingly kind and respectful in his treatment of 'country folk,' be they his servants or his equals. But, he always saw himself as a loyal British subject. Edwina's ardent discourse, however, betrayed that she felt a kinship with the Indian that went beyond the benevolent patronage of the ruler towards the ruled. To her, they were her countrymen. Rather than being shocked by it, however, Davenport saw this is as entirely reasonable. *For*, he thought, *it is only right, when we have established ourselves as the new rulers of the land, that we see the ones we rule as subjects of the empire, and consequently, our fellow citizens.* No sooner had this reflection presented itself than an uneasy conviction settled upon him, that reality diverged quite sharply from this ideal state.

Conquerors of old have come to this land and been seduced by it, making it their home. The European, however, has never fully submitted himself to this land, never really adapted to it as to a new home. Instead, we have isolated ourselves from it, fearing its influence on us, rejecting its customs, fiercely clinging to our own, and building fortresses of self-contented superiority, he thought.

He thought uneasily of how often he had heard the members of his club jeer at the Indian. He recalled the words of an acquaintance describing them as a 'filthy, foul band of natives, ungrateful for the kind patronage of their masters, unwilling to let themselves be civilized by a race vastly superior to their own.' He thought of how this race of people had endured for centuries, with customs, laws, trade and practices so lofty that a good many men and women from Europe had come to its shores, seeking to share in its wealth. *Somehow, we have failed to comprehend the merits of this people and have forfeited the opportunity of becoming enriched by their customs*, he reflected unhappily.

He was only partially correct in this assumption, however. The current state of relations between the Indians and the Europeans were not reflective of the past. In the early stages of the European incursions into India, a good number had indeed succumbed to the charms of this new land and quickly adopted its customs. Many had adopted the religions of the land and married well, often the daughters of nobles. Some threescore and ten years ago, as many as a third of all British men who came to India were said to have had Indian consorts. Such was the extent to which many men from England found themselves changed by their new country. In fact, Sir David Ochterlony, the Resident of Delhi forty years ago, was said to have been so taken with Moghul court customs, that he had acquired for himself a harem with thirteen concubines. He was wont to take a promenade around the Red Fort each evening, followed by his wives, each mounted atop her own elephant!

'No sooner does he reach his home, than he discards English attire to be clad like a Musselman, in loose flowing robes of cotton, sitting in *durbar*, with his servants in attendance and smoking his hookah, while reflecting on the music played by his women,' a secretary had written about this superior to his wife in England.

The affections of these men towards their wives and half Indian children were deep and enduring. Agreements were made to raise their offspring as Christian or as Mohammedan. Children of such unions were often sent to Britain for their education and for a Christian upbringing. Some men returned to England with their families, who rapidly adjusted to life in a new world. Others died in India, leaving their wives and offspring to the care of trusted friends, who acted as executors of their estate.

But, somewhere along the way, the people of Great Britain had become wary of these developments. Much was made of the apostasy of the men who deserted the faith of their fathers to respond to the charms of India. Yet others were concerned about the debauchery that the young men of the Company instigated on the young women from villages surrounding the cantonments. Women had to be sent from the empire to ensure the wayward man did not stray from his origins and heritage. Over time, the Indian and the members of the East India Company had become more and more distanced from each other. Still, Davenport could not conceive a reason for civil unrest on the scale he had been informed of.

'Why is this trouble brewing?' he asked Kartar Singh, as they rested in the shade of a *pipal* tree in the heat of the noonday.

They had reached Solan[2], some thirty miles distant from Simla, in the foothills of the Himalayas. There was an abundant supply of fresh spring water there, and Dyer Breweries, which made the famous Lion beer that many English swore was as good as any ale to be had in England, was situated not far away from where they rested.

'It is hard to say, *Sahib*. Perhaps it is some troublemakers who are

---

[2] A map of the mutiny, along with the route traversed by Mr. Davenport, may be found at the end of the book.

inciting the people,' replied Kartar Singh, looking very much as if he wished to change the subject.

Aware of his circumvention, Davenport pressed, 'But surely a few troublemakers cannot cause such mayhem, without sympathy from the *sepoys*? Why are the sepoys so enraged? Are they all involved?'

'We have ridden with you to this place, *Sahib*. We know no more than you, for we have been in Simla with Knowles *sahib* the whole time this has been brewing,' he replied quietly.

Davenport did not reply. Instead, he opened the *tiffin* they had brought with them.

Taking a *roti* out, he passed the container to the men, asking as he did so, 'Do you have an onion or a chilli with you, which we might eat with the *roti*, for it is dreadfully bland by itself!'

The men were as taken aback by the question as by his action. To share his food with his men was one thing, but to eat from the same container, was quite another. The men had brought their *rotis* wrapped in a cotton cloth, and had not expected the *sahib* to share his portion with them. In their haste to depart, they had brought little else but the bread and some water. There was no curry to accompany the *roti*. And, to their astonishment, the *sahib* had asked for the accompaniment that the poorest folk often partook of at noon with their *roti*—an onion and a green chilli.

Perhaps this sahib is not much different from Knowles sahib, thought Kartar Singh.

As if reading his thoughts, Davenport offered his bottle of water to the men, allowing them to take a drink first, and then gulping a mouthful himself. He knew the men were Sikhs and would not consider their caste defiled by sharing the container of water with him, for the Sikhs do not espouse caste separations. They, on the other hand, were considerably astonished to see him drink the water himself, for in their experience, the *gora sahibs* did not share food and drink with Indians, and certainly not from the same container!

'We must fill our containers in the nearby spring and then we must each take no more than a sip every hour once we quit this place, until we get to a place where we find another spring or a lake, to refill our container' he said shrewdly, conveying to them a notion of camaraderie, by stating that the rations were to be shared equally between them.

As those who have lived in India for any length of time will attest, such simple acts of kindness and respect can earn the fierce and undying loyalty of its inhabitants. He treated the men as his companions, not as his inferiors, and in doing so, he won their hearts that day. He could not yet know how this simple gesture of respect would hold him in good stead in the days to come, for his very life would hang by a thread that the two men would have to power to preserve or break.

For now, the ill tidings that had come from the plains seemed idle tales, as they sat in a calm dell. They had left home yesterday, and had travelled some twenty miles. They had arisen early this morning, before the break of dawn and in the cool part of the day, had traversed some ten miles, reaching Solan, where they partook of their simple meal. Danapur was over eight hundred and fifty miles away and as yet, they had much ground to cover. Davenport, having set the impulse of panic aside, pulled out his maps. He gestured to the men to come closer as he pointed out the route they should take. Still close to Simla, they had not traversed very far. Once the momentum afforded by terror had lulled, the need for refreshment, for they had had none that day, forced him to stop and take stock of their predicament. With meagre rations and limited information about the state of affairs, Davenport thought it wise to examine the map carefully.

'We should travel west and take the Grand Trunk Road, perhaps joining it at Umbala. We can stop at Kalka, for there is a stable there and its owner will gladly give us a change of horses.' he said, chewing on his pencil.

'No, *Sahib*,' said Kartar Singh at once.

Makkhan Singh refrained from commenting, but shook his gravely to indicate his dissent as well.

'Why not?' asked Davenport puzzled. 'It is the quickest route to our destination. It will take us no more than two days to reach there, for the horses are yet fresh.'

Kartar Singh coughed, as if to buy time, so that he might choose his words well.

But before he could speak, Makkhan Singh said vehemently, 'That would be perilous, *Sahib*. We must at all costs avoid Umbala and indeed the Grand Trunk Road itself.'

'But Umbala is a good distance from Meerut, where the trouble has brewn. We could easily use the Grand Trunk Road for a portion of the journey—for that will be far more convenient—and depart from it when we approach Meerut, could we not?' asked Davenport.

'No *Sahib*!' said Kartar Singh with vehemence. 'The Grand Trunk Road travels along the entire path of the unrest. We must at all costs avoid Umbala and any of its neighbouring towns, for there is great danger there. It was not but five weeks ago that the sepoys there rebelled against the *sahibs*. They were defeated by the *sahibs*, forewarned by a loyal sepoy. All the rebels were hanged at the bridge by the cantonment,' he finished, quite forgetting his assertion made not twenty minutes ago, that they were quite ignorant of the happenings of the plains.

Davenport was stunned. He had not calculated that the tumult had come within a hundred miles of Simla. It was unsettling to come to terms with the idea that one's very home was under threat of destruction.

'Why this disquiet now? All I have heard is that the men are furious about the grease on the paper encasing their cartridges that they must tear open with their mouths. Surely they cannot be revolting over a simple matter of grease?' he asked dumbfounded.

'It is anything but a simple matter, *Sahib*!' retorted Makkhan Singh. 'Are you unaware that consuming the fat from a cow is sacrilegious to the Hindu and the fat from the pig defiles the Musselman? That is to defile their very existence and deprive them of salvation! What has been honoured and reviled by their ancestors as sacred or vile since ancient times is now overturned and reversed by the *sahibs* with no thought for the souls of their men,' he said.

'That is true,' replied Davenport in a conciliatory tone, adding, 'But surely, the matter was attended to. I know for a fact that the cartridges were ordered to be made ungreased. Why then is there this unrest over a matter that has been long since successfully resolved?'

'Because that is surely a sign that the damage has already been done! The men would stand no more for this assault on the ways of their ancestors.' replied Makkhan Singh gravely.

'It is more than that!' said Kartar Singh irritably. 'The sepoys are tired. They have no hope of advancement. A nephew of one of our hill-people in Simla told me that his cousin is in the Bengal army. They are being forced to fight overseas. Everyone knows that the sepoys of the Bengal army are of higher caste, as that is who the *sahibs* sought to recruit. They have been loyal and brave fighters for the *sahibs*, but now their caste will be defiled if they have to fight overseas. The *sahibs* threaten to replace them with others, and their past loyalty is forgotten. No wonder they rise in revolt,' he declared.

Davenport drank this in, reflecting on the ill-advised nature of the Company's actions. He was well aware of the policy of 'Divide and Conquer' ruthlessly adopted by the East India Company. Upper caste men were recruited as sepoys and the interests of the Company became synonymous with the maintenance of caste boundaries, for the upper caste sepoys, finding themselves in oversight of lower castes, were quick to protect the interests of the body that had invested them with these powers.

'Who leads the sepoys in their revolt?' he asked.

'Some lead themselves, *Sahib*,' said Makkhan Singh.

Kartar Singh added, 'There are also some kings who lend their support to the cause of the sepoys. Nana Sahib *Peshwe* the adopted son of *Peshwa* Bhaji Rao lends his support, as does the *Ranee* of Jhansi, Lakshmi Bai. It is their hope that they will restore the glories of the Maratha kingdom by acting at this hour.'

Davenport was not ignorant of the significance of these circumstances. The Maratha Empire, once renowned and a formidable challenge to the Moghul Empire, and which had over time evolved into a loose coalition of small kingdoms, had been routed by the British in a series of wars, with the Third Maratha War providing them the decisive victory. Now the heads of these assorted kingdoms found themselves at odds with the British Empire as the East India Company sought steadily to rid the land of them by invoking the Doctrine of Lapse.

Davenport's thoughts returned to Edwina's heated words to Captain Lovelace, when she had condemned the law as imbalanced and unjust. Indeed, it was a scandalous law, practised by Lord Dalhousie, as a scarcely concealed attempt to expand the power of the East India Company and enhance its revenues. It stipulated that any kingdom defeated in battle and made a vassal state, finding itself under the paramountcy of the East India Company, could be annexed if the ruler of that kingdom were to die childless, or if the Company deemed that the rulers thereof were incompetent and consequently unable to rule. This device for usurping kingdoms had been practiced earlier by the East India Company, but Lord Dalhousie, perhaps eager to reinforce his reputation as a capable administrator—for the policy netted the Company millions of pounds in revenue—came to be most associated with it, for it was implemented most heartily in his tenure.

Things had come to a head when the Maratha *Peshwa* Baji Rao II, defeated in battle and pensioned off in exile had passed away. In keeping with the traditions of his ancestors, he had adopted Nana Sahib as his son and heir. But the British refused to acknowledge his position as his adoptive father's heir, ostensibly to avoid continuation of the pension. Nana Sahib had sent an envoy to Britain to plead his case and to impress upon the powers there that ancient traditions granted him the rights of an heir, but he was scornfully rebuffed. Queen Lakshmi Bai had faced a similar fate at the hands of the East India Company, for her adopted son was refused the recognition due him as her heir. What rankled for these and other monarchs was not the deprival of their pensions, for many were enormously wealthy, but the impunity and heavy handedness with which the foreign invaders had imposed their unjust rules and stripped them of their royal titles.

This is infinitely more than the question of grease on cartridges, and the catchpenny solution of ungreasing them has not served, Davenport reflected gloomily.

As if reading his thoughts, Makkhan Singh softly added, 'It is not just a few sepoys who are discontented and idle who create this storm, *Sahib*. Many in the land have been dissatisfied by the way the winds blow. The poor have nothing to eat and the *sarkar* is callous in demanding higher taxes. The brother of one of the women who works in Knowles *sahib's* bungalow is a farmer who was unable to pay his *lagaan*. He ended his life by jumping into the river, for the moneylenders vexed him so. The *sahibs* have set the *sahukars* moneylenders loose on the poor and there is no respite for them.'

Davenport listened as a sense of remorse crept over his heart. Perhaps he had contributed to this man's wretched end in some way, he wondered. *While I have been benefitting from a lively trade in cotton and indigo, men have been starving and driven to death on account of our administration's lack of foresight. I am a direct beneficiary of their cruelty, and we are all of us to share in the blame,* he thought. But presently, his mind returned to his sister.

'If the peril is so great, I must make greater haste than ever. We have faced danger together in the past, but perhaps this journey has more than its fair share of terrors. I would not fault you for deciding to return to Knowles *sahib's* bungalow, for it is perhaps not to your liking to aid a *sahib* at this time,' he said gravely.

'Ha! You would not survive a day without our aid, for it is a dangerous thing for a *sahib* to be wandering alone through the plains now!' retorted Kartar Singh, not insolently.

'Besides, *Sahib,*' added his more restrained colleague, 'Knowles *Sahib* has entrusted you to our service and care. We have never disregarded or betrayed his wishes and we shall not do so now. As to our desire to dissociate ourselves from the *gora sahib,* you may rest assured that you have nothing to fear from us. The Sikh Empire would never have been defeated and Punjaub never annexed by the Company, had it not been for the treachery of some of those who now revolt. Their cruelty has torn our beloved Punjaub from us and the Maharaja Duleep Singh is now a prisoner in your land. The wounds of that betrayal are still fresh though a decade has passed. We are still aching from it and cannot fight. Besides this, we have eaten your salt and will not betray you. Recall we have known you from your childhood. You are safe with us.'

'That I am indeed and have never doubted it for one moment. It was not your loyalty that I questioned, old friend, but whether this exercise would be of any concern to you,' Davenport responded, touched by the older man's sincerity.

'Any command from Knowles *sahib* is of concern to us. We would lay our lives down to fulfill his wishes,' Kartar Singh said, somewhat impatiently.

'Then we should be on our way without further delay!' Davenport declared. 'If, as you say, the Grand Trunk Road is now fraught with danger, we shall have to bypass it. I had hoped to connect with my men in Delhi, but that hope must now be abandoned, for the situation is worse that I had ever imagined. Let us skirt the highway and make our way through the villages that border it. We shall have to be on our guard when we approach them, for the revolt may have spread there too and my presence would occasion notice,' he continued.

The men nodded and they saddled the horses. Davenport marveled at how much information they had divulged, while seeming unwilling to do so at first. That they were privy to so much information in such short time, however, did not surprise him at all. News travelled fast in the hill country among domestics and if one wished to find out about anything, he only had to solicit the servants of his own household for it. They could be counted on to enlighten one, provided one had earned their trust!

Skirting the main roads, they travelled from Solan towards Nahan, which was a good fifty-six miles away. They would reach their destination by sundown the following day, taking care not to overtax the horses. From Nahan, they travelled to Dehradun, another two-day journey. Once there, they rested for a half-day for the grazing was plenteous in the Doon valley. The valley itself, lush and fertile, was nourished by the two mighty rivers of India, the *Jumna* and the *Ganges,* which came closest to each other in this valley. Resting under the shade of a *sal* tree, Davenport asked the men of the state of their rations.

'They are meagre, *Sahib,*' responded Makkhan Singh.

'We should hunt, for the game is plenteous here,' suggested Kartar Singh.

They were interrupted by the sound of cattle bells approaching. They were seated at the edge of a cattle track that led into the forest. Soon, a herd of around fifteen buffaloes, prodded on by a stout young lad singing lustily emerged from the cattle track. Seeing Davenport, he stopped in his tracks.

Then, after a moment's hesitation, he warily approached, greeting Davenport with a '*Salaam, Sahib!*' sweeping his hand to his forehead.

'*Salaam!*' responded Davenport with a smile.

The *sahib's* friendly demeanour put the boy at ease and he approached closer. He appeared to be a lad of fifteen or perhaps sixteen.

'The buffaloes are returning from their grazing,' he said, pointing from the direction of the jungle from which he had emerged. 'I am the cattle herder,' he informed Davenport, quite unnecessarily.

'Ah! So you are,' responded Davenport genially, 'How many cattle do you have in your herd?'

'Eighteen, *Sahib,*' he replied. 'We had twenty- four, but four were killed by a tiger that roams by our village.'

'You have a large herd, and you are a brave lad to venture with your cattle alone into the jungle, when there are tigers close by that are hunting your cattle,' replied Davenport.

The boy's chest swelled and he answered, 'But I must be brave, *Sahib*, for my father was a *sepoy*. He has retired now and I will someday follow his footsteps and myself become a sepoy. Furthermore, my buffaloes can chase the tiger away in the daytime, *Sahib*. They are as brave as the tiger.'

Evidently, the news of the mutiny among the sepoys had not reached the hill-folk in this region. Feeling encouraged by Davenport's friendliness, the lad proceeded to inform him about the cruel way the tiger had decimated herds of buffaloes in the villages in the vicinity. They were fortunate that only four buffaloes in their village had been taken so far. Still, considering how poor they were, he lamented that it was liable to ruin them in the long run. He then proceeded to inform them about how they cut leaves from the trees for fodder each day and how the trees near the village had become bare and each day, they had needed to risk going deeper into the jungle to gather leaves. Lately, however, they feared to venture into the jungle, for the men of the neighbouring village had carried a report to them that a man had been killed by what appeared to be a tiger and carried off into the jungle. The terrified villagers had not yet mustered the courage to venture into the jungle to retrieve his remains. But, go they must eventually, for the man's soul would never rest if he were not cremated properly.

'That is why I take my buffaloes with me now, *Sahib*. They will at least try to resist a tiger if they are attacked, and I can find refuge if I huddle in their midst,' said the lad.

'Where is your village?' Davenport enquired.

'Over there, *Sahib*, by the edge of the fields,' he replied, pointing in the direction of a valley where a stretch of flat land of some four acres, lay.

Beyond that was the village, a collection of thatched huts, surrounded by the jungle. The path between where they sat and the patch of cultivated land was a good mile-long, and wound through a dense *deodar* jungle.

'Do you plan to remain here, *Sahib*?' the lad asked, looking uneasily at the horses, tethered loosely to a tree.

They seemed placid, and gave no indication of smelling danger. Still, they would make an easy target in the night, thought Davenport. Finally, the lad broached the question he had wished to ask when he first encountered them half an hour ago.

'What do you do here, *Sahib*?' he asked.

'And what is that to you?' growled Kartar Singh.

He had been eyeing the boy distastefully and was annoyed by Davenport's encouragement of his garrulousness. The lad, however, seemed unfazed. He was duly impressed with the two men who accompanied the *sahib*. They were evidently his retainers and consequently, important personages in their own right!

'We are here to hunt,' said Davenport affably, hurriedly adding, 'for some deer,' lest the lad presume that they were here to rid the village of its predator. 'Do you know where the Forest Bungalow is?' he asked.

'That is at least a *kos* from here, *Sahib*.' he responded, adding 'But, there is a forester's hut on the edge of our village. The *shikari sahibs* who hunt for tigers stay there often. You could tether your horses by our cattle for there is a fence around the cattle shed,' he volunteered.

The men were inclined to reject his offer, for fear was alien to them, and they were disinclined to see a local predator as a threat. But Davenport did not wish to court the risk of the horses being injured in any way, for there was little hope of procuring a change soon, and their loss would further delay their journey. He also did not wish to see the lad walk alone through the remaining jungle, to his village.

'Lead the way, then,' he said. 'We shall tether our horses and return to hunt. May we purchase some food and some milk for my tea at your village?' he asked.

The lad joyfully asserted that both were plenteously available, glad for the company of three fearless men. By the time they reached the village, there was a small army of persons collected at its edge. Seeing the approach of the lad with three men who were evidently foreign to these parts, a man ploughing his field had alerted the others. An excited buzz made its way through the crowd as they realized that one of the men was a *sahib*. The headman of the village greeted them with a courteous bow and folded palms. Davenport reciprocated the traditional greeting and a hum of approval passed through the crowd. They were invited to sit on the headman's *charpoy* and water was duly produced for them. When asked if some milk might be purchased for their tea, the headman looked horrified declaring that it would be a sin to take money from their guests. Food and drink, humble as it was, would promptly be made available for them. Accordingly, a large pitcher of milk was fetched and Makkhan Singh proceeded to make some tea. The man had asserted that he would himself make the *sahib's* tea, rebuffing the villagers' eager offers to be of service.

Again, there was much commonplace conversation, following which the men enquired why their guests had honoured them with their presence. Davenport informed them that they were here to hunt small game. The men quickly advised him that there was an abundance of *sambar* and *nilgai* in the neighbouring jungle, adding sadly, that the presence of the tiger prevented them from hunting.

The headman duly stated, with evident pride, that he was in possession of a hunting rifle and was not a bad shot himself. Perhaps the *sahib* would be brave enough to venture into the tiger's lair? Davenport agreed, stating that he would go right away with his men to sit up on a tree, for there were but a few hours left before the daylight would be gone. Leaving the horses in the care of the villagers, the three men trekked back in the direction they had come, into the jungle. Talking loudly would keep the tiger away, but possibly also scare away the deer; so, they kept a sharp lookout, making as little noise as possible.

They selected a section where a number of large *chanchri* trees stood. They had selected well for its long ivy-like roots made climbing easy, while the lush foliage of the tree provided ample cover so that, remaining still, they were entirely undetectable. They sat there, motionless, for about three hours, until an orange light began to bathe the forest. It was six-thirty and nightfall would shortly follow. Davenport did not relish the idea of remaining up there all night. They would have to descend soon, to take advantage of what little light there was in order to return to the village. He decided to wait for a few more minutes, desperate to make the most of whatever light they got. He was rewarded for his tenacity, for just at the very last possible moment, two *nilgai* appeared. They were young males and oblivious to the danger nearby.

After signalling to the men, Davenport took aim at the larger one, which was closest to the tree upon which he sat. He had the satisfaction of seeing his shot reach home, with the animal crashing to the forest floor. Another shot rang out simultaneously—from Kartar Singh— and the smaller antelope fell likewise. The men cheered exultantly, for at the last moment they had managed to bag, not one, but two antelope. The bounty at their feet presented a fresh problem. How would they transport the meat to the village? One *nilgai* itself presented quite a challenge, and needed to be carried by two men. Fixing the larger one to stout saplings, Davenport and Makkhan Singh shouldered the burden of the first one with some difficulty. Kartar Singh lobbed the second one onto his shoulder and declared he would carry this one by himself. That was an impossible feat, however, as he frequently needed to stop, to prevent his burden from sliding off his back. The scent of blood had no doubt filled the air and Davenport did not wish to attract the tiger that was known to frequent these parts.

'Leave that one concealed in these bushes. We will come back for it in the morning,' he ordered, aware that it would likely be consumed by then.

Happily, he was interrupted by a shout from the ridge below. A band of villagers, armed with axes and *kudaal*s emerged around the path. They had heard the report of the two guns and hastened to see what was shot. Emboldened when in numbers, they hastened towards the forest. Kartar Singh, loath to leave his kill, hailed the men and asked them to make haste if they wished to eat some meat before the tiger got their share. Thus spurred on, the men ran up the slight slope, grabbing the second *nilgai* and quickly making off in the direction of the village with it. They were overjoyed by the appearance of the antelope, for meat had become scarce ever since the men began to avoid entering the jungle for fear of the tiger. Davenport gave them most of the meat, taking only what would last for their journey without spoiling, for the heat would be pernicious in the plains, and foodstuffs were apt to deteriorate quickly in the summers in India.

With the antelope roasting on a spit, the men sat around talking, and the women giggled in the shadows. Their presence and voices reminded Davenport of his mission. A heaviness descended on his heart as he wondered about his sister. Jane Davenport had turned sixteen that month. She was of a most gentle and delicate disposition and his mind could not fathom her state in the present crisis. Feeling overwhelmed by a sense of powerlessness, he slept poorly that night, tossing and turning, awakened frequently by the grim forebodings generated by malignant dreams. The villagers bade him a sad farewell the next day, pleading with him to change his mind, and abide there a few more days, so that he might rid them of the fearsome predator that now threatened their livestock. He regretted having to part from them so abruptly, but go he must.

They now made their way to Almora arriving there ten days later. They had travelled for fifteen days and Danapur was yet six hundred miles away.

'Travelling in the mountains slows us down. We need to move closer to the plains to reach Danapur! As it is, it will take us an entire month to reach there,' he declared with some frustration, as they pored over the maps. 'I must take any risk, if that will help me to reach Miss Davenport sooner,' he continued.

'Then you will be of no use to her, *Sahib*, for you will surely be dead before very long' answered Makkhan Singh.

The older and cooler of the two retainers, he was not given to exaggeration or impatience, and Davenport was forced to acknowledge the truth in his statement.

'Still, I cannot just sit back and do nothing, when my only sister is in mortal danger, can I?' he asked bitterly.

'You are not sitting back, *Sahib*. You are making your way to the plains with the utmost urgency,' he replied calmly.

'What I am doing, is crawling with the utmost vacillation,' retorted Davenport, adding, 'Perhaps we should travel by night, for then I can move undetected.'

Makkhan Singh shook his head, proceeding to point out that they would need to find shelter in the day, which would prove virtually impossible, travelling as they were, on horseback. Listening to their exchange, Kartar Singh suddenly sat up erect. Thinking he had sensed some danger, they grabbed hold of their rifles. To their surprise, he rose and wordlessly made his way into the jungle, unarmed except for the scimitar—a weapon worn by every Sikh male—draped across his person, paying no heed to their calls. They looked at each other puzzled, wondering if they should follow him; but he was soon gone, vanishing into the mysterious jungle. To follow him without knowing where he was would prove foolhardy. They lit a fire, for nightfall was fast approaching and looked anxiously in the direction of the dense undergrowth. Suddenly, after the space of about a half-hour, he emerged from the forest, carrying an abundance of twigs and roots, swaddled in his cummerbund.

Waving away his companions' queries about what he was up to, he proceeded to sit by the fire, scraping away at the twigs and vigorously grinding the roots he had gathered. The two men looked at him mystified, wondering if he had gone mad suddenly. He seemed to be in quite a frenzy, sweating profusely as he fashioned a concoction of some sort in a small dish. Both men wondered what the unappetizing creation might be, hoping he would not demand that they partake of it, for he was occasionally characterized by the greatest impetuosity. Reaching towards the fire, he grabbed a charred twig and by degrees added portions of it into his brew. After a while, he heated it in the fire and when he seemed satisfied by it, he quite abruptly lay down and proceeded to fall asleep.

Shaking his head at his younger friend, Makkhan Singh said in a low voice to Davenport, 'I have always suspected that he is a little mad.'

Davenport involuntarily smiled at the momentousness with which this declaration was made. He nodded and winked at his friend and lay down, soon finding himself drifting off to sleep.

He was awakened by a clammy sensation on his hand the next morning. In the murkiness of half awakened thought, the possibility that a snake was crawling on his hand presented itself to him. Possessed with this thought, his eyes widened and he restrained the impulse to jerk his hand and jump upright. He could hear the men speaking to each other in hushed tones. No doubt they had seen the reptile and were endeavouring to assist him with caution, so as to prevent it from striking. He felt no small comfort at the thought that help was on its way, lying perfectly still, when, to his horror, the clamminess descended on his neck. Unable to lie still any longer, he lunged, with a great roar, tugging at his neck to rid himself of whatever malignant creature had placed itself there. To his amazement, instead of a snake, which he fully expected to find, on his neck was some sort of slop, that had somehow adhered itself to him. His men, completely startled by his eruption had scattered to the side.

'What are you doing, *Sahib*? We need for it to last for the entire month, and perhaps longer,' shouted Kartar Singh.

'I told you not to do it until he woke up. Look! You have angered him. He meant no harm, *Sahib*,' declared Makkhan Singh, with some agitation.

'What are you doing? What is this substance, and why do you smear it on me? I thought a snake was crawling up my arm. Why, this is the very stuff you were concocting last night, is it not?' Davenport demanded.

'It is not a snake, *Sahib*. It is just some harmless pigment,' replied Kartar Singh with a guffaw. The situation now appeared quite amusing to him, and he could not cease laughing.

'You were quite right about him. He is definitely mad,' Davenport said to Makkhan Singh, with some asperity.

That served to dampen the other man's hilarity somewhat, as he cast a severe look upon his colleague, demanding whether the man had indeed declared him to be mad.

'And if he did, who could blame him? For behold yourself, since yesternight, you have behaved in the oddest fashion. And now, perhaps you will enlighten me as to what this is all about?' Davenport demanded firmly.

Breaking into a smile again, Kartar Singh responded, 'Why *Sahib*, this is our way into the plains. Do you not see? These pigments that I have prepared will turn you into the colour of a Hindustani! We shall spread this on your person and tie a turban on your head and declare you to be one! It is a pity that you have no beard, for then we could pass you off as a Sikh. Still, we shall say you are from our village in Punjaub. We are each possessed of a change of clothing. You can choose one to your liking, and dress as one of us, though perhaps you should choose Makkhan Singh's clothing, for he is cleaner than I,' he finished hastily, with thinly veiled self-interest.

Davenport's creased brows slowly gave way to widened eyes as the audacity of the suggestion became apparent to him. Kartar Singh was proposing that he disguise himself as an Indian and ride with impunity through the plains!

'What shall we do if someone asks about our horses, for we do not look very wealthy?' he asked.

'If we are stopped by the sepoys who mutiny, we shall say that they horses were snatched from *sahibs* whom we have killed, and if an English *sahib* asks, then you can reveal yourself to be a *sahib* too,' said Makkhan Singh coolly.

Davenport sat down suddenly, leaning his chin on his hand, quite overcome by the unexpectedness of the plan. Feeling the coldness of the dye on his palm, he glanced down at his hand. It was brown and quite a similar hue to the men's hands. He threw his head back and laughed, delighted with the simplicity and the daring of the plan. They proceeded to swiftly smear the pigments upon his person. The task of transforming Davenport into an Indian was accomplished within the space of an hour. After the slop had been washed away in the stream and Makkhan Singh's clothes been donned, he looked remarkably like an Indian.

'Remember to be cautious in your speech, *Sahib*,' Kartar Singh warned. 'For there are many dialects and languages spoken along the way we shall take, and you must not let your speech betray that you are not from the Punjaub, for our language is different from Hindustani.'

'Why do we not say that he is mute if anyone speaks to him?' asked Makkhan Singh brightly.

The two men unanimously agreed that this would be the most expeditious course to follow and solemnly charged Davenport not to speak, should they encounter anyone but the British.

Sticking to their scheme to avoid large towns, they decided to make their way to Pilhibeat, situated one hundred and ten miles away. It was smaller than the city of Bareilly and surely the mutiny would spare it, they hoped. Making their way through Nainital, Davenport was relieved to find that Major Ramsay, the newly appointed Commissioner of the Kumaon District had taken firm command of the city and order appeared to prevail. He had hastened from Almora some three days ago, on May 22, and appeared to be doing everything in his power to prevent unrest. The 66th Gorkhas and the 8th Irregular Cavalry were stationed in the Kumaon District and were successful thus far at preserving the peace. Despite the prevailing calm in this region, Davenport opted to retain his disguise as the men purchased rations, to prevent exposure, should any men from Nainital make their way to the plains to join the discontent there. They feigned that they were travelling a day's journey, to Haldwani, to avoid attracting attention to themselves. This would turn out to be a wise precaution, as it was not until they reached Haldwani that they, at last, began to lend credence to the truth that there was a mutiny afoot.

The city was largely quiet as they approached it. However, very quickly they heard shouting and a mob appeared to be leading a riot. They seemed to be led by *pahari* men and there was a good deal of shouting. They quickly dismounted, keeping away from the main street, and endeavouring to remain at the very outskirts of the city, departing from the Kaladhungi road, which they presently travelled on. They arrived at the edge of the surrounding forest, by means of a cart track. Nevertheless, they were privy to the violence occurring within the city, as they witnessed smoke rising from within it. A building of some sort had been set on fire, and the flames had spread across two other buildings in the centre of the town. The building that had been set ablaze was a treasury of some sort from which the men appeared to be making away with considerable sums of money.

'There is great chaos and looting there, *Sahib*,' reported Kartar Singh, as he descended from a tree that he had been scouting on.

He could not know it at the time, but the chaos in the city was indeed so great that the District Magistrate had fled and made his way to Nainital to seek refuge there.

'We would do well to avoid the city all together,' Makkhan Singh said.

Davenport nodded and they continued to make their way through the jungle, until there was no more daylight. To prevent their fire from being observed in the city—for create a fire they must—they journeyed further into the cover of the jungle. The howling of some strange animal piercing the night air oddly seemed more comforting than the horrendous howls that had emerged from the city as they had passed by it. Davenport felt a chill run through him, partly because the night was cool, and partly because the dangers of the situation were becoming apparent to him. It was not his own safety that he feared for, but rather that of Jane's. He tried not to think of her for the construing of what her present circumstances might be inevitably led to a suffocating sense of desperation in him that drove away all sleep and deprived him of the ability to think. He must keep his mind on the journey, for the planning thereof would enable him to preserve his sanity.

Tonight, a fresh problem had presented itself to him. That the mutineers had made their way to Haldwani was chilling, for Simla was but a fifteen days' journey. What was to stop the mutineers from reaching Simla? Praying fervently for Major Ramsay to be guided in his efforts to preserve order in the region, he fell into a troubled sleep, dreaming about Edwina Hardingham, beckoning to him with the palest countenance, and appearing to be in the greatest distress. Disturbed by his dreams, he awoke in the middle of the night, and was relieved to find Makkhan Singh awake and stoking the fire. Grateful for his company and glad for the warmth and protection afforded by the fire, he enquired whether he thought the disturbance would make its way to Simla.

'It is too early to tell, *Sahib*. But, I wish with all my heart that it does not, for I would wish to be at Knowles *sahib's* side, were he to be in any peril,' he responded, with the utmost sincerity.

Davenport was suddenly struck by a thought. 'What about your family? Do you not have a wife and children that you wish to protect?' he asked.

The man remained quiet for many moments, so that Davenport believed he had fallen asleep, when at last, he replied quietly, 'No, *Sahib*. They are no more. They died of *haiza* many years ago, as did Kartar Singh's parents. He was just a boy then. I took him under my care, but when there was a drought one year, we were forced to wander away from our village in Punjaub, in search of food. After wandering many days, we reached Sehranpour, for we heard the famine was not as severe there. We heard one day that the *tahsildar's* friend was looking for some men to employ. I went early to the *sahib's* bungalow. Knowles *sahib* was there and he looked at Kartar and me. Before he said anything to us, he ordered the servants to feed the child and me. I never forgot that act of kindness and many such that he has shown me. I have eaten his salt ever since and have been his faithful servant. Apart from them, I have no one I need protect. Except for you, at this moment, of course,' he added.

Davenport was moved by the poignancy of the man's tale, and pondering over how impartially tragedy finds its way into the lives of the rich and the poor, he fell into another troubled sleep. Their journey had taken them to the east of the city, and the next morning, they gradually made their way to the south, continuing on towards Pilhibeat, which would take the better part of two days, situated as it was sixty-five miles away. They stopped at the village of Sunpar before approaching Pilhibeat, wary from their expedition into Haldwani, and keeping a sharp lookout for any signs of unrest. All seemed well in the sleepy village, as they approached it. The sounds of village life permeated the air. Someone was chopping wood with an axe, occasionally drowning out the unmistakable sound of a spinning potter's wheel. In the distance, the humming of women grinding wheat could be heard. No one was in sight and the three men debated on the best course of action. They were in need of provisions and as such, must seek nourishment here.

'Better to seek food at a small village, *Sahib*, than in the city,' said Makkhan Singh.

'What ruse shall we employ here to explain the presence of the horses?' asked Kartar Singh.

'There does not appear to be the hint of mutiny here. I would hide from them that infection as long as I could. Why do we not say that we are traders and are travelling southward?' suggested Davenport.

'Perhaps I should lead the horses away from the village and await you by the road yonder. Once you have obtained refreshment, you could meet me on the path, for there is but one road that leads from this village,' said Kartar Singh.

Davenport did not believe this course of action to be wise, for if it were detected by the villagers, it might make for a most suspicious interpretation. They were prevented from coming to a unanimity of opinion, when, as if out of nowhere, a lad appeared, chewing on a twig, and making his way to the stream by which they stood, a small collection of goats following him closely.

'Remember, *Sahib*, say not a word in his presence,' cautioned Makkhan Singh under his breath.

The lad stood arrested, looking wide-eyed at them. Three men on horseback approaching the village were an odd sight. Approaching warily, he stood, staring at them for some time.

He opened his mouth and then shut it again, when Kartar Singh gruffly asked, 'Do you live here, boy?'

The boy nodded, awestruck at the size of his examiner, for Kartar Singh was a tall man who—when he stroked his moustache and sat erect in his saddle, as he now did—struck a rather imposing figure. His piercing gaze, now directed at the boy, served to impress him further.

'We wish to buy food at your village. Where can we find the elders of the village?' he asked.

The boy, still awestruck pointed wordlessly in the direction of a clump of trees about a hundred yards away.

'Be off with your goats then,' Kartar Singh said as he nodded in acknowledgement. 'Do they live up in the trees, then?' he muttered under his breath.

But, the boy, now relinquishing the twig in his mouth, and possessed by the urge to be hospitable, volunteered to take them to the headman's hut. The hope of quietly riding out of the village died quickly, for that was sure to cause alarm. They dismounted and followed the child, finding behind the clump of trees, an assembly of around twenty huts. A wall surrounded the settlement, seemingly to ward off wild visitors from the jungle. The sounds of axe and wheel abruptly stopped as the villagers beheld their unlikely callers. An animated hum of conversation was ignited, as news travelled from door to door, and soon, even the humming of the women behind the walls ceased, and the three men found themselves suddenly besieged by the members of the village. The headman scurried out from his hut, hastily donning his turban, and folding his hands in greeting.

He invited them to sit with him on his *charpoy* in the shade of a large mango tree in the centre of the village. The boys of the village who sat feasting on fruit on the branches were shooed down, as the men made their way to the *charpoy*. The headman beckoned the oldest of the three, Makkhan Singh to be seated at his side, for it is customary in India for the elder to have precedence over the younger. The rest of the men squatted on the ground around them, in the manner that perhaps only the men and women of India can squat. Kartar Singh made himself comfortable on the ground, beside the *charpoy*. It was a small one and only two men could reasonably be seated on it. Davenport hesitated as Makkhan Singh sat down. For a moment he stood awkwardly, looking down at the men as they seated themselves. Accustomed to the privileges of race and rank, he fully expected to be seated by the headman. Suddenly, he seemed stripped of both, and Makkhan Singh must have precedence over him, for he was the elder. This was a truly novel circumstance and he stood pondering on it so that, in a few moments, he remained the only one standing.

With a puzzled look, the headman asked, 'Why does your companion not sit?'

'He is deaf and mute,' said Kartar Singh quickly, taking a firm hold of Davenport's hand, and dragging him to the ground beside him.

Unaccustomed to squatting, Davenport found himself landing awkwardly on the ground, with his legs flailing, much to the amusement of a small brood of children who sat nearby.

'He is also somewhat feebleminded,' added Kartar Singh, prompting Makkhan Singh to clear his throat reproachfully.

Smiling genially at the children, Davenport squatted as best he could, swearing to himself to give Kartar Singh a sound thrashing as soon as they exited the village. The men sitting around clucked and nodded sympathetically at Davenport. They had a simpleton in their village too. This tall stranger however seemed to be more in possession of his faculties than their unfortunate associate who spent the principal part of the day chasing the goats in the village.

The headman proceeded to make conversation with them, informing them that soon it would be the *kharif* season, and the men would plant their wheat as soon as the rains came.

'The rains appear to be lagging this year,' he lamented, for it was already the first day of June, but no sign of the monsoons had come.

He then proceeded to ask the men about their families, whether they were wed, whether they had any progeny, how many, etc. After as much circumventing as was polite and expected of well-bred men in the villages of India, the headman broached the subject of the reason for their visit.

Makkhan Singh informed them that they were traders from Almora and had become slightly lost in their journey towards the plains. At this, they became curious. Where in the plains were they journeying to? Makkhan Singh responded that they sought to go to the faraway city of Calcutta.

The men gasped in awe, for that was an impressive destination indeed. What did they trade? They would trade in cotton and dyes, Makkhan Singh informed them, drawing on his knowledge of Davenport's extensive trade across India. But, what were they going to barter and sell so that they may buy these items?

'Oh, we are not actually buying and selling anything, for our *seth* is sending us to assist his men who already conduct trade for him in Calcutta,' improvised Makkhan Singh.

He proceeded to inform them that the matters of trade were complex and highly intricate, such that, even their local grocer would be hard-pressed to comprehend them. Suitably impressed, the men's eyes widened.

'But why do you carry guns?' the headman asked, gesturing at the Enfield rifles hanging from their saddles.

'Those are to hunt game,' said Makkhan Singh.

Enthralled by the notion that their visitors were truly superior men, the headman invited them to stay at their village for as long as they wished. They would be welcome at his own humble home. Refreshments were procured and the men sat in the shade, fanning themselves as the noonday sun made the air unbearably hot. Davenport nodded imperceptibly at Makkhan Singh, who made no motion, but, clearing his throat a few moments later, suggested to the headman that if they might purchase some provisions, they would prefer to continue their journey as soon as they partook of their meal. The man looked somewhat taken aback and had the air of someone who is on the verge of taking offense at something that is put to him, when, without warning, a series of shots rang out in the air.

Numerous birds, taking sanctuary from the blazing sun, suddenly scattered from every tree in the vicinity, and suddenly the air was filled with the deafening roar of a thousand beating wings and startled squawks. The sound of thundering hooves soon followed as dozens of men on horseback descended upon the village, emitting fearsome howls as they rode into the centre of it, brandishing guns and swords. The men seated around the headman's *charpoy* yelled, scrambling to get on their feet. Pandemonium ensued with some men trampling on others. The intruders randomly fired their guns into the assembly, felling several souls in a moment. Children screamed in fear, calling for their mothers. A shrieking woman rushed from within her hut, towards her child who stood wailing in the centre of the commotion, only to be beheaded by a man with a sword. The child stood frozen with terror and was soon run down by a man on a horse. Davenport leapt in the direction of the child, but it was too late, and the child lay lifeless on the ground.

A man dragged a woman by her hair, carrying her away on his horse, after shooting her husband down with what appeared to be a duelling pistol. Everywhere, men and women ran, scattering like mice as the men went from house to house ransacking them, taking what little they could find. In one house an old woman lay, too feeble to rise to investigate the cause of the commotion. She lay helpless on her cot as a villain burst into her house, pillaging and smashing everything in sight. Enraged at finding nothing of value there, he sank his sword into her, cursing her as she died. Davenport and his men tried to rush to their horses where their weapons were, but were prevented by several men on horseback who brandished swords. The men shepherded the villagers that remained alive into a tight circle, circling them like a pack of wild dogs. Some of them dismounted and began to search the persons of the men and women who stood trembling. The women shrieked in terror and were killed without mercy. Standing among the villagers, Davenport studied the men carefully. It was not clear who they were. They did not seem to be sepoys, for they did not operate in an organized manner and not all of them were armed with rifles. Some carried swords and daggers, all of which carried the same inscription, suggesting that the men were in the employ of someone, perhaps a local *zameendar*. Unarmed, they stood little chance of overpowering their attackers and he cast about desperately in his mind what to do.

A hush had descended on the village like the stillness that descends on prey before a predator that is about to spring. One man dove into the crowd, dragging a young woman of about nineteen who stood behind Davenport. She screamed pitifully, begging for mercy, pleading with him to spare her. Enraged, and with nothing but his fists to fight with, Davenport lunged at the man with a swift uppercut. He reeled back momentarily, releasing his grip on the unfortunate woman who, pushing back with all her might towards the back of the crowd, made her way to the hut behind where they stood. The marauders, temporarily distracted by the audacity of Davenport's attack, seemed confused. Seizing his advantage, Davenport followed with another swing at the man's jaw, successfully knocking him unconscious. With the speed of lightening, he grabbed the man's sword, and swung in the direction of another man who rushed at him, in defence of the unconscious man. His sword found his mark and severed the man's hand. Reeling and staggering he fell on his knees, howling in pain, unable to display manliness in the face of the agony he so unflinchingly had inflicted on others just a few moments ago.

The men had not counted on resistance from the villagers. They were the armed fighters in the service of the neighbouring *zameendar* and such, were not accustomed to encountering defiance from their victims when they engaged in acts of pillage and plunder. One of the men on horseback raised his rifle in Davenport's direction, but before he could fire, Kartar Singh dispatched his dagger straight into his heart. The man collapsed, sliding off his horse and with a roar akin to that of a lion, Kartar Singh lunged at him, savagely pulling out his dagger that was implanted in the man's chest. Quickly, Davenport seized the dead man's rifle and fired at one man who took aim at Kartar Singh. The crowd of villagers scattered as a hail of gunfire emitted from the plunderers. Arming himself with a sword, Makkhan Singh planted himself firmly in front of Davenport, swinging wildly and injuring several horses as he did so. Panicking, the horses reared, unseating their riders as they did so, trampling on them as they turned and fled. One man bellowed and charged at Davenport and found himself shot in the belly for his efforts. Reloading his rifle and shooting was not expeditious, for the men attacked them from all sides. Taking positions from behind trees and alternating between the use of guns and swords, the three men engaged the marauders effectively.

Meanwhile, the villagers, taking advantage of the distraction created by their valiant guests, turned in all directions and fled. Doing so was a fatal error, for had they stayed in the vicinity of the three men who battled the brutes, their lives would have been spared, for between the three of them, they had killed eighteen of the invaders. The remaining attackers had fled, for it had occurred to them that the two Sikh men were not natives of the village and along with the third who fought in their midst, had the demeanour of warriors. They would not easily be cowed into terror as the villagers would, and they now had a battle on their hands that they had not bargained for. They had looted as much from the village as they could possibly hope to, and calling for a retreat, the one who appeared to be their leader hastily fled.

However, not all the marauders heard his call or indeed were apt to respond to it. For a handful of them had followed the fleeing villagers, and in the blindness of cruel rage, had hacked them to pieces. Hearing desperate cries from behind the village, Davenport charged in that direction.

'Do not go alone, *Sahib,*' Makkhan Singh warned, to no avail.

He was forced to let Davenport go alone, for there were four malevolent persons presently advancing on their position. Kartar Singh fired on them killing two of them and quite effectively convincing the others that further aggression on their part would prove to be most unwise. The men backed away to join their colleagues who were fast fleeing the scene.

Behind the village, Davenport found himself facing one man who had attacked and most cruelly stabbed the young woman he had rescued earlier. Not content with having snatched the necklace around her neck, he endeavoured to cut the remainder of her jewellery from her person. She lay in a heap on the ground and he prepared to slay her when Davenport commanded him to desist from so dark a deed. The man fired in his direction, and while he missed, he hit the sword that Davenport carried. Although no lasting harm was done, the impact of the shot painfully wrenched the sword from Davenport's hand and, for a moment, his wrist seemed numbed by the impact.

With a malignant growl, the man grabbed it and lunged at Davenport who, thinking very quickly indeed, unfurled his turban, and swathing his hand in it, grabbed the man's sword by the blade. He held it with all his might, wincing as the sharp blade tore through the cloth, but earning himself enough time to kick the man to the ground. Perhaps taken aback by this audacious defence, or perhaps because the blow stunned him, the man hesitated for the smallest moment. Spinning the sword into his left hand, Davenport swiftly plunged it into the man, mentally thanking his fencing master for insisting that he practice his skill with both hands. The man gasped as he fell to the ground, and Davenport averted his eyes as he wallowed in his blood, turning his attention instead to the unfortunate woman who was his last victim.

Gently grasping her shoulders, he raised her off the ground and found to his great shock, that she had been shielding an infant with her own body. She cringed at first, as if to break free from his grasp, and then recognising that it was the man who had tried to save her twice, leaned into his arms. Davenport glanced desperately around for some shade, for they sat in the blazing sun. He felt a twinge in his heart as she leaned over her infant to provide him shelter from the sun. He picked up the child, and with his other arm, raised the woman as gently as he could, to prevent her from suffering further pain, and found that this was impossible. Leaving her on the ground he ran to place her infant in a shady spot under a tree and then returned to carry her thence. Finding a mud pot of water in a nearby hut, he searched about for a utensil and seeing there a mug, he carried the water back to the wounded woman. Holding her up in his arms, he brought the water to her lips. Gasping as he held her in his arms, she took a small sip of the water he offered her but seemed unable to swallow it.

'Where are you, *Sahib*?' came Makkhan Singh's agitated call. 'Those devils are gone. They have turned and fled. We had better …' he said, stopping halfway at the sight of the wounded woman leaning on Davenport's shoulder.

He felt pity for the wretched creature, but he speculated that it was possible that the men had not left for good and that they might possibly return with reinforcements. Her injuries were too grave for her to survive and they could be of no further assistance to her. They must proceed without delay and this he attempted to convey to Davenport.

'Where is Kartar Singh?' Davenport asked urgently.

'He is by the mango tree, *Sahib*, keeping watch lest they return. And we would do well to make haste and leave this place, for they might return with others,' he said.

Ignoring his suggestion, Davenport asked, 'What of the rest of the villagers? How do they fare? We must attend to the wounded.'

His friend lowered his eyes and shook his head sadly. 'There are no wounded ones, *Sahib*,' he replied softly.

Davenport looked at him with horror in his eyes, exclaiming, 'No! You cannot mean. …'

Makkhan Singh simply shook his head again.

'Is my husband alive? Please, you must find him!' gasped the woman, straining to breathe as she spoke.

'Who is your husband, Daughter? How shall we know him?' asked Makkhan Singh.

'He and I ran together in that direction, before the man caught up with me. Perhaps he is hiding there,' she said, pointing in the direction of a grove of trees to their right.

Davenport signalled to his friend and the man rose, with little hope, to see if someone had taken refuge in the grove. He did not traverse very far, when he stumbled upon something on the ground. Looking down, he saw the severed head of a man. As he continued into the grove, he saw men and women lying everywhere, viciously hewn to pieces, and although a fearless fighter in battle, his heart was sickened at the sight of the carnage that lay at his feet.

He returned hastily, as if to flee the site of such grotesque happenings, returning to the spot where Davenport and the woman sat in the shade of the tree, lowering his eyes as the woman's hopeful eyes met his.

'There is no one there, my child,' he said quietly as he knelt beside them.

Her eyes welled with tears as she correctly interpreted that her husband lay dead in the patch of ground between the trees, and she coughed, gasping for air and from grief.

Davenport tried to soothe her saying, 'I am certain your husband will return, and if not, we shall go and search for him when you feel a little better. Do not gasp so violently, for you will hurt yourself more,' knowing that the hope he attempted to give her was the veriest falsehood.

They were joined in a few moments by Kartar Singh who urged that they depart the place with the greatest urgency, for he had heard rumblings in the distance that sounded like artillery fire. Makkhan Singh nodded in agreement for he had heard them as well. The woman had closed her eyes now and only the faintest tremor from her body every few moments betrayed that life was left in her. A profusion of blood had covered her garments and it did not seem possible that she would survive her injuries.

'Every moment we tarry here enlarges the risk you face, *Sahib*, for consider how vicious these brutes have been against their own countrymen. Think you that they shall deal any kindlier with you? She will not live very long, *Sahib*. There is nothing more that you can do for her,' said Makkhan Singh gently.

'Then we shall stay and give her comfort as long she remains alive,' said Davenport firmly.

The child that was laid on the ground, mercifully asleep thus far, whimpered and the woman's eyes fluttered open. Kartar Singh and Makkhan Singh started for they had not realized that there was a child with the woman. She made as if to pick up her child, and Davenport assisted her, cradling her head on his lap, and placing the child in her bloodied arms. She looked at the child with exceeding tenderness, and with great effort handed the infant back to him, folding her hands in silent entreaty, her eyes beseeching, making an unspoken request. He nodded and she closed her eyes with the smallest sigh, and was gone.

The three men looked at her with moist eyes, for despite being frail, she had fought valiantly to protect her infant, shielding her from the sword and the sun, and with her very last breath, sought protection for the babe. The child had awoken, even as her mother's soul departed, not realizing that in this rather large and terrifying world, she now found herself quite alone. Her cries brought their present difficulties to mind, for now they must find someone in the village to whom they must entrust her. The task proved to be truly horrendous, for as they walked around the village and its environs, they discovered nothing but pools of blood in which lay the bodies of hapless villagers who had met their end in the cruelest manner. Suddenly, the men stiffened as they heard the report of guns being fired in the distance.

'We must depart, *Sahib* for they are returning,' shouted Kartar Singh.

Without delay, Davenport created a sling from which to affix the child to his person as he rode, while the men soothed the frightened horses that had stood tethered to the trees in the village through the entire ordeal. Thankfully, they had not suffered injury and their assailants had not had the opportunity to steal them. They were entirely taken aback when Davenport mounted, the child attached firmly to his chest with his cummerbund. His hand was slightly injured, and having torn off a piece of cloth from his turban to bandage it, he managed with some difficulty to set himself on his mount.

'Surely you do not plan to take the child with us, *Sahib*?!' Kartar Singh asked incredulously.

'What, pray, must I do with her, if not?' Davenport asked tersely.

'There may be some members of the village who have managed to escape and shall return eventually. They would perhaps take the child in. She would be better off amongst her own, rather than with us, going as we are, at the peril of our own lives,' said Makkhan Singh.

'She will be happier amongst her own, but what if there remains none of them to return? And what if they do not return until several days are passed, for terror? Shall we leave her to the jackals or to die of starvation until someone ventures to return to this unhappy place? And what if the marauders return first? Do you think they will spare her life? And perchance the villagers return sooner, what if no one wishes to take her into their care? No, my friends, leaving her here would be a death sentence, as cruel as the one already meted out to her by those murderous thugs. We shall take her with us, until we find a suitable place where she may be left in safety and treated with kindness. Do not forget, her mother pleaded with us to guard her, as she breathed her last. To deny her would be almost too cruel to imagine. Come, let us be going, for I am certain that I hear muskets and they appear to be approaching nearer!' he exclaimed, spurring his horse on with the greatest urgency.

'Wait, *Sahib*!' shouted Makkhan Singh as he ran towards one of the huts.

Reining in his horse, Davenport looked over his shoulder to see him hurrying into a nearby hut. They could hear him move within, where he seemed to be turning over a variety of pots and pans, making no small commotion as he searched desperately for something.

Kartar Singh clucked impatiently, saying, 'We shall never be able to escape for the road is surely blocked by those murderers now! We shall have to retreat into the jungle!'

Davenport shared his impatience to flee, as the horses apparently did, but he had developed a profound respect for his older companion by now and was sure that he tarried behind for some reason of the utmost importance. Finally, the man emerged from the hut with a look of triumph, carrying something that he secured very carefully with his cummerbund before placing it into the bag that hung from his saddle. He had correctly surmised that he would find some milk within the hut and having found it, he emptied the water from his bottle, which he had sagely brought with him when embarking on this expedition, and proceeded to fill it with milk.

'We shall need this, for the child will soon be wailing for nourishment,' he said, as he hurriedly mounted his horse.

Nodding approvingly, Davenport said quickly, 'Let us make for the jungle, for we shall certainly be safer there.'

The men rode furiously through the groves at the edge of the jungle until they were out of sight of the village, slowing down to a canter as they approached it. It loomed before them large and ominous. It was unlike the forests on the Himalayan foothills. The vegetation here was thick and the undergrowth dense. *Sal* trees and *pipal* trees filled the surroundings and a great variety of birds sat perched atop them. They pressed into the undergrowth, Davenport taking care to mark a subtle trail that none but the keenest tracker would be able to follow, and which would nevertheless aid them in their eventual exit from the jungle. If they pressed eastward for a few days, they would eventually reach Nepal. The border between India and Nepal had been left open by the government to promote trade and there would be safety there. But, Davenport did not seek safety. He pressed on, braving the stifling heat until they were a good distance into the jungle. He shrewdly assessed that only the most bloodthirsty fiend, desperate for vengeance, would venture this far, into forests inhabited by fearsome beasts. The babe attached to his person had made the riding somewhat difficult. While she had started to whimper, she soon quieted as they rode, entranced by motion, as infants generally are.

Now, however, as they rested by a *nulla* that gurgled with incongruous mirth on this hot and bloody day, she took up a wail and appeared to be freshly aware that something was awry in the world and the person seated by where she lay resembled her tender mother not at all. Davenport looked at her greatly disturbed. Never in his twenty-seven years had he found himself playing the rôle of nurse and comforter to an infant. He vaguely remembered comforting Jane when she had hurt herself in childhood games, but she was so much younger than himself that her care and company were largely outside the purview of his interests. Desperate to rid them of what had now become a shrill crescendo of wails, he patted her head and cooed at her, and when that failed, picked her up for she had been quiet whilst they rode. He found that he had stumbled upon a most acute course of action, for she instantly ceased to wail, contenting herself with unhappy whimpers. Emboldened, he gently rocked her, dipping his cummerbund in the water and mopping down her brow. The evaporating water cooled her somewhat but she remained fretful and whimpering.

'She is hungry, *Sahib,* and the milk I have carried shall make her happy now,' said Makkhan Singh, reaching forth into his bag to retrieve its precious cargo.

'How will you feed her? And, can *we* partake of some of the milk too, for I am hungry and we cannot very well hunt here for a shot would be heard for miles,' grumbled Kartar Singh.

The men shook their heads at him. The milk would scarcely calm the infant for a few hours and none could be spared for him, and should he not make himself more useful? Retrieving a spoon he had stowed away, Makkhan Singh gently poured a few drops of milk gingerly into the child's parted lips as Davenport nervously cradled her. To their joy, she sucked up the nourishment greedily and soon, she had emptied the contents of a quarter of the bottle. The three men laughed with relief, for by this time, even Kartar Singh had become engaged in nourishing her. Makkhan Singh sagely informed Davenport that having partaken of the milk, she would soon be desirous of relieving herself, kindly taking her away from Davenport who declared that he had done quite enough of his share of the job of protecting her thus far.

Kartar Singh chuckled and then enquired, 'The milk shall not last very long without spoiling in this heat, *Sahib*. And what shall we do then? Infants, in my experience, usually desire to be fed a great many times!'

His question brought their present troubles to the fore. From seeking to be reunited with his sister at the earliest possible instance, their undertaking had now turned into one of protecting the young infant in their care with the need to procure sustenance for her becoming their most urgent concern.

'We should make haste to leave the jungle then, and find Pilhibeat,' Davenport suggested.

Debating on their best course of action, they agreed that it would be wisest to quit the jungle while there was yet light left. It was three o' clock presently and with another eighteen miles to traverse, they would certainly not be able to reach there before nightfall. But perhaps that would be fortuitous for surely they could travel undetected and enter the city in the dark. But, what of the infant? How could they explain her presence? Perhaps they could pass off as mutineers and state, if accosted, that they had rescued her from a village that had been plundered. But what if their assailants earlier in the day had verily been the mutineers? That might arouse the whole town against them. No, that course of action would court far too much risk.

'Why do we not declare that we are mutineers, and one of us is her father and that her mother was killed in a raid near Umbala? We can say that we have travelled thither to take up arms against the government,' suggested Davenport.

The men debated the merits of this plan, but finally, it appeared to be the only one that was tenable among the options before them. Perhaps they could find kindhearted persons at Pilhibeat who would give the child refuge.

They made their way again through the jungle, in the direction they had come from, carefully keeping watch for signs of trouble. Davenport had marked their way well, and their expert eyes were deft at detecting the little signs that indicated the direction they should proceed in: broken twigs, small branches that were placed by trees and other innocuous objects that belonged readily in the jungle. Within the space of a half hour, they were back at the edge of the forest, facing the grove of trees that stood between them and the village. All was quiet, but they could detect the faint sounds of human voices in the distance. Taking care to avoid detection, they skirted the village, darting in and out of the cover of trees at the jungle's edge. When they had reached as far as they possibly could travel in this manner, they approached a narrow road that emerged in between the trees. It was the road that they had taken to come to the village of Sunpar earlier that day.

Keeping a sharp lookout for their erstwhile attackers, they travelled slowly along the road. Mercifully lulled by the motion, their ward had drifted off to sleep again, but Davenport prayed under his breath that she would not awake nor betray their presence. His fears appeared needless at present, for the road was deserted and not a soul was in sight. They spurred their horses to a steady trot and traversed for a space of a few hours when the child awoke and began to whimper. Eager to calm her before she became greatly distressed, Davenport ordered the men to enter into the cover of the trees by the road, to allow themselves a brief rest. Having become acquainted with the infant's disposition, the men found it easier to attend to her in this instance, for she eagerly partook of the refreshment they proffered, grasping Davenport's face as she sucked on teaspoonfuls of the milk that had mercifully not curdled, owing to Makkhan Singh's wise stratagem of enrobing the bottle in his wet cummerbund to keep it cool.

Suddenly, the men stiffened, as the unmistakable sound of riders approaching in the distance could be heard. From his shady resting place, Kartar Singh leapt up and led the horses deeper into the woods that lay around. Davenport moved slowly to avoid alarming the child, for her cries at this time would be most inopportune! She began to whimper when temporarily deprived of her sustenance, but soon quietened when the men hastily restored it to her when once in the cover of the jungle. The men stood silently, not daring to breathe. The sound of the riders became louder until a profusion of horsemen appeared to have passed them. Mercifully, the sound had not agitated the child and with the exception of a few curious snorts, the horses had remained calm as well.

'Who were they?' asked Kartar Singh, as curiosity replaced a sense of danger.

'They appear to ride in the direction of the village. They could very well be the assailants we encountered this morning, intent on retribution, in which case, they appear to have taken an inordinate amount of time to return with reinforcements,' Davenport suggested, somewhat puzzled.

Who then were the men whose voices they had heard in the village as they returned from the jungle?

'Perhaps there were villagers spared who returned to the village, and now these devils are returned to punish them again?' wondered Makkhan Singh aloud.

Davenport shook his head. The voices they heard in the village as they emerged from the forest were not hushed in fear. Neither were they raucous or enraged. They were men speaking to one another in serious and quiet tones. Surely, had they been villagers, their voices would be more panicked? And surely, had they been the marauders returning for vengeance, their voices would betray violence. But they had heard neither panic nor wrath in their voices. As to the identity of the riders who had just passed them, that was a mystery as well.

Waiting until they were sure that not a sound could be heard, they ventured back towards the road. Pushing Davenport towards the rear, the men approached the road first, satisfying themselves that the danger was now past. When they ascertained that it was safe, the three men mounted and continued on their journey. Their charge was now cooing as she was bundled into Davenport's cummerbund, and it was another hour before she fell asleep. They had travelled for four hours and the terrain began to change as the road moved further away from the forest. Gone was the promise of concealment afforded by the trees. But providentially, the sun had begun to set at this time, and while its orange glow would bathe the horizon for a good while yet, a coolness had begun to descend upon the earth.

Still, the threat remained, for although the darkness would conceal them somewhat, it would also conceal a foe that approached. They had no other option, however, but to continue to ride, stopping only once to give the child the remainder of the contents of the bottle. Their case was now desperate for with the milk gone, they would need to reach some human settlement quickly. It was not until eleven o' clock that night that they reached Pilhibeat, fatigued and worn from their day's undertakings. The city was surrounded by dense jungles. Still, they became aware of it a great while before they reached it, for the lights from fires within it lit up the night air, hovering like a halo upon the city and causing it to stand out like a beacon against the blackness of the night.

As they approached, they marvelled at how bright the light was that emanated from within, realizing soon, that the city was yet awake and alive, as people milled around dozens of campfires that appeared to be lit on streets and squares. That this was no ordinary night was quickly apparent, for instead of a lone night watchman who habitually proclaimed the hour and the state of wellbeing in the streets as he made his rounds, there appeared to be some sort of guard posted at the fringes of the city, with four men marching to and fro in each direction. The night air was filled with the acrid odour of smoke and with the sounds of a multitude of men arguing, exulting and declaring their thoughts on something of importance. That the news of the revolt had reached here was obvious, but what was unclear was the extent of the turbulence. Had the men of the city taken up arms against the government, or was the guard posted an indication of its defence against potential rebels?

Standing silently in the invisibility offered by the blackness of the night, the three men stared intently at the tableau in their view. Their horses, smelling the smoke, and rightly divining the signs of battle stood alert and restless. Davenport sensed danger but was willing to confront it for he had much at stake. However, he was not inclined at the present moment to rush into battle unless he could be very certain indeed of a favourable outcome.

Unflinching courage was natural to his disposition, as when he had flung himself at the tigress that threatened Miss. Hardingham on that *shikar* that seemed to have taken place a lifetime ago. What was infernally difficult for him was to shirk from danger, as he did now, for although he felt no fear for his own life, he wished at this moment, above all else, as he sensed the desperation in the air, to emerge from this ordeal unscathed. He must stay alive, and ascertain the fate of his sister. He realized also that the two men who had willingly followed him thus far would plunge into any peril unquestioningly at his behest. A sense of obligation and restraint flooded him and when Kartar Singh, as he was wont to do, urged that they proceed towards the city, he shook his head saying that they must think over this course of action very carefully indeed. The men barely concealed their impatience at his hesitation, with the intolerance of fearless men who are unaccustomed to caution.

'We have gone from village to village with you and you have been safe with us. Sitting under this tree in the darkness of the night will not get us closer to the *memsahib*. We should proceed with haste, and employ the ruse we have thus far,' chided Kartar Singh.

'That would very likely earn us a beheading. Take care, for it is not a few brigands we face now, but a city filled with armed men who carry themselves as those who have a taste for blood. Give me time to think and do not clutter my ears and thoughts with your rash ideas, for we will need our wits as much as we do our hands in this battle!' returned Davenport somewhat sharply.

Makkhan Singh looked at the *sahib* with great surprise, for he had never rebuked either of them in the past. He prepared to lay a restraining hand on Kartar Singh's arm as that rash young man stiffened. But happily, the man was at last possessed of good sense and restrained himself as he sensed that Davenport would not be trifled with.

After a space of fifteen minutes, Davenport offered, 'Let us keep to the darkness and go around the city, looking for unguarded entrances into it. If we cannot find one, we will return and stick to our plan of declaring ourselves as mutineers. But I wish to know which way the wind blows here before we place ourselves in peril. Realize too, that the infant's presence makes ours harder to explain.'

The men nodded and staying as far from the light as they could and making use of the dense forest cover on the outskirts of the city, silently inched their way around. The access to the city was not restricted to the large gates in the front. Looming in the distance was the northernmost of the four gates constructed by the Moghul *soobedar*, Ali Mohammed Khan, who ruled this place over a hundred years ago. Named the Jahanabadi *darwaza*, it was a magnificent edifice, rising over seventy feet into the air, with domes and minarets that gleamed in the night fires. Thankful for the light reflected from within, they realized that the northeastern aspect of the city provided a much easier access into the city even as the guard here was thinly spread, for no one anticipated an incursion from the direction of the jungle that stood there. Walls loomed in front of them that were high enough to ward off wild beasts from the jungle, but these could easily be scaled by three determined men. They moved closer to the city, relatively undetectable now, for the walls concealed their approach and no one sat atop them to monitor the city from this aspect of it.

They could hear the chatter of men within but these were drowned out by occasional shouts and sounds of explosions from within. Handing the sleeping infant to Makkhan Singh and hoisting himself over Kartar Singh's shoulders, Davenport cautiously glimpsed over the walls and noted to his great satisfaction that the guards appeared to be sitting around a fire at a distance of approximately fifty feet. What was greatly encouraging was that they appeared to be drinking heartily and several danced around the fire and made many speeches. From his vantage point, he spied a cluster of small houses on the right, perhaps some forty feet away. One of them was a guardhouse, for it stood beside a small gate that was built into the wall and allowed access for horses. A stable stood not far away and it was rapidly becoming apparent that the area was comprised of homes for the guards.

Descending from his perch, he whispered to the men that they could enter the city with their horses no more twenty feet away. This was most fortuitous for they were unwilling to leave their mounts unguarded at the jungle's edge. The gate was locked from within, as could be expected, and Davenport, intending to hoist himself over the wall, beckoned to the men to provide him a foothold. However, Makkhan Singh firmly pushed him aside, and thrusting the infant back in his arms, assisted Kartar Singh up instead. Once inside, the revelry in the city ensured that he and the two men noiselessly entering the city remained undetected, despite his having to force the lock open with a large stone.

CHAPTER SEVEN

AT SHAHJEHANPORE

The infant who had been awakened when removed from her comfortable position in Davenport's cummerbund uttered a sleepy cry, but the noise of excited conversation arising from the men seated around the fire was too great for it to be heard. Davenport cradled her comfortingly as they stayed close to the shadows and darted between the tiny homes, making their way to a street on the other side of the houses. They had chosen their entry well and this part of the city was fairly deserted. As they came to the end of the street, they found themselves standing before a palatial house, surrounded by imposing walls.

The street ended at this house and it was evidently the home of a Moghul official of some importance as evidenced by the size of the home and the stately marble gateposts whereon stood elegant inscriptions in Persian. A house of this size was bound to be guarded and yet, it appeared to be entirely deserted and only a few flickers of light emerged from latticed windows in the distance. Peering through the gates, they saw large gardens, fountains and an orchard, which extended outside the boundary walls, on their left. A house this large was certain to contain a supply of food, and once its walls were scaled, it could be effortlessly penetrated without detection. The circumstance of the road ending at this house made it a choice target, unlike the tiny homes that dotted the street earlier, where they would be sure to awaken the inhabitants as well as their neighbours, should they attempt to enter them.

After ensuring that no one was within sight or sound, they tethered their horses to the mango trees outside, well out of sight of the street, and with some difficulty, managed to scale the wall. It was easy enough for Kartar Singh to climb up, hoisted by the others. It was Makkhan Singh who had the greatest difficulty in climbing, as he did not have anyone to assist him below. With the aid of ropes that the other two men had let down, he reached the top with considerable effort. Hauling a large man atop a wall by means of jute ropes, with an infant affixed to one's back by means of a cummerbund, is no mean feat, and Davenport struggled for a moment to regain his breath, as his hand, injured by the sword earlier that day, began to bleed again. They could not afford exposure, however, and tightening bandage across his palm, he moved quickly, jumping into the compound within, followed by the men.

The child rudely jolted thus began to protest and for the next few moments, exposure seemed imminent. However, no sound came from the house and Davenport desperately attempted to calm her.

She whimpered and fussed, causing Makkhan Singh to declare with an agitated whisper, 'She will cause us to be caught, *Sahib*!'

Taking her from Davenport's arms, he rocked her with the expertise of one who had rocked his own offspring a long time ago, and before long, she became quiet again. Making their way towards the house, they realized that it had appeared deceptively close to the walls because of its largeness. In reality, it was close to a half mile away from the walls, allowing the infant's cries to remain undetected. As they reached halfway, Makkhan Singh suggested that to avoid courting the risk of detection should the child take up a wail again, he would remain in the gardens while they proceeded to enter the home and obtain some refreshment.

Thinking this a sound strategy, Davenport and Kartar Singh proceeded towards the rear of the house, which was more likely to house the kitchen. To their surprise, as they rounded the corner, they were confronted with another wall which prevented their access into the rear of the house. This wall, however, was conveniently in possession of a gate that was unlocked and upon entering within, the men found themselves in another garden that was filled with a profusion of flowers, the scent of which clung to the midnight air.

'It is the *zenana*,' Kartar Singh said, with a sudden flash of insight.

Davenport nodded with sudden comprehension. He knew that the *zenana* was a customary feature of a Musselman household, but had never imagined himself entering one. For that matter, neither had Kartar Singh, for entry into the *zenana* in a Musselman home was strictly forbidden to all males except the immediate relatives of the women within. Thankfully, there were no women to be seen at the moment. As they approached the house from this aspect, they heard a series of chirps from the verandah. In the moonlight that bathed the marble walls and floors, they saw cages of birds one of which had been awakened by their approach.

At the same time, they heard sounds from without the *zenana* walls. A heavy set of iron gates appeared to be opening in the distance, filling the night air with a deep groan.

Almost immediately, Makkhan Singh entered the *zenana* gardens, saying in an urgent whisper, 'It appears that the men have returned. I saw seven or eight of them enter on horseback through the main gates. There were four servants on foot.'

Taking stock of the situation, Davenport calmly said, 'Make sure to shut the gate to this garden, for no one will expect anyone to be hiding here in the *zenana*. We shall be quite safe here for the present moment, at least.'

He was partially correct, for although no one suspected the presence of intruders in the *zenana*, the current tumult in the city caused the men of the household sufficient anxiety to send a servant to ensure that the *zenana* was secure. This worthy retainer, when he saw the gate unlocked, entered within to ensure that all was well within the gardens. Having heard his approach—for he lustily sang to himself as he walked up the path—Davenport cast about desperately for a place to hide, when he spied a large, half-shut window by the verandah. With the same mixture of quick thinking and brazen courage that he had displayed at the *shikar,* he thrust the large window open and stepped within, beckoning to the two men to follow and shutting it after they did so.

They were not a moment too soon, for the man who had been dispatched to secure the *zenana* had at that same moment entered its gardens, and casting a cursory glance around him, he quit the garden, taking care to shut and lock the gate behind him. As the heavy iron key clicked audibly in the lock, the men realized they were trapped—and in the women's apartments, no less! No matter how fine a tale they fabricated to explain their incursion into the house, their very presence in this area would indicate the deepest malevolence on their part. At that moment, they heard a sound from their right, emerging from the interior of the house. A dim light appeared through the doorway, as if finding its way through several corridors and they realized that they stood in a drawing-room.

They could see divans spread across the room and cushioned seats and pillows dotted the floors. Great glass lamps stood on the floor and, catching the tiny flicker of light through the doorway, appeared to come alive. They made ready to hasten back into the garden when they realized that the window, which they had pulled firmly shut, was stiff and would not give way without some violence, which would certainly alert whoever was approaching, to their presence. The light in the doorway was steadily getting brighter and in the distance, the jingle of bangles and anklets could be heard.

Aroused from her sleep by the men who had returned to the house, the woman who approached was a maid who had also been dispatched to ensure that the *zenana* entrance had been secured. She had taken to leaving the large window in the drawing-room open, for when shut, it became stiff and impossible to open again and it was a great nuisance when the women had to leave this section of the house and the men had to be called in to force it open. That put the eldest mistress out of humour and she was apt to berate all the maids then. She bitterly reflected to herself that she was harangued when the room became stiflingly hot when the windows were shut, and then she was harangued when the men had to be called to pry it open, and now, she had been aroused rudely and ordered to ensure it was firmly shut. And worse, she would surely be harangued the next morning when the mistress found the room too hot! She was quick to admit to herself, however, that it wasn't her own mistress who berated her, but rather her mother-in-law, the senior most member of the *zenana* and the one who ruled it with an iron hand. She was the one who kept the women in the harem—there were four wives and a multitude of maids—in check. Her own mistress, Zeenat Begum was by far the kindest and arguably the fairest woman in the household—and her husband's favourite. But sadly, she was childless, a circumstance that cast a shadow on her consequence and although none of the younger women dared accord her the slightest disrespect, she spent less and less time these days in the company of the other women, choosing instead to retreat to her own rooms, in the company of none of the maids save this particular one, Noor-un-Nissa. But being her mistress' favourite maid counted for nothing, for she had been roused anyway, and age and consequence seemed to matter little these days, she thought bitterly, as she made her way to the drawing-room.

She stopped suddenly, hearing a sound in the distance. So faint was it that she was fairly sure that she had imagined it, when she heard it again, emerging from the kitchen, which was at the end of the long corridor outside the room to the right of the drawing-room. For a moment, her heart stood still and then took to pounding wildly in her ears, so that she could hear nothing though she strained to catch the tiniest sound. She hesitated, wondering whether to turn and flee. However, at thirty and having been a longtime member of the household, she was acutely concerned about her prominence. She saw herself as someone of stature amongst the other vacuous females who had been added to the retinue of servants. She did not wish to flee like a headless chicken to the interior apartments, unless she was sure there was danger.

Besides, if there was nothing there—and she had heard almost nothing—no one would take kindly to being scared out of their wits in the middle of the night, and that would give the other unintelligent females enough fodder for gossip. No, she must make sure she had indeed heard something. So she stood still, with bated breath, for what seemed like an eternity and then she heard the smallest whimper and what sounded very much like a mew.

Her knotted brows relaxed and with clenched teeth she muttered, 'Curse that cat! And that good-for-nothing cook, she has probably left the window open in the kitchen and now I have almost been killed with fear,' quite forgetting that it was very likely through the window that *she* herself had left open in the drawing-room, that the feline had probably entered.

She marched into the drawing-room, undaunted now, and as the light from her lamp filled the room, saw to her great surprise, that the window was shut firmly. She was sure that she was the last maid to leave after the ladies had finished their game of *shatranj* that day, and could not remember having shut it, but it did not preoccupy her a great deal. For her mind was now occupied with thoughts of triumph, for it was the ruinous cook who had let the cat in, and not herself. With a triumphant gleam in her eye, she marched down the corridor towards the kitchen, muttering threats under her breath rapidly. Standing at the threshold of the kitchen, she glanced around, but saw nothing amiss. Nevertheless, she was a persistent woman and raising her lamp towards her face, she strode in purposefully, swinging the partly opened door inwards, and noting that it swung partly back as if obstructed by something behind it.

Aha! There's that accursed cat, she thought, starting to swing around the door, when she felt a vice-like clamp around her mouth and around her person.

At the same time, she felt the lamp being grabbed out of her hands. She struggled wildly, but was no match for whatever had her in its grasp. Superstitious as most women in India are, she felt a great terror descend upon her, for she was sure that a devil had her in its grasp and would devour her on the spot, when, out of the corner of her eye, she caught sight of Davenport. This caused her to cease her struggle somewhat, and she felt an inexplicable sense of relief that it was a mere man standing before her. However, the terror came rushing back as she realized that their intentions were surely vile. To her horror, another man—Kartar Singh—appeared, approaching her with a drawn scimitar. But he was quickly thwarted by the tall man she had seen first.

Addressing her in chaste Hindustani, the tall man said quietly, 'Do not fear, for we mean no harm. Please do not scream. We do not wish to hurt you, but if you do scream, we will be forced to restrain you! Will you remain quiet if we release you?'

She glared at him with enraged eyes, when Kartar Singh interjected softly, '*He* means you no harm, but *I* would be glad to slit your throat.'

So malevolent was his voice and manner that she froze in terror and became limp.

'Stop it! She is a woman and we ought not to terrorize her thus, having broken into her home. Listen, Sister, we wish you no harm. We only came hither to seek food. We have taken nothing and shall leave with nothing but half a *seer* of milk, for which we shall gladly pay you,' Davenport pleaded.

A look of suspicion and derision filled her eyes and finally, exasperated by Davenport's unwillingness to frighten her into submission and entirely mistrustful of her, Kartar Singh came nearer and deftly gagged her with his cummerbund. So terrified of him was she that she did not so much as breathe as he completed the exercise. He then proceeded to shut the door and secure it from within, dropping the large bar that served as its bolt. Satisfied that she would not be able to alert the remainder of the household, Makkhan Singh relaxed his hold on her and she rubbed her hands to allow the blood to flow back into them. She glanced in the direction of where the knives were kept, but in a voice akin to a growl, Kartar Singh promised her that she would not live to see another day if she so much as twitched a muscle.

When Davenport said, 'We should move fast, for she will soon be missed,' her eyes glinted maliciously.

Still, she did not dare move, for Kartar Singh hovered over her, scimitar drawn. She looked away from him, for he was truly fearsome, when, to her astonishment, she saw as Davenport turned his back to her, a young infant strapped to his back. Makkhan Singh had busied himself around the kitchen and finally, in a corner, in a large earthen pot of cold water, they found several small pots filled with milk. Taking only one pot, as he had promised, Davenport, to the woman's great surprise, proceeded to feed the infant who had become quite awake by now.

Perhaps it was because they hurriedly fed her, she choked a little, and they stared at her in panic. When patting her head did not relieve her, Davenport looked at the men, alarm creeping into his eyes. The woman, quite forgetting herself and the danger she was in, moved closer, and gesturing to them crossly, took the child out of Davenport's hands and held her upright, resting her head on her shoulder and tapping her back gently, until the choking fit had passed. Kartar Singh who had been momentarily distracted by the infant's distress was upon her in a trice, dagger drawn, but was restrained by Davenport who had sensed accurately that she had come to aid the infant. Before very long, she gestured to Davenport to take off her gag and despite the reservations of the others, he nodded and proceeded to do so. She seemed unable to speak for her lips were sorely bruised from having been gagged so severely. Once she had recovered the power of speech, however, there was no stopping her, as they soon found out.

After berating them for injuring her mouth thus and declaring that never in her life had she, Noor-un-Nissa, been subjected to such abuse, not even at the hands of *badi begum*, she demanded to know who they were and who the child was. A redoubtable and most unusual woman, she did not seem to want to scream anymore, so intrigued was she by the sight of the babe they held. Davenport quietly informed her that they had found it on the way and its parents were dead. For some reason, he did not wish to deceive her, for her genuine concern for the child pleased him and he was sure that a woman who could forget her own peril to aid an infant she had never set eyes on before, must truly be a rare one indeed!

'But,' she demanded, 'why did you see fit to break into the *haveli* to procure milk? Surely you could have obtained some from the market? Decent men do not break into respectable homes and then proceed to enter the *zenana* of all places, and then harass innocent and weak women like myself, do they? Surely you are not good men! How could you be, having behaved in such a shabby manner?'

Kartar Singh, tired of her relentless harangue, begged to be allowed to slit her throat, while Makkhan Singh firmly declared that she would have to be gagged again. However, by now, she had lost her fear of them, for she realized that they would have surely killed her twenty minutes ago, were they so ill intentioned. And, men who broke into houses to steal a half *seer* of milk for an orphan they had picked up on the way could not be so wicked, after all.

'Be quiet! First you steal from me, and then you try to puff your chest out at me?!' she scolded.

Entirely taken aback by this line of attack, the men meekly obeyed. While they would not think twice to face a charging tiger unarmed, a nagging woman was quite another matter.

Davenport chuckled and then, in response to her statement, said more seriously, 'You must know of the unrest that has taken hold of the city. I did not dare take such a tiny infant into the tumult. I had promised her mother that I would save her life. Do you know of any place where I may safely leave her?' he asked.

She had avoided looking at him directly thus far, for it would be altogether too immodest for a woman to look into the eyes of a strange man. When he said this, however, she looked directly at him, and having met his eyes, continued to stare at him with a strange expression as he spoke, a thought dawning on her suddenly.

'Wait here. I shall be back presently. Do not make a sound, for the men are yet awake and are presently ensuring that the house is secure. If you try to leave, you will surely encounter the watchman who has been posted within the walls,' she said in an urgent tone.

Makkhan Singh stood in her path, barring her way as she approached the door. But the woman insisted that he get out of her way at once, before all the men descended upon them, which they were very likely to do, since she had been gone for a good while. Seeing the wisdom in her words, Davenport nodded to him to let her pass.

'What if she sounds the alarm, *Sahib*, he asked,' biting his tongue even as he spoke, realizing that he had betrayed Davenport by addressing him thus.

But the woman said nothing, and when Davenport asked what she had planned for them, she merely told him that he would have to wait and see. Makkhan Singh reluctantly stepped aside. He did not wish to kill such a fine specimen of a woman, but the moment she was out of earshot, he urged Davenport that they should make themselves scarce for they could not risk placing their lives in her hands.

Davenport looked uncertainly at him, pointing out that she had informed them that the compound was now being guarded by a watchman. Still, he agreed that it was entirely too risky to await imminent capture and certain death. They might be forgiven for most crimes, but certainly not for the one of invading a *zenana*! They made their way to the drawing-room when, to their horror, through the window, they saw men standing in the garden, torches in their hand.

'She has betrayed us. Why did you not let me silence her when we had the chance?' Kartar Singh demanded through clenched teeth.

They withdrew back to the kitchen and looked for means of escape. The window there was small and would certainly not permit a grown man passage. Helpless, they prepared themselves to fight their way out, as they heard the woman return. Certain that she had brought someone with her, they charged towards the door, but to their surprise, found that she was quite alone.

'Follow me!' she commanded.

But, the men did not budge.

'Do you think we are foolish enough to follow you to our deaths? And are the men of your household wearing bangles and hiding in the harem, that they send a woman to do their job? No! You go back and tell the men who sent you and the ones lurking about in the garden that if they want us, they must come and get us, whoever gets past the threshold alive, that is,' said Makkhan Singh angrily.

The effect of this proclamation on her was quite the opposite of what they had expected. Remaining quite unfazed, she proceeded to scold them for leaving the kitchen when she had told them not to, and for being so obtuse. Did she not need a ruse so that she could guide them out through another part of the house? Yes, she had sent the men there claiming to have heard a sound because they would all congregate out there and the rest of the house would remain unguarded! The *zenana* garden had been locked from the outside, and they would need to find another escape anyway. Now, did they want to help the child and find her a refuge or not?

This last question succeeded in arresting their attention, and despite his present suspicions of the circumstances, Davenport, upon weighing his options, felt that following her would be the most prudent course of action. They found themselves passing through several corridors and walking through several large and stately rooms with yards of muslin curtains which fluttered as they moved past them, past fountained courtyards, and up several flights of stairs, when at last, they found themselves standing in front of a large *purdah* that hung from the ceiling and that was made of an exceedingly opulent fabric with gold and silver threads woven into it.

Noor un Nissa coughed and a soft voice from within said, 'Enter!'

She parted the curtain, making room for them to pass, but the men were reluctant to do so. They had evidently reached the boudoir of some woman of consequence and they did not wish to be trapped in that sanctum sanctorum. But, the woman pushed them in, urgently whispering that they risked the chance of being seen if they stood gawking in the hallway.

Inside, the room was only dimly lit and Davenport noted that it was richly furnished with muslins and silks of the finest quality while a profusion of Persian rugs graced the floor. The scent of perfume filled the air and on a large cushion on the floor, and leaning on a great number of pillows, sat a woman, with a bejeweled dagger in her hands. Averting their eyes instantly, the men bowed in greeting and the woman's demeanour became more relaxed.

'My maid informs me that you have a child with you that you wish to get rid of,' she stated directly in soft but firm accents.

'Not precisely, *Begum sahiba*,' returned Davenport. 'She was left in my care when her mother died and we have been taking care of her, but three men are unfit to nurse a child of such tender years, so we wished to find a safe refuge for her. To that end, I am willing to pay for her care.'

The woman laughed softly, saying, 'So, my maid was right: you are indeed an English *sahib* trying to escape this tumult and finding it hard to do so, saddled with a babe. Tell me, is she yours, or did you kill her parents? Is it guilt that makes you carry her about?'

At this, the three men turned to look at her in great astonishment. That their ruse had been uncovered by two women in a *zenana* was greatly troubling. How could they hope to escape detection by the sepoys they would undoubtedly encounter?

'Did I not say it was a trap?' growled Makkhan Singh and he and Kartar Singh placed themselves in front Davenport with their scimitars drawn.

'Do not be so foolish! A sneeze from me would bring the entire household here and none of you, including that child would leave this room alive,' she said contemptuously.

'How do you know who I am?' Davenport asked quietly.

'My maid recognized you were a *firangi* when she looked in your eyes. You are dressed and appear as shabby and lowborn as them and your speech is as one of us, and yet, your man called you a *sahib*. You offered me money for the child's care, and yet, you appear desperately poor. You are able to pay for the child to be cared for, and yet, you steal milk to nourish it. Shall I go on?' she asked.

'No, you have explained the matter quite satisfactorily,' said Davenport averting his eyes again. 'But allow me to enlighten you,' he continued, 'I am not fleeing this tumult. Rather, I am making my way through it to find my sister who may be in mortal peril. I did not kill the child's parents, but some *zameendar's* men did, men perhaps not unlike those in this household. Finally, I did not offer *you* money for her care, but thought you might know someone in your household who wishes to take a child in, for I thought that was why you invited me here. But, perhaps I mistook your intentions! Why *did* you invite me here?' he asked with a glint in his eye.

She paused, greatly astonished by this unlikely Englishman and at the strange circumstances surrounding him. His words and his actions had hinted a man of most noble character, and yet, the tales she heard everyday told of myriads of hardships perpetuated by those of his race on hers. She mistrusted him, but as she gazed at the child he held in his arms so tenderly, her yearnings overcame her and she finally relented.

'I summoned you here to ask you how much money you wanted to part with the child. But now, I am simply begging you to give me that infant, for you have no use for a child and I am childless,' she said, spreading her veil before her as she spoke, in a symbol of entreaty.

Taken aback, Davenport looked at her with puzzlement. How would she explain the sudden appearance of a child to the household?

'I will keep her hidden in my rooms until noon. I shall say in the morning that I have a headache and do not wish to be disturbed. I shall permit no one to enter my chamber. In the meantime, I shall send Noor-un-Nissa to the *dargah* to offer prayers for me in the morn. When she returns, it shall be with a bundle in her arms. She will proceed directly to my room in a state of agitation, and after a suitable length of time has passed, I shall call out for all the women to make haste and come hither. When they are arrived, I shall say that a *fakir* delivered the child to her, and she then brought her to me, knowing how greatly I desire a child. Have no fear, I shall raise her as my own child and will not let a hair on her head be harmed. Give me this child, Englishman, for she can be of no use to you, and my arms ache to hold a child.'

So fixed and assured did she seem in her plan, and her words so compelling and uttered in tones so plaintive, that Davenport handed her the infant without any further hesitation. Watching her as she gazed at the now sleeping infant and tenderly caressed her face, he felt satisfied that placing the child in her custody would be the best course of action.

'It is a good plan you propose, *Begum Sahiba,* and I feel certain that this child could know no better fate, given her present circumstances,' he said softly.

The lady nodded, tears streaming down her cheeks, all former suspicion of the men having disappeared by now. The circumstances they found themselves in could not be forgotten, however, and Noor-un-Nissa abruptly told the men that they should get out now before disaster struck and they were discovered, whereupon, the lady Zeenat added that this was true. She cautioned them that the city of Pilhibeat had received a *paigam* early that morning from Bareilly that the troops there had risen in rebellion against the British, and had now proclaimed the Khan Bahadur Khan Rohilla as their new leader. He was the grandson of the *Nawab* of Bareilly dethroned in battle by the *Nawab* of Oude, with the aid of Warren Hastings, then Governor-General of Bengal. His kingdom, Rohilcund, handed to the *Nawab* of Oude, was soon forfeited to the East India Company when Oude fell greatly behind in its payments of subsidies to the Company. British aid in the time of battle had, as it always did in those days, come at a heavy price for the self-indulgent prince.

At present, it was not entirely astounding that the deposed heir to Rohilcund should join the fray and demand his due when others had raised their voices in revolt. Davenport was troubled by this report, for it indicated that the entire territory they must cross was now embroiled in the insurrection.

The lady Zeenat further warned them, 'Beware that you do not reveal yourself, for the city was in great upheaval this day. It is well that you are disguised as one of your men and your speech, fluent as you are in Hindustani, will not betray that you are English. It is imperative that you do not let anyone discover that you are English, for then, your life would surely be imperiled. The English ruler, the magistrate, fled for his life today, some say to Nainital. Much looting and rioting has occurred today and people will molest any Englishman with impunity. The villages that surround the city have been ransacked. Some say by the *Angrez*, and others say by the *zameendars*. In fact, this afternoon, men rode from Sunpar to tell us that the entire village had been hacked down by they knew not whom. The *Hindoo* menservants were dispatched then, to render aid to those who cremated the dead.'

Noor-un-Nissa nodded, adding 'The men are only just returned from thence and the funeral pyres of those miserable souls shall probably burn till tomorrow, but that is how you managed to gain entry into the house undetected, for even the master has left to discover what transpires in Bareilly.'

At last the mystery of the unknown riders who had approached the village as they journeyed to Pilhibeat was unveiled.

Davenport shook his head, exclaiming, 'What strange and serendipitous circumstances are these! For it was in that very village that we encountered the fiends who unleashed the terror we described and cruelly massacred this unfortunate child's parents. Surely we have been guided by the hand of Providence in coming to the very household where the men have been dispatched to cremate her dead!'

The others nodded their heads in agreement, much struck by this thought. However, Davenport turned his thoughts to their present circumstances. They must not tarry any longer, and thanking the two stalwart women who were now unmistakably well disposed towards them, Davenport begged to be allowed to depart. They were guided by the worthy Noor-un-Nissa through a series of secret passages, through the *mardana*—abandoned tonight, for the men had gone to Bareilly—and then through an underground passageway, cleverly dug into the ground. The end of this passage emerged outside the compound walls, concealed by vines growing on the wall, and into the orchard where the horses stood, grazing peacefully.

The woman had managed to procure some refreshment and this she handed to them as they departed, urging them on before they were heard by the watchman who stood within the walls. Departing the city proved to be far easier than entering it, for they were now familiar with the path they must take and arriving at the point where they had first gained access into it, they slipped out as unobserved as they were when they had entered in, for the *sawars*, now considerably under the influence of spirits, had descended into a deep slumber from which not even the report of a rifle would awake them.

'What dark days these are, *Sahib*,' complained Makkhan Singh, 'for the jungles filled with wild beasts are safer than the cities of men.'

They passed the night in the relative safety of the jungle, eschewing a fire for fear of being spotted from within the city and choosing instead to take turns to man a watch while the others slept. They were awakened by the oppressive heat of the morning and the distant report of muskets. Kartar Singh had taken this last watch and he shook his companions urgently, as the shots rang out. They hurriedly made their way forward, setting their faces towards the city of Shahjehanpore. Hoping to reach the city before it too was infected with rebellion, they rode hard, for a good part of the day, traversing a distance of forty miles. Resting in the jungles, during the night, they navigated the fifteen miles that remained, the following morning, arriving near the city by noon. As before, they hoped to make their approach gradually, skirting the city from the outskirts, and ascertaining whether they may attain safe passage through it, failing which they would undertake to journey circuitously through the jungle.

Although this had allowed them to evade the pandemonium that prevailed in each place, it also served to slow their journey considerably. Danapur was still a good four hundred and thirty miles away. Journeying at the rate they were, it would take the good part of a month before they reached it. This reflection served to lower Davenport's spirits considerably and the result was that he was desperate to ride into the city to make his way speedily through it. Perhaps it was because of this, or perhaps because the good fortune that had attended their way thus far deserted them, but through a great misfortune, they were spotted on their arrival when still in the cover of dense trees. Two woodcutters, having seen the three men on horseback making their way through a meandering path around the city hastened back into it and informed the men within that some suspicious men were seen lurking without, whereupon a troop of twenty horsemen emerged from the city, riding with the utmost urgency and overtook the three men before very long.

Instantly, Davenport found himself flanked by the two men who, shielding his person, prepared to engage the approaching menace. Recognizing that the men were extremely likely to be followed by reinforcements from the city, Davenport adjured his men to stand back in a low voice. They would need to engage their wits to the highest degree, for they were clearly outnumbered. They sheathed their swords and gesticulated a *salaam,* the effect of which was to diminish somewhat the murderous look on the faces of some of the men approaching. As they drew near, their leader demanded with great ferocity who they were. The three men soon found themselves surrounded by men with drawn swords and *lathis.*

Again, their leader, a man of roughly forty-five and wearing regimental uniform, spoke saying, 'Hand over your weapons, or you will be cut to pieces.'

Emboldened by the fact that the lady Zeenat had described his diction as chaste the previous day, Davenport decided to abandon the pretense of muteness that he had adopted before in Sunpar.

'Certainly, *Huzoor*!' he said affably, 'We mean no harm; we simply wish to rest here awhile and then be on our way.'

'Whence do you come?' demanded their leader.

'From the north,' said Davenport, guardedly, adding, 'we did not know that it would cause you offense if we came hither. We shall depart if our presence offends you, *huzoor.*'

His placating manner served to calm the man somewhat, but he remained hostile, demanding to know why they had come there. Unable to diagnose whether the winds of rebellion had blown this far, Davenport cast about in his mind for answer. Should he declare that they had come here fleeing the mutiny? That answer would suffice if the European officers still held the command of their regiment. But, in the event that the uproar had visited this city as well, that answer would cost them their lives, for the mutineers would surely despise any who absconded from embracing their cause.

If he declared that they were mutineers, and the city were still commanded by English officers, he could very easily reveal himself once they were taken in custody. But, if the rebellion had reached this place, the wrong answer would cost them their lives. Recognizing that the men belonged to the 28th Regiment of Native Infantry, the only one likely to be in Shahjehanpore, it flashed through Davenport's mind that there was virtually no possibility of this region having remained uninfected by the malcontent.

'We are here to join the revolt, *Huzoor*. We rode from Pilhibeat. We fought some *Angrez* there. Look what the beast did to my hand,' he said smoothly, showing them his bloodstained and bandaged hand.

The answer satisfied infantryman only partially.

'Why did you not stay there and fight, then?' he asked, his penetrating eyes peering from beneath bushy brows.

With a sinking heart, he realized that the sepoys confronting them had mutinied.

'There was no real army there, *Huzoor,* and no one to fight. So we came here,' he replied.

Before the man could answer, one of the men with him demanded in rough speech why a Hindoo like himself was in the company of the *two dogs* beside him.

Placing a firm restraining hand on Kartar Singh, Davenport spoke in a high plaintive voice of one deeply wronged, 'What are these rash sayings, *Huzoor*? These are men with the courage of lions. Do not speak so unjustly of them for they have killed five *Angrez* between them, but yesterday!'

Makkhan Singh, hand on his sword looked menacingly at the men. So ferocious was his glare that the ones who stood the closest to him backed away a little.

'Why, that is a strange occurrence, indeed,' declared the man who stood the furthest from them. 'For it was but yesterday that a hundred sepoys adhering to the same faith as these two defended the *Angrez* officers. They allowed the women and children to get away, instead of cutting them down to pieces,' declared the man accusingly.

After this awful pronouncement, he spat on the ground, declaring his disgust at the men who had refused to join their just and worthy cause. Davenport, resolutely banishing the images conjured within his mind of his own Jane being in a party thus persecuted, shook his head in horror.

He was prevented from answering by Makkhan Singh who spat with greater vehemence than his antagonist, declaring fiercely, 'Then those men deserve to die! We do not know about those sepoys. We know this, that we are here to do battle against our enemies. Any man who accuses us of lying shall face us and fight us to the death!'

His violent tone, coupled with Davenport's testimony that the men had hacked down five Englishmen the day before served to finally convince the men that they were indeed loyal to the cause of revolt. Having relaxed their hostile stance, they guided the men into the city. So complete was their trust in the men now, that they surrounded them from all sides, eagerly asking for accounts of the scenes of any violence against Europeans. The hope that Davenport bleakly cherished, of riding furiously away, vanished as they were shepherded into the city. Within, it was a scene of great tumult and it became quickly apparent that the city had been witness to a great carnage.

There were men milling all around. Some were inebriated, and the acrid smell of smoke filled the air as several small huts with thatched roofs were ablaze. The act of mutiny, although resulting in the overthrow of a tyrannical power, had unleashed a state of lawlessness and the mutinying sepoys appeared to be halfheartedly preserving the semblance of peace. Muskets were set off every few moments and panicked citizens were seen rushing off to enlist the aid of the sepoys against ruthless pillagers. The grocers appeared worst affected for, everywhere, signs of grain, fabrics and dry goods being looted became apparent. One man desperately cried for help as a drunken sepoy threatened to ravish his daughter. Mercifully, two sepoys rushed to his aid and dragged their intoxicated associate away.

Even so, it was forcefully discernible that pandemonium prevailed, and while some sepoys, believing in the justice of their cause, and seeing themselves engaged in a righteous struggle, clung to some semblance of organized action, many others had simply cast all restraint off, and the abrogation of authority brought to the fore the basest impulses in their nature. There seemed to be a struggle of some sort between the two factions, with no clear tactic visible. They had overthrown the government with ease.

But, when Davenport, with feigned fervour, asked eagerly, 'What do we do next?' not one of the men he encountered had an answer beyond the assertion that they had killed their officers and would kill any others they could lay their hands on.

The day dragged on and the carousing amplified as more and more sepoys succumbed to the seduction of drink. Sitting around campfires on the city square and on the streets, they recounted gaily the atrocities they had committed in the previous days. One boasted that two days ago, he had barged into the church (for it was a Sunday) and had killed the priest of the *Angrez*, cutting off his arm first. He also claimed to have killed the magistrate and his clerk inside the church. This was quickly gainsaid by another sepoy who asserted that the man he slew in the church was not the magistrate. Rather, he had killed the two clerks. It was he himself who had killed the magistrate. This account of the day's events was not accepted without antagonism from the first sepoy, but that boastful man was silenced by the latter when he made the following announcement.

'I have often seen the magistrate spying on us in the past weeks, and being the *Soobedar Major*, the senior most native office here, would I not be more apt to recognize the magistrate rather than you, a lowly sepoy? And what's more, it is I who shot the Captains *sahib* on the parade ground today!' declared the *Soobedar Major* with no small pride.

Thus silenced, the other offered no rebuttal.

'What became of the rest?' Davenport enquired.

'One ran to the vegetable patch to hide. The villagers cut him down with pickaxes. We invaded the cantonment, but the women and the children had all taken shelter in the church. We went to get our muskets when they locked themselves within, for the officer present there began to discharge his weapons. They fled from hence in carriages, but we were not able to destroy them, as the Sikh sepoys stood around their carriages, preventing us from attacking them,' came the reply.

'It was not just the Sikh sepoys who hindered us. Even the *sahibs'* servants hastened to the church with their rifles to attack us,' declared another bitterly. 'Had it not been for these traitors, we would have eliminated every single one of the *Angrez* here today!' he continued.

'You are fortunate that at least the villagers from the area are honourable and have aided you in destroying them!' Makkhan Singh remarked, with feigned sympathy.

'That is true,' he was told, 'for the villages have been destroyed by the *Angrez*. Our *zameendars* have lost their lands and the villages that have lived in their benevolent shadow and patronage for centuries have been broken into smaller *jagirs* and sold off to other landlords, who neither know nor care about the condition of the villages they now own. These new landlords are cruel and indifferent to the hardships of the villagers. And then there is the matter of the revenues they demand. It is no wonder that all share their hatred of the *Angrez*!'

By far, this was the only reasonable explanation for the mayhem that had ensued in these parts, and while Davenport was deeply sympathetic to the legitimacy of these claims, it perturbed him greatly that the people who had been killed, while certainly acting as representatives of the government, were none of them personally responsible for the outrages perpetuated on the peasants or the sepoys. None of those who had made uncaring and coldblooded decisions were near enough to the heat of the battle to be singed by its fires. Many of them had retired to Britain and were enjoying the wealth they had accrued from India. And sadder yet was the fact that women and children who had nothing whatsoever to do with these matters, were drawn in as pawns in a deadly game.

'What became of the women and children?' Davenport asked at last, when he could bring himself to speak.

He was told that while one—whose husband had been shot—was injured, the rest had fled, with the aid of the perfidious sepoys loyal to them.

A sense of relief flooded him until one of the sepoys said, 'They will not get very far. I heard today that the Raja of Powain whose refuge they have fled to in Oude has refused them shelter.'

This announcement was met with a rousing ovation by the men. Powain was little under a day's journey. Surely they could be overtaken and cut down as they attempted to seek shelter elsewhere? Plans began to be drawn up, and to his great horror, Davenport found himself being included in them. Providentially, the sepoys were far too intoxicated to make coherent plans and Davenport, signalling the men to stay alert, bided his time.

They hoped to steal away when an opportune moment presented itself. However, none presented itself for a very long time. For, although many sepoys had collapsed in a drunken stupor, many others remained vigilant. Sitting around campfires, they talked of rebellion. In hushed tones, they spoke of the great Khan Bahadur Khan who had now proclaimed himself the ruler of Rohilcund. There was also talk of visits to Shajahanpur by Nana Sahib, *Peshwe* of the Marathas and by the *Ranee* of Jhansi, Laxmi Bai.

It was impossible for Davenport to ascertain whether they had already visited the city, or whether they planned to visit it soon. Not wanting to seem unduly curious, he contented himself with whatever morsels of information fell on his ears. He leaned back against a pile of straw, closing his eyes in silent prayer. When he opened them, it was early morning and Makkhan Singh was urging him under his breath to awaken quickly. Bewildered as he accustomed himself to his surroundings, he soon became aware of a great deal of activity around him.

'Awaken quickly, lazy one, we must go afar today. And you and your companions shall ride with us and prove your words, whether they be true or not!' declared a sepoy with great zest.

Begging to be allowed to freshen himself first, Davenport made his way to the well nearby, followed by Kartar Singh.

As he splashed some water across his face, he heard Kartar Singh caution in an urgent whisper, 'Beware, *Sahib*, the colour is changing on your palms. Take care that you do not wash away the dye.'

Hastily dabbing himself, Davenport asked where they were being led to.

To his relief, Kartar Singh replied, 'To Sitapore.'

Sitapore was fifty miles away and definitely in the direction they were following.

His relief was short lived, however, as Kartar Singh announced, 'The English who fled from here and who were denied refuge by the Raja of Powain are believed to be proceeding in the direction of Sitapore. These men aim to overtake them and slay them.'

Davenport stood frozen for a brief moment, but then, with an impassive countenance, mounted his horse as their leader bellowed for him to hurry. Riding in silence, a profusion of thoughts churned through his mind. This was possibly the hour when his mettle would be tested to the greatest degree. Denouement was now inevitable, for they could not continue to maintain their stance of mutineers. They must, with all their might, defend any women and children they overtook, and that end seemed unachievable, riding as they were with a troop of over a hundred men.

However, the element of surprise might work in their favour and if they were dispersed amongst the sepoys, it was conceivable that they could generate the illusion of a breaking away among the ranks and in the confusion, manage to delay the inevitable. But, he did not feel very secure that they would indeed manage to escape alive. He communicated to his two companions that when they reached Sitapore, they should disperse themselves among the crowd of revolting sepoys and generate as much of mayhem within the ranks as possible, as that was their only hope of providing any assistance whatsoever to the hapless wretches they came ever nearer to with each passing hour.

Makkhan Singh, however had plans of his own. He had vowed when they set out from Simla, to guard the *sahib's* life, and this he proposed to do, with all his power, even if it required that they disobey his orders. Die they must, but he privately resolved that he himself would do so defending the *sahib*. Wisely refraining from gainsaying, he nodded his head and conveyed quietly to Kartar Singh that under no circumstance were they to leave the *sahib's* side. Reaching Sitapore, they discovered, to their joy, that the European women and children had indeed reached there, but had departed the day before, in the direction of Aurangabad. The sepoys were sorely disappointed at the loss of their quarry and some talked of pursuing them in that direction.

'We should wait till daybreak, perhaps. For, the horses have travelled far today,' suggested Davenport, in a self-deprecating manner.

He was angrily brushed aside by the *Soobedar Major* who had led the expedition thus far.

'Do not be giving us advice on these matters, for we are far more experienced in battle than you!' he declared imperiously.

'It is as you say, *Huzoor*,' said Makkhan Singh hastily, 'but the English women are surely accompanied, by now, by more men who would have joined their party from these parts. If we wait until morning, they will surely be overtaken easily, for I am certain that none of them shall sleep peacefully this night. Nor will they venture to travel in the night. No! I am certain that when we overtake them, they shall be worn out, and ripe for the picking. Their loot that they no doubt carry must surely slow them down.'

The *Soobedar Major* was disinclined to give weight to words from men he had not proved, but his words seemed judicious. English women and children, in his experience, were extremely delicate and would certainly not have managed to traverse very far without the escort of their men. That they were possessed by great terror and would not sleep a wink that night was also entirely reasonable. They would surely have the advantage if they pursued them tomorrow, having had the benefit of a restful night's sleep themselves. Besides, he did not at all feel certain that they should proceed as far west as Aurangabad, for they had not received news of whether the British had been completely overthrown there. Undecided as to the best course of action, he ordered the men to set up camp, but they seemed reluctant to do so, distracted by the promise of treasure. They had mutinied once and to do so again would not be very farfetched. However, the *Soobedar Major* retained some prominence in the men's eyes and after much haranguing on his part, the men decided to settle down for a night's rest.

'Shall I fetch some food and water for you from a home nearby, *Huzoor*?' Kartar Singh enquired genially.

The *Soobedar Major* agreed, dismissing him with a curt nod. Kartar Singh made his way down a narrow street, apparently looking for a grocer, or even for a home where they could obtain a few *rotis*. The scene at Sitapore appeared vastly different from the one at Shahjehanpore the night before. The streets were deserted, and no one answered the knock on their doors. Perhaps this was due to the lateness of the hour, or perhaps due to the fear of looting. When he did not return for half an hour, Makkhan Singh and Davenport began to walk in the direction he had gone, when they were accosted by some sepoys, who demanded to know where they were headed.

'Our friend has not returned, and we are afraid that some harm has befallen him,' said Makkhan Singh.

'Or worse, that he has stumbled on drink, for he is quite a drunk!' interjected Davenport with chagrin.

The *Soobedar Major* appeared to be satisfied with this explanation, but as soon as the men left, he ordered a handful of men to follow them. The two men proceeded to walk down a narrow street, the light from their lanterns casting long shadows before them. When quite out of view of the rest, they proceeded to extinguish the light from their lanterns. Standing in complete darkness, they quickly stepped into the shadows, standing frozen, until their eyes became accustomed to the blackness of the night.

They realized that they were standing in a street lined with houses on one side and a large cattle shed on the other; to the right of the cattle shed, there appeared to be an open field, lined with trees that began at the cattle shed and made their way to about a quarter of a mile. Guessing that Kartar Singh had either taken refuge in the cattle shed or proceeded to the shelter of the trees, they approached the cattle shed cautiously. There was no indication that anyone was present within. Makkhan Singh prepared to call out in a low voice when Davenport squeezed his arm, dragging him inside the shed. Listening with bated breath, Davenport felt quite certain that he had heard a sound without. For what seemed like an eternity, but was in reality no more than five minutes, they stood with bated breath, hearing nothing but the sound of their own hearts beating rapidly. The cattle, although largely calm at their intrusion, uttered low calls. Could the sound have emanated from the cattle?

Deciding that he was mistaken, Davenport prepared to call out for Kartar Singh, when they heard a man speak in a low tone, saying, 'They have disappeared. We haven't seen their lanterns for some time now. We should go back to the *Soobedar Major*.'

Another interjected, 'No, we should pursue them now, for they will escape before we return and then the *Soobedar Major* will strip our hides.'

'Perhaps some harm has befallen them,' suggested another, with some fear in his voice.

'No, that cannot be, for surely we would have heard some signs of a struggle as their lanterns went out?' objected the first.

Suddenly, there was some commotion outside, and the men began speaking all at once.

'What was that sound? It came from behind me,' said one man in an agitated voice.

'Where did Hari Charan go?' asked another in a fearful voice.

They did not attempt to conceal their presence anymore. It appeared as if some scuffle had taken place and one of their party had disappeared. It was entirely possible that the man had headed back to the safety of the troop while the others were arguing, but the men appeared to be rather panicked over a sound they had heard.

'It is Kartar Singh,' whispered Davenport. 'And somehow, he has managed to get rid of one of the men. There remain only three now. Perhaps we can overcome them?' he suggested.

Before they could act, there was a shout and someone fell to the ground with a great thud.

'Light your lantern!' shouted the man outside to his only remaining companion. 'Someone is trying to kill us!'

The other man lit his lantern and beholding his colleague on the ground, began to run, shouting with all his might, when a dagger speedily dispatched from Makkhan Singh sent him to his death. Davenport quickly overcame the last man with a stunning blow to his head. They surveyed the two men who lay dead and the two who lay senseless, when Kartar Singh emerged from the shadows, urging them quietly that they would need to depart from the city with the utmost haste, for the alarm would be sounded when the men did not return.

'Proceed to the field. But take care to keep to the shadows of the trees,' he said in a low voice.

Dragging the men into the cattle shed, they fled quickly into the fields, which were connected, one with another. Soon, they were near an orchard and at its edge, tied to some mango trees were three horses, whinnying at their approach.

'There was no hope of recovering our own horses which were right at the entrance of the city, *Sahib,* so I stole out of the city and found three horses which belonged to the men at the rear. They had left the horses to graze and had gone inside the city in search of food,' he informed them with pride.

'Well done!' declared Davenport. 'We shall have to make haste, for we shall soon be missed.'

'Which direction shall we proceed in, *Sahib?*' asked Makkhan Singh somewhat unhopefully.

'I have a plan,' replied Davenport with some excitement in his voice. 'I was listening as the men talked of pursuing someone last week and finding it hard to cross some river. Why don't we travel by boat?' he asked.

'But, where will we find a boat?' Makkhan Singh demanded.

'And where is the river exactly?' asked Kartar Singh.

'It is to the east. We shall have to travel a little to reach the River *Chauka.* It is a tributary of the *Gogra.* If we follow it to the River *Gogra,* and remain on that until the confluence, we shall find ourselves on the River *Ganges.* Once we are on the river, we should find ourselves in the vicinity of Danapur in no more than a fortnight. As to how to procure a boat, that is something we shall have to discover when we arrive at the river's edge,' Davenport elaborated.

The plan seemed absurd in its simplicity. There was no time to lose. Ride away from the city as fast as they could, they must. Riding east towards the river seemed logical, for the troops, if they pursued, would not think to go thence. Instead, they would seek them out in the cities and villages around them. Once they reached the open plains, filled with paddy fields and dotted with tiny hamlets on their fringes, they would find themselves relatively safe and out of the cauldron of the mutiny. The river would certainly take them through many cities that were apt to be rife with revolt, but they were no safer on land than on water.

They rode on wordlessly for some miles, grateful for the monotonous landscape that afforded them speed as they rode across the countryside bathed in moonlight. The campfires of the city became increasingly distant as they headed in the direction of the river, whilst Davenport continually consulted his compass. They had lit a lamp now, which they kept underneath Kartar Singh's shawl, for in the dark, even a tiny flicker of light can be seen across a very great distance. Soon, they were rewarded with the sight of the river in the distance, placid and shimmering in the moonlight like a giant enchanted mirror on the earth. The grassy, featureless landscape gave way to arid patches of land and gradually to sandy banks. Davenport wisely decided that they should dismount and make their way to the river banks on foot. As they approached the river, the sandy earth appeared white, and Davenport recognized it as containing *reh*, the salty surface soil that is characteristic of the Ganges plains. Tethered to a sturdy bush, the horses whinnied, nibbling patches of earth for the minerals they contained, seemingly uninterested in the three men walking away. Two boats stood on the sandbanks, to their delight.

'Said I not, that we would procure a boat once we reached the river's edge?' asked Davenport, with as much triumph in his voice as a whisper could convey.

'We have not procured the boat yet, *Sahib*,' came Kartar Singh's gloomy reply. 'The boats are sure to contain the boatmen in them. How shall we persuade them to give us a boat and not raise the alarm?' he asked pessimistically.

His observation regarding the presence of the boatmen was accurate for these boats that traversed along the Ganges and its tributaries were constructed to allow a boatman to cook and sleep on them. Presently, Davenport puzzled over the matter of the boatman. By what artifice could they hope to convince this person to part with his boat? If they awoke the man and offered to purchase the boat from him, he would experience no small alarm and suspicion at the sight of three men wishing to purchase his boat, in the dead of night, no less. Should the boatman go into the city and inform the sepoys of what had transpired, they might have a boatload of sepoys in hot pursuit of them by dawn. Worse, the sepoys might suspect that the three men were no ordinary travellers, but rather, were possessed of some intriguing secret.

Furthermore, what if the sepoys spread the alarm to the cities ahead? They should be hunted at every *ghat* and bank along the cities that sat on the river.

As things currently stood, the only information the sepoys in the city possessed was that two among their number were killed while the three strangers had disappeared. Their horses remained in the city—and Davenport hoped the three stolen horses would wander back to them by morning. He felt that there was a good chance that they would not have a clear idea of where to direct their pursuit, for he was sure that the *Soobedar Major* was not likely to take their treachery lightly and would be in hot pursuit as soon as their disappearance was detected. If an agitated boatman hastened into the city, reporting that three strangers had bought his boat, disclosure and pursuit were inevitable.

'What shall we do, *Sahib*,' asked Makkhan Singh urgently, interrupting Davenport's ruminations.

'We shall have to go near the boat to discover if, indeed, the boatman is present. If he is, we shall overpower him and take his boat, for I do not think we should place ourselves in his power by trying to reason with him to part with the boat or explain ourselves to him. Two of us should enter the boat and ensure that the man is overpowered in his sleep, and neither sees nor hears his attackers. Keep silent, and take care to blindfold him. Gag and bind him as well, so he does not alert the boatman from the other boat. Release the horses, so they may wander back to the city,' ordered Davenport.

He hoped fervently that they would wander back to the camp by morning and leave no clue about the direction their riders had gone in. Kartar Singh complied, although the horses seemed not to have the slightest inclination to escape. They continued to nibble on the earth, contented to remain where they were. The three men descended on all fours and began to creep towards the boats. As they reached within five yards of the first one, Makkhan Singh drew out his dagger, but Davenport squeezed his shoulder, gesturing to him to put it away. The mettle of a man may be measured in moments of utmost distress, as can his honour. Desperate though he was to reach Jane, Davenport would forsake neither his honour nor his kindness. He would not murder a man in his sleep and rob him, no matter what his present predicament. And although the three men would be sure to put up a stiff fight should the need arise, he wished to avoid harming the sleeping man who was neither his friend nor his foe.

Silently they crept to the side of the boat. These type of boats commonly had no keel, and were wide by the stern. The bow narrowed to an elongated point and a domed covering stood on it, inside which the boatman evidently was asleep, letting out intermittent snores and grunts. As they prepared to mount the boat, it occurred to Davenport that he had read somewhere that the *Chauka* river, and indeed all rivers along the Ganges were filled with crocodiles! He could not remember precisely where he read this, and indeed, it did not signify. He did not wish to leave the boatman lying on the shore as an easy prey for the crocodiles of the river!

He whispered urgently to Makkhan Singh that the other boat would also need to be secured, but again, no harm was to come to the boatman. He was only to be overpowered in his sleep and never to know who or what had attacked him. Makkhan Singh nodded, and without questioning Davenport's reasons, crept noiselessly towards the other boat. Once he reached it, Davenport and Kartar Singh silently climbed into the boat that stood by them. It leaned slightly to the side as the sand below gave way to the shifting weight of the boat. They stood still and listened, and were greeted with the sounds of muttering as the sleeping man turned to find a more comfortable position. Silently, they approached him, ropes, gag and blindfold in hand. Their task proved easy, for the man did not awake before they managed to blindfold and gag him.

Before he could comprehend that someone or something was constricting his mouth, the blindfold had been placed and Davenport proceeded to tie his hands and feet. To their surprise, although he initially resisted, he became deathly still and did not twitch a muscle. Worried, Davenport leaned forward, planting his ear on the man's chest. The man appeared to be breathing rapidly, and his heart beat at a furious pace. Relieved that the man was not dead, they wrapped the blanket around him and proceeded to carry him off the boat. They spied Makkhan Singh's silhouette in the moonlight, beckoning them to approach.

The three men struggled to haul their cargo into the second boat. Their boatman was rather heavy set and it was only with the greatest exertion that they managed to hoist him into the boat. Once in, they placed him beside the boatman in this boat who was also trussed up, quite efficiently, by Makkhan Singh. The two men lay very still, as if afraid that greater harm would befall them, should they resist. Soon, the boatman in the first boat attempted to speak in a voice that sounded strained. Satisfied that the men were safe from crocodiles and unable to sound the alarm, the men prepared to depart and board the newly vacated boat. Before they left, Davenport leaned forward and deposited a pouch of money into the cummerbund of the erstwhile owner of the boat, evicted so unceremoniously.

The boatmen, terrified as they felt someone or something overpower them in their sleep were each convinced that an evil force had taken possession of them and out of sheer terror, did not put up any further resistance. One attempted to recite the few scriptures he knew in an attempt to ward off the evil, but found this exceedingly difficult an exercise, given that his mouth was quite expertly gagged. The result was a chortling, strangled sound that the other boatman unfortunately interpreted as the blood curdling growl of some foul spirit. He lay there, trembling in silence, until he quite fainted. In the morning, after being discovered and rescued by some men who had come to employ their services, each man learned that he had actually been lying next to the other and mistaking the other for some strange fiend, waiting to devour him!

To their consternation they realized that they had very likely been overpowered by a human force, who also stole a boat. The boatman who had lost his boat further discovered a handsome sum of money fastened to his cummerbund. Who had done this? Why had they not simply killed him and taken his boat away? Why had they overpowered his colleague and then left him in his boat? Why did they simply not awake him and offer him the handsome sum of money he now found himself in possession of? He reflected he could purchase another boat, if not a house with it! Perhaps a deity had done this, for did they not sometimes jest with mortals to prove them? Unable to explain the source of their predicament, the men resolved to make extra offerings of coconuts at the temple that very day!

Once they had effected their escape, the night passed rather unremarkably for Davenport and his two companions. They unfurled the sail that stood in the center and owing to a favourable breeze, drifted uneventfully some twenty miles away from the sandbanks that lately beheld such excitement, towards the river's right bank. Davenport fell into a deep sleep, feeling for the first time since their journey began, a sense of relief and security from danger. His worthy retainers took the watch in turns, never waking Davenport from his rest. As dawn broke, they realized that to their left was a deep jungle. The unmistakable call of a tiger sounded from deep within, punctuated by howling from startled monkeys and the calls of myriads of birds. Davenport's mind was drawn to the safari he had undertaken, seemingly an eternity ago. He recalled Edwina's perilous encounter with the enraged tigress and his countenance darkened. Had it not been for Grayson's foolhardiness, they should never have found themselves at the centre of so hair-raising a tale!

'The jungle is dense around us, *Sahib*,' remarked Makkhan Singh, who had been watching the *sahib* for the past few minutes.

Noticing his scowl, he construed that the man was worried for his sister's safety. The thought that Davenport's mind was actually elsewhere would not have crossed his mind. Thus startled from his contemplation, Davenport sat up with a start, awakening Kartar Singh as he did so.

'Where are we, *Sahib?*' enquired Makkhan Singh, genially.

'I believe we are near Bairach,' replied Davenport, poring over the maps in his possession.

They beheld the densest jungle they had ever encountered. The grasses were tall enough to easily conceal a herd of elephants. Doubtless, the jungle held an abundance of game. They had already heard the tiger's call. They had also heard the unmistakable howling of wolves.

'It is said that the soil here is rich and fertile, but the *talukdars* are very cruel to the small farmers and exact inordinate fees and revenues from them—sometimes as high as a quarter of their entire earnings,' Makkhan Singh informed Davenport. He continued, 'The poor farmers have forsaken cultivation to flee the *talukdars*. It is said that they imprison men who cannot pay the rent on the land, in dark dungeons, for days on end. They are treated worse than animals!'

Davenport drank in this information, nodding silently. He had read of Lord Cornwallis' Permanent Settlement Act, enacted over sixty years ago. It was designed to maintain British control over revenues and to protect farmers from unscrupulous exploitation. In reality, however, the *zameendars* were—by virtue of being responsible for gathering rents—given the power to decide on rents and revenues that farmers owed. Furthermore, they were left in charge of day-to-day administration and were consequently a powerful force to reckon with. They greedily demanded more and more from the hapless farmer who could not escape their demands, supported as they were, by the British.

'No doubt, this is another of the provocations for this revolt, *Sahib*,' said Kartar Singh sadly.

'That is true. Wherever we have been, I have seen some regrettable affair or the other that is the direct result of ill-advised decisions made by the government. And here we are, made to suffer by their foolish actions!' replied Davenport.

Both men felt sorry for their friend—his burden seemed to be heavy, witnessing on the one hand, the excesses of his people, and worrying, on the other, for the safety of some of them. In an attempt to distract him, Makkhan Singh asked if they might not anchor the boat to the bank and hunt for some game? They could rely on the river for several days for a bountiful supply of fish, but this might very well be their only opportunity to eat meat for a while. The idea seemed to appeal to Davenport and in the space of an hour, they had shot three wild ducks and Makkhan Singh was well on his way to cooking them a meal.

CHAPTER EIGHT

ALONG THE RIVER

They drifted thus, aided by favourable winds for a bulk of their journey, for a space of two weeks. When the winds were uncooperative, the men rowed with all their might, taking care to avoid shallow sandbanks. On the way, their river, meeting with other rivers, transformed into the *Gogra* river and thereafter joined with the confluence of rivers that forms the mighty Ganges. They determined that at the rivers' confluence, they would reach their objective of Danapur in a matter of a few hours. Along the way, they had crossed many ghats and banks, witnessing as people in villages and cities came to the river's edge to bathe, wash their clothing or to offer prayers as they greeted the rising sun. They were often hailed by friendly persons, and returned their greetings with folded palms.

Not wishing to delay their journey, they relied on the river for sustenance, stopping only once, at a remote village near the river's edge to purchase some provisions. On that day, the three men relished their tea, as they were able to purchase some milk. As they neared their destination, they hastened their pace, rowing harder while keeping a keen eye upon the shallows. Davenport was filled with a mix of excitement and trepidation as he wondered what outcome they would discover at their journey's end. At long last, they reached the confluence. Having passed it, after some thirty miles, they approached Danapur, where a large garrison of soldiers was known to be stationed. Davenport was most anxious to discover the state of the town before they made a foray into it.

'It is not safe to venture into the city just yet, *Sahib,*' said Kartar Singh.

Davenport nodded in agreement, adding, 'We must first determine whether it remains secure. Very likely it has been also overthrown, situated as it is, between the Meerut and Barrackpore.' 'However,' he continued, 'If the city has been reclaimed, it will mean that the mutineers have possibly been checked and military reinforcements may have been dispatched to Calcutta. We should approach cautiously, until we have determined the state of affairs here.'

Danapur was a centre for trade and export, and one of the oldest ghats, Flagstaff Ghat, welcomed them in the distance. They could see a large sandy outcrop and beyond it, at some elevation, stood a large white bungalow with red tiles on its roof and with an inviting verandah. There appeared to be a guard post nearby and no doubt, this was an official residence or government building of some sort.

'Perhaps we shall not need to journey to the barracks, which are located some two miles away, as someone in the bungalow there is bound to know the state of affairs in Danapur, and possibly beyond, in Calcutta,' Davenport suggested.

But, hardly had the words left his mouth, when they were hailed by a barrage of shouts. Their boat, which had begun to approach the banks, appeared to have attracted the attention of some persons standing on the banks who were gesticulating rather wildly. They stared hard at the banks with narrowed eyes, attempting to discover whether they were being greeted in the distance by friend or foe.

'Slow the boat down and prepare to move farther into the river,' commanded Davenport, 'We need to flee if these are sepoys.'

As they drew parallel to the men on the banks, they recognized that they donned the sepoy uniform, but had discarded their characteristic red coats and were simply wearing *dhotis*, the long loincloths that men wore in India, resembling the knee-length pantaloons worn by men in Europe. The men brandished drawn swords and rifles. They beckoned to the three men to bring the boat to land. Kartar Singh, who manned the oars, swiftly proceeded to move farther away from the banks. As he did so, Makkhan Singh and Davenport smiled genially at the men and waved at them with great gusto, appearing not to comprehend their signals.

'Bring the boat to land, if you value your lives!' shouted one man. 'We need to chase the cowardly English Major-General Lloyd who escaped this place by boat. We have overthrown the English and will not spare a single one of them.'

'Bring your boat hence, or we will slit your throats!' roared another.

'What?! What did you, say, Brother? I cannot hear you for the roaring of the river!' answered Makkhan Singh, making a great show of cupping his hands to his ears.

He was rewarded for his trouble with a volley of shots, as the men took aim at them and commenced firing their rifles.

'There is no point firing back, *Sahib*,' growled Makkhan Singh, sounding very much like an enraged tiger, even as they ducked for cover, lying flat in the boat. 'We must save our bullets and these rogues are too far away to hit,' he said in muted rage.

Davenport nodded, clenched teeth and fists notwithstanding. They must conserve their ammunition, for who knew what battles lay ahead of them? The frenzied shooting soon grew sporadic and diminished entirely for the boat had moved too far away from the banks for the sepoy bullets to reach them. Valiant men who stood their ground in battle, the three men were furious on being forced to flee when they had been subjected to so unprovoked an attack.

'Well, that answers our question then—Danapur has also revolted! It appears that these men have won an easy victory and received very little resistance, for their Commanding Officer appears to have fled,' said Davenport gloomily.

He was partly correct in that, the Major-General on that particular day, at half past one in the afternoon, had stepped on a steamer, knowing that his native regiments had revolted. He had not returned to assume command, but instead, had left Danapur and apparently, there was not a clear chain of command established to take matters in hand. Consequently, the sepoys found themselves unexpectedly victorious and facing very little resistance from the English, as they revolted against their Commanders.

'It appears also that they have acquired a great deal of ammunition, for they did not hesitate to fire upon us. No consideration of rationing their ammunitions appears to have weighed with them,' continued Davenport.

He was correct on that score as well. Although an attempt had been made that morning to divest the sepoys of the percussion caps that they required in order to fire their rifles, the manner in which this occurred resulted in the sepoys unanimously rioting. Davenport would discover later that a detachment of the 5th Fusiliers had arrived from Calcutta but the Major-General had not seen fit to detain them in Danapur. He did not believe that the rebellion would reach their town.

Consequently, the 5th Fusiliers continued on their journey to aid other areas affected. The sepoys, having routed their quarry with little resistance, attempted to chase down Major-General Lloyd who, they had heard, was at the river's edge, preparing to board a steamer. They were rebuffed and then stood there, uncertain on how to proceed. They had stood discussing the matter for a good two hours, at the end of which Davenport and his men arrived on the scene. Now, they could see no point in remaining at the river's edge, as no other boats appeared to be coming by.

Davenport and his companions continued on the river, until out of sight of Flagstaff Ghat. They would need to find a more opportune entrance to the city. Enter it they must, especially if the revolt had only just broken out, as it appeared to have. While it was entirely fortuitous that they had arrived there at its very inception, it was vital that they reach Jane at the earliest. The three men, not being privy to the facts of what had happened in the town that day, speculated on what carnage was occurring there. Recalling the words of the men on the river banks, Davenport began to face the possibility that he would not reach his sister in time.

Faced with the prospect that some ill may already have befallen her on this very day, a deep sense of dread and loneliness descended upon him. His only relation in India (with the exception of Mrs. Edens, who was quite distant a connection), Jane Davenport held a fond place in his heart and he felt the greatest solicitude for her. For the first time since they had begun their journey, he began to wonder if she were even alive. He shuddered, even as the possibility that some calamity could have already occurred, began to take hold of his mind. The prospect of life without her seemed dismal and intolerable. And what of Edwina Hardingham's sisters? How would the Hardinghams endure it if their children had suffered harm? A dark foreboding gripped his heart. He put his face in his hands, as if to block the painful images that were conjured in his mind at these ruminations.

'In just a while, *Sahib,* we will have accomplished our mission, for we are very near the end of it,' said Makkhan Singh gently, correctly guessing that his friend was engulfed with a profound sadness.

'Do not assume she is dead, *Sahib,*' added Kartar Singh, with equal kindness, if somewhat less tact.

Makkhan Singh glared at the younger man.

'Hold your tongue, man! Why should such inauspicious words escape your mouth? May anyone wishing to harm a hair on her head be dead, and may the child be preserved unscathed!' he admonished. 'Besides, the *sahib* was thinking no such thing. He is merely tired, for he has not had any tea for a fortnight,' he finished, somewhat lamely.

Unabashed, Kartar Singh retorted, 'Do you mistake the *sahib* for the fragile Diana *Memsahib* who was with us on the *shikar,* that you suggest he would have a fainting fit for the lack of tea? He is doubtless pensive, for he thinks of the young *memsahib.* Are you not, *Sahib?* Do not fret! Instead, turn your fears into great resolve and anger, so that when it comes time, you will be able either to rescue her or to avenge her!'

Makkhan Singh glowered at him, wishing he could slap the back of his head, as he was wont to, when the man was younger. He signaled to him to be silent. But, having collected his thoughts, Kartar Singh would not allow his eloquence to be stemmed.

'Besides,' he continued, 'What if Jane *Memsahib* is like Edwina *Memsahib?* Then, she will probably fight her way through and remain unscathed. Recall, how that lady stared down the tigress, as if daring it to attack!' he finished, with the air of one who has proved a point beyond the possibility of contradiction.

An involuntary smile escaped Davenport at these comparisons. Clearly, Edwina Hardingham had established herself in their imaginations as an epitome of courage! The idea sent a flutter of pride across his breast. Cheered by these images, he resolved not to underestimate his sister's mettle. True, she was a most gentle creature, but he was sure she was possessed of a great deal of courage as well.

The two are not contradictory virtues, he reflected. *Besides, we are also fortunately arrived at Danapur at the very hour of the revolt. I cannot but believe that God has brought me here in time, that I might rescue her,* he thought.

They arrived at a sandbank which was by a lonely and serene stretch of land that belied the tumult that was occurring not even a mile away, and began to make their way to the cantonment.

Davenport and Kartar Singh were correct in assuming that Jane Davenport was possessed of a good deal of courage. She had undertaken her journey to Mrs. Edens' lodging at Danapur in the company of her childhood nurse and an elderly male retainer. Both these persons had served her since her childhood. The nurse, who went by the name of Bibi, had nurtured Miss. Davenport since her infancy, and like most Indian nurses, watched over her charge with the tenderness and ferocity of a tigress with cubs. Likewise, the manservant, Ram Singh, who had taught her to ride, served as a guard for the Davenport children and devoted himself to their care.

Both of these worthy persons were typical of the servants of India. Deeply loyal and grateful for any kindness they were shown, they made lifelong attachments and served their masters with the deepest of dedication, even at the cost of their own happiness. While some, like the Davenports and Hardinghams, were cognizant of the great value of these people and made sure to treat them with kindness, courtesy and respect, many Europeans believed that such reverence was owed them, by virtue of their conquest of the land. Thus it was that in these times, some sought to overthrow the oppressive regime they found themselves under, slaughtering any European within reach, whilst others sought to protect friends and employers who had made them a part of their homes and families.

Bibi and Ram Singh had both heard the other servants discuss the trouble that was brewing, for some weeks now. They had heard talk of a great rebellion at Delhi and some said that the English would no longer be the rulers of the land. Sitting around after dusk in the courtyard of the servants' quarters, they talked much of these matters.

'They deserve to be killed, every one of them,' pronounced one manservant whose employers had been particularly harsh in their treatment of him.

'No, they are not all bad. My Davenport *Sahib* has never mistreated anyone on his staff. He often remarks that he has relied upon me ever since he was a lad. In fact, he offered to buy me a plot of land in my village when I retire from service,' replied Ram Singh.

The other men looked at him in wonder. They agreed, some men were reasonable and kind and others not so.

'It is all in our fate, whether we have a good employer or not,' remarked one.

Matters seemed to approach a climax beginning the previous evening, when an agitated hum of discussion could be heard among the servants across the cantonment.

'They are trying to kill all the sepoys,' declared one maid, in an excited undertone, 'They are taking away their rifles!'

'That cannot be so; they are still in possession of them. My husband's cousin is a sepoy and still has his rifle,' replied the other.

Another asserted, 'It is indeed so! They most certainly *are* trying to kill the sepoys. My husband told me that they have taken away some weapons today and left the sepoys with only a few parts that they need to fire their rifles. My husband says that it is time to act. If we do not, they will slaughter us in our beds!'

'If they have left the rifles with the men, they cannot intend to kill us. My husband says that even with the parts they have, the rifle can be discharged four times,' said the first, adopting a more reasonable stance.

As Bibi listened, she heard talk of the need for firm action against the British increase, until a revolt seemed inevitable. She relayed this information to Miss. Davenport, taking care not to betray her sources. Jane felt a growing uneasiness as well, for there was a great deal of discussion among the officers about the wisdom of continuing to allow the native regiments to carry arms, given the news of the revolts in faraway places.

On the evening before the revolt in Danapur, she had conveyed to her hosts that it was conceivable that a revolt was imminent, whereupon Mrs. Edens took up a hysterical wail and began to lament that their throats would very likely be slit that very night. Captain Edens, once she had been prevailed upon to take to her bed with some smelling salts, soundly admonished Miss. Davenport for heeding the idle tales of a servant that were liable to spread panic among the families of the officers, should they have been repeated.

'At this hour of difficulty, it is of the greatest import,' he said, 'that the women remain calm and unruffled, for the present difficulty is all but over, since the percussion caps have been secured from the munitions storehouse, and plans are being laid of relieving the men of any remaining caps in their possession, the very next day.'

He declared his intention of soundly punishing Jane's maid, whereupon the young woman in a firm and grave voice informed him that such a course of action would distress her greatly. She begged her host to refrain from chastising her maid. She also informed him that she regretted that she had agitated his wife in this manner and would be happy to effect her departure from his household the next morning, in the company of her servants—for she had several friends in the cantonment who would be delighted to welcome her into their establishments.

Captain Edens was somewhat taken aback. He was in awe of Davenport's fortune and influence and consequently, did not wish to antagonize the man by causing his sister—whom, by all accounts, he was dreadfully fond of—to flee his household! Reassuring her that her well-being was his only concern, he announced that it was best to let the matter lie. He urged her to rest, for he was sure that her nerves must be overwrought with all this excitement!

Jane Davenport complied, with a demeanour that belied the agitation she felt within. In her bedchamber, she listened as Bibi recounted what the servants had said.

'Do not be afraid, Missy *Sahib*. I have a plan. But you must do exactly as I say,' she began, addressing Jane in the affectionate manner she did when she was a little child.

Jane nodded for her to continue. 'I have a *saree* for you to wear. Ram Singh will keep close watch and at the first sign of trouble, he will signal me and you must wear these garments. We will feign that you are a washerwoman and place a great bundle of clothes on your head and we will flee the house. Ram Singh says that there is a large pile of hay by the stables behind the quarters of the servants. You can hide there and when it is safe, we will flee and make our way to safety. You must not remain in this house if a revolt breaks out, for many *sahibs* and *memsahibs* and their little ones have been killed as they attempted to hide in their homes. But, do not fear, Ram Singh and I will not let any harm come to you. If you disguise yourself as one of us and flee this house, you shall be safe,' she said.

Jane listened to this scheme with widening eyes.

She saw the wisdom of it, and although she had become somewhat pale, she asked in a level voice, 'How shall we escape this house, for shall we not be seen to be quitting it by the sepoys?'

'We shall leave by the servants' entrance by the kitchen, child. And, Ram Singh and I shall carry daggers, just in case we are followed,' replied the redoubtable Bibi.

'And I shall carry the little pearl-handled pistol my brother gave me,' came the cool reply.

The following morning, a tense calm prevailed upon the Edens household.

It is akin to the calm before a storm, thought Jane, who very much sensed that there was some strife brewing.

Unlike the Edens and quite like the Hardinghams, she had, from her earliest memories, held a keen love for the land and its people. She was fluent in Hindustani and her soft grey eyes had a penetrating quality that seemed to instinctively grasp what was happening around her. While Mrs. Edens sipped on her tea with the air of one who was being subject to inordinate suffering, noticing nothing but how hot it was and how slowly the maid tugged on the *pankha*, Jane Davenport perceived the furtive glances the servants exchanged with one another. It did not escape her notice that the food had been hastily prepared. The kedgiree seemed somewhat uncooked, and her eggs had not been poached correctly. The air of suppressed agitation amongst the staff was patent and after the maids glanced at each other with an air of great significance for about the fourth time, she could bear no more. Excusing herself, she made her way to her bedchamber, and asked Bibi if she knew if anything was afoot.

'Something surely is afoot, Missy *Sahib*,' replied Bibi, adding, 'but no one will tell us anything anymore, for they are sure that Ram Singh and I are loyal to the English. The Captain *Sahib* berated his staff this morning, telling them that I was spreading rumours of trouble and that if anyone else was caught doing so, they would be flogged.'

While this did not provide any comfort to Jane, she resolved to not permit herself to be beset by worry and instead picked up her newest book, *Aurora Leigh*—it had been brought from London that very month, on a ship carting supplies for her brother's many business ventures. Soon, she was lost in Elizabeth Barrett Browning's stirring romance and it was only the sound of two shots fired in the distance around noon, that brought her current circumstances forcefully to her mind.

Rising hastily from the comfortable chair wherein she had lately been ensconced, her book falling unheeded from her lap, Jane Davenport launched herself behind the large screen in her bedchamber, and with the assistance of her maid, robed herself in Indian attire, drawing the long fabric that hung over her shoulder as a veil around her head. Bibi had kept a large bundle of clothes, as well as a smaller bundle of valuables and items they would need, at the ready. The women made their way to the kitchen in haste. As they did so, Ram Singh hurried in, out of breath and declaring that a group of sepoys with rifles was making their way to the quarters of the European officers.

Jane darted towards Mrs. Edens' bedchamber to warn her. At that moment, Mrs. Edens called out for the servants, a hysterical note rising in her voice. When none answered, she ran out of her bedchamber, demanding that they present themselves at once if they did not wish to be horsewhipped. Catching sight of Jane, she shrieked, asking Jane what she was about and why she was dressed in that manner.

'My man has spied a group of sepoys making their way towards this place. Let us flee to the stables that are beyond the servants' quarters. Come quickly with us,' Jane pleaded.

Mrs. Edens, who by this time was quite overwrought with fear, became possessed of a most irrational distrust of Indian servants, a tendency that was present in her nature for some time now.

'Are you quite mad, Jane?! Pray, come away from those vile persons and take off those disgusting clothes. Do not trust them for one moment, for they will rob and murder you the moment you turn your back to them,' she said with a strange sob that sounded like a laugh.

'These people have cared for me my entire life and I think of them as my own family. Come with us! It shall be well!' pleaded Jane.

Mrs. Edens ran to her room and came back with a pistol, screaming, 'Stand back, Jane, for I must protect you from yourself. I cannot let you leave this house with those murderous devils!'

She aimed the pistol at Ram Singh, and Jane, who had planted herself firmly in front of the old man, was quite in danger of being shot by her friend who was threatening to have the hysterics, when the front door burst open.

A group of sepoys barged in, yelling, 'Kill the European women! They are tyrants like their husbands.'

Mrs. Edens swung in their direction, quite ready to faint. Unfortunately, seeing a pistol in her hand, the sepoy who had shouted his murderous intentions earlier, shot her with his rifle. Poor Mrs. Edens sank down and appeared to be quite dead. A scream died in Jane's throat, as the men barged into the home. She felt Bibi and Ram Singh grab her arm and resolutely drag her towards the kitchen.

'There is another one living here. The maid told me there were two women in this house,' said one, as he began to search the bedchambers for Jane.

The sepoys ignored the two veiled Indian women who scurried to the kitchen, followed by the manservant. Having been rescued from being shot by the crazed Englishwoman, it did not seem surprising to the sepoys that they wished to flee from the house. Indeed, most of the women and old men had taken refuge in the servants' quarters as the trouble broke out, for none wished to be caught in the crossfire.

Rushing through the rear entrance of the house, the three fugitives fled towards the stables. Their progress was somewhat hampered by the fact that Jane struggled to run in her *saree*, perching a large bundle of clothing on top of her head. As the bundle was necessary to maintain the disguise, she was forced to content herself with a slow trot, which could not have been avoided anyway, as Ram Singh, who was somewhat advanced in years, could not run very fast either. The result of this was that while Jane and Bibi reached the stables and found a suitable hiding place for Jane atop a loft covered with hay, Ram Singh was spotted making his way to the stables by the sepoys who were ransacking the European cottages. One of them was familiar with him, and he had heard a manservant from a neighbouring officer's household remark that Ram Singh was loyal to the English and had claimed that his master had offered to buy him a tract of land when he returned to his village.

The sepoy said something to the men beside him and soon, three men began to make their way to the stables. Bibi, who was unable to alight the steep loft and preferred to keep a lookout, sat beside Ram Singh as he caught his breath. While she was also getting on in years, Ram Singh had the advantage of a good twenty years over her. She remembered coming to work as a wet nurse in the Davenport household when Ram Singh was a senior member of the household staff. He wore a stately uniform and was in charge of the other servants. Once Jane had been weaned, Bibi had been retained as her *ayah* and over time, she had become acquainted with the man. Now, she was like a daughter to him, and they had both been entrusted with Jane's care on numerous occasions. She was glad to be in his company at present, for he did present a somewhat formidable appearance with his large moustache and beard. She prepared to ask him if he wished for a draught of water from the well nearby, when to her horror, three sepoys rushed into the stable.

'Old man! Where is the Englishwoman from the house?' demanded one.

'We found only one woman there and I know you were the servant of the other one. Where is she?' asked another.

'I do not know. Some men came into the house and we ran away because there was fighting and we did not wish to be harmed,' replied Ram Singh, who had by now, risen to his feet.

'You lie!' roared the third sepoy. 'We heard that you are a loyal dog to the British, and were defending them but this past week!' he thundered.

Choking back his rage, Ram Singh answered in a reasonable tone, 'How should I know where the *memsahib* is? As you can see, we are but servants here and when the fighting began, we fled for our safety, for the *sahibs* and the sepoys are both likely to shoot us.'

'Where is the third servant who left the house with you?' asked one of the men sharply.

The men suddenly narrowed their eyes, as the possibility of the subterfuge that had occurred began to dawn on them.

'She was a washerwoman and ran to her quarters yonder to the left just a few moments ago. Perhaps you can see her if you go that way at once,' said Bibi, desperately hoping that the men did not detect the panic that raged in her breast.

The men looked around them and unfortunately, spied the bundle of clothes that Jane had carried as part of her disguise. The loft was a good six feet off the ground and Jane had used it as a ladder of sorts with which to ascend onto the loft. They had not had time to conceal it, caught as they were in the chaos and terror of their present circumstances. Furthermore, they had scarcely managed to conceal Jane before the men arrived.

'I believe I shall be able to loosen your tongue presently,' said one sepoy in a rather sinister tone. Armed with his sword, he came towards Ram Singh, and grabbing him by his shirt, demanded again, 'Tell us where the woman is, or you die!'

'Have you no respect for the aged, you accursed one,' shrieked Bibi. 'Is that any way to treat an old man who is old enough to be your father?' she asked.

One of the men struck her on her face and she fell to the ground. Ram Singh struggled to fight the man, but was held in place by his captor with the drawn sword.

The man said, 'If you will not stand with us, you must die.'

Forcing the old man to his knees, the man lifted his sword, taking aim at his neck. Suddenly, from somewhere in the stable, a shot rang out. The man with the sword fell, senseless, while the other two raised their rifles. The shot had come from above and they could see a thin line of smoke at the spot where it had been discharged. Someone had fired on them from the loft. They prepared to shoot in the direction of the loft, when both men suddenly became arrested in motion. Their eyes widened and the rifles fell from their hands. Both crashed down onto the ground, on their faces, and each had a dagger planted in his back.

Ram Singh and Bibi stood silent and petrified, too afraid to move, lest they should be the next targets of the daggers whose owner, it was more than likely, would soon wish to reclaim them.

'Stay where you are,' said Bibi in a low voice to Jane, as a shadow fell across the stable entrance.

Three tall men strode in, two of whom were Sikhs.

'Are you hurt, Father?' they asked Ram Singh.

The man shook his head, unsure of what to expect from these three formidable seeming men.

'Where is *Memsahib?*' asked one of the men.

Ram Singh and Bibi looked at each other, expecting fully that they were in the hands of some other sepoys who would mete some harsher penalty to them.

'We know not where she went. When the Englishwoman was shot in the Captain's house, we fled and came hither, for we are both too old to be involved in these troubles. Then the three sepoys came and one of them shot at us,' said Bibi, quickly thinking of a way to explain the shot the men had undoubtedly heard and that had very certainly drawn them hither.

'Bibi! Has Jane been shot? Where is she?' came the anguished reply from one of the men.

The two servants looked speechlessly at the man. Finally, Bibi found her voice again.

'Who are you? How do you know my name?' she asked in a trembling voice.

'Do you not recognize me, Bibi? It is I, Davenport!' came the answer.

This pronouncement had the unlikely effect of causing the indomitable Bibi to open and close her mouth several times in succession. For his part, Ram Singh sat down suddenly on the ground with his head in his hands, shaking silently, as if sobbing in relief. It also produced an unexpected squeal of joy, mingled with a sob, from above, in the general vicinity of the loft. Someone appeared to be squirming there and tufts of hay began to make their descent onto the ground. Makkhan Singh and Kartar Singh grabbed their rifles, approaching the loft with caution. But, Davenport, rightly discerning that the source of the strange sounds was his sister, threw his head back and laughed for joy! Striding towards the loft, he received what appeared to be a tumbling roll of hay, into his arms.

'Thanks be to God! You are alive and apparently quite well!' he exclaimed joyfully.

Jane Davenport clung to her brother and kissed his cheeks several times in succession. Kartar Singh laughed and Makkhan Singh wiped his eyes quietly. A huge sense of relief washed over them, resulting in a temporary sense of disorientation and impassiveness, as usually happens when one has come through a great ordeal. The need to plan and strive disappears and the soul wishes to rest in the joy of the moment, often unable to think or decide on the next course of action. This intermission was rather short-lived, however, and the company soon heard shouts and shots in the distance, reminding them that they were still very much in peril. Unsure of whether the sounds were being created by those headed in their direction, the whole party suddenly became animated, attempting to effect their escape instantly. Davenport ordered them to steal away from the side entrance towards the mango orchards in the rear, taking pains first, to ensure that the bodies of the three men who had lately assailed them were concealed from view. He did not wish to alert anyone about what had happened, and wished to avoid at all costs, the possibility of their being followed.

Unbeknownst to them, the European soldiers were resisting the sepoy incursion into their quarters and the violence that began quickly also was stemmed quickly, with the result that the sepoys, changing direction, determined to go to Arah instead. Why Arah? They had chosen that place because its *zameendar*, the honourable Kunwar Singh, had lately become disenchanted with British rule, owing to oppressive revenue practices that had led to a great decline in his wealth. He had offered his support and the services of his armed servants to the cause of the revolt. The sepoys planned to besiege Arah and defeat the government there. This proved fortuitous for Davenport and his company, as they were able to retreat back to the river's edge, by the way they had come, unspotted. Kartar Singh wondered if they should go to the European officers at Danapur and reveal themselves to them. But, Makkhan Singh was quick to point out the defects of such a plan.

'How will we get within even ten steps of a British solider? Will they not fire upon us as they spy us coming? What good would it do to tell them what we are about? Will they lend us their aid and escort us to Calcutta?' he asked.

'That they most certainly will not do,' replied Davenport, adding, 'Go to Calcutta we must, and it is certain that we must do this on our own strength, for the authorities are now unable to provide us assistance.'

He was correct in this assumption. The British soldiers were sorely outnumbered. Following Major-General Lloyd's orders, the sentry at the cantonment hospital had fired two shots when he witnessed the native regiments take control of the store of percussion caps that had been secured the previous day. The Europeans were having their lunch at that time and upon receiving no resistance from them, the sepoys gave chase to Major-General Lloyd. Having been rebuffed by the men accompanying him, they returned to attack the European quarters, when their leaders, having proceeded to pouch all the caps in the regimental store, made the decision to set off with haste to Arah. They had succeeded in getting no further than the residence of Captain Edens. His wife, they would discover later, had been grazed by the bullet, and received no greater injury than that. Her life had been spared by the shock that made her faint. Jane Davenport's disappearance was greeted with no small alarm, for they were sure that she had been beset upon by her servants, into whose hands she had most unwisely placed her life.

Unaware of all of these developments, the Davenports and their retainers departed in the direction of the river. Reaching the river unspotted was easy enough, as the attention of both, the sepoys and the British soldiers, had been claimed elsewhere. They quickly made their way down the river, moving away from Danapur rapidly. Once out of sight of the town, they stopped to fish at a calm stretch, and Davenport and his sister recounted their adventures. He listened with great surprise as his sister explained that she had shot the soldier in the stable.

'It seemed as though he was going to kill Ram Singh and then he struck Bibi and so I had to shoot him. I am sure it was a wicked thing to do, for I was hidden, and the man had no idea what hit him, but I did not feel certain that had I revealed myself to him, it would make matters any easier,' she said, with the air of one attempting to reconcile a disagreeable course of action with one's conscience.

'To be sure, there was nothing else you could do. He deserved to be shot for striking a woman and trying to kill an old man. You saved their lives, as was your duty,' Davenport soothed.

Kartar Singh, who had a fairly reasonable grasp of English, smiled genially at them, saying, 'Said I not, *Sahib*, that your sister would fight bravely?'

Davenport nodded, a pleased smile spreading across his face and erasing the lines that had lately marked his brow. He thought to himself that his sister had become a fine young woman, without his noticing it. She was no longer the little child he was wont to think of her as.

She did not seem very astounded by his adventures, on the other hand, accustomed as she was to his courage and maturity. She had grown up thinking of him as a parent and he had always conducted himself with honour and bravery. And so, it did not seem very remarkable to her that he should have traveled across a strife torn country to find her, although, to be sure, she found it rather thrilling.

The accounts of the people who were killed by the three men enroute, did not perturb her in the slightest. James was nothing if not good and kind. If those men were killed, she was sure that it had been done under great duress and for reasons that were most pressing in nature.

'Why do we not simply return to Simla, following the same route you came by?' she asked, for she was quite certain that her brother could effortlessly lead them back home.

'No, we must first go to Calcutta,' he answered.

'But, what if the revolt had broken out there as well, *Sahib*?' asked Kartar Singh, who was inclined to agree with Jane.

'We need to ensure the Hardinghams are safe,' said Davenport quietly.

'Who are they?' Jane asked, in some surprise.

'They are John's relations who reside in Simla. I promised them that I would determine how their relations in Calcutta fare,' he answered.

'Is Uncle John out of harm's way? Is he in Simla? How came you to make the acquaintance of his family? I believe he has a cousin there, does he not?' asked Jane.

Davenport informed her that he had accompanied Mr. Knowles to a ball at their residence and to a *shikar* that members of the family had attended.

Hearing this, Kartar Singh volunteered, 'It was only Edwina *Memsahib* who was at the *shikar*. You are very much like her. I told the *sahib* that I was sure you would be so!'

At this, Jane turned to her brother, enquiring who the lady was.

'Edwina Hardingham is a woman with a good deal of sense and courage and she is also enormously pr—er— prudent, a—and quite a good shot,' he said, with uncharacteristic diffidence.

His sister gave no response, but she did take note that a change had come upon her brother's countenance. Davenport cleared his throat and looked carefully at his hands, as if noticing something there for the first time. He made a show of studying them carefully in the fading light and Jane stared at him, with widened eyes.

'When shall we meet her?' she asked with a twinkle in her eye.

'Meet whom?' asked Davenport nonchalantly.

'Miss. Hardingham, of course! Oh, I cannot wait to make her acquaintance!' she replied.

'I expect we shall meet them sooner or later when we are in Simla. They are year-round residents there and one cannot but run into people one is acquainted with in Simla,' he answered absently, as if preoccupied with some other matter.

The task of settling down for the night appeared to consume him, and Jane was unable to pursue the matter further. They partook of the fish that they had caught and as the dusk settled around them, Jane drifted off into a deep slumber, wearied by the day's events.

The days that followed passed uneventfully. It was near the end of July and the drenching monsoon rains, deceptively shy at first, finally arrived on the plains, first in the form of a steady downpour, and eventually as torrential rains. The river began to swell, but showed no signs of flooding yet. They maintained their pace as they traversed along the *Ganges*, careful to avoid the cities on their way. Despite the threat of dangers that lurked ahead, a sense of calm prevailed, as Davenport and Jane were no longer plagued by the fear of what may have befallen the other. He hoped fervently that no catastrophe had befallen the members of the Hardingham family in Calcutta. When they passed Barrackpore, all seemed calm, and they hoped fervently that it was a sign that all was well in Calcutta.

They approached Calcutta cautiously, some three weeks since their incursion into Danapur, making their way down the Hooghly river, as the *Ganges* was known, in Calcutta. They approached the magnificent Prinseps Ghat, built sixteen years ago and flanking the large park that was surrounded by the best homes in Calcutta. If anything was amiss, it did not appear to be so at this ghat. They were close to the Chowringhee area, where Davenport's residence was located, adjacent to a park that stood nearby.

Considering his options, Davenport said, 'All seems calm ahead of us, but we must be vigilant. Kartar Singh, you go into the park and discover the state of affairs there and when you return, we shall determine what course of action we must adopt.'

The man nodded, leaping off the boat and making his way up the steps of the ghat. They were at a quiet stretch of the river banks. It was yet dawn and although worshippers would dot the river's edge to offer prayers to the river, the area which they stood at was rather abandoned. Kartar Singh had been gone for the space of about two hours and

Makkhan Singh and the Davenports began to feel alarm over what might have delayed him.

'Perhaps he has been caught?' Jane suggested in a worried tone.

Davenport shook his head saying, 'No, he is unlikely to have allowed himself to have been captured. Besides, the sepoys have no quarrel against other Indians. There should have been no cause for them to have captured him.'

'What if it is the *sahibs* who have captured him, suspecting him of being a part of the revolt?' asked Makkhan Singh.

'If he does not return in half an hour, I shall go and discover his whereabouts. If he has indeed been taken by the Europeans, I shall be able to secure his release without any difficulty,' Davenport replied.

He did not need to execute this plan, however, as Kartar Singh returned in fifteen minutes. He quickly proceeded to give them an account of the state of the city.

'When I first arrived, all seemed peaceful, but I could not be sure. I could not find anyone to make small talk because it is yet so early, so I had to loiter around till someone passed by. Soon enough, a man selling milk passed by and in the guise of purchasing some, I asked him about the state of the city. It appears that there was the threat of violence two months ago, but the *Nawab* of Oudh was taken prisoner by the government to prevent his followers from joining the revolting sepoys against the government. So, no mutiny broke out here,' he reported.

Surprised, Makkhan Singh turned to Davenport, saying, 'It is strange that the revolt spread as far west of Barrackpore as Delhi, but Calcutta, which is quite near, has been unmolested.'

Davenport nodded. 'Well, we are safe, at least presently! Secure us a carriage while we secure the boat,' he ordered.

They hurried up the steps leading to the city and were presently hailed by a shout from Kartar Singh. A carriage awaited them and in the space of half an hour, they found themselves at Davenport's residence, knocking on the imposing doors flanked by two lions on either side. Davenport's butler, a Bengali man with a most affable disposition, greeted them with some surprise.

'You must make deliveries at the rear entrance. Go around the street and knock on the third door you see,' he said politely.

'It is I, Chatterjee! Open the door!' declared Davenport.

'And who might you be?' asked the greatly puzzled Chatterjee, searching his mind, for this bedraggled person at his doorstep looked and sounded very familiar.

At this, Jane Davenport giggled and asked, 'Surely you recognize us, Chatterjee! We cannot have changed all that much, even though we are not washed and are quite shabby.'

At this the man gasped, and with a look of great astonishment, flung the doors to the stately home wide open, stepping aside to let his master and mistress in.

A few hours of rest and a hearty lunch having been partaken of, the company soon felt refreshed. The tension of the past weeks appeared to have vanished, for all appeared to remain unruffled in this part of the world. Davenport lost no time in sending his card to Markham's residence and begged to be permitted to call upon them that very evening. He was known by reputation and Markham was honoured to welcome him. Davenport was not surprised to see Captain Lovelace in attendance as well. After pleasantries had been exchanged, he enlightened them on the purpose of his visit.

'Have you been able to send word back to Simla?' he asked.

'No, the *dâk* runners are notoriously slow, as you know, and the present crisis makes them even more untrustworthy,' Markham replied.

'What about you? Have you received word from Simla?' he asked.

He was greatly astonished when Davenport informed him that he had actually been in Simla and had left the Hardinghams safe and sound in Simla around ten weeks ago.

'As far as I know, the revolt has not reached Simla,' he informed them.

Anne and Kate were overjoyed to hear this news.

'I wish I could be home with dearest Mama now,' said Anne, hastily adding, 'But of course, I am glad that I am able to be with Kate this hour.'

Kate, taking no offence, replied, 'But of course, dear. I too would wish to be with Mama at a time like this. But, I am delighted to hear that they are quite safe.'

They eyed Davenport with awe, wondering what sort of man would undertake and complete such a fantastic mission.

'How was it that you managed to make your way here unscathed?'

asked Lovelace. 'The reports we have received tell of nothing but murder and looting along the way,' he added.

Davenport informed them of the disguise he donned as he traveled.

'What a capital idea! Dress like one of the savages and you will be quite safe! 'Pon my word, all Europeans need to do that,' cried Lovelace.

'But,' asked Markham, 'tell me, did the natives not recognize you? And did you not worry that your servants would betray you?' Kate and Anne were both horrified at such unmitigated hostility.

'Surely that is a most unchristian way to describe the native country folk,' murmured Kate in a shocked voice.

Markham looked sheepishly at his wife.

Anne, adopting a decidedly sterner tone, said with flashing eyes, 'Our servants have been nothing but loyal and kind. We are kind to them and they have always regarded us with affection. I beg you not to refer to them or even to the mutineers as 'savages,' for they are no such thing!'

Captain Lovelace flushed, but was prevented from answering by Davenport, who said, 'It was actually my man who suggested the disguise. I would not have arrived here alive with my sister, had it not been for the kindness and loyalty of our servants. We are very much in their debt, and I fear, it is a debt I can never repay.'

Captain Lovelace opened his mouth as if to reply, and then closed it into a hard line. Davenport guessed that if the revolt were crushed, the retribution meted out to the sepoys would be harsh and unrestrained. He suspected that Captain Lovelace would be at the forefront of many acts of vengeance that would occur.

'Have you made the acquaintance of my sister, Edwina, Mr. Davenport,' inquired Anne politely, veering the conversation away from its present unhappy tenor.

'Yes, I have indeed had the honour of making Miss Hardingham's acquaintance,' replied Davenport with a slight bow.

Collecting himself, Lovelace interjected, 'Mr. Davenport has neglected to tell you of the friendship he has with your sister, Miss. Hardingham, for he actually escorted her and her friends on a tiger hunt. I believe they bagged a tigress and its cubs, did you not, sir?'

Anne looked horrified, asking, 'They killed the cubs of a tigress? To be sure, that sounds rather cruel, does it not?'

Before Davenport could explain the circumstances, Lovelace answered, 'My dear Miss. Hardingham, I hope you will allow me to prevail upon you to see that your sympathies are rather misplaced. When one's life is placed in peril—whether by man or by beast—it is most expedient to refrain from seeking reasonable behaviour where none should be expected. A wild creature, whether human or animal, must be made to submit or be destroyed. Ferocious beasts cannot be made to restrain their viciousness any more than persons of races that have not become civilized, despite the benefits of training and patronage by those who are inherently superior in their fibre. Take, for instance, your sympathy for the natives. It is as much misplaced as your pity for tiger cubs, who will one day grow up to be ferocious beasts who will probably hunt people or their cattle. It appears to me that you speak from a lack of experience of the world and its ways and perhaps, your views have been formed by those who lack a precise understanding of our function in this country as a superior and civilizing force. It is to be hoped that you will see the wisdom in my words.'

He had very much wished to say these things to Edwina, but had restrained himself. Now, her sisters displayed the same lack of understanding of the importance of keeping the natives in their place. Having displayed so much forbearance—or so he thought, he no longer could contain himself and sincerely believed that it behooved him to counteract the dangerous liberal tendencies that the Hardingham family had a proclivity for. He imagined that Anne Hardingham naturally appreciated the superiority of his mind, and while she had been brought up to think the most unconventional thoughts, he was sure that his influence would erase the shortcomings of her upbringing. Indeed, she would certainly allow herself to be guided by him in matters such as these.

Consequently, he was most surprised when she turned crimson red and, sitting up very straight, said in a wrathful tone, 'Captain Lovelace, you are absolutely correct, one should not seek for reasonable behaviour where none can be expected. Therefore, I shall refrain from trying to reason with you. I shall also go further and release you from our engagement, as it is apparent that anyone who does not submit to your barbaric view of the world must very likely suffer destruction at your hand.'

She rose, and curtsying formally to him, said in crushing accents, 'I bid you goodbye, sir!' leaving him no room for retort.

He looked at her with a shocked expression. And then, as his pride discovered it had been injured, he rose, a look of anger crossing his face. For a few moments, Davenport, who had watched the entire exchange with some amusement, believed that Lovelace would suffer an apoplectic attack.

Markham appeared entirely bewildered, and Kate, horrified at her sister's lack of discretion in the presence of a complete stranger, blushed and stammered, 'But, Anne, only consider. ... Please, Captain Lovelace, you must not. ...'

Captain Lovelace, however, was beyond the reach of reason.

He bowed stiffly and said, 'I shall not impose on your kindness any further. I beg your leave.'

From her earliest years, a deep sense of uprightness had been inculcated in Anne Hardingham, causing her to bristle at Lovelace's words. Moreover, she was a Beauty and unaccustomed to being lectured to—by a man, at that. Worse still, he had insinuated that she had been poorly informed by her parents, and that had enraged her. She felt vindicated in her actions by a sense of righteous anger. However, as Lovelace left the room, it dawned upon Anne that Mr. Davenport, a stranger to her and this home, had been the unwilling witness to a most awkward exchange on a matter that was entirely private between her and Captain Lovelace. She glanced at the door, as if considering an unladylike flight to her bedchamber, but to her relief, Davenport, as if nothing out of the ordinary had just occurred, turned to Markham, asking in a most genial manner, 'Shall we be seeing you in Simla next year, Mr. Markham, providing, of course, that peaceful travel is once again possible?'

Markham, stolid and unimaginative though he was, was excessively well-bred and found himself answering him. Davenport proceeded to invite them to hunt with him if ever they were in Simla again, and within ten minutes, Kate and Markham were discussing their next journey to Simla. Anne marveled at the finesse with which he had countered her clumsy performance. Then, with the hint of the faintest yawn, he rose, and begged to be allowed to take their leave.

'I am much fatigued by my journey. Now that the thrill has passed, I feel nothing but the need to keep to my bed for many days,' he said with a smile.

Inviting them to dine at his home the following day, he bid them good night and departed in the direction of his residence.

The following evening, Markham and the ladies were very gratified to be presented to Miss Jane Davenport who had reportedly had her share of the adventure, the account of which was now spreading across the drawing-rooms of Calcutta. They found her manners very pleasing, and while she was reserved, she was not in the least aloof, and easily conversed with all present. After dinner, when the gentlemen returned to the drawing-room, Anne approached Davenport nervously, to apologize for the events of the previous evening. Mr. Davenport gallantly forestalled her, informing her that her father had shared the news of her engagement with him. He smiled reassuringly at her, promising to treat the matter with discretion, and in fact, he said, he had already put it out of his mind. Mr. and Mrs. Markham also took it upon themselves to apologize for the embarrassment that the incident had most certainly caused Mr. Davenport.

But, he replied calmly, 'On the contrary, it was excessively gratifying to witness Miss. Hardingham champion the cause of kindness and decency. In my business endeavours as well as during my recent adventures, I have witnessed the best and the worst of behaviour from men and women of both races. In my view, respectability and strength of character are not the sole purview of the Europeans. Human beings, as we all are, share vices and virtues alike, and time and circumstances shape us all. We choose actions based on our experiences and our circumstances, whatever they may be, and that has very little to do with our race or our sex. I am grateful to Miss Hardingham for her uncompromising scruples. Had she not challenged Captain Lovelace's assumptions, I most certainly would have. But then, given his temper, he would probably have called me out and we should have had a duel in your drawing-room, Mrs. Markham, which could not have boded well for your magnificent silk rug,' he finished with a twinkle in his eye.

Anne giggled at the image conjured up in her mind at this remark. She looked up at Davenport and it occurred to her that he was extremely handsome. Although not quite as striking in appearance as Edwina's beau, Mr. Grayson, she reflected that he made one feel at ease instantly. He was a master at conversation and seemed highly knowledgeable about a variety of subjects. And although she would be loath to admit it to herself, his considerable wealth, manifested in the magnificence of his dwellings, added greatly to his charm! Markham stood a little in awe of him, and seemed willing to be influenced by him in the matters being discussed. Presently, the conversation turned to more serious matters.

'I intend to return at once to Simla, to discover whether any unrest has reached there, and to bear news to your family, for I had promised Mr. and Mrs. Hardingham that I should bring them news of your state at the earliest. As you cannot be certain that the *dâk* runners have reached them with your messages, I shall leave within the week,' he informed them.

'Oh James, is it perhaps not wiser to wait a little before you place yourself in jeopardy again? When you quit Simla, matters were certainly in hand there. Of what advantage can it be to return there at the peril of your life? And, I should make myself ill with worry if you were to leave, for I am certain you shall not permit me to go with you,' Jane said, her voice trembling.

Markham concurred, saying, 'Consider, Davenport, we have received no word that the Central line has been secured. Indeed, Delhi, Lucknow, and Cawnpore are still out of the Company's control. And besides, the monsoon is underway and you would very likely find yourself swept away should the rivers experience flooding. I urge you to postpone your departure, at the very least until the rains have ceased. Your life and the lives of your men will depend on it!'

Davenport agreed to consider the matter carefully. He was anxious to return to Simla. However, there was, as yet, no cause for alarm and it did not seem just to imperil his men when there was no instant urgency. He resolved to return as soon as the monsoons abated. It was now the beginning of August and in a month and a half, the rains would cease and allow them to make their journey back. He was not troubled by the possibility of battle on the way, as he was sure that they could make their journey back in much the same way as they had on their way here.

CHAPTER NINE

STARTLING REVELATIONS

As these momentous events had unfolded on the plains, life in Simla continued unperturbed. Nothing caused very much anxiety to the British there, save the reports that wafted from the plains. Disconcerting though it was, most felt a sense of security, as if, like the mighty mountains in the distance, they too were sure to endure the ravages of changing times. Those who awaited news from the plains of loved ones, however, experienced no small strain, among whom were the Hardinghams. The gradual, albeit intermittent, supply of news in the hands of the *dâk* runners had brought them some respite from the relentless dread. But, owing to the delay in the relay of such news, one could never be sure how accurate the events and experiences detailed in such letters possibly could be.

On this morning, Edwina sat in the library staring absently at the fire crackling in the hearth. Her attention was soon commanded by a disturbance on a tree branch by the window. There appeared to be a battle of some sort being waged among the beings that had taken up residence on it. Two squirrels quarreled over a heap of nuts that one had reserved to tide him through the winter. The interloper who had attempted to commandeer the stash for himself was angrily driven away from the tree with a great deal of scolding. Edwina felt pleased that the intruder had been routed, relieved for any justice that was meted out in this world. The one who had stored the nuts was the rightful owner and she was gratified that the would-be burglar had been forestalled.

It was October and although it was still autumn, Edwina felt that winter had already taken the world captive. Life in Simla was harder in the winter. The excess of snow made travel difficult and they found themselves living in seclusion for weeks. But, that is not to say that they existed in continual isolation. While practically everyone in the town left for the plains in October or November, many clerks and government officials continued to reside there during the winter, for the business of the government must of necessity be transacted during the winter months, as it must during the summer. Accordingly, the Hardinghams found themselves in the company of friends in the winter, as well. In years past, the family had made its journey to the plains in November, along with the majority of Simla's summer residents. However, when their children had grown up, the Hardinghams began to spend Christmas in Simla, and eventually chose to simply reside there throughout the year. Edwina, usually loved these months when the summer visitors had departed and they enjoyed the town in seclusion. But this year, the autumn air appeared colder and the shortened grey days had a somewhat dampening effect on her spirits. Currently, her temper appeared somewhat more depressed than usual.

The source of her present dissatisfaction lay on her lap, taking the shape of one of several letters the family had received that morning. She glanced down at them, re-reading their contents for possibly the twentieth time. One was from Davenport, addressed to her father. He had read it aloud to her, but she had brought it with her to the library requesting that she be allowed to read it again—to comprehend, she said, more fully the news it carried. The other was a note to her from Anne, and it was the contents of this letter that were a source of some consternation to her. Davenport's letter had brought much joy to the family. It had been sent in the middle of August and, by a miracle, had reached them in October. It announced that he had, after many adventures, reached Danapur safe and sound and, having found his sister unharmed, had escorted her to Calcutta to determine the condition in which the members of Mr. Hardingham's family there found themselves. To his great joy and relief, he said, Calcutta had been spared, by the grace of God, and Markham, the two ladies and the children were in the very best of health.

'*It was my intention,*' he wrote, '*to make my way back to Simla the very week I reached Calcutta. But, I was prevented from doing so by the entreaties of your kind family and my sister, who implored me to remain in Calcutta, at least until the end of the monsoon rains, and return to Simla in October. Knowing the constant anxiety you must find yourself in, only the consideration of my men's wellbeing and my reluctance to drive them through inhospitable terrain – for, I am certain you are well-acquainted with the perils occasioned by the flooding in the plains of the Ganges in this season—have compelled me to delay my departure to Simla. As I cannot be sure that you have received this missive, I am resolved to venture to Simla to echo its message to you in person. I shall set out from Calcutta sometime near the end of October and, having devised a means of travelling without drawing attention to myself, hope to reach Simla no later than the end of November.'*

There were other details in the letter concerning the state of affairs in Calcutta and the effects on trade of the events of the previous months—matters that were of importance to her father, but which Edwina cared nothing about. She was greatly relieved that Davenport had reached Calcutta unscathed and that his sister and her family were all out of harm's way. The news that he intended to arrive in Simla no later than November had greatly pleased her. She stared at the letter, noting the masterful strokes and the neat penmanship. She touched the pages tenderly several times, as one attempting to reach through the distance to touch someone cherished.

Then, against her will, she read Anne's note again. Unbeknownst to its author, its affectionate message produced a great deal of anxiety in its recipient. It said:

Dearest Edwina,
I am overjoyed to write to you, for I have received reassurance that all of you are safe and have been spared the horrors of the trouble that sweeps across our land. News of your condition was brought to us by Mr. Davenport, who has undergone the most fantastic adventure to reach his sister—a most amiable creature. I must own that I am inclined to scold you, for I discovered from Mr. Davenport that you have been acquainted with him for some months now. He has informed us that you were a member of a shikar escorted by him and Uncle John. What a thrilling adventure! But why did you not write to us about it and indeed, why did you not wait for us to return to Simla to be a part of this grand scheme? I should very much have wanted to join a shikar! I have been wondering why you have not taken the pains to write to us since you left Calcutta. I vow it is most provoking, for as the youngest, it is your duty to write to Kate and me. Kate declares that you

had hardly any time to write to us for the rebellion broke out a very short while after your departure for Simla. Nevertheless, I find your reserve quite provoking! But, I shan't scold you too much, for I am certain that you have found yourself quite engaged, in the company of a certain Mr. G who, I was informed by another source, also arrived in Simla not long after you. I hope we shall hear some News from you soon on that front.

As you are probably aware, Papa gave his blessing to an engagement between me and a Captain L. However, since our engagement, I have found that I cannot consign myself to a life of unhappiness with one so incompatible. Indeed, we are wholly unsuited to each other. He has turned out to be quite overbearing and disagreeable. The very night of our acquaintance with Mr. Davenport, he spoke most disrespectfully of our native countrymen, and I was forcefully brought to observe the disparity in our temperaments. I released him of his pledge to me and have since felt a great relief that I can only ascribe to a hitherto unrecognized dread on my part, of ever being united to him!

But, I am not in the least bit unhappy. Having met Mr. D, I have forcefully been made to recognize the virtues that make a man stand above other men. Indeed, it is not fortune or worldly position, but rather, a nobility of character and kindness of temperament that elevate a man's stature. I see now that it is of great import that one be discerning and guarded when selecting a companion. How fortuitous that he should have come into our drawing-room in Calcutta on the very evening I broke off my engagement to Captain L! We have prevailed upon him not to return to Simla for, noble man, he wished to be off to Simla, the moment he entered Calcutta, to reassure Mama and Papa of our wellbeing. He has agreed, quite unwillingly, to tarry here until the monsoon has concluded, but I hope very much that I shall be able to persuade him to remain in Calcutta for a while longer. I am determined to cultivate his acquaintance further and am certain that he will bring himself to be swayed by my entreaties.

I hope that the present difficulties will come to an end rapidly. We have heard of horrible tales of great massacres but I shall not allow them to dampen my spirits. We are all well and I end my letter to you on that cheerful note. God bless you all. Give my love to dearest Mama and Papa and kiss them for me!

Ever your affectionate sister,
A. Hardingham

Edwina stared at the letter with a sense of foreboding. To be sure, she was relieved and gave thanks to God that her sisters and brother-law and the children were safe. Her joy over this circumstance was surpassed only by the fact that Davenport had reached Calcutta unharmed. For months, she had walked around with the greatest dread and only a stubborn reliance on God's mercy on her part, had afforded her any solace. Today, however, as she read Anne's letter, the revelation that Anne was beginning to develop a partiality for Mr. Davenport had the effect of greatly upsetting her. It was evident that she herself was believed to have a partiality for Mr. Grayson. Indeed, Mr. Davenport had appeared to be convinced of that when he last dined with them, and now, the giggling references that would no doubt be made on the subject by Anne, would only cast the idea more solidly in his mind.

Edwina cringed as the sound of Anne's tinkling laugh resonated in her ears. She stood up and walked to the mirror that hung on the wall. A slight, unremarkable and frankly bleak figure stared back at her forlornly. Suddenly, she collapsed on a nearby chair, giving vent to the tears she would not shed for months, as she held resolutely to the conviction that Davenport was alive and would reach Calcutta unscathed. But today, when she had felt love's joy at hearing that he was well, she felt great despair wash over her, as she had simultaneously received the intimation that Anne, who was Beauty personified, had set her cap at him! Anne, with her golden hair and fluttering eyelashes, who could rest her fan across her right cheek and then across her left, dragging her gentlemen through crests and vales, would have no difficulty whatsoever in capturing Mr. Davenport's affections. Besides being vastly pretty, she had the advantage of having his company at her bidding, for the monsoons had collaborated effectually with her to detain him in Calcutta. She wished very much that she could chatter and scold, like the squirrel on the tree, and shoo away all who came in between her and Davenport. She sat sobbing noiselessly for several minutes, when the door to the library opened and Christopher walked in. Pleased to see his cousin, he was about to speak, when it occurred to him that she was in some distress.

He stood silent for a few moments, drinking in the scene and then strode to her, saying with great concern, 'Eddie, my dear, what has occurred?! Why do you weep?'

Edwina started and hastily attempted to dry her tears, but the streams that flowed down her cheeks were already observed and Christopher put his arms around her shoulders as he knelt by her chair. Overcome by his kindness, she collapsed into his arms, sobbing inconsolably. Her cousin was considerably disconcerted by this, for he had known her, for their entire lives, to be a rather tenacious person, never wont to give in to fits of melancholiness. Edwina Hardingham was not known for having overwrought nerves, no matter the adversity that presented itself. The present deluge, he was sure, must have its source in some great misfortune.

After the space of ten minutes, she collected herself, and having pulled herself away, began to dry her tears, saying, with a chuckle, 'Do not panic, dear brother. I have not the slightest intention of having the hysterics!'

'Well, what made you weep, in the first place?' he asked.

'Oh, nothing! It was just silliness on my part. Perhaps the news from Calcutta has overwhelmed me with joy and relief,' she answered with a forced smile.

Saying nothing, Christopher glanced down at her lap and surmised, quite accurately, that the contents of the letter were responsible for the sorrow manifested on his cousin's countenance. Picking up Davenport's letter, he read the contents, finding nothing exceptional in there to warrant such a demonstration of feeling.

Perhaps her dislike of Davenport has upset her, for she feels guilty for it, given the extent to which we are obliged to him, he mused.

He shook his head, for that explanation did not serve to explain the very heartbreak that appeared to be etched across her face. Then, he spied the other letter, from Anne.

Very likely, it is that letter that has made her unhappy, he thought.

With her permission, he began to peruse the contents of this letter, but it too held no explanation that was readily apparent, for the dark mood that had descended over Edwina.

'Perhaps you are hurt by Anne's scolding you for not writing,' he speculated. 'Do not be grieved by it, for I am sure Anne says a hundred cross things in a day without quite meaning half of them. I daresay she was in some petulance over how her hair was dressed that evening, or some such trifling matter, and turned her annoyance in your direction,' he said soothingly.

She looked at him absently and nodded. He re-read Anne's letter, thinking that Edwina ought to be pleased by the broken engagement to Captain Lovelace, if anything.

'What has upset you, Edwina? You well know that you can pour your heart out to me!' he said.

Again, she shook her head, saying, 'It is nothing, Chris. I am simply being a peagoose. That is all!'

Suddenly, as he read the letter for the third time, convinced that the source of her sorrow lay within it, he stiffened.

'Can it be—Edwina!' he said in shocked accents.

'You cannot be in. ...' he said, with widened eyes.

'But, I thought you. ...' he tried again.

Perplexed by these half-uttered interjections, Edwina looked up at him in puzzlement.

He got up very quickly and with dancing eyes, pulled her up by the hands, exclaiming, 'Oh it will do! Indeed, it will do! Well done, Edwina! You have chosen well! Davenport of all persons! You shall get along famously—when you stop quarrelling, that is!'

'What on earth are you talking about, Chris? And pray, do stop hauling me about the room in this unbecoming fashion. It is most unsettling!' she replied indignantly, trying desperately to conceal what he had just discovered.

He laughed and pulling her to sit beside him on the sofa, asked her softly whether she was unhappy because it appeared that Anne was very much in danger of becoming rather fond of Mr. Davenport. She abandoned all pretense at this direct approach.

'Yes, that is very likely, for as you know, he is quite dazzling and no girl could help it but that she should find herself falling quite in love with him! And consider, Chris, that Anne will have whomever she pleases for she is so handsome,' she replied in a forlorn but breathless voice, relieved to be able to unburden herself of the great secret that she had held onto for all these months.

'But surely, you recognize, my dear, that Davenport is a gentleman and you have no cause to doubt his constancy towards you. Depend upon it that he will remain true to you, even if Anne has set her heart upon him and flirts endlessly with that silk fan of hers!'

'But—but,' she stammered unhappily, 'I do not think he has reason to remain constant to me. Indeed, I do not think he has a very good opinion of me. In fact, I do not believe he has more than a cursory awareness of my existence.'

'So you have not pledged yourselves to each other?' asked Christopher, sounding very disappointed.

She shook her head.

'If he has no more than a cursory awareness of your existence, which I find hard to believe, it is unlikely that he would have thought enough of you to have a bad opinion of you,' her cousin said, matter-of-factly. 'I would venture to say that he either likes you very much, or dislikes you intensely. But, I doubt that he is indifferent to you!' he continued.

The conviction that Davenport probably disliked her a great deal had taken firm hold of her mind and this pronouncement had the effect of driving her to tears again.

Quite annoyed at herself for this missish display of tears, she shook herself, and straightening her shoulders, said in weary but firm voice, 'It does not signify. He is presently at Anne's side. She seems rather captivated by him. It is unlikely that he would discard her attention to gain mine, unexceptional as I am.'

And when Christopher opened his mouth in indignant retort, taking umbrage at her words, she raised her hand, saying, 'It does not matter. Pray, let us not discuss this anymore. I am resolved to live a happy life and I refuse to give credence to the notion that it is impossible in Mr. Davenport's absence to do so. I should have found life most pleasant at Mr. Davenport's side. But who is to say whether we are truly compatible or not? After all, we never made any declarations to each other that gave us leave to be frank in each other's company.'

She gave him a tremulous smile and, with a confidence without that she was far from feeling within, she squeezed his hand and put the letters aside. Christopher found her calm acceptance of Anne's conquest unsettling. After all, they did not know anything about Davenport's feelings on the matter. But, Edwina was nothing if not clearheaded and was very unlikely to entertain notions that were impractical and improbable. Still, he wished that there was some means by which he could unite these two remarkable persons! He had the greatest respect for Davenport, and apart from his aunt, there was no one he loved quite as much in this world as his youngest cousin. He smiled at her, according her an affectionate peck on her cheek. Hearing her mother call, she composed herself and they made their way to Mrs. Hardingham who had also received a letter from Anne.

Mrs. Hardingham appeared to be in some disarray, for Anne had relayed much the same message to her mother, as she had to her sister. However, she was noticeably less reserved about her regard for Davenport, when addressing her mother. All the Hardingham children had a deep affinity towards their mother. They were wont to confess things to her that they did not share with each other. Throughout their childhood, she had been their confidant, their champion and the witness to their jealousies and petty quarrels. They quaked when she admonished them and doted on her with a jealous love. She, for her part, was a devoted parent, patient and kind, but also firm and occasionally, exacting. She loved her daughters impartially and unreservedly, to the dismay of some of her friends, who found her unabashed adoration of her offspring quite unfashionable. Her impartiality—for she would never prefer one child over the other—was tempered by great love, good judgment and a sense of fairness.

She noticed that Edwina was sometimes put upon by the others and quietly championed her cause. She chuckled as Edwina, unaffected by their overbearing actions, held her own and quietly pursued her own interests. While she was aware that her youngest child had a steely backbone, she also knew that Edwina was possessed of a good-natured and generous temperament that often led her to capitulate to the will of the ones she loved. Presently, she was concerned that Edwina stood in very great danger of being besieged by her sister.

'My love, I have news from Anne,' she said, in somewhat heightened colour.

'Yes, Mama! Indeed, she has written to me also,' replied Edwina.

'Well, my letter has some fantastic news—that I have just now shared with your Papa.'

'Is it about her engagement? That she has released Lovelace from it?' asked Edwina.

Her mother nodded impatiently, saying, 'Yes, yes, but there is more. She says that she has taken a liking to Mr. Davenport—she declares that she is *quite in love with him*!'

231

Edwina paled imperceptibly, but answered impassively, 'Yes, she has hinted of that, although not quite as *bluntly*.'

Mrs. Hardingham clucked disapprovingly.

'That will not do, it will not do at all! Oh, it is most unsuitable, and so, *so* provoking of Anne!' she said.

Edwina looked at her with disbelief.

'But surely, Mama, you cannot believe that Davenport is unworthy of Anne?! On the contrary, he is every whit her superior!' she declared, rising hotly to the defense of her beloved Davenport, and quite forgetting that she was championing the cause of her rival in love.

'Aye, silly chit, that is what I am trying to say!' retorted Mrs. Hardingham with some asperity. 'Davenport is a good man, and *almost* worthy of you! Anne is but trifling with him, and she will soon find her fan broken by him! Depend upon it, she will blunder with him with her coquettish ways and he will give her a stern dressing down ere their vows are spoken! A more unsuitable pair I have not met, and what's more, I daresay he and you are quite in love with each other! Really, Anne must be quite obtuse not to notice that his heart is elsewhere engaged. But then, he is a gentleman and she has never beheld the two of you together,' she lamented.

Edwina listened to this outburst with great astonishment. Her mouth had fallen open and she shut it, swallowed a few times and opened it again to speak, but was prevented from doing so by a hoot of laughter from Christopher who had listened to their exchange with knotted brows at first, but with an ever-widening smile, eventually. Edwina cast a disapproving look at him, but he was not crushed in the least.

Instead, he pressed on, 'Oho! So this has been common knowledge, has it, Aunt? I have only just guessed this great secret, while you both have been secretly planning the wedding! Is my uncle privy to this wonderful news?' he asked.

Mrs. Hardingham was forced to smile at this.

Looking disapprovingly at Edwina, she remarked, 'Oh, Edwina has been disagreeably reserved on this matter, as you know—having only just discovered the information yourself! *I* guessed it when he came to dine and she was tongue-tied in his presence. Have you ever known Edwina to be at a loss for words? But that was what she was that evening! Of course, I must point out that this effect only lasted in our poor Edwina when she was in the immediate vicinity of Mr. Davenport, for it was not five minutes after he had left her side and walked to the other side of the sofa that the effects wore off. I dare say none of us shall quite forget the tongue-lashing she gave poor Captain Lovelace when that happened, despite being desperately in love, and quite tongue-tied on account of it!' she finished with a twinkle in her eye.

'Upon my word! Has she been in love with him all this time?!' Christopher asked, looking at Edwina in some confusion.

'But of course, she has, dear Christopher—ever since Mr. Davenport rescued her from the tiger. I am astonished that you failed to grasp what transpired beneath your very nose,' replied Mrs. Hardingham, the laughter brimming in her voice and eyes.

Christopher turned to his cousin with a look of bewilderment, saying 'Why on earth did you then want me to detain the men at their Port that night, Eddie? I thought it was because you couldn't stand the sight of the man and wished to be miles away from him!'

Edwina had, by now, turned a bright and becoming shade of crimson and was studying very intently the patterns on her dress. She carefully plucked a loose thread, taking care not to create a run in the fabric. But, Christopher tugged her arm impatiently, demanding an answer.

Abandoning her façade of indifference, she replied with exasperation, 'I didn't want you to *detain* them. Rather, I wished you to *hasten* their return to the drawing-room. It was really most disappointing to have to wait for *hours* for you to return. I was very close to boxing your ears!'

Hearing this, her mother and cousin erupted in a chorus of laughter that accentuated her present discomfort.

'There is really no cause for merriment here. Mr. Davenport has made no pledge to me and indeed, there is no evidence that he has any affection for me. He is very likely to fall head over heels in love with our lovely Anne and she may cast aside all her wilful ways for him and they shall live happily ever after, whilst I shall die of a broken heart,' she said severely.

'Oh, I don't suppose you shall *die* of a broken heart, my love. One never does, you know. It is considerably more likely that you shall *live* with one—to a very ripe old age, and have seven cats and carry a cane,' pronounced Mrs. Hardingham cheerily.

Despite her despondency, Edwina giggled at the images this remark conjured in her mind.

Her mother stroked her cheek affectionately, saying, 'Come, this is much better, for that is the first time I have seen laughter in your eyes for many months!'

'What is to be done?' asked Christopher seriously.

'I shall persuade Anne that they are unsuited to each other—for he is entirely too serious to make her happy. She will be unhappy unless she is endlessly at balls and routs and none of those will do for Davenport for very long, unless I am mistaken,' she replied.

'There really isn't anything to be done, Mama. I beg that you will not interfere for I will not have Anne's unhappiness on my conscience. We will learn, when Mr. Davenport returns, of how things stand. I had lief as not have his affections through manipulation or artifice,' said Edwina firmly.

She was resolute in this and at last, her mother and cousin agreed to let matters rest, although Mrs. Hardingham was privately resolved to discourage Anne's interest in the man, for her own good. When he came in November, all would be clear. For her part, Edwina sat down to write a long letter to her sister, disabusing her of certain notions she appeared to cherish regarding herself and Mr. Grayson.

October dragged on into November and then into December and still, there was no sign of Davenport. Finally, they received a letter from him in the middle of December, intimating that he had postponed his return to the hills until the spring, for he was unavoidably detained in Calcutta on matters of business. Having received their letter of reply that reassured him that they were aware of how matters stood in Calcutta, he no longer felt a sense of urgency to return and was able to attend to matters that were pressing. His business affairs in Delhi had been affected by the revolt and he needed to tend to matters at once, he said. Edwina, privately concluded that Anne's charms had made their mark and that he had chosen to remain at her side.

They would not receive any letters until the spring, for the snows made it nigh impossible for the *dâk* runners to make their way up the hills. Instead, it would be collected and remain at the government bungalow at Haldwani, and someone would collect it, once the snows melted and the path became clear. The delay in Davenport's return and the absence of letters convinced her that her cause was lost. Her heart felt gripped by a cold hand, a feeling that was doubtless exacerbated by the coldness of winter. She alternated between moments of great regret at her circumstances and a resolve to be joyful, regardless of her circumstances.

Sometimes she thought, *Why did I not convey to him my feelings in some measure? Why would I not permit Uncle John to censure Grayson, for then, he would not believe that I continued to harbour a fondness for him! Oh, why was I not born beautiful and charming and witty, so that the charms of a thousand other beauties could not rival mine?!*

At other times she thought, *Had he any affection for me, neither the presence of Grayson nor other enticements would suffice to keep him from me. If he does not care for me now, it is because he never has and one must never repine over unrequited love, for that is the greatest waste of time. There can be no compulsion in matters of the heart and one cannot help whom one loves and neither can one be reproached for whom one does not.*

And so, her thoughts and emotions went back and forth in the endless vacillation known to all who are afflicted by unrequited love and its accompanying heartache, until one day, she was more inclined towards the conviction that life was to be enjoyed to its fullest, regardless of one's setbacks, than towards an overwhelming sense of regret. Perhaps it was the promise of change in the seasons, or perhaps it was the inevitable cure that time affords, but she felt herself less depressed as February began to dwindle down. Mrs. Hardingham was exceedingly gratified to note that Edwina did hum as she flitted around the house, taking a greater share than ever in managing the affairs of the household.

And one evening, Christopher was delighted to hear her make plans to ride the following day, 'For,' said she, 'the snows are almost melted and if we stay on the road, perhaps we shall enjoy a morning of good riding!'

The proposal was well-received and soon, plans were made to go riding the following day, if the weather permitted. The roads were relatively clean, with the exception of accumulations of snow in some places. The air was crisp and the horses, delighted to be about, snorted and shook their heads in delight. Edwina inhaled the crisp spring air deeply, savouring its scent and blinking at the sunshine that danced on her eyelashes. The whole family had set out and they rode for the space of twenty minutes, when they caught sight of the smoke drifting from the chimney in the Vicar's cottage, in the distance. The Reverend Gladstone and his wife were some of the few year-round members of the British community in Simla. The Hardinghams rode towards their cottage, intending to access the open meadow that lay beyond it.

As they drew closer, perhaps a quarter of a mile away from the cottage, Christopher exclaimed, 'There is something on the ground by the clump of trees.'

The rest of the company, following the direction of his hand, beheld what appeared to be a scarlet heap, fluttering upon a clump of snow and dried leaves near a thicket that bordered the road. The men dismounted and approached slowly, when Mr. Hardingham gave a shout.

He declared with some agitation, 'It's a lady—she has collapsed and is unconscious. Quick, my dear!'

Christopher aided his aunt and cousin, as they dismounted and hurried to the inert figure. Sure enough, it was a lady in a grey walking dress. A crimson scarf, fluttering in the breeze, obscured her face, but highlighted golden hair that glistened in the morning sun. Mrs. Hardingham lifted her by the shoulders and gently placed her fair head on her lap. Edwina let out a gasp as her scarf slid off her face.

'It is Miss. Johnson!' she said in great astonishment.

'Are you acquainted with this lady, Edwina?' asked Mr. Hardingham with no small surprise.

'Indeed, Papa! It is Miss. Johnson. Do you not remember her? She is my friend—she accompanied me on the *shikar* with Uncle John and Mr. Davenport,' replied Edwina.

Picking up a clump of snow, Christopher melted it in his hands and sprinkled it upon Miss. Johnson's face, whereupon, she moaned. Taking off her gloves, Edwina chafed her small hands and after a few moments, Miss. Johnson's eyes fluttered open.

'Wh—who? … Wh—where am I?' she stammered.

Her eyes widened in recognition, as she beheld Edwina and Christopher. She sat up in some confusion, clutching at her scarf and trying desperately to regain her composure. It was then that Edwina saw that her belly appeared to be swollen. Startled, her eyes flew to her mother's face, and she saw a look of great concern written across it. Mrs. Hardingham motioned to the men to assist Miss. Johnson to her feet.

'Miss Johnson, were you walking to your home?' Christopher asked with great solicitude.

'N—no—that is—I—er—I was going to the Vicar's house. That is, I am currently residing with the Gladstones—for—for the winter, that is,' she said, with some confusion.

'Ah! That is most fortunate, for that is the general direction in which we are headed. We would be honoured to escort you there,' said Christopher kindly.

At this, Miss. Johnson looked alarmed and said she would prefer to continue her walk.

'Miss Johnson, that can hardly be wise, given that you have just been revived from a state of unconsciousness. Come, walk with us, so that you can reach safely home,' said Edwina coaxingly.

Miss. Johnson forced an unnatural laugh and said with some stubbornness, 'Why, it was the veriest little fainting spell. I am quite well. In fact, nothing would be better than for me to walk, for the fresh air is bound to do me good.'

Then, as a thought crossed her mind, she added, 'Pray, do not tell the Vicar or his wife that you ever saw me. I beg you will promise to keep this a secret!'

Her voice carried a note of desperation and she looked pleadingly at them.

At this, Mrs. Hardingham intervened and said firmly, 'Nonsense, child! You have had a fainting fit and in this condition, you shall not be allowed to wander about the countryside unaccompanied. Mr. Hardingham and my nephew will aid you and ensure that you reach home safely. Come, let us be going, unless you would prefer to be carried by them, Miss. Johnson.'

The note of decision in her voice left no room for gainsaying and Miss. Johnson, her countenance becoming paler by the minute, meekly surrendered her arm to Mr. Hardingham. They walked to the cottage in silence disturbed only by bird calls and the chatter of squirrels. Edwina looked at her mother, an unspoken question in her eyes, and Mrs.

Hardingham nodded, answering her wordlessly. Edwina's eyes widened and her hand flew to her cheek in dismay, but she said nothing. She glanced at Christopher who, along with his uncle, was holding Miss. Johnson's arm and leading her gently to the cottage, but his face remained impassive.

Leaving the men's horses tethered to a tree, Edwina and her mother made their way to the cottage to alert the Reverend and Mrs. Gladstone about what had occurred. Mrs. Gladstone, a thin, birdlike woman who was given to spells of nervous agitation, wrung her hands nervously.

'Oh dear! Whatever shall I do? I warned her not to go out by herself. I told her this was how it would be. She would not listen. Oh, if word got out, Reverend Gladstone and I would be hard-pressed to explain. ...' she trailed off, with a nervous air.

She shook her head and paced nervously, groaning under her breath intermittently, muttering something about being ruined. She looked anxiously out of the window and shook her head nervously as the two men escorting the lady neared the house.

'Perhaps we can make a cup of tea for Miss. Johnson, and one to steady your nerves, my dear Mrs. Gladstone,' suggested Mrs. Hardingham taking charge of matters.

The Vicar nodded, as he stoked the fire. A somewhat bookish man, he had chosen the life of a clergyman—to serve God, as he put it. This, he was perfectly content to do, as long as it did not entail dealing with predicaments involving his parishioners. While he took great pleasure in discourse on the finer points of doctrine—and his sermons were rather rousing—he demurred from dealing with the murkiness of human tribulations. Not for him was the knowledge of the sordid circumstances people were likely to find themselves in when sin had completed its ravages on them. He had an innate horror of the base, and squalor appalled him. Like his wife, he was strongly of the opinion that transacting with the sinner could taint one's own reputation, and he was a firm believer in eschewing all appearance of evil—although it must be pointed out that he had a sadly deficient notion of what eschewing the appearance of evil might entail. He spoke eloquently of God's mercy, but shuddered at the thought of any involvement with sinners. The lost sheep might find itself a place in the fold, as long as it could demonstrate great penitence, but he could not, as a respectable clergyman, go after such sheep, and certainly not succour one in its hour of suffering the consequences of sin.

Consequently, he felt himself inconvenienced by Miss Johnson's presence at his home. He had agreed to her presence as a guest after some pressure from Colonel Pendleton, who had promised vague advancements and promotions, should they house his wife's cousin in their home for the winter. He remonstrated with Miss. Johnson as she entered, looking pale and worn.

'Well, really, Miss. Johnson! I wonder at you, going off by yourself for a walk! May I remind you that this is a clergyman's establishment and we cannot have you—you. ...' he stopped abruptly, not wishing to reveal the reason for his indignation.

Mr. Hardingham stared at him with some amazement and said, 'Surely the lady can have meant no harm to you by going for a walk, and perhaps she is in need of assistance now?'

Tears welled up in Diana's eyes, but before she could speak, Mrs. Hardingham led her to a chair by the fire, offering her a cup of tea.

'You are right; come on Miss. Johnson, sit by the fire,' said Mr. Gladstone in a somewhat resentful tone.

Christopher receiving a cup of tea, walked to where Edwina stood, and in the guise of pulling her a chair, whispered in her ear, 'This is bad business, Eddy! I dislike having to tell you something this indelicate, but poor Miss. Johnson is with child.'

Before she could stop herself, Edwina let out a smile. She bit her lip to keep herself from laughing, for Christopher with his earnest air, declaring to her a circumstance that she and her mother had noticed at the outset, seemed rather comical.

'And what, pray tell, do you know of such matters?' she whispered back.

He looked down at her in some surprise, but refrained from answering. The room had fallen silent and Mrs. Hardingham urged Diana to rest awhile in her bedchamber. Overcome with embarrassment, the lady was glad to oblige and excused herself from their company.

Mrs. Gladstone sighed as soon as she left the room, remarking, 'Oh, whatever shall I do, Mr. Gladstone, for this will certainly not do. We shall be undone by this very great scandal!'

'Hush, my dear! Do compose yourself, for we must be mindful of our guests,' replied Mr. Gladstone, wanting very much to keep the matter concealed from the Hardinghams.

But Mr. Hardingham, who had thus far failed to notice the hapless Diana's altered appearance wished to know what scandal Mrs. Gladstone was referring to.

'Oh! Can it be that you have not noticed, Mr. Hardingham?' said Mrs. Gladstone in a dramatic voice.

Before he could answer, Mrs. Hardingham said, 'Perhaps you should tell us, Mrs. Gladstone. You may depend upon our silence and our discretion!'

This assurance served as an invitation for Mrs. Gladstone to unburden herself of the great secret she had hidden for some five months. Speaking rapidly and continuously for the space of fifteen minutes, she apprised them of the unfortunate Miss. Johnson's predicament. The lady, she said, was found to be with child seven months ago. The blackguard responsible for her condition had deserted her, and was very likely to have been killed during the fighting in the plains. Colonel Pendleton and her cousin had all but cast her off, paying the Vicar handsomely to keep her in their home and to remain discreet. Once her confinement was past, she would be sent with the child to England. No harm would come of it, promised Colonel Pendleton, for the lady would remain in Simla for the winter, and given the relative isolation forced upon them by winter, none would be the wiser.

When the worthy clergyman had balked at the notion of tainting himself by involvement in such a scandal, Colonel Pendleton, always a rather forceful man, offered up vague promises of putting in a word with the Viceroy's Private Secretary, who was an old friend, for a possible appointment in Calcutta. They needed someone of Reverend Gladstone's calibre in Calcutta, suggested the Colonel vaguely, and Mr. Gladstone would possibly be able to procure a position on the Viceroy's staff the following year.

While Mr. Gladstone did not wish to be corrupted by associating with the fallen, the inducements proffered by Colonel Pendleton proved to be too great and he would after all, he thought, be assisting a soul in error to find the path to repentance. But, this task proved to be too exacting, as he discovered. For with each passing month, Miss. Johnson's secret became more apparent and the risk of exposure increased. Furthermore, she appeared not to see herself as one terribly stained by wickedness and who should consequently remain hidden from Polite Society. She was given to walking about in public and artlessly coming into the sitting room whenever they had visitors. The respectable Vicar and his wife were most certainly inconvenienced by her presence in their home. Mrs. Gladstone concluded her account of the affair by declaring that she thought the young woman a perfect hussy who should not be permitted into such respectable and polite company as theirs. She was interrupted by a great sob from Miss. Johnson who, having come unobserved into the sitting room in search of a book of sermons that she had lately been perusing, stood by the door listening to the invective against her.

Clasping her hand to her mouth, she fled back to her bedchamber, declaring, 'I shall have to kill myself! Oh whatever shall I do!'

At this awful pronouncement, Mrs. Hardingham and Edwina went after her quickly, followed—somewhat halfheartedly—by Mrs. Gladstone. They found the unhappy lady wailing in her bedchamber, beating her breast and rocking to and fro on a chair. Mrs. Hardingham, recognizing correctly that she was on the verge of hysterics, went straightaway to her and enveloped her in the most motherly embrace. This had the effect of increasing Miss Johnson's agony, and she began to wail louder. Mrs. Gladstone then began to feel a strong bout of hysterics coming on herself.

Seeing her dismayed and overwrought appearance, Mrs. Hardingham declared, 'Hush, child! Do not weep, for you must remain calm in your condition. Perhaps we can be of service to you? Would you do us the honour of being our guest? We shall take very good care of you and poor Mrs. Gladstone, who has taken very good care of you thus far, shall have a chance to recover her nerves.'

At this, both ladies cheered up considerably. Mrs. Gladstone, who had not considered the possibility of liberation from her circumstances, eyed Mrs. Hardingham with considerable awe. Diana, who had correctly surmised that Mrs. Hardingham was a compassionate maternal figure, was likewise noticeably consoled and dried her tears instantly.

Leaving Edwina to assist Diana in packing her things, Mrs. Hardingham returned to the sitting room and informed her husband in soft accents that Miss. Johnson would be a guest in their home until her confinement. Mr. Hardingham, a firm believer in the wisdom of minding one's own business and refraining from meddling in those of others', opened his mouth to protest, but encountering a stern look from his wife, closed it again. He was a kind and patient man, but he had no desire to intermeddle in the affairs of those around him. If the lady was entrusted to the Vicar's care, then why interfere with the arrangement?

What if Colonel Pendleton took it into his head to take offense at the change of plans that was occurring without his having been consulted? His practical nature gave him pause for thought, but that side of him was soon overruled by a deep affection for his wife. He had been married for a sufficient length of time to recognize the gleam of crusading kindness that entered his beloved wife's eyes when she championed the cause of the underdog. Nothing in that hour would suffice, but to carry out her mission of compassionate rescue. He nodded resignedly and began to make plans for transporting the young woman to his home.

The next morning, Diana awoke to the cheery sounds of a Himalayan *bulbul* outside her window. She stared uncomprehendingly at her surroundings for a few moments, before recalling that she was now very comfortably installed in the establishment of Mr. and Mrs. Hardingham. A sense of sadness and mortification washed over her, as she realized how distressing her circumstances were. She recalled the ball she had attended here, seemingly a lifetime ago, where she had danced and flirted and had such a glorious time. She shed tears recalling how Christopher was one of her set of admirers. Sadly, here she was now, by all accounts a *fallen* woman, depending on the charity of these very persons.

Her contemplations were interrupted by a gentle knock on the door. She called to the person to come in and was somewhat uncomfortable to see Edwina enter, followed by the maid carrying a tray of tea and breakfast for her.

'We were not sure what you would desire for breakfast, so we brought you some toast and eggs. I am sorry to have woken you up, but Mama says it will not do for you to abstain from nourishment in your present condition,' she said, motioning the maid away. 'Do you feel well, Diana?' she continued, as she plumped the pillows behind her head.

Grateful for such kindness, Diana began to weep again and Edwina, every bit as compassionate as her mother, folded her into her arms.

'Do not weep, dear Diana. It shall be well. You shall get through this by the grace of God,' said she.

'Oh, what would God have to do with a wretch like me? Oh no! I cannot expect his mercy, for I have behaved in a most wanton manner!' wailed the unhappy Diana.

'Oh but you must not say so! The mercy of God is precisely for the very persons who have behaved unseemly, for did not our Lord say that it is not the healthy who need a doctor, but the sick? Be assured, my dear Diana, that God's grace is verily for those in the greatest need of it!'

This heartening discourse had its desired effect upon Diana, who soon dried her tears and partook of some toast and tea.

'What shall we do this morning?' asked Edwina cheerfully. 'Let us take a turn about the lawn. We must not venture too far from the house, for Mama says that is not safe to scurry around when one is *enceinte*. Have you any names picked for the baby? I must own, I am most excited to meet him, or perhaps, her,' she said with a twinkle in her eye.

This elicited a worried smile from Diana who, although stirred by instincts of maternal love, was also troubled by the circumstance of being unwed.

'Oh, I try not to think of the baby. In fact, I sometimes wish it were not. I wish for my life to be returned to me, for in coming into my womb, this child has ruined me,' she cried, feeling a pang of guilt race through her heart as the words came out.

Edwina looked at her with great distress, declaring, 'Oh, do not blame the poor child. It is not its doing. It shall have plenty of hardship in its life and many who shall reject it. Only let not one of those persons be you!'

Diana had not considered this point of view. She had spent many nights alternating between a deep love for the child and a desperate resentment of it. In Edwina's company, she began to feel the former sentiment overwhelm the latter so that, by the day's end, she was happily debating on the excellences of several infants' names for each sex.

Eventually, she became silent, and after dinner, as the men lingered over their Port, she asked in a quiet tone, 'Do you not wish to know who has placed me in this predicament?'

Mrs. Hardingham and Edwina looked at her in some surprise.

Edwina replied, 'We wish to know only that which you wish to confide in us. Do not tax yourself by worrying about our thoughts or conjectures on the matter. You are among friends. You shall not be gossiped about. Indeed, you shall only divulge to us whatever details you choose.'

Mrs. Hardingham nodded in agreement and Diana, tears welling up in her eyes, declared, 'Oh, you are angels of mercy, and I have served you so ill!'

The two ladies looked at her in some puzzlement, but said nothing, waiting for her to continue.

She swallowed and then, said in a soft voice, 'By one whom you have held in some esteem, Edwina, am I in this state. Mr. Grayson is the one who has ruined me. And, while I deeply regret that I interfered in your friendship—for I was aware that he held you in some regard—I am glad that you, my dearest friend, for that is what you are now become, have been spared the ignominy of his affections. He is a most unscrupulous, mercenary man, and while it is true that you might have experienced a kinder fate at his hands, I am excessively gratified that you have been preserved from the dishonour of association with him! All that pains me now is the notion that you have been hurt by my interference.'

Mrs. Hardingham and Edwina, entirely stunned by this announcement, said nothing for several moments.

Then, as Diana began to look pale with anxiety, Edwina said in a soothing tone, 'My dear Diana, it is I who am to blame. I became acquainted with Mr. Grayson's character after our *shikar*. I noticed also, the transference of his affections from me to you. Instead of warning you of the dishonourable character of the man, I chose to heave a sigh of relief that he was gone, and was distracted by—by—other circumstances. You have nothing to reproach yourself for. The only person who is worthy of reproach is Mr. Grayson. He alone has done what is abhorrent. Rest assured that I have, for many months, not experienced the smallest trace of affection for Mr. Grayson!'

CHAPTER TEN

A GREAT MISUNDERSTANDING

Miss. Johnson's astonishing revelation, while occasioning great surprise among the Hardinghams, did not exactly come as a terrible shock. They had by now formed a rather accurate image of Mr. Grayson's character and Diana's predicament, while quite distressing, appeared entirely in keeping with it. When they thought they had plumbed the true baseness of his character, however, they were once again given cause for astonishment. This occurred by means of a letter that Edwina received the following day. Warmer weather had permitted the servants to be sent to Haldwani to purchase provisions for the household. They returned with several letters that had been deposited there during the winter. Some were from Mr. Hardingham's business manager in Calicut while others were from Kate and Anne, apprising the family of events occurring in the plains.

Markham wrote a complete account of the outcomes of the revolt in his letter to Mr. Hardingham. Delhi had been reclaimed by the British. While Lucknow was still being fought over, the European women and children there had been rescued and moved to safety. Cawnpore had also been secured and the great leader Tatya Tope had been defeated there. The most awful tales of the slaughter of women and children at Cawnpore had emerged, which were now fuelling the British thirst for vengeance as never before. Countless Indians had been killed as a result, and it was all so deeply distressing! What caught the attention of the Hardinghams, however, was a very startling revelation in Anne's letter to Edwina.

My Dearest Edwina,

I am just now made aware of News of a most shocking nature, which gives me great reason to thank God for His kindness to us. I have been terribly distraught since hearing it and cannot stop trembling. A great anger fills my heart, along with a desire for retribution upon the head of him who is at the centre of it. But, I digress and shall presently come straight to the point, as soon as I am able to collect my thoughts and describe the events of the past few days to you.

A few days ago—perhaps on Wednesday—Markham returned from his club in some agitation, informing us that a scandal of a most peculiar nature was unfolding in Calcutta. He claimed that an Englishman had lately been arrested by the police on grounds of suspicious behaviour. He would not divulge anything further without evidence, he said. He came home to dine today in some agitation and revealed all to us.

Some days ago, a band of robbers held up a carriage in Chowringhee and made away with the valuables of an elderly Indian lady of some means and importance in the city. An English gentleman made an appearance, seemingly out of nowhere, and played the part of the lady's rescuer. He fought bravely against the robbers and they fled, but not before they snatched a box of jewels in her possession. The lady was most grateful for the intervention of the Englishman who had, by all accounts, put up a stiff fight against the villains. She rewarded him handsomely with a ring that was upon her hand and which the robbers had not time to relieve her of—for they beat a hasty retreat in the face of the Englishman's wrath.

She then proceeded to invite him to her haveli for a greater reward. However, one of the lady's servants recognizing a bracelet on the hand of one of the miscreants— for it was a particularly unique bracelet—was able to disclose to the police later, the identity of this robber and the location of his dwelling. The Inspector of Police, upon hearing of the incident, became extremely suspicious of the circumstances. He called on the Englishman for his account of the events and then, without the man's knowledge, posted two men to follow him about. A few days later, the men followed him to the very location of the robber's residence that the lady's servant had informed the police about.

As the Sergeant's Station was not but two streets away, the men sent word to the Sergeant, who rushed thence with a body of men and apprehended the man, who was busy dividing the loot with the robbers and devising plans for another robbery. The Englishman, who was caught with a share of the lady's jewels on his person, attempted first to deny his complicity with the robbers. He endeavoured to convince the Sergeant that he was here to attempt to recover the jewels for the lady, as they were heirlooms and consequently, of some sentimental value to the family, whereupon the robbers promptly denounced him to them and revealed all their past undertakings with the man. They revealed to the Sergeant—who had already deduced this fact, leading him to be suspicious of the man in the first place—that they had done this very deed the previous year in March, and on that occasion, an Englishwoman had been their victim, whose elderly coachman had been murdered (or so they thought!). The entire band was arrested at once, as the Sergeant's suspicions were now confirmed. That Englishman was none other than Mr. Grayson!

When I received your previous letter intimating that your acquaintance with Mr. Grayson was of a most short-lived nature, I own I was greatly disappointed for you. But today, I thank God from the bottom of my heart for preserving you from the clutches of that wicked man. Truly, the wisdom and knowledge of God are deep, His judgments unsearchable and His ways past finding out. No one can claim to be His counsellor, and His plans ever surpass those of our own! Had our wishes been granted for a future for the two of you, I shudder to think of what might have resulted. For now, the dreadful creature is in custody and can do no harm to others. I pray for my heart to be possessed of charity whereby I might forgive him for his actions against you and indeed, all of us!

I hope that we shall soon see you and dearest Mama, Papa and Christopher. Markham means to bring us to the hills for the summer, for it is dreadfully hot here and he says that the mutineers who blocked the Grand Trunk Road near Delhi have been dislodged. We are apprehensive, but emboldened by Mr. Davenport's success at traveling through the country during the revolt. He deems it safer now and will depart soon for Simla with his dear sister Jane. Give my love to Mama and Papa and Christopher.

Your loving sister,
A. Hardingham

Edwina had read the letter aloud and its effect upon the family was rather marked. Having surmised its conclusion halfway through the reading, they had become speechless with disbelief, listening in horror, as when one stares at an unfolding scene of destruction, unable to look away, and unable to bear the sight. They exchanged shocked glances, looking frequently at Diana, for they worried about the impact of this intelligence upon her. She appeared impassive, looking down at her knitting. A tiny frown creased her brow, as if she were attempting to resolve some difficulty with the pattern. Only a slight tremor in her lower lip gave away the agitation she was experiencing. Mrs. Hardingham sat down beside her on the couch and embraced her, whereupon she dissolved into tears.

'I had the smallest hope that he would return, prompted by his conscience to do what is right. However, he has turned out to be a greater villain than I imagined. Furthermore, he is a criminal and I have no hope of any future redemption!' she cried.

Edwina looked at her with the greatest compassion, as did Christopher.

'As long as you have the breath of life in you, child, you have hope for redemption. Redemption is the very gift our Saviour came to bestow upon us. Trust in the mercies of God and it shall be well. Look to your soon-to-arrive child at present, for that is sufficient care for the hour,' replied Mrs. Hardingham.

'If he is such a blackguard, perhaps it is well that you and the child are divided from him,' added Mr. Hardingham, as he and Christopher left the ladies to console Diana.

Privately, he resolved to do what lay in his power to assist the child, for he had become fond of her. She had vastly pretty manners and despite her forlorn condition, it had appeared to him, that she had considerably cheered Edwina up since her arrival. His youngest child's despondency during the winter had not gone unnoticed, although Mr. Hardingham had attributed that to her concern over the state of the family in Calcutta. To this end, he wrote a lengthy letter to Markham, followed by one to his steward in Delhi.

Edwina, enthralled by the news that Davenport had at last made his way back to Simla, awaited his return with all the eagerness and anxiety that characterizes love that is as yet unrequited and insecure. Her attention was mercifully diverted, however, by Diana. Over the next month, Diana kept increasingly to her bed as the hour of her confinement drew nigh. She experienced a great deal of discomfort from being unable to sleep at night, along with a disconcerting shortness of breath. She was warned to rest continually, for it would be any day now. They did not have to wait long, for by the end of April, an infant girl arrived—in the dead of night—as infants are wont to do, reflected

Edwina. Mother and child were both well and presently asleep. Edwina yawned as she had her morning tea, reflecting that Diana appeared to be none the worse for the wear, while she herself seemed quite ragged. A warm glow hovered about the mother's face, and it was as if the presence of the infant had dispelled all thoughts of hopelessness and gloom from her mind.

Shanta, who had worried endlessly over Edwina's forlorn air these past months was convinced that she was affected by some malady. Moreover, to her, the presence of this unwed mother was a certain blot on the family's honour—for she had guessed that the *memsahib* who had come to have her baby in their household, with no *sahib* in tow, had come to be a mother through disreputable means. But being acquainted with the compassionate ways of the Hardinghams, she knew it would be futile to point the obvious out. She was not an unfeeling woman herself. However, when it came to Edwina, her protective instincts asserted that this woman's presence in close proximity to her charge could not possibly have a positive effect.

Presently, she urged Edwina to go to bed, hoping to purge the haggard look from her eyes, promising to take care of the infant, should she awake. Mrs. Hardingham nodded in agreement and Edwina obeyed, glad for the chance to lie down for a little while. Instead, she slept soundly, for the space of three hours and woke up feeling very refreshed and rather starved. Shanta obligingly brought a tray of tea and sandwiches to her bedside, which she devoured in a decidedly unmaidenly fashion. It was three o'clock in the afternoon and having ascertained that Diana and her child had awoken, she returned to her friend's side, relieving Mrs. Hardingham, who insisted that one of them should always be at the girl's side for a few days.

In a few weeks, Diana was able to join the family as they dined. The infant endeared herself to everyone in a very short time, especially to Mr. Hardingham and his wife, who missed Kate's children dreadfully. Diana, utterly devoted to the child, had little else on her mind. A general sense of domestic harmony and blessedness prevailed upon the company for several days.

One morning, Edwina and Christopher, desirous of riding—for it was a glorious day—ventured to the stables, where they heard an animated discussion among the menservants. Drawing nearer, they overheard the men discuss something with some excitement. They conversed in loud voices about the events on the plains and Christopher and Edwina heard their entire exchange with some amazement.

'The revolt has been crushed in Delhi and the *sahibs* are winning everywhere,' declared Manohar Lal.

'I have heard tales of great bloodshed and violence, and that at one point, the *sahibs* fled Delhi at the peril of their lives. Besides, I have heard that hundreds of *memsahibs* and their children were killed in Cawnpore, which was extremely cruel, for one ought not to attack women and children in battle,' said Madho, the head groom.

'Perhaps it is not as bad as they say, for would the *sahibs* here not have fled for their lives if it were so?' asked Manohar Lal doubtfully.

'Ha! Then you do not know *Hardeeengham sahib* very well, if you think thus!' scoffed Haridas, the senior steward. 'He is a brave man and would not run. Also, he had nothing to fear, for any one of us should have laid his life down to protect him and the young *sahib* and the *memsahibs*. I do not care what cause they fight for, but no man shall harm a hair on the heads of anyone in this household. But I do not doubt your account of the events on the plains, for the two men who told you about them are noble and brave fighters and they should have no reason to lie to you. They are the only ones in these hills who have seen firsthand the troubles down below in the plains and we can have no cause to doubt their word.'

The wisdom of this appealed to the younger men and Manohar Lal opened his mouth to reply, when Christopher interrupted him, saying, 'You seem to have received word of goings on in the plains from someone who has been there. Tell me more about it. Who are these people who have seen the fighting on the plains?'

The servants were surprised to see Christopher and Edwina, but soon began to share with them the information they had received. Much of it he had already heard from Markham, but what interested him and Edwina the most was the identity of the persons who had divulged this news to them.

To their great surprise, Madho responded, 'It is the two noble Sikh men who are Knowles *sahib*'s servants who have shared these things with us. You know them from the *shikar, Memsahib*. You know they are brave men and have no cause to lie.'

'Are those two men back? Where did you meet them? What of Davenport *sahib*? Has he returned too?' asked Edwina a little breathlessly.

'I met them when I took the horse to the blacksmith to replace his shoe a week ago. The *sahib* has returned too, along with his sister, a young *memsahib*,' replied Madho.

Edwina fell silent, as Christopher asked, 'When did they return from the plains?'

'Three weeks ago, *Sahib*,' came the reply.

Christopher nodded to Madho to fetch their horses. He and Edwina rode in silence for several minutes. The fact that Davenport had returned to Simla three weeks ago and had not called on them, weighed heavily upon Edwina's heart. Her downcast countenance was not lost on Christopher.

'Perhaps his business affairs have become tangled and that is what has kept him from calling on us?' he ventured.

'No,' said Edwina in a small voice. 'The man who rode to the plains in a tearing hurry, promising to discover whether our family in Calcutta was unharmed, would certainly have called on Papa. He was kind enough to add our interests to his mission of securing his sister's safety. Something has occurred and he has changed,' she finished dully.

'Well, it cannot very well be on account of the formation of an affection on his part for Anne, for in that case, he would have been at our doorstep post-haste, calling on my uncle,' said Christopher, hoping to elevate her fast-plummeting spirits.

Mr. Hardingham discovered the news of the Davenports' return to Simla that evening from Mr. Knowles, who dined with them. Having been relieved of some of his responsibilities upon the return of his two brave Sikh servants, he ventured to call on the Hardinghams. He regaled the family with a brief account of the tales of derring do that the men had told him. They were naturally reticent and did not give him a great many details. Further, as brave men generally are, they were reluctant to boast about their own feats of courage. But they unhesitatingly had shared a truthful account of Davenport's exploits, which Mr. Knowles was delighted to relate to the family. The result was that the evening passed rather unhappily for Edwina, who could not but hear of Mr. Davenport's adventures. It was Mr. Davenport did this or that for the entire evening, so that she felt quite faded by the end of it and begged to be excused to retire early. Christopher and his aunt exchanged knowing glances but said nothing. Mr. Knowles, who always stayed until morning when he dined with them, kissed her cheek and declared that he hoped she would be better by breakfast.

The morning brought no cheer to Edwina. She had tossed and turned and angrily brushed away an odd tear for several hours before falling into a deep slumber. She was awakened by the persistent chirping of birds outside her window, which annoyed her excessively. Sitting up, she discovered a stiffness about her neck and shoulders from sleeping in an uncomfortable position, as usually happens when one falls into an exhausted slumber. She winced, thinking she quite hated birds and their chirping. This thought brought a reluctant smile to her face in a few moments.

I must be uncommon disagreeable and out of sorts to think such a thought! she reflected.

Then, remembering the cause for the general sense of sadness that seemed to have taken hold of her heart, she frowned.

Wretched man, I was a joyful soul before I met you, she thought resentfully.

It occurred to her next, that her peace of mind could not possibly be wrested away from her without her consent.

I have need of such peace as transcends Mr. Davenport's treatment of me. And indeed, it is I who must guard my heart and not permit it to be disturbed. I must face this moment with fortitude and resolve to be happy, for it shall soon pass, she thought.

Stepping out of her bed with effort, she said firmly to her reflection in the mirror, 'I am resolved to be joyful this day. I shall not let Mr. Davenport's absence hurt me. I do not need him to be happy!'

Her resolve soon faded away, however, as she discovered Diana and Mr. Knowles engaged in an involved discussion on Mr. Davenport's merits. With Diana's permission, Mrs. Hardingham had discreetly shared Diana's plight, as well as Grayson's perfidy, with Mr. Knowles, for he was of a most sympathetic nature and known to the family as one who could be counted on to hold their secrets intact. Diana's changed demeanour since the hour of their last meeting had pleased him and now, they appeared to have become the very best of friends!

Edwina eyed them with some disfavour as they tried to draw her into a discussion of Mr. Davenport's superiority. She mumbled into her teacup that his pleasing attributes were too many to recount. That assessment appeared to satisfy them and they resumed their discussion. To her great dismay, she heard that her father had sent Davenport an invitation to dine at their home the following evening.

I shall have to have a decline and keep to my bed all summer! she thought bleakly.

Wishing to break free from their unabashed admiration of the man, she declared that she would go for a short walk, for she desired the exercise. Shooting a quelling look at Christopher, who was on the verge of accompanying her, for he and her mother well knew the state of unrest her heart probably was in, she resolutely set out for the meadow that skirted the woods beyond, a short distance from their home. As she walked, she reflected that Christopher had seemed quite content to stay by Diana's side, after she had discouraged him from accompanying her. She thought she had seen a glimpse of admiration there, very similar to the adoring glances he had directed at her at the beginning of their acquaintance.

She worried about Christopher, for she perceived this to be quite a hopeless situation. What if Grayson did return with an expectation of being united with his daughter? She was not at all certain that Diana's heart had relinquished its partiality for Grayson. She herself had cooled towards the man instantly upon beholding his cowardice, but perhaps Diana was not so particular? On the other hand, a great change, fostered by her close encounter with the cruel nature of the world, had come upon her. Gone was the shallow young woman who giggled and glanced coquettishly over her fan. In her place, a serious and grave person, very timid and shaken by circumstances, had come to stay with the Hardinghams. It was only recently that her serious air had given way to a charming and quiet countenance, for she was cheered by the good friends she had met, besides which, the baby was no small comfort to her soul.

Regardless, the gossip that Chris should be subjected to—were he to form an attachment with Diana—would be considerable. What if Grayson resorts to blackmail, for he is base enough to do something that odious! Where would they go to escape scandal and certain persecution? It will not do, she thought as she bit her lip, looking very troubled.

Presently, the surroundings she found herself in and the steady pace at which she walked calmed her mind greatly. She walked for half an hour, by the end of which, she had made her peace with the chirping birds and flitting butterflies. Taking care to avoid the roads, for the summer residents had started to return to Simla, she stayed close to the trees, walking along a mud path created by the woodcutters who forayed daily into the forest. She heard a horse in the distance and stepped back into the open meadow, to ensure that the rider caught sight of her well in advance of his approach.

She turned to look at the horse that approached and to her very great astonishment, beheld a resplendent man with broad shoulders and an excellent seat, riding a magnificent black horse. On beholding her, he reined his horse in, perhaps a little too sharply, for the animal reared a little, adding to his dazzling appearance.

He dismounted quickly and with a sweeping motion of his hat declared, 'Miss. Hardingham, it is an honour indeed!'

His raven locks glistening in the sun, the movements of the folds of his cape and his deep voice were not lost on Edwina, who—with a wildly thumping heart—thought that she had never seen him look quite so imposing. When she spoke, her voice sounded alien, and she fully expected that he had heard the deafening roar of her heartbeats.

'Mr. Davenport! H—how do you do?' she asked faintly, clearing her throat and wishing desperately for a draught of water, for her mouth was now unaccountably dry.

He looked at her in an appraising way and then, noting the warm colour taking hold of her countenance, declared, 'You appear to be in the best of health, which I am pleased to see. I had not thought that you would be permitted—that is—that you would be abroad so soon ... I mean, that you would be able to venture forth away from your home.'

With a puzzled look, she replied, 'Oh, the snow melted some weeks ago and once the ground dried, we have been able to walk about quite freely. But I imagine you were aware of that, given that you reached Simla a few weeks ago.'

He seemed surprised at this and she said, 'The servants met your men, and besides, Uncle John dined with us last night. Indeed, my father had announced his intention of inviting you to dine with us.'

He nodded and they walked for a few moments in silence. After several minutes, he informed her that he was, in fact, heading to her home to call on her father.

'In that case, you are proceeding in the wrong direction,' she pointed out, for she was walking away from home, and he with her.

'That is true,' he agreed, continuing to walk in her direction.

'And, you wish now to walk in my direction?' she enquired with a faint smile.

'Perhaps,' came the enigmatic reply.

They walked together for another fifteen minutes in silence. Edwina, once the first rush of excitement had abated, started to feel exhausted. The fatigue of the morning returned with great force and soon, she wished very much that she could sit down.

Spying a log beside a thicket, she sat on it, saying, 'I have walked further than I supposed I should. Pardon me, but I require a little respite.'

He looked at her with great concern, helping her to her seat.

'But of course, please rest awhile. I shall conduct you to your home. My horse can easily carry us both, or I can walk beside you, if you prefer,' he said.

'Oh, that will not be necessary, Mr. Davenport. I shall be myself presently. I slept poorly last night and woke up feeling rather tired. But in a moment, I shall feel quite refreshed and walk home, and you—you can ride to see my father,' she said.

She was not surprised when he shook his head firmly. She had not expected him to ride on and leave her to walk back home. But what he said next astounded her greatly.

'How does the child do?' he asked in a soft voice.

She looked at him incredulously.

'What child? How do *you* know? How have you heard?' she asked in considerable confusion.

He looked down at his feet uncomfortably and replied, 'Grayson told me about it.'

'*Grayson?*' she asked, in shocked accents. 'What have you to do with Mr. Grayson, and why should he tell you of his despicable behaviour?' she demanded.

'He told me when—you see, he was imprisoned for—'

'Yes, yes, I know!' she interrupted. 'My sister gave me the entire account. But what possessed him to reveal his dissolute tale to you, of all people?' she asked impatiently.

'He told me about it when I secured his release from prison,' he answered quietly.

'*YOU?* You secured his release from prison? Why, in heaven's name, did you do such a thing?' she asked, beginning to feel quite mystified and greatly exasperated.

'I did it for you,' he replied quietly.

'*For ME?* Mr. Davenport, whatever can you mean? Pray enlighten me!' she cried with great annoyance.

He replied, 'When I heard that he had been imprisoned, I thought of your affection for the man and went to see him. At first, I was incensed at him and sought to punish him for his actions, for I had come to realize that he had effected the very same crime on you last year, in Calcutta. However, when I began to remonstrate with him, he begged for my mercy, and divulged to me the—er—*predicament* that he and you found yourselves in. Thinking of myself as your friend, I had no choice but to secure the man's release. Before I did so, I exacted an oath from him that he would return to Simla and—'

But he got no further, for he was interrupted by Edwina, who said in a strange voice, 'Mr. Davenport, before you relay any other facts to me, allow me to enlighten you that I have not the slightest affection for Mr. Grayson. Owing to his craven conduct on the *shikar*, I had ceased to think of that person as my friend. I am glad that he was apprehended by the police and had quite hoped that he would be taken to task for his villainy. However, that does not signify. What puzzles me is...pray tell me, Mr. Davenport, what *predicament* do you imagine *me* to be in?'

He looked at her strangely for a few moments and then said, 'Miss. Hardingham, do you wish to have no connection with Mr. Grayson?'

'No, I do not!' she declared impatiently, adding, 'I have not the slightest idea why so many people wish to foist that odious creature upon me! I was delighted to hear that he had left Simla and was even more delighted that he was to be brought to justice—that is, until you took it into your head to have him set free! But, that does not signify— you have not answered my question.'

He stared at the trees beyond, as if not hearing her voice, causing Edwina to wonder if he had gone quite mad. Perhaps someone had hit him on his head during his adventures. She had heard that people went mad from blows to the head. She looked at him with some concern in her eyes.

And then, quite suddenly, he looked at her, and with something in his eyes that made her stomach twist itself into a large number of knots, said, 'Miss. Hardingham, this changes the matter entirely. Will you do me the honour of becoming my wife? I am aware that I should seek your father's permission before paying my addresses to you, but given the circumstances, I would prefer to ascertain your feelings on the matter before addressing him.'

She felt a glorious thrill surge through her and her heart took up that tiresome pounding again. She could hardly hear from the commotion it made! She opened her mouth to blurt out her answer, but—but, something nagged at the back of her mind.

'What precisely did you mean by *my predicament*? And what exactly do you mean by the matter being entirely changed,' she asked in an uneven voice, trying to hear her own thoughts above the pesky din in her heart.

'Grayson informed me about your condition. He said that he was now reformed but forced by adversity into one last criminal act so that he might secure a comfortable living for both of you,' he answered, looking somewhat embarrassed.

She blinked at him, uncomprehendingly and asked, 'M—my *condition*? Whatever did he mean? And why should he want to secure a living for me? He made me no offer and I should never have accepted one, had he done so. Mr. Davenport, I am most puzzled and I do not know what Mr. Grayson has told you, but apparently, it is the source of some confusion. I should inform you that I am delighted beyond words that you have made me an offer, but I find your manner of doing so extremely odd. Pray, have done with these enigmatic riddles and tell me plainly what is afoot!'

He looked at her in surprise and then, with a pained expression said, 'Grayson informed me that you were—er—*enceinte*. He said that he was trying to effect one last robbery so he might have enough means to procure a living for himself and marry you at once. Although I despise his methods, I believed this to be the only possible outcome in your circumstances, until you informed me that you have no affection for Mr. Grayson and indeed, appear to quite despise the man. In that case, having admired you for a long time now, I should be honoured if you will let me give you and the child my name.'

Edwina sat very still for a few moments. The miserable pounding in her ears had resumed. However, what washed over her now was a great rage, perhaps such that she had never experienced in her young life.

Sitting upright on her log, she asked in quiet but extremely forbidding accents, 'Mr. Grayson told you that I was with child by him?'

Misreading her demeanour as indicative of embarrassment, he blundered on, 'Well, he did not mention you by name. He is not entirely a cad, thank God!'

'Oh?' came the reply in a dangerously quiet voice, 'What *did* he say? Pray, tax your memory, sir, and repeat to me his very words.'

In the heat of anger, she became very calm and wished to have complete evidence before she unleashed her wrath upon the wretched man who stood before her now. Sadly, Mr. Davenport, having spent very little time conversing cordially with his beloved Edwina had no notion of the effect of his words. He had devoted most of his dealings with her to quarrelling, and was thus inadequately acquainted with the deceptive calm that preceded her fury. True, he had encountered it once when they first met, but then, he was so struck by her dark hair and heightened colour, that he had not paid attention to much else. Besides which, at that first meeting, he was keen on goading her because he wished to conceal how tongue-tied she made him feel. In sum, he could not be faulted very much for his misconstructions on this particular morning.

He cast about in his mind to gather together the scattered fragments of information that were contained therein, and then, with great sincerity and veracity, replied, 'He said that he had compromised the honour of a certain lady in Simla, with whom I was well-acquainted. He described the lady as being gently-bred and exceedingly beautiful and declared his deepest devotion to her. He vowed that she returned his affections and it was the greatest blot on his honour to have recently discovered that he had ruined her. He had left her with the promise that he would return the following year and implore for her hand. But now, news that she was with child put the matter in a different light. He wished to rescue her and marry her, and to that end, he required a reasonable sum of money quite desperately. He begged me to aid him in whatever manner I could.

Naturally, having loved you since our first meeting, I did whatever was in my power to secure the man's release. I offered him a sum of money, which he would procure from me, were he to come to Simla and ask for your hand—for I did not fully trust him. I then secured his release and he agreed to come at once to Simla, once he had set his affairs in order in Calcutta. He said he had some gambling debts to take care of and once those were discharged through the sale of his remaining possessions, he would make his way to Simla and call on me—after he had secured the lady's hand. Understand me, Miss. Hardingham, I have never held the man in any regard from our first acquaintance. I did not wish to be of any service to him and mistrusted him entirely. You alone were my motive for interceding on his behalf.'

He stopped and looked at her with a warm glow in his eyes. She waited to see if he had anything further to say, for Edwina was nothing if not just. She believed that a condemned man must have his uninterrupted say when he stood trial. Besides, she was too angry to be able to speak, yet.

He continued, 'But now that you have declared that you feel nothing for the man, I am proud to offer you and your child my name and my protection.'

He looked at her questioningly and was surprised when she stood up in great agitation and paced about for a few moments.

Then, turning to him, she said in great wrath, 'You insolent, hateful man! How *dare* you insult me so! Marriage to you would be the greatest affront to any dignity I possess. You have insulted me beyond words can describe and were I armed, I should make you pay dearly for your stupidity!'

Now, it was Mr. Davenport's turn to wonder if his beloved had gone mad. He took a step in her direction, whereupon the incensed Miss. Hardingham, who now perceived her beloved as a prime villain, delivered a resounding slap upon his cheek.

He stepped back and asked in great astonishment, 'Good heavens! Have you gone quite mad, Miss. Hardingham?'

This had the effect of causing her to stamp her foot and say in a voice that was quite louder than she was accustomed to employing, 'Have *I* gone mad? It is not I, but rather *you* who have gone mad, you foolish man! You accost me in the woods and cast aspersions on my honour and then call me mad! I shall ask my father to call you out and my cousin too. Do not think me a weak female, sir. I shall call you out myself. I shall shoot you and run you aground with a sword and dance upon your corpse and—and murder you!' she finished breathlessly, having run out of tortures to accord him, dimly aware that some of her schemes, if not all of them, were quite impossible to execute.

Her face was now crimson red, and several wisps of hair had made their escape from her bonnet, while her eyes danced with fury. The intended cumulative effect of this display of passion went sadly awry when Mr. Davenport, having recovered from his initial shock, began to find her entire demeanour and haphazard plans for his extermination vastly amusing, despite being quite perplexed by it all.

A roguish smile hovered around the corners of his mouth and he asked with maddening calm, 'If you have already danced on my corpse, madam, I shall already be quite dead. How do you propose to murder me again after that? I think you have not given much thought to the sequence of events that must occur in this scene. You must first choose your weapons. I recommend a pistol first. If you are careful with your aim, I should die instantly and you shall have no need of further violence by means of a sword. After that, you may dance upon my corpse to your heart's content. But do not, I implore you, once I am dead, hope to murder me again, for you shall be sadly disappointed.'

'Don't you *dare* mock me, you—you *vile* creature!' she said through clenched teeth.

He laughed softly, but the laughter did not reach his eyes.

He regarded her cautiously and then, stepping aside, swept his arm towards his horse in invitation, saying, 'Now, madam, perhaps you will allow me to conduct you back to your home?'

'I shall conduct myself home. Now, be so good as to get out of my way, or do you propose to heap more dishonour upon me than you already have?' she replied contemptuously.

A look of great anger swept across his face, and she took an involuntary step back, a look of alarm flooding her eyes. He wheeled around, however, mounted his horse, and without looking back at her, rode away at a furious pace.

She noted that he rode in the direction of her home. She did not believe that he would have the temerity to call on her father after this encounter, but she hoped fervently that he would, and that she herself could reach home in time to call him to account for his words. She began walking in the same direction, as fast as her legs would carry her. Anger made her fatigue disappear and she walked very fast indeed, reaching the house in twenty minutes. She was out of breath, extremely hot and uncommonly cross. To her great satisfaction, Davenport had indeed acted upon his intention of paying his respects to her father. No doubt the villain would be taking some tea and cakes, laughing and talking genially to her father, as if he had not just humiliated her, not quite an hour ago!

She charged into the sitting room, trying desperately to catch her breath, and trying to present a poised appearance. Mr. Davenport looked at her quizzically, one eyebrow faintly raised. She thought she read a challenge there and was about to rise quite fearlessly to it, when she caught sight of Diana sitting by her mother. That artless young lady had thought nothing of happily joining the family in the sitting room. Mrs. Hardingham had debated on suggesting to her that she retire to her bedchamber until their guest had departed, but thought better of it, for she instinctively trusted Davenport. Besides, the child was asleep and Diana's presence there would seem harmless enough. Mr. Davenport would simply assume that it was just a case of Diana paying a visit to her friend. Consequently, her presence cast a damper on Edwina's plans of humiliating Davenport. The heat of the battle having dissipated, it dawned on her that it would cause her friend great humiliation and hurt if she were to relate her encounter with Davenport that morning.

She sought to leave the room, thinking wrathfully, *Well! So you sit here and partake nonchalantly of my mother's tea and cakes, as if you were not the most insufferable of all men!*

However, Mr. Davenport rose, and with a bow, proffered his greetings, accompanied by a bland smile.

Oho, so now you are our very own court jester, are you not? she thought, wishing very much to fling a vase that stood nearby, at him. Unable to satisfy herself in this impulse, she glared at him and with a stiff curtsey acknowledged his presence, preparing to mumble her excuses and leave the room.

At this, Mrs. Hardingham who had been eyeing her offspring quite disapprovingly ever since she had rushed into their company presenting so dishevelled an appearance said, 'Edwina, do sit down!' in faintly reproving accents.

Her father was less subtle.

'Don't go away, child. We have waited so long to see Mr. Davenport and declare our gratitude to him. Sit down,' said her father.

Flinging her bonnet aside in a most unmaidenly fashion, she sat down heavily, muttering, 'Very well, then, although I should like very much to attend to a matter of great importance, and shall have to excuse myself shortly from the very great pleasure being offered me of conversing with Mr. Davenport!' causing great surprise to everyone present—except Mr. Davenport, of course.

He looked at her with an air of polite interest that was carefully studied, for now, his pride wounded, he intended to goad her further. He was not a vain man, and had she rejected him outright, he would have received her reply as a gentleman ought to and not troubled her ever again with his attentions. Instead, she had declared herself to be delighted beyond words at first, and then for some inexplicable reason, had become infuriated at him—perhaps, he thought, because he had discovered her circumstances. He appreciated that she had felt no small degree of embarrassment upon discovering that the matter had become known to him, but it irritated him that she felt the need to maintain the façade before him—after he had declared his love for her!

'Ah! I am devastated that you wish to escape, Miss. Hardingham. I shall be desolate if you leave us. Are you keeping well?' he asked with exaggerated politeness.

'Yes, I am, thank you. And you, sir? How have you fared? Perhaps you have news from the plains of our acquaintances?' she asked pointedly, as if daring him to reveal his interactions with Grayson to those present.

He smiled at her, his eyes saying, *Bravo*! and replied, 'Ah yes, but no doubt you are rather more keen to hear about the state of your dear sisters and brother-in-law, are you not?'

'We have already received accounts of them, sir! I beg you will not trouble yourself any further on that score,' she answered waspishly.

His eyes danced and it occurred to her that he seemed to be daring her to expose him to her family.

Stupid, odious, hateful man! she thought.

Mrs. Hardingham looked greatly puzzled and said, 'Oh, but indeed, we should be delighted to hear an account of your latest meeting with them, for letters from those you love seldom convey sufficient information to the reader, do they Edwina?'

'I had the great felicity of dining on several occasions with Mr. Markham and with your charming daughters, Mrs. Hardingham. I should be delighted to share with you any details of their wellbeing that you wish to be in possession of, that is, if Miss. Hardingham does not find it too tedious to hear of it again, for you seemed to be in receipt of news from the plains,' he said, the challenge returning to his eyes.

'Why, of course, we wish to get every bit of news we possibly can, Mr. Davenport, and are indeed grateful to you that you are here in person to describe to us the state of our children in Calcutta! Pray, let Mr. Davenport know how anxious you have been to receive word of their state, Edwina,' said Mrs. Hardingham, quite embarrassed by Edwina's ungracious remark.

Mr. Hardingham who had listened to their exchange with some surprise and had assumed, quite correctly, that his daughter was out of sorts, said reprovingly, 'Edwina, perhaps you might muster a little more interest in the affairs of your sisters? Why, you have scarcely smiled for many months now for great worry, and how does it come about that you have so little concern for Mr. Davenport's account of them? I do believe you are acting uncommon strange today! And do stop clenching your fists that manner. You put me in mind of a boxer!'

Turning an attractive shade of crimson, she stammered, 'Oh, P— Papa—' but was interrupted by the maid who, with a look of great concern declared softly to Diana that the baby had woken from her sleep crying, and seemed quite feverish.

Davenport looked impassive, as if he had not understood what she had said. However, Diana let out a gasp and, looking very pale, jumped up and begged their leave, hurrying after the servant to her bedchamber. A flush crept across Christopher's face, but as Mr. Davenport seemed not to have noticed anything, he relaxed momentarily. Mrs. Hardingham appeared to be at a loss as to the next course of action. She did not wish to draw attention to the fact that their young guest was now the mother of an infant, but she felt she might be needed, particularly if the child was unwell. Casting a warning look at her husband, she rose, and on the pretext of needing to speak with the cook and promising to return in but a moment, she left the room.

On her way out, she whispered forbiddingly to Edwina, 'Don't come after me, for that would attract more attention. But *do* try to be more civil, child. I do not know what the matter with you is, but pray, call to mind how you positively *pined* for this man all year. Oh, how I wish I could shake you!'

Then, with a radiant smile at Mr. Davenport, she made her way to Diana's bedchamber.

Partly from a desire to deflect attention from Diana and partly to placate her father, Edwina asked in a strained voice, 'Pray, do tell us, Mr. Davenport, how my sisters and Markham and the children fare?' And then, in a level voice, she continued, 'Have you had the good fortune of meeting any other persons of our acquaintance in Calcutta?'

She had hoped to discomfit him by this question, and noted with great satisfaction that a look of great consternation had descended upon his face.

She arched an eyebrow, challenging him to go on, but he remained silent. It dawned on her that the maid's incursion into the drawing-room and its subsequent effect on Diana had not gone unnoticed by him. She read in his countenance that the truth of the matter had dawned on him. She was correct in her assumption. Davenport appeared to stare at his shoes for a few moments.

Then, collecting himself, he cleared his throat and replied, 'Your sisters and Mr. Markham are in the very best of health, ma'am, as are the children. No doubt they have apprised you that Calcutta was spared of the violence that swept through the land.'

His manner seemed absent and although the others waited for him to continue, he did not add anything further to the conversation. When he had met Miss. Johnson in the company of the Hardinghams that morning, he was mildly surprised. He had wondered if she had come to render her assistance to her friend. It had bemused him somewhat, for he had not thought her to be very close to Edwina, or even a person who could be depended upon in a delicate circumstance like this. He then concluded that he was not well-enough acquainted with the lady to appreciate her merits. However, all that had changed when he beheld the episode that had just unfolded in his presence.

Diana's reaction upon hearing about the infant and her instant departure from their company had forcefully brought to his awareness the fact that he had been very much mistaken in his understanding of the matter. He thought hard about the last time he had met the lady. He recalled that, feeling humiliated at his own cravenness at the tiger hunt, Grayson had devoted his attentions to Miss. Johnson. In a flash of sudden insight Davenport deduced the matter in its entirety. How could he have been so blind! He had read Grayson correctly in that, the man was indeed speaking the truth about having compromised a lady's honour. But the lady in question was not Edwina Hardingham, but rather, Miss. Diana Johnson. His brows knotted together, as he tried to recollect what it was that had made him assume that the lady was Edwina. Had Grayson deliberately led him to believe a lie? The man had not precisely mentioned the lady's name. Grayson had said she was lovely—and in his passionate love for Edwina, he had not stopped to think of any other lovely woman of his acquaintance. ... He raised very contrite eyes at Edwina, but she looked at him with the most unrelenting severity.

He opened his mouth to say something, but was interrupted by Christopher who asked, 'Mr. Davenport, pray, how does your sister do? I trust she is not too overwrought from her journey?'

Mr. Davenport's sudden reticence and his impassioned glance at Edwina had not gone unnoticed by him, nor had Edwina's inexplicable antagonism this morning. Something was afoot, although he could not be sure precisely what. His question forced Davenport to collect his thoughts.

'My sister is very well, thank you. She was indeed rather fatigued by the entire ordeal, but her spirits have remained unflagging. Miss. Hardingham, I beg that you will allow her to call on you, for she is most desirous of making your acquaintance,' he replied, wishing quite desperately to be alone with Edwina for a moment.

She looked at him in some surprise. The warmth of his appeal disconcerted her and she began to feel a little confused.

Before she could consider her words, she answered with icy politeness, 'Indeed! And to what do I owe the honour of Miss. Davenport's regard? Surely it cannot be anything *you* have said, Mr. Davenport?'

'On the contrary, Edwina, I am certain that Mr. Davenport has conveyed—quite truthfully—your excellent merits to Miss. Davenport,' interjected Christopher, warmly.

Mr. Hardingham, who was also beginning to feel rather annoyed by his daughter's inexplicable truculence, added, 'We would be most delighted to make the acquaintance of your sister, Mr. Davenport. Perhaps you may be prevailed upon to bring her to dine with us tomorrow night? We are all eager to meet her!'

Edwina felt the colour rush back to her face. She bit her lip, regretting that she had rebuffed him in a manner so uncivil.

Mr. Davenport responded with great enthusiasm to this scheme, adding, to everyone's surprise, 'Indeed, sir, we should be most delighted to. Jane wished most earnestly to join me today and will no doubt be desolate that she will have to wait an entire day to meet you all.'

Hearing this, Mr. Hardingham suggested, to Edwina's dismay, 'Then, perhaps, Mr. Davenport, you can be prevailed upon to join us this very evening. Do, sir!'

The scheme was welcomed by Mr. Davenport and Christopher with nods of approbation. Plans were made and it was agreed that Mr. Davenport would ride home and return with his sister to dine with them that evening. Mr. Hardingham said that it was too bad that Mr. Knowles had already taken his leave of them that morning, although Davenport was secretly relieved, for he wished to be able to find an opportune moment that evening to pay his addresses to Edwina. Everything was arranged and when Mrs. Hardingham returned to the drawing-room, having ascertained that Diana's child was not ill, but had simply become too warm from the blankets around her, she was faced the delightful prospect of meeting Jane Davenport that evening. Furthermore, she was relieved that Davenport would have another opportunity to meet Edwina, who she hoped fervently, could be induced to act in a more civil and maidenly manner.

As he prepared to effect his departure from their company for the present, Mr. Davenport suddenly appeared to be struck by a thought.

Looking at Mr. Hardingham, he coughed and said, 'I wonder, sir, if I might have a word with you in private—about matters of business and how the recent events in the plains may affect them.'

Although he was slightly surprised by this request, Mr. Hardingham was pleased to be able to confer with Davenport about matters of business, for he had been concerned about whether there would be any change in the direction of the unrest. Contained as it was in some cities, his trade had remained unaffected, but he wished to hear Mr. Davenport's thoughts on the subject of the future direction events might take. Bowing to the ladies, the two men made their way to the library.

Mrs. Hardingham lost no time in setting out to determine the source of Edwina's discontent. She took a direct route and mounted a frontal attack.

'How wonderful that Mr. Davenport should call on us today! Are you not greatly relieved to see how well he looks, Edwina?'

'Oh, I am feeling a great many things now, Mama, but relief is certainly not one of them,' she replied. Then, as her mother began to ask her what she meant, she declared passionately, 'I wish I had never set eyes on Mr. Davenport, for he is verily the vilest creature I have met. But, I beg you will not tease me on this subject, as I do not wish to speak of it, or indeed, of Mr. Davenport!'

Greatly astonished at her words, Christopher and Mrs. Hardingham glanced at each other, wondering what had transpired. That Edwina should abruptly detest today the man whom she was deeply devoted to until yesterday, seemed the most mystifying of contradictions.

'Edwina!' Christopher said, with some dismay, 'How can you say that?! Mr. Davenport is a gentleman and, you will agree, a true friend to all in this home!'

'Oh indeed, the man is no gentleman, Chris, and should you become acquainted with the extent of his incivility towards me, you should, I assure you, cavil at calling him your friend,' replied Edwina, becoming increasingly incensed at the man who appeared to have turned all her relations against her in the space of an hour!

'Edwina, what has occurred to put you thus out of humour?' asked Christopher greatly concerned.

Mrs. Hardingham's countenance became grave and she said in a quiet voice, 'Edwina, perhaps you had better tell us what has occurred to put you out of humour with Mr. Davenport in this manner. Did he communicate with you before calling on us today?' A thought dawned on her and she added, 'Perhaps you encountered him on your stroll?'

Edwina nodded with a flush. She stood up and paced the room angrily for a few minutes and then sat down again. Mrs. Hardingham and Christopher waited, somewhat anxiously, for her to continue.

After several moments, she cleared her throat and in as calm a tone as she could muster, said, 'Indeed, I did have the misfortune of running into Mr. Davenport this morning. He appeared surprised to see me abroad, a fact that I now understand, having conversed with him. He informed me of Grayson's transgressions and then indicated to me that he was aware of Grayson's having trifled with the honour of a certain lady.'

At this, Christopher drew in a sharp breath, declaring, 'How on earth did Mr. Davenport find this out?'

Mrs. Hardingham had made known to the gentlemen the identity of the man responsible for Diana's predicament in the hopes that something could be done to induce him to come to her aid. Anne's missive detailing the extent of his dissipation had rendered that course of action unsuitable. Christopher was most taken aback by the fact that others were now privy to this great secret.

'Grayson told him,' replied Edwina drily.

'What a blackguard! What possible motive could he have for exposing her to public disgrace?!' he asked fiercely.

'I intend to tell you, dear brother, if only you stop interrupting me,' replied Edwina somewhat tersely, and then, beholding Christopher's hurt countenance, added, 'Oh, I know, it is most provoking. Do forgive me, Chris, for my unkindness. The man has left my nerves quite overwrought. But, I digress. Grayson, it appears, confessed all to Mr. Davenport, for Mr. Davenport visited him as soon as he heard of his arrest and was responsible for securing his release.'

'Why on earth should he wish to do something so odd?' asked Mrs. Hardingham, greatly flummoxed.

'Our good friend, Mr. Davenport, has been belabouring under the misapprehension that I bear a—a *tendre* for Mr. Grayson. He wished, accordingly to secure the man's release, as an act of goodwill towards me,' answered Edwina bitterly.

'Oh! That is most unfortunate, indeed!' declared Mrs. Hardingham beginning to realize that perhaps Edwina had just cause for feeling quite aggravated.

'Oh, but that is not the whole story, Mama. Mr. Grayson's confession of his wretched dealings with a lady were assumed by Mr. Davenport to implicate me!'

'Eh?' said Christopher, uncomprehendingly.

'Mr. Davenport was so kind this morning as to offer me and my—my *ch—child* the *protection* of his name! You will pardon me, Mama if I take to my bed tonight with a headache of a most distressing nature, for that is what the man has given me!' she finished, looking very much as if she would burst into tears any moment now.

Christopher stared speechlessly at her, a look of great dismay written across his face. Mrs. Hardingham appeared impassive. She had walked to the open window and stared abstractly outside, inhaling deeply, as if to capture the scent of the roses growing in the garden.

'It is too bad,' she said in a dreamy voice.

Edwina nodded, swallowing back the tears that threatened to engulf her.

Mrs. Hardingham continued, 'I shall never know if your dear Papa ever loved *me* as much!'

Edwina drew in a sharp breath, but before she could speak, her mother said hastily, 'Of course, I do not wish you to think that your Papa's love for me is lacking in the least! But, how *wonderful* for you to witness your beloved's constancy put to the test and his steadfastness to you in the face of what appears to be utter perfidy on your part. Oh, 'tis the stuff of the great romances!' she finished, somewhat wistfully.

'Mama! How can you say such a thing to me? You know very well that Mr. Davenport has insulted me most unimaginably. It is he who is perfidious—and—and utterly *despicable* in thinking such a thing of me!' declared Edwina wrathfully.

'But, Eddy, consider how much this man adores you for him to. …' Christopher began, but trailed off as Edwina directed her irate gaze at him.

She tried her best to compose herself, for she did not wish to be unkind to her cousin, and said gravely, 'I am certain my dear Chris, that it is every whit as clear to you as it is to me, why it is impossible for me to accept Mr. Davenport's offer.'

They said nothing for a few moments and then, Mrs. Hardingham looked frankly at Edwina and said, 'I understand. He has most dreadfully impugned your honour by assuming you to be in Diana's circumstances.'

'Oh, it is not that simple!' declared Edwina impatiently, as she strode to the door. 'He did not think well enough of me to know that I *could* not possibly love a man as base as Grayson after his character had become known to me. That he should cherish such great misconceptions in the face of Grayson's craven dealings with me at the *shikar* serve to tell me beyond all doubt that there is no real sympathy between Mr. Davenport and myself. He does not understand my character and has no conception of my true nature.'

'But you do love him, Edwina! Of that I am most certain, for had you no feelings for him, you could not be hurt by his misjudging the situation,' declared Mrs. Hardingham with a firmness that surprised Edwina.

Edwina was prevented from answering by Diana's return. Grateful to be liberated from this discussion of a most disagreeable nature, she mumbled her excuses and fled to her bedchamber. There, she paced most fretfully, for the better part of an hour, alternating between moments of great fury and despondency. Finally, she threw herself upon her bed, sobbing into her pillow, raising her head once from it, to dismiss the maid who had arrived to call her to luncheon. On her pillow her head remained, until she fell into a troubled and uncomfortable sleep, from which she was roused a few hours later by Mrs. Hardingham who brought her a tray of tea and sandwiches.

She clucked at Edwina's dishevelled appearance, saying, 'Tut-tut! This shall never do, my dear, for your eyes are quite swollen and you appear rather raggedy! Whatever shall our guests think of you! Come, now, you must rise and partake of some refreshment for you shall be quite miserable if you do not eat until supper.'

At this, Edwina eyed her with some disfavour and replied, 'Oh, I do not intend to appear at supper, Mama. Therefore, our *guests'* opinions of my appearance are of no consequence.'

With a sharpness in her voice that belied the kindness in her eyes, Mrs. Hardingham scolded, 'Pray, have done with these megrims, Edwina. Have you forgotten that Miss. Jane Davenport is to dine with us as well? It will not do for you to be uncivil to her or indeed, to Mr. Davenport, for that matter, for he is your father's guest and we owe the man a great debt for coming to our aid at our hour of need! Do stop acting in this childish manner.'

As soon as she had spoken, Mrs. Hardingham regretted her words, for a mulish look had taken possession of Edwina's face, one that Mrs. Hardingham had encountered on a few rare instances before. The generally pliable Edwina was wont, on extremely rare occasions, to dig her heels in when goaded beyond endurance, and nothing would fortify her resolution at these moments, than to goad her further. Mrs. Hardingham hastily altered her plan of attack.

In a most sympathetic tone, she continued, 'But that is not to say that you are not to be pitied, Edwina, for you have had a most trying day! In fact, the more I think of it, it is perhaps best that you remain in your bedchamber for the evening. That will show Mr. Davenport rather forcefully how deeply he has wounded you. Let us make him regret his words and actions! I shall tell him that you are keeping to your bed today, owing to some great agitation of the nerves. Of course, I shall not breathe a word to him that reveals that I am aware of what has transpired between the two of you. Instead, I shall speak of how your poor nerves have suffered all day from some unknown vexation. It will do famously, don't you think? I shall send you tray of supper, which you must promptly send back down with a message that your nerves are too anxious to permit you to partake of any refreshment. Perhaps I should declare then that you seem very much in danger of going into a decline!'

This last salvo had its intended effect on Edwina, who sat up very straight in her bed and replied scornfully, 'Mama! You cannot be serious. The very last thing I would wish in the world is for Mr. Davenport to think that he has injured me in some way. On the contrary, I wish him to recognize how very beneath my contempt he is and how very insignificant he is to me. I should vastly prefer to snap my fingers at him and marry Grayson just to spite him, than to ever concede to that pompous, conceited wretch that I have even a shred of interest in what he thinks of me!'

Her mother replied with a look of great innocence, 'Oh, my dear, I had not considered that. If that is how matters lie, then perhaps you should come downstairs and show him that he is indeed a person of no consequence to you.'

'Do you think that would teach him a lesson?' she asked uncertainly.

'But of course! It is the veriest thing that shall punish him for vexing you so! I wish I had thought of it first. Clever girl! You should wear the pink taffeta gown we purchased at Calcutta. It is most becoming and I am convinced that it is the very gown that will punish the man for his indiscretion. Dazzle him, Edwina, and then devastate him with supreme indifference!' replied Mrs. Hardingham reassuringly.

This last course of action appealed vastly to Edwina and Mrs. Hardingham lost no time summoning the maid to assist her in her toilette. Cool poultices of muslin were placed on her eyes to eradicate all traces of weeping. The maid fetched a brass incense burner and soon, the scent of musk and sandalwood filled the air, as she waved the smoke from the incense through her hair, as was the custom of the ladies of India. Mrs. Hardingham dressed her hair in an elegant chignon, adorned with a pearl encrusted pin, that complemented the pearls sewn onto her gown. The result of these manoeuvres was that Edwina, her eyes flashing and colour considerably heightened, presented a most resplendent figure when she descended into the drawing-room an hour later.

She was gratified to observe Mr. Davenport's eyes widen for the smallest moment before he schooled his features again. She greeted him with icy indifference, noting with pleasure the disappointment in his eyes as she carelessly gave him her hand. She was forced to abandon her disdainful demeanour momentarily, however, for she found herself being presented to Miss. Jane Davenport next.

With a soft, shy laugh, Miss. Davenport grasped both of Edwina's hands, declaring, 'Miss. Hardingham, how delightful to meet you at last! I have heard tales of your great beauty and courage, and I have waited most anxiously to make your acquaintance!'

Disarmed by her charm, Edwina found herself involuntarily squeezing her hands in return and saying, before she could stop herself, 'Indeed, Miss. Davenport, the honour is entirely mine! I have wished these many months to make your acquaintance, even as tales of your adventures on the plains have made their way to these hills. Come, sit down beside me and tell me how you have fared! Are you quite recovered from your arduous journey?'

The two women chatted prettily and Davenport noted, with some surprise, that his customarily reserved Jane was freely regaling his beloved with an account of their home in Calcutta. They appeared to be commiserating greatly with each other that they had not thus far had the honour of making each other's acquaintance. Their conversation turned to the subject of reading and Miss. Davenport lamented that she had forsaken her copy of the *Aurora Leigh* at Barrackpore the day the rebellion broke out. Their library in Simla was woefully inadequate, she complained, whereupon Edwina begged her to visit their own library before dinner so that she might take as many books with her as she wished. They could be returned when next she came to tea, for the two ladies had by now already traded several invitations to tea and luncheon.

Jane consented to this scheme most heartily and the two ladies set out, arm in arm, to the library, followed by Christopher and Diana. With some annoyance, Edwina noticed that Mr. Davenport had followed them as well. She ignored him and continued to discourse animatedly with Jane and Diana on the subject of a number of books in their possession. Jane was most impressed with their vast collection of books and asked hopefully if, perchance, they had a copy of Dicken's tome, *David Copperfield.* Edwina replied that indeed, their father had procured them a copy when he toured England for trade the year before.

'I have just finished reading that very book, Miss. Davenport,' declared Diana. She continued, 'It is in my bedchamber and I shall bring it to you this instant. Perhaps you will assist me in carrying a pile of books to my chamber and we shall extract the one you wish to read from there?'

'But, of course, Miss. Johnson. I should be delighted to do so. James, do help dear Edwina put these last two away, for I shall take the one from Miss. Johnson instead,' said Jane.

Turning to her brother, she handed him a pile of books that she had selected from the shelf beside her. She hurried off, followed by Christopher who announced that he had a book by Charles Dickens in his possession that might be of interest to Miss. Davenport as well.

And in that manner, Edwina, most unexpectedly found herself standing alone with Mr. Davenport in the library. It occurred to her that the entire exercise had been carefully orchestrated by one or all of the persons who were present in the library a few moments ago.

Was Miss. Davenport also involved in this contrivance? How much does she know? she wondered, with rising ire.

273

Mr. Davenport wasted no time, even as fortune dropped the opportunity for a private conversation with Edwina in his lap!

'Miss. Hardingham,' he declared, 'I have longed for a moment of privacy with you. I beg you to allow me the opportunity of explaining my actions this morning. I was labouring under the greatest of deceptions, one of my own making, I am afraid. But I spoke in ignorance, and with the very best of intentions and I beg your leave to pledge my troth to you again.'

'Mr. Davenport, this is most trying of you! I believe I made my disapproval of your suit quite evident this morning. I do not wish to discuss the matter with you any further. Pray, get out of my way!' she replied wrathfully.

Undaunted, Mr. Davenport continued, 'You were not at first averse to my suit, which gives me hope that my cause is not entirely lost. It is the false impressions that I laboured under that have offended you, and I implore you to give me the chance to explain and beg for your forgiveness, for I cannot imagine living a life from which you are absent!'

This was said with so much tenderness that Edwina burst into tears and declared, 'Go away! I hate you! You believed in Grayson's veracity but did not for one moment stop to think that I had any integrity of my own! You believed the very worst of me. I shall never speak to you as long as I live!'

At this, Mr. Davenport knelt in front of her and said simply, 'It was my jealousy that blinded me. I thought you cared for the man and when he described his—his *object* as exceedingly beautiful, and someone I was acquainted with, no other possibility occurred to me but that the man was referring to you. I could not think of any other woman who answered to that description!'

His words were sincere and without flattery and she could not help feeling quite gratified that he thought her excessively beautiful. Still, as if reluctant to relinquish a hard-won victory, she refused to concede.

'You are quite a wicked person for having thought so about me,' she insisted.

'Very true, my love, and you should reform me,' he answered soothingly.

'You deserve to be severely punished!' came the reply.

'Yes, I do, my dear. Consider, if you were to marry me, you could torment me for as long as you wished. In fact, if you agree to marry me, I shall help you create a list of chastisements you could mete out to me. Please say you will marry me, Edwina!' he said humbly.

She laughed involuntarily and soon found herself in his arms, wondering if her ribs would break in his embrace, for he held her tightly, as if he would never let her go.

'We shall have ask Papa for his blessing. I do not think he shall object. Indeed, he is very likely to turn me out of the house if I were to reject you, for you are an odious and disagreeable man who has turned all my relations against me!' she announced with a laugh.

He released her in a moment, and clasping her hand, walked to the door, saying with a laugh, 'My darling Edwina, I did secure your father's permission to present my suit to you and I believe he did look on my cause with favour. Where do you think we shall find your parents?'

'In that case, they are all very likely to be awaiting our return in the drawing-room. You must allow me to tease them, for you have, all of you, managed to tease me very much today,' she replied with a twinkle in her eye.

They returned to the drawing-room where Edwina was not at all surprised to find Jane, Diana and Christopher huddled together in conversation. Squeezing Mr. Davenport's arm, she stormed into the room, and looked very severely at the entire party.

'I am shocked that I have been neglected by you, my dear Diana and Jane, for I awaited your return to the library,' she announced coldly.

Mrs. Hardingham sighed, whilst Jane and Diana appeared noticeably crestfallen.

'Oh, do forgive us, dear Edwina!' declared Jane contritely.

'Only if you kiss me and declare that you shall be delighted to have me as your sister,' said Edwina, a torrent of giggles bursting forth from her.

Mr. and Mrs. Hardingham fairly crowed, overjoyed at the prospect of Davenport for a son-in-law.

'I *knew* you both were destined to be together! If you only knew how devoted she has been to you and how heartbroken at being far away from you, and how eagerly she has awaited your return, sir!' declared Christopher shaking his hand joyfully.

At this, Davenport turned to Edwina in some surprise, asking 'Is that so? You—you were ... awaiting my return?'

Mrs. Hardingham interjected with a sigh, 'Ah, but indeed it is so! If you only knew the vapours we have all been subjected to, my good James—I may call you that, yes, since you are to be my son?'

'*Vapours*, Mama! Indeed no such thing ever occurred. In fact, I recall threatening to live happily for a very long time!' declared Edwina indignantly.

'Yes, dear, and to take in a large number of cats to keep you company in your dotage, as I recall,' sallied her mother.

While this gave Davenport much amusement, he was also quite wonderstruck that this lady, whom he had adored from a distance, the thoughts of whom had accompanied his every waking moment and given him courage—often in the most perilous of times—had been reciprocating his devotion the entire time. If he had only known! He could not wait to speak to her privately. But for now, he took his leave, promising to bring his sister to dine again the next day, declaring that he was so pleased to be able to provide Jane with a sister at last!

Edwina watched as he rode away, a contented smile on her lips and a faraway look in her eyes. They returned inside, and Mr. Hardingham, shrewdly realizing that the women would now wish to inevitably discuss the subject of the wedding that must be planned, and earnestly enumerate the many merits and virtues Mr. Davenport possessed, declared that he regretted very much that he and Christopher would have to retire to his business room. Diana had joined them, and Mr. Hardingham noted, as they walked away, that Christopher had looked at her in the most singular manner. There was something in his eyes these days. ... Mr. Hardingham wondered if the lad was starting to form an attachment to Miss. Johnson. That seemed to be a complicated matter. He put it out of his mind and the two men walked on in silence, one quite determined to engage for an hour or two in uninterrupted labour and the other, lost in thought. Diana was overjoyed on hearing the news of Edwina's engagement to Mr. Davenport.

'The two of you shall be so happy, possessed as you both are with a unity in mind and purpose!' she declared, adding, 'Why were you so cross with him?'

Edwina looked at her friend seriously. She bit her lip, wondering if she should narrate the whole matter to Diana. Feeling it was only right that Miss. Johnson be made aware of how things stood with Grayson, she told them what Davenport had said to her in the woods. Diana looked very pale after all was said.

'Whatever will Mr. Davenport think of me? He shall probably implore you to turn me out and have nothing to do with me. Perhaps it is time we talk of my departure from here, Mrs. Hardingham. You have been most kind, but I cannot stay here forever. It was my intention to leave your home as soon as the baby was a few months old and able to undertake the journey back to England. Perhaps that time has come and I should make my way back to England.'

Mrs. Hardingham looked at her in some surprise asking, 'Where will you go? Do you have relations who would welcome you and Mary?'

'I have no one, except my cousin, who wishes never to see me again. I shall work as a governess, for I am quite accomplished at singing and the pianoforte and drawing. Perhaps, you will be so kind as to provide me a reference, Mrs. Hardingham?' she said in an uncertain voice.

'And where will you leave the child? No one would offer you a position as a governess if you had a child!' declared Mrs. Hardingham, not unkindly.

This possibility had not presented itself to Miss. Johnson, who had planned on declaring herself a widow, hoping that no one of her acquaintance from this corner of the world would ever find their way to the particular corner of England that she retreated to.

'I had not thought of that … perhaps I shall engage someone to care for her in the country whilst I earn a living,' she said, uncertainly.

'Perhaps you could, but such an arrangement might prove excessively difficult on a governess' wages, don't you think?' suggested the pragmatic Mrs. Hardingham.

Miss. Johnson had not considered this and her spirits were considerably dampened.

'Perhaps Mr. Grayson shall come here after all, and—and—perhaps. …' she trailed off in a small voice.

'Diana! Do not speak such nonsense! Would you still have Grayson, after he has ill-used you so? Do not worry yourself about what Mr. Davenport thinks. Indeed, at no time did I breathe your name to him, and no mention of it came from him.' cried Edwina.

'I have left myself with no choice, Edwina. But, I shall point to you that Mr. Davenport must love you very much indeed if he offered for you, being mistaken of the facts,' replied Diana sadly.

'That is true, Edwina, and I am surprised that it did not occur to you when you were quarreling with him!' Mrs. Hardingham agreed.

Edwina nodded meekly and said nothing, for she did not wish to say to her friend how mortified she had been when she discovered Mr. Davenport's assumption, for that reflection would no doubt greatly intensify her friend's mortification. Despite her displeasure at his conclusions, it did offer her great satisfaction that he had loved her in spite of them. She reflected that a love that was willing to come with one to the extremities of scandal and disgrace must indeed be a great one and she felt vastly gratified by it.

As if reading her thoughts, Mrs. Hardingham said, 'I am certain your union shall be a blessed one and your domestic bliss great. He is a good man and would try very hard to be a kind husband to you, my dear!'

Edwina smiled, her heart soaring at the recognition of the truth of her mother's words. She wished very much that her friend too would find such love!

The next day, Edwina was delighted to further her acquaintance with Jane Davenport. They begged her after they dined, to recount her journeys on the plains. They listened with bated breath as she narrated to them her adventures, how she had shot the man who had attacked her *daye* and manservant, and how Davenport had intervened at the very moment that their attackers had sought to exact vengeance for this. Edwina declared that she was possibly the bravest lady of her acquaintance.

To this, Jane replied, 'Oh! But I have it on very good authority that you are the most courageous person of our acquaintance. Your conduct at the *shikar* is now quite famous!'

Edwina blushed and retorted, 'My dear Jane, you have been sadly misinformed. I stood there looking at the tiger because I was too afraid to move or even faint. Had I a jot more courage, I should certainly have taken off, running as fast as my legs could carry me—and then I would quite properly be the lady whose timidity was famous!'

They laughed at this, Jane marvelling at how simple choices made in desperate moments greatly affected their outcomes. What if one had chosen a different course of action? Each course of action presented varied outcomes that vastly affected the lives of the players. Edwina listened as Jane spoke, pleased by her charm and wisdom. She felt deep gratitude for the happiness that lay before her.

She could not believe that Davenport had fallen in love with her and not with Anne! When they had had a few moments of private conversation, Davenport had sat beside her and she asked him, very shyly, about what he thought of Anne. He replied unhesitatingly that although he hadn't really thought much about her, he could say with certainty that she was very charming and definitely possessed an enormously kind heart. But, he declared, he had tried very hard to stay away from their home as much as he could, for meeting her sisters haunted his heart with memories of Edwina. He had missed her so desperately, he said, that he could not bear to be around them, and after a while, had ceased to call on them. He hoped that Anne and Kate would not disown him as a ramshackle person with sad manners! Edwina laughed, declaring that they quite loved him and would be much delighted to discover that he was to be their brother!

CHAPTER ELEVEN

CONCLUSION

The following Sunday, they were gratified to see many soldiers returned alive and attending services. There were still battles raging; but, overall, the balance of power had tipped back in favour of the British, and men who had been badly wounded were allowed to seek respite in the hills. This was certainly disappointing news for the sepoys in India who had mutinied against a government whose actions were often characterized by cruel indifference and excess. Nevertheless, a strange new realization had taken possession of the people; perhaps it was a nascent recognition that their subjugation by this foreign force that had begun its ascendency over the land a quarter of a century ago, was not as insurmountable as they had supposed all along. They had risen in revolt and their voices had resounded across the land. The most indifferent and careless observer of these events— Indian or English—could not disregard that cry. Matters had changed, perhaps forever, although it remained to be seen whether this would effect any change of heart in the rulers of the land. On the other hand, for the British, the turn of events in their favour proved to be a relief, if a somewhat unsatisfactory one—for their pride had been greatly stung by the losses they had suffered.

Life began, once more, to approximate what had formerly been its normal state. The summer visitors to Simla were fewer this year, but not conspicuously so, for Delhi having been secured, many families were able to travel to the hills unmolested. They greeted Mrs. Parks whose husband had sent word that he was safe, but going forward to

Cawnpore. She seemed distressed, but greatly relieved to have received some word from him. As they made their way home from church, it was decided that they would walk the short distance home, for it was a beautiful day. To their great astonishment, as they prepared to leave, Mr. Grayson appeared before them, embarrassment written all over his countenance. He seemed to have been seated in an obscure corner of the church and had been present for the entire service.

Resisting the inclination to send him on his way, Mrs. Hardingham nodded and he greeted her with a low bow. The others nodded at him and he, spying Davenport and realizing that the tales of his deeds in Calcutta had made their way to Simla, begged Miss. Johnson to take his arm as they walked home. Diana complied, causing Edwina to become quite alarmed.

'Do *not* trust him. Whatever he says to you, tell him you need time to think on it!' she whispered to Diana, quite fiercely.

She hoped desperately that Diana would not allow the man to deceive her again. She was aware that no other solution presented itself to her in her present predicament, but that she marry Grayson. However, Edwina greatly feared that outcome. While it would truly be a magnificent thing for Grayson to atone for his behaviour and to offer his protection to Diana and his child, Edwina was convinced that it was only Davenport's offer of money that had induced Grayson to come hither. She felt sure that the man had simply used Diana as an excuse to avail of Davenport's good graces.

Diana had long since communicated to him the wretched condition he had left her in, but he had paid no heed to it and shrugged her off as a castaway. Today, he appeared to have come to her to make reparation for the harm he had done, but Edwina did not trust that he intended to stay long enough to do so once he availed himself of the money promised him. She prayed that the hand of God guide her friend in choosing the path most wise.

They walked home, ostensibly enjoying the beautiful summer morning, but in fact, keeping a close eye on Grayson, lagging slightly behind with Diana. They appeared to be talking animatedly and Diana appeared to be remonstrating with him. He seemed discomfited and steadfastly kept his gaze on the ground as they walked. Their conversation completed, Grayson took his leave from the party, and they continued their walk home, at a considerably hurried pace now, for Mrs. Hardingham and Edwina were greatly desirous of hearing what had transpired.

When they reached home, after ascertaining that Mary was well, Diana begged that she be allowed to divulge the details of their conversation before lunch, for she did not, she said, believe that she could swallow a single morsel of luncheon without getting the matter off her chest! They nodded, eagerly awaiting her report.

'Mr. Grayson has asked me to marry him,' she declared in a trembling voice.

'What have you decided to do?' asked Mrs. Hardingham, not in the least bit surprised.

'I believe I shall have to marry him, given my circumstances,' replied Diana despondently.

'Forgive me for prying, but do you love him, child?' asked Mrs. Hardingham kindly.

'I hated him at one time, and then, I forgave him. Now, I feel nothing beyond Christian charity for him. But I don't believe I shall ever love him again,' she answered softly.

'Then you should not marry him, I think, my dear!' declared Mrs. Hardingham.

Mr. Hardingham, realizing the delicacy of the matter had not ever discussed it with Diana.

But now, he felt compelled to speak and said, 'On the contrary, my love, I believe Christian charity is the very thing to build a marriage upon! Granted, Miss. Johnson has been greatly wronged by this person, but consider, he is Mary's father and the only logical solution to this unhappy situation is for them to be wedded and form a household. The child will be ostracised at every turn and every corner of this cruel world if Miss. Johnson were to remain unmarried!'

'Miss. Johnson is not so utterly devoid of friends that this fate must inevitably be hers! In this corner of the world, Uncle, she shall never be ostracized!' said Christopher warmly, considerably troubled by the possibility presented by his uncle.

Diana raised her downcast eyes and looked at him with a mixture of reverential admiration and sadness.

'Alas! I do think your uncle speaks the truth, sir,' she said quietly.

'Yes he does, but have you considered, Diana, that this man is not to be trusted?' said Edwina. 'After all, had Mr. Davenport not made him an offer, would he have made *you* one?'

'That is true. I do believe that he made me the offer in view of the bargain he struck with Mr. Davenport. But what of it? I have ruined myself and there is nothing else to be done. I am most fortunate that he *has* made me an offer, whatever the circumstances may be!' said Diana sadly.

'What offer has Davenport made him?' asked Christopher sharply.

Edwina was obliged to reveal some of Mr. Davenport's remarks to her father and her cousin. Mr. Hardingham shook his head sadly but agreed with Diana that there was no other possible outcome.

'I have ruined myself beyond hope of redemption,' lamented Diana.

'That is nonsense! How can you speak of Christian charity towards the man, but have none for yourself? God has forgiven you, and indeed, you should do the same! If you do not love the man, Diana, by all means, do not marry him! You shall stay here with us as our guest!' replied Mrs. Hardingham with great firmness.

'Oh, but I cannot do so, Mrs. Hardingham! I cannot continue to live on your charity and bring disgrace to your household. I cannot forever hide Mary at home whilst I go to church!' cried Diana.

'Have a care, dearest, I am afraid you are giving poor advice to Miss. Johnson,' protested Mr. Hardingham.

'No I am not!' declared his wife. 'Think about it, my dear. What do you think will happen if Grayson were to indeed marry Diana? Do you think they would go to England and live in wedded bliss forever? Do you believe that Grayson is a reformed person who would carry out his duties as father and husband in an honourable manner? Indeed, no! I predict that the moment the money he obtains as a result of James' generous promise to him is over, he would cast her off in some shabby lodgings in London and be gone forever. Why should this poor girl live her life in squalor and loneliness? She must not be sacrificed on the altar of Propriety! If you do not wish to be recipient of our charity, Diana, then let me employ you as my companion and you and Mary can live with us. Please, do this for me, Mr. Hardingham, for you know I am right. We shall think of some excuse to silence gossiping tongues!' she declared.

Mr. Hardingham was much struck with this line of thought.

'I do not care about the gossip of idle tongues! What strikes me is your perception of the dubiousness of Grayson's penitence. You are quite right, my dear. Dissolute young men seldom are reformed by marriage! It would not do to let Miss. Johnson become permanently entangled in this man's deviousness! I would not wish that for my daughters and no daughter deserves such a fate. Nay, do not cry, child! You can take the man, if you wish. But, be advised that you do not need to do so, for you can stay here or any place of your choosing,' he consoled, for Diana had now collapsed weeping into Edwina's arms.

'I am crying because of the kindness you have shown me. Indeed, it convinces me, beyond any doubt, that God is good and kind and full of mercy!' she replied.

'Miss. Johnson,' said Christopher in a trembling voice, 'I had hoped to speak to you on this matter at a more opportune moment and in private, but I believe I can hold my peace no longer. I have admired you greatly for a very long time. Would you do me the honour of becoming my wife? Take my name for yourself and Mary and make me a very happy man! And pray, forgive me, dear Uncle, for I did not seek your permission first.'

Miss. Johnson stared at the man in horror declaring, 'Oh no! Indeed I shall not marry you! I *could* not ruin you in such a manner!'

Before Christopher could reply, his uncle said dryly, 'You shall, of course, marry whoever you please, but as your guardian, I have to ask you, have you considered the matter carefully?'

'Indeed, I have thought of nothing else since Miss. Johnson came into our home. At first, my thoughts were to provide comfort to her and the child, and then, I wished very much to keep her and the infant with us forever. I cannot bear the thought of her marrying Grayson, and I cannot bear the thought of her going away from this house. If that is not love, Uncle, I do not know what is!' he answered with great passion.

His aunt answered with some severity, 'And if all one needed to be happy in life was love, that would certainly suffice! But, have you thought about the scandal? How should you explain having a child ere you were wed? What if Mr. Hardingham and I withhold our consent?'

'That would indeed be regrettable and give me pause, for I am sure that my kind and wise guardians would never withhold their consent to my happiness for so trivial a cause as petty gossip. If you were to refuse to give us your permission to marry, then I do think it would be for a very unprejudiced reason, Aunt,' he replied sadly.

'That is indeed wise of you, Mrs. Hardingham, for nothing in this world would induce me to accept your offer and ruin your life, sir,' interjected Diana in a tone of great relief.

'Do not speak such fustian, Diana! The man is head over heels in love with you and has been for as long as I know you! And well you know that you return his regard, for I see the look that comes over your face when he speaks—for indeed, no one looks at Christopher with so much admiration!' declared Edwina, much annoyed.

'Love is not everything,' answered Miss. Johnson defiantly.

'On the contrary my dear, love is everything! If a man were to exchange all his riches for love, they would be despised, so the scriptures teach! Its absence creates a void of all happiness. If you were to marry Grayson, feeling no love for him, I am convinced that you would be desperately unhappy, as you should be—if you rejected Chris, knowing that you love each other. True love is rare and one ought not to turn it away when it spreads its arms before one in entreaty! Do not worry about the gossip. I have an excellent plan. Only, say you will marry Christopher. That is, if you wish to,' Edwina finished, conscientiously attempting to refrain from cajoling her friend.

Greatly moved by this speech, Diana looked at Mrs. Hardingham uncertainly.

To her relief, Mrs. Hardingham said with a twinkle in her eye, 'If Edwina has a plan, let us hear it, for it appears she is quite the expert on the matter of love!'

This caused Christopher to stride up to his aunt and give her a kiss of gratitude. Diana burst into joyful tears, as Mr. Hardingham resigned himself to his nephew's resolve on the matter.

'Thank you very much for your offer, sir! I gratefully accept—that is, if Edwina can come up with a plan to make sure that no dishonour is ever attached to your name because of it!' she said prettily.

'No dishonour shall be attached to his name,' said Edwina gleefully. 'Here is what we shall do. We shall have the vicar perform a private ceremony and then, the two of them shall leave with Mary for a honeymoon on the Continent, where they shall stay for the better part of two years, after which they shall return here. No one would know them abroad and anyone beholding Mary would naturally assume Christopher to be the father. When they return home from their honeymoon, no one would question that they returned home with a child. Perhaps they could even spend some time in our estate in Berkshire and that should satisfy anyone that they had the child in England. Papa, perhaps you could put an announcement in the paper— after they leave, of course—announcing the marriage, and when they return in two years, no one would suspect anything. No one knows the circumstances—apart from Grayson and the vicar. We may depend on the former's absence if he were to be given a sum of money, and the latter's discretion, for he would not wish to be connected in any way to such a great scandal!' she finished quite breathlessly.

'Bravo! I had not thought you to be quite so devious, Edwina,' chuckled her father as he listened to this scheme.

Ever practical, Mrs. Hardingham wished to know how Edwina set such store by Grayson's honesty.

'What if he returns when the money is exhausted, and wishes for more? What if he resorts to blackmail and threatens us with scandal?' she asked with annoying perspicacity.

'Well, here is what we shall do. We shall not breathe a word of our plans to him. Instead, James shall act as if he meant to fulfill the promise he made to Grayson in Calcutta. He shall offer him the money, admonishing the man most earnestly to marry Diana, and then have him sign an agreement to discharge some business for the payment that has been made to him. James will inform him that the agreement is a formality and simply a way to exact the money back from him—with the assistance of the Magistrate—should he break his promise to marry Diana. This part is crucial and Grayson must sign a pledge promising to perform some duties of trade at James' bidding, and he most certainly will, for he is a greedy man who will do *anything* for money, as we have all witnessed. In reality, James will keep the signed promise from Grayson as an assurance against blackmail!'

'If we know Grayson well, he will take the money and disappear from Simla. After a few weeks, Christopher's marriage shall be announced and Mr. Grayson would either be unaware of the development, or simply be too far away to be able to act upon it. He will never have the courage to blackmail us, for he would never dare show his face here again, for then, James shall want to reckon with him concerning the money he was paid. Grayson is afraid of James—of that I am certain. Having swindled him of money by failing to marry Diana, he would not dare reappear before him, knowing fully well that James would not hesitate for a moment to turn him over to the Magistrate here in Simla, under the pretext of his failing to have discharged the business he was paid to! Is it not a grand scheme? I have every confidence that James can execute it. He is quite intimidating when he wishes to be, you know. I doubt very much that Mr. Grayson would dare cross him, craven as he is,' replied Edwina triumphantly.

This explanation satisfied her parents who were beginning to thoroughly enjoy the adventurousness of the undertaking of marrying off their nephew.

Christopher appeared to be considering something and with a frown, he said, 'There is one problem you have not paid heed to, Eddy. If we leave in a few weeks, how shall we be at your wedding?'

'Do you mean to say you wish to postpone your own wedding so you might attend mine?' asked Edwina with an air of great innocence.

'N—no … er—that is—' he stammered.

She laughed and said, 'Just so Chris. I shall have the joy of being at both your wedding and mine, while you shall simply have to enjoy becoming a parent before I do!'

'Perhaps you and Davenport could wait until we return?' he asked with a twinkle in his eye.

'No, my dear Christopher, I do not think that would be possible. I have waited for him through wars and the rumours of wars. I shall wait no more for now, 'tis the time for love. Given this sad revolt we have witnessed, perhaps the world in which we live is not what we imagined it to be. It is filled with uncertainty and the promise of change. What *is* sure is the promise that love brings.'

She could have no notion of the truth of her words for, although two years after it had begun, the revolt was declared to be over and peace proclaimed, life in India could not be quite the same for the British. Always, there would be the rumblings of a people groaning under the pressure of servitude to a foreign master, and demanding their freedom and their homeland back.

For their part, the British retaliated against the revolt with an unyielding thirst for vengeance. Some just punishments were meted out. But, most often, soldiers simply ran amuck, perpetrating injustices on the countryside, causing many honourable officers to recoil in shame at their unfettered display of savageness. Some decency prevailed, even as the Governor General, Lord Canning proposed a clemency for those who had never participated in murder either directly or by aiding someone committing murder. The powers of the East India Company were passed on the British Crown, creating the hope that under Her Majesty's care, India would receive her patronage and Indians be treated as her subjects, with the same rights and dignity as the British. Time would tell whether this would indeed be so. For now, a temporary and uncertain peace appeared to hold sway and Edwina Hardingham was right to hold on to love very firmly indeed.

GLOSSARY

Abba	Father
Angrez	English
Anna	Former currency unit of India and Pakistan
Attar	Perfumed essence
Ayah	Maid or nursemaid
Babu	Gentleman or an educated man
Bada Sahib	Senior master
Badi begum	Senior mistress
Begum Sahiba	Aristocratic title for a woman; Muslim woman of high rank
Chanchri	*Ficus gibbosa* (a fig tree found in Asia and other regions)
Charpoy	A bed with ropes woven across the frame
Chital	Species of deer native to south Asia
Dâk	Post
Dâk runner	Postman
Dâkwallah	Postman
Dargah	Muslim shrine
Darwaza	Gate
Dawat	Feast

Daye	Wet nurse
Deodar	Conical cedars native to the Himalayan region
Dhobi	Washerman
Dhotis	Men's garment worn in parts of south Asia resembling pantaloons
Durbar	Court
Durzi	Tailor
Fakir	Mendicant ascetic
Firangi	Foreigner
Ghat	Steps leading down to the banks of a river
Gora	White
Gora sahib	White master
Haiza	Cholera
Haveli	Mansion
Hindostan	Former name of Persian origin of the Indian subcontinent; present day India
Hindustani	Language used in the Indian subcontinent, comprising of Hindi and Urdu; person of Hindostan
Howdah	Carriage used when riding an elephant
Huzoor	Master; sir
Jagirs	Land tracts
Kala titer	Black francolin (bird of the pheasant family)

Kharif	Planting season that stretches between July and October
Kheer	Sweet rice pudding
Kichidi	Dish made from lentils and rice
Koel	Cuckoo found in India and other Pacific regions
Kos	A distance of approximately two miles
Kudaal	A spade
Lagaan	Tax
Langur	Wild monkey inhabiting the Indian subcontinent
Lathis	Stout sticks
Machans	Perch constructed at a height (such as a tall tree) upon which one hunts in the jungle, usually for tigers or similar predators
Mahout	Elephant trainer and driver
Mardana	Men's apartments
Memsahib	Mistress; lady
Monal	A bird of the pheasant family
Muggurmuch	Crocodile
Munshi	Clerk
Nawab	A Muslim ruler in south Asia

Nilgai	Asian antelope
Nullah	Stream
Paan	Betel leaf
Pahari	Of the mountains
Paigam	Message
Pakoras	Fritters (usually made from vegetables)
Pankha	Fan
Parchisi	A board game of Indian origin
Peshwe	Title of the Prime Minister of the Maratha Empire
Pipal	Species of banyan fig found in southeast Asia
Purdah	Veil
Reh	Soil crust composed of salt, found in India
Ranee	Queen
Roti	Bread
Sahukars	Moneylender
Salaam	Greeting, usually involving a gesture of sweeping one's hand to one's forehead
Sambar	Species of deer in southeast Asia
Saree	Woman's garment consisting of a long piece fabric draped around the body
Sarkar	Government

Sawars	Soldiers; horsemen in the army of the British East India Company
Sepoy	Soldier in the army of the British East India Company
Seth	Merchant
Shatranj	Chess
Shikar	Hunt
Shikari	Hunter
Soobedar	Viceroy
Soobedar Major	Senior Indian officer in the British army in India
Tahsildar	Revenue administrator
Talukdar	Landowners
Thuggees	Dacoits that were members of a cult in India, exterminated around the 18th Century
Tiffin	Midday meal
Vaid	Doctor practicing Indian medicine
Zameendars	Feudal landlords
Zenana	Women's apartments

Map 123

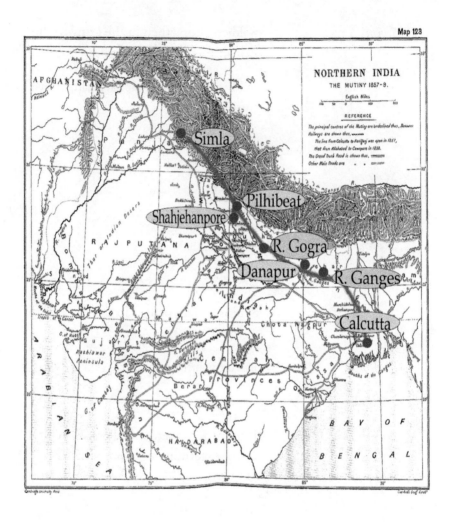

Map of the great mutiny of 1857, highlighting northern India and the regions traversed by Mr. Davenport. Ⓢ

Source: University of Texas Libraries

Dear Reader,

I hope that you enjoyed reading Love and Mutiny: Tales from British India. If you liked the book, please take a few moments to leave a review on Amazon.com or any book-related site of your choosing. I would truly love to hear your thoughts. I hope this will be the beginning of a good friendship, where you enjoy many books I write.

Sincerely,

Anne George

ABOUT THE AUTHOR

Anne George grew up with a profound love of history and English literature. She spent her childhood devouring books. Yes, she was *that* child who had to be forbidden from borrowing any more books from the local library until she finished her homework (her mother was very grateful for the one-book-a-week policy enforced at the strict convent school she attended). Her love affair with words has persisted through the years. In addition, she developed a fascination with storytelling. In the course of her career as a professor of education for several years, her students often applauded the narrative storytelling in her lectures. She has finally indulged in her passion for storytelling by crafting a work of historical fiction. This book is a representation of stories that have been woven over several years of reading, imagining and storytelling.

CPSIA information can be obtained
at www.ICGtesting.com
Printed in the USA
LVHW04s1728141018
593571LV00002B/311/P